GHOST
FLOWER

GHOST FLOWER

MICHELE JAFFE

razOr
bill

An Imprint of Penguin Group (USA) Inc.

Ghost Flower

RAZORBILL

Published by the Penguin Group
Penguin Young Readers Group
345 Hudson Street, New York, New York 10014, U.S.A.
Penguin Group (USA) Inc., 375 Hudson Street, New York, New York 10014, U.S.A.
Penguin Group (Canada), 90 Eglinton Avenue East, Suite 700, Toronto, Ontario, Canada
M4P 2Y3 (a division of Pearson Penguin Canada Inc.)
Penguin Books Ltd, 80 Strand, London WC2R 0RL, England
Penguin Ireland, 25 St Stephen's Green, Dublin 2, Ireland (a division of Penguin Books Ltd)
Penguin Group (Australia), 250 Camberwell Road, Camberwell, Victoria 3124, Australia
(a division of Pearson Australia Group Pty Ltd)
Penguin Books India Pvt Ltd, 11 Community Centre, Panchsheel Park,
New Delhi – 110 017, India
Penguin Group (NZ), 67 Apollo Drive, Mairangi Bay, Auckland 1311, New Zealand
(a division of Pearson New Zealand Ltd)
Penguin Books (South Africa) (Pty) Ltd, 24 Sturdee Avenue, Rosebank, Johannesburg 2196,
South Africa

Penguin Books Ltd, Registered Offices: 80 Strand, London WC2R 0RL, England

10 9 8 7 6 5 4 3 2

ISBN 978-1-59514-396-9

Library of Congress Cataloging-in-Publication Data is available

Printed in the United States of America

A heap of broken images, where the sun beats
And the dead tree gives no shelter, the cricket no relief,
And the dry stone no sound of water. Only
There is a shadow under this red rock,
(come in under the shadow of this red rock),
And I will show you something different from either
Your shadow at morning striding behind you
Or your shadow at evening rising to meet you;
I will show you fear in a handful of dust.

—T.S. Eliot, *The Wasteland*

PART I
ASLEEP

Her body wakes up before her mind. The air is warm and still against her skin. A truck groans by somewhere in the distance. But then it's gone, and silence settles back over her like a soft quilt. Her cheek rests on something cool and smooth, and her legs are curled up under her chin.

This isn't how she usually sleeps. She turns slightly to stretch out, and her shoulder screams in agony.

She opens her eyes and sees white tiles, a streak of something blue across them, the underside of a sink. Her heart starts to pound as her mind takes in the details, eleven grey wads of chewing gum stuck to the bottom of the sink, a gallon jug of bright pink disinfectant, a purple nail tip next to the base of the toilet.

One of her eyes won't open all the way, and when she reaches up, it is puffy. She grabs the white porcelain of the sink, and pain lances across the back of her head, blacking out her vision for a moment. She holds on; the pain passes. She's on her feet now, but the room is swaying beneath her.

In the dented mirror she sees a person with the beginnings of a black eye and mascara running down her face. It takes her a moment to realize it's her, it must be her. She feels something poking her thigh, and she reaches into her pocket and finds $18.75, a broken piece of gold chain, and a receipt from a car wash convenience store for a Diet Coke.

She pushes the door open and stumbles outside. The sunshine is piercing. She squints against it and gazes 360 degrees around. She has no idea where she is.

She starts running.

CHAPTER 1

I t started with a new dawn.

I awoke with the sound of a girl's laughter in my ears. A shaft of sunlight slanted across my face, painting the space behind my eyelids golden. I stretched, fingers and toes uncurling against rumpled sheets toward the other side of the bed.

Empty.

It had been a dream. There was no laughing girl. The air filtering through the fly-specked screen of my rented room was still and silent and warm already at 5:03 a.m.

I had been asleep for more than a thousand days. Not technically, that's just how it felt.

There were still two minutes until my alarm would go off. That had been happening to me more and more recently, waking up sixty, ninety, one hundred seconds early, as though some part of me was issuing a warning, telling me to stop dawdling and leave.

I am an imposter. A fake. A fraud. But everything that follows is the truth and nothing but the truth. I have no reason to lie anymore.

Dawn is special in Tucson. It doesn't arrive gently with the sweet smoldering quality it has at the edges of the country. It comes on all at once, a thin, sharp light the color of corn silk that gives the impression of being more honest than its afternoon butter yellow cousin. It may not always be flattering, but it doesn't pull any punches.

I yawned. A fat bumblebee hummed outside the window. Down the street I could hear the sound of a sprinkler watering a thirsty lawn, clicking one, two, three, four, five, six, seven and then *seven-sixfivefourthreetwoone* as the automatic arm swung back fast. The warm air settled over me like an extra blanket, and I gave myself a moment to savor it. Then my alarm began to beep, and I pulled myself out of bed.

The light did my room no favors, picking out every scar and gash in the battered night table and dresser with the drawers glued shut—$53.50 a week didn't entitle you to drawers—and making the tiny blue flowers that dotted the yellow wallpaper look even more like flu germs. I could have spent ten hours cleaning the place, and it wouldn't have looked any better or any less lonely.

It was Mother's Day, and by nine thirty the Old Town Starbucks where I worked was filled with well-fed white men with thick gold bands on their fingers wearing cargo shorts and U of A T-shirts, pushing strollers and taking extra care to get their wives' double chai latte with wings, light foam, just right. Like this would make up for all the nights they didn't get home to help with dinner or the way they winked at me when they came in weekdays alone wearing suits. The wives played along with the lie, doing their best to look as if a coffee shop with the family was where they most wished to spend their special day.

Who knows, maybe it was. I should say upfront that I don't really understand how happy families work. My experiences in foster care gave me a view of "family" as an organism knitted together by convenient lies and inconvenient needs that bristled porcupine-like with protective quills if you dared to point that out.

My third foster mother, Mrs. Cleary, couldn't understand why fitting in was so hard for me. "You need to learn to think of someone besides yourself and have compassion for others," she said, leaning back in her La-Z-Boy chair with the bowl of popcorn on her lap and a glass of bourbon in her hand. My stomach growled audibly, but we both ignored it. "All you have to do is put yourself in someone else's shoes."

I tried, but her shoes were black pointy-toed three-inch heels with garish buckles on them that squished the front of her feet and made her red painted lips draw into a tense line every time she stood up. Looking at them made me feel like screaming.

That was the last foster home I lived in.

I had just finished attempting to put myself into the Lilly Pulitzer lime-green flip-flops of a woman with a Botox permasmile—"Have a super day!" I chirped—when the guy and the girl reached the front of my line.

"Hi, remember me?" the guy said, shooting me a conspiratorial smile and leaning close to the register.

I treated it as a rhetorical question. It would have been as impossible to forget him as it would have been to not notice when he and the girl next to him had walked in that day. For one thing, they blended in with the Mother-Father-Stroller crowd as well as sand in a Frappuccino. For another, he looked like he'd stepped out of an advertisement, the kind with the half-naked guy with abs like the sculpted bottom of a riverbed squinting at the horizon. Rich. Spoiled. With a perpetual expression of being pleased with himself. The kind of face that could easily haunt your dreams.

Plus he had been in five times during the last two weeks. I felt like I might have seen the girl recently as well, but I wasn't sure.

"I'm Bain," he said when I just kept looking at him. "Bain Silverton. And this is my sister Bridgette."

"Eve," I told him, nodding my head toward my name tag. "My name is still Eve Brightman. The same way it was the other times you asked."

"You do remember me." His eyes lit up with pleasure. "I believe you, I do. It's just—damn you are a dead ringer for someone I used to know." He turned to the girl next to him. "See, Bridge? Isn't it weird? I mean the hair is short, but it could seriously be her."

She nodded. Like him, she had early-morning-blue wide-spaced eyes with heavy lids and a perfect oval face, but while his gaze was mischievous and warm, hers was cool, appraising. I'd guessed she had his same light brown hair that mellowed to gold in the sun, but she'd dyed it a subtle red and had thick bangs across her forehead. I had the sense that in her world, this was an act of thrilling rebellion. I watched her place my Target jeans and T-shirt with a two-second glance. She was wearing a denim shorts jumper with a loose cashmere sweater over it, driving moccasins, a large leather bag with subtle hardware, and aviator glasses on top of her head. On the pointer finger of her left hand, she wore a Cartier triple-band gold ring. Simple, understated. I guessed the outfit, not counting the ring, cost four thousand dollars. Mine cost $34.53.

Bain said, "I told Bridgette all about you."

I couldn't imagine what he'd told her, and before I could ask, Roman, my boss, came up. "What have I told you about chatting with your friends at the counter, Eve?" he asked in his nasal voice, somehow managing to glare at me and smile smarmily at Bain and Bridgette at the same time.

"We were just ordering," Bain said and proceeded to do it. He and Bridgette took their cappuccino (him) and mint tea (her) to a table that a family of five had just vacated in the corner.

Roman rounded on me. "You're on probation, you know," he told me, his little eyes flashing. Out of the corner of my eye, I watched Bridgette carefully brush the crumbs the family had left behind into a napkin and fold it precisely into a little envelope before throwing it away. "We'll discuss this after work."

The anger on his face was just a mask for the excitement beneath it. Roman knew I needed this job. He suspected there was something hinky about my ID, that I should probably be in school, which meant he felt he had power over me. In the past he'd tried to use that power in ways which—

Well, in ways. And even *I* wasn't lonely enough to want that.

I'd managed to avoid his attempts through a combination of skill and luck. But it was getting harder.

Bain and Bridgette sat, heads bent together, talking earnestly for fifteen minutes, glancing over at me every few seconds. They reminded me of sleek, well-groomed mountain cats—they were beautiful, but there was something predatory about them. I pretended not to notice, but my heart was pounding, and I'm pretty sure several people got their coffees for half price because I wasn't paying attention to what I was doing.

Bridgette's grey stingray Filofax was on the table, and Bain grabbed it. From the corner of my eye I saw him take out a piece of paper, scrawl something on it, push his chair away, and stand up. As Bridgette gathered her bag, sweater, and sunglasses and moved to the door, he walked to the front of the line and slipped me the paper.

"We have a proposition for you. Call if you want to hear about it."

I quickly palmed the paper into the pocket of my apron, aware of Bridgette's eyes on me. There was something unreadable in her expression, something I couldn't put my finger on, but it wasn't friendly. She was toying with the ring on her finger.

When I got my break, I pulled the paper from my pocket. On one side was some kind of list written in pencil. On the other, in pen, two numbers. One was a phone number. The other was "$100,000 cash."

I could hear Nina's catcall whistle, the one she was so proud of having perfected, as if she were standing next to me. God, I wished she were. "You must have something they *really* want," her voice marveled in my head.

I must, I thought. I flipped the paper back over and scanned the list. I assumed it was in Bridgette's writing; it certainly seemed to fit what I'd seen of her. The top said "For Marisol," and below it: "Remove contents of spice rack, wipe with damp cloth, replace in alphabetical order. Remove contents of medicine chest, wipe with Clorox antibacterial wipes (blue not yellow), and replace in chrono-logical order from earliest expiration date to latest." I had a sudden vision of her doing the same with me, remove contents, wipe clean, and replace in a new improved order.

This is a person I don't want anything to do with, I thought. I shoved the note into my pocket, rearranged my face, and went back to work.

CHAPTER 2

"Forgetting is harder than remembering," Miss Melanie liked to say. She lived next door to my last foster family at the Efficiency Suites Apartments. She was the oldest resident in the complex and kind of our unofficial caretaker. I picture her sitting on the scarred Naugahyde armchair that she'd had us move onto the flat roof of the building, sectioning and braiding my foster sister Nina's hair. Nearby some of the indistinguishable boys who also lived in the complex kicked a half-inflated ball. The dusty summer night hung around us. It was hot, scorching, even with the sun down, but you could catch a slight breeze if you got up high enough.

Miss Melanie's hands worked like hummingbirds, darting in and out, up and around, pausing only so she could reach for her Kent 100 and take a deep sizzling drag. "You can try and try," she said, "but the memories are still there, waiting for you like thugs out behind the liquor store."

I laughed and said, "I wish."

"Yeah, that doesn't make any sense, Miss M," one of the boys who'd been playing soccer shouted over. "If that were true, I woulda been an A student acing my exams instead of hanging out with these losers."

There was a chorus of jeers, but Miss Melanie ignored them. "Just wait."

I'd been waiting, but I'd still found the opposite was true. I was a professional forgetter. My memory seems to have been ransacked, not with professional precision but crudely. I'm left with pieces of memories dangling like the red fleshy sinews of the severed limbs in zombie movies—streaks of headlights on wet pavement or "Tom Yaw" or the line of my real mother's jaw as she is about to turn toward me.

I can't remember my actual mother's face. When I see her in my mind, it's always from the back, her standing in front of something, a painting, a window, but mainly the ocean. Walking not away from me but toward it, to put her toes in and feel the glittering chill of sand gathering between them as the cold water hits and the crabs run tickling along the bottom. Without turning, she holds out her hand to me to join her, but I stay on the shore watching the long-legged birds, trying to figure out why some fly and some stay. When I ask my mother, she says, "Everyone has a choice."

She flew. I stayed. Although I suppose you could see it the other way as well.

There's no ocean in Tucson, but there are still plenty of ways to drown yourself. I'm not talking metaphorically—life is complicated enough without word play. I mean the way that you can drown in something as mundane as a plate of chicken soup. Essentially you are always just one inch of liquid away from death. That's why I've never understood why people make such a big deal out of planning suicide. Even generic store-brand soup will do.

The triggers for a memory can be obscure, mossy little embankments with unexpected wormholes that lead you into unknown regions of your psyche, but there didn't seem to be much mystery to why my thoughts would turn to my mother on Mother's Day. I've wondered, though, if there might not have been some tiny groove I stumbled into without knowing, some part of me that longed for family, that also got touched off without me realizing it. If that's what ultimately made me do it.

CHAPTER 3

The rest of the day was a blur until closing time. That's when Roman struck. "The cash drawer is ten dollars short," he announced, eyeing me. "I think you know what that means."

He took a step toward me. I took a step back.

"I had nothing to do with that."

"Then who did?" Another step toward me. The coffee grinder was pressing against my back now.

"I don't know." I reached behind me to steady myself, and my fingers closed around the handle of one of the ceramic Easter mugs we were putting on sale.

"Well, what do you propose to do about it?" One step closer and his body would be pressed against mine. His breathing was already heavy, and his eyes were locked on my breasts. They're not big, but his expression said they would be adequate. "I think we'll have to do a whole body search."

I lashed my arm forward, sending the heavy mug bashing into his cheek where it met his eye socket. The mug shattered, and he reeled backward, gasping.

"You stupid bitch," he said, gripping his eye. "You stupid bitch, you could have blinded me."

I wanted to correct him. I knew what I was doing, and it wasn't anything that dangerous. But he was recovering, and it was time for me to go.

"You stupid bitch," he repeated, apparently liking the sound of it, lurching toward me. He was between me and the exit. "I'm going to make you pay for that. I'm—"

His meaty hand reached for me, and I ducked, throwing him off balance. As he stumbled, I shot toward the end of the counter. I felt his fingers close on the back pocket of my jeans, but I kept going. My heart was pounding in my ears so loud I only barely heard the rip of fabric, but the release sent me sprawling forward.

"I'm going to call the police. You stupid—"

On my hands and knees I crawled for the opening of the counter. He tried to pin my foot, but I kicked up and was rewarded with a groan. "You stupid bitch, I'm going to have you arrested. You're going to—"

I didn't hear the rest. I was on my feet and at the door, fumbling with his keys in the lock. *God, why wouldn't my fingers work? Work dammit wor—*

And then I was outside, in the warm night air, the mountains' dark silhouettes against the blue and gold of the late dusk sky. I ran—I don't know for how long or how far. Finally I had to stop, leaning against a rust-red boulder, panting, crying. I looked down at my hands, and they were pocked with shards of pink and lavender and green and white ceramic from crawling over the mug I'd broken. A small yellow daisy from the rim was dangling from my left palm at a weird angle. I looked around and had no idea where I was.

I had no idea about anything. The only clear thought I possessed was that I could not go back to my room in case Roman really did call the cops. There wasn't much there, nothing anyone could use to find me, but it also meant I had nothing except an ID in the name of Eve Brightman and the clothes on my back. I certainly couldn't plan to pick up my last paycheck.

The wind changed, bringing the smell of desert sage, which meant it was raining somewhere nearby. I looked up and saw the eerie grey shapes of storm clouds massing around the mountains on the horizon. I looked down and realized I was still wearing my apron. Reaching in, I felt a crumpled-up bill and the piece of paper Bain had given me.

"We have a proposition," he'd said. "$100,000 cash," the note read. There was a crack and a rumble of thunder. The storm was getting closer.

He didn't ask questions when I called, just told me to sit tight, he'd be there as soon as he could. I used three of the ten dollars I'd stolen and stashed in my apron to buy an ice tea and sat on the side of the road waiting, watching the storm clouds crawl closer. My mind should have been going a mile a minute, but instead it was just . . . blank. My eyes focused on the silvery-white cocoon of a moth or butterfly beneath the boulder next to the one I was sitting on. Apparently I wasn't the only one making a new start at this particular intersection.

Forty-five minutes later a silver Porsche Carrera did a U-turn and stopped like an impeccably trained panther coming to heel in front of me. Bain rolled down the window and gave me a smile. "Ready for the ride of your life?" he asked.

A voice in the back of my head whispered that this was too smooth, too easy. My hand hesitated on the door handle for a moment. If I did this, whatever it was, there would be no going back. No escape.

You can keep running, the voice said. *There's no reason to stop now. Turn and run away again.*

I opened the door and dropped into the seat. "I'm ready."

At the time I thought I was.

He made another U-turn and headed west, toward the clouds.

CHAPTER 4

I watched the raindrops slide down the window, finding pathways through the dust. It's fascinating to watch how they do that—one of them leads the way, and then the others follow in that path, perhaps veering slightly and making it wider, but generally sticking to the same direction unless acted on by something powerful like the wind picking up or a sudden turn. Watch them sometime; their reluctance to chart their own course is remarkable. And if raindrops exhibit that—raindrops that have nothing at stake in their brief lives—how unsurprising is it that people do it too, following paths carved by others, even if it leads nowhere good.

Surface tension was what did it, held them in place, I knew. They stayed that way because of the cohesion of molecules, their attraction to the surface, the superficial.

Bain said, "Do you need to go to Van Cortland Street to pick anything up?"

"You know where I live? Did you follow me?"

"It's called due diligence. I wanted to make sure you were suitable."

The word *suitable* sent a creepy chill prickling between my shoulder blades. "And what did you learn?"

"That you've been living there for a month, during which time no one has come to visit you, you told the landlady you're an orphan, you have no cell phone, and you've never gotten a phone call there."

I stared at him for four breaths until the creepy feeling receded. I said, "No, I don't need to get anything."

He changed lanes, getting on the ramp to the highway, the clicking noise of his blinker the only sound in the car. Once he'd merged into traffic, we drove in silence, heading north. After about a mile he glanced over at me. "How long have you been on your own?"

I paused, deciding which story to pluck from my quiver and shoot in his direction. I said, "My mother drove me to a Greyhound bus station when I was ten, said to wait there while she went to get Twizzlers, and didn't come back." It wasn't the whole story, but it was true.

I could tell I chose well by the way his lips compressed and his fingers curved over the mahogany inlay on the steering wheel. The atmosphere in the car shifted slightly, the way it does when someone burps and is embarrassed. "I'm sorry," he said.

"I managed."

"I had no right—"

"No, you didn't." There would be no more questions about my childhood, I was sure.

The windshield wipers traced smooth overlapping semicircles out of the raindrops on the glass, like a flamenco dancer opening and closing her fans. Lightning flashed in shining silver veins across the sky, and thunder rumbled far away.

I picked out a question with care. You have to be careful with strangers; questions can reveal as much as answers. "People always say it never rains in the desert."

"You're not from here," he said, almost to himself, like he was filing it away. "You've never seen a thunderstorm in the desert then?" He glanced to see that I was paying attention. "They can be pretty amazing. Wild and out of control until suddenly, abruptly, they just stop. Ro—Aurora—loved thunderstorms. She'd run outside in them and just stand there for as long as they went on, getting soaking wet."

"Who?"

"My cousin. The one you look like. I sometimes wondered if it was because she was kind of like a storm. Sounds stupid, probably." The last part seemed more directed at himself than to me.

"You say 'was.' What happened to her?"

His lips compressed. "That's what you, Bridgette, and I are going to talk about." He frowned. "Why haven't you asked where we're going?"

I kept my eyes out the front window, but I was watching Bain in my peripheral vision. "It wouldn't matter. I don't waste my time with superfluous questions."

"Superfluous. Fancy word. Where did you pick that up?"

"I have a library card."

A billboard for the Highway Motel—"Next exit. Best in class!"—seemed to catch Bain's eye as we went by it, and I felt his gaze rest on me for a moment, appraisingly. I pretended not to notice, watching the scenery pass, Mary Ann's Diner, Citco Gas, the Rub-a-Dub Carwash.

Bain shifted his weight in his seat. "Are you always this calm when you get into cars with strange men?"

We sped by the exit for the motel. I said, "I'm fairly certain there's nothing you and your sister want me to do that I haven't done before."

A parenthesis formed at the corner of his mouth as it rose in a small, pleased smile. "Oh, I think you might be surprised."

Out of nowhere, my mind flashed back to earlier in the day, him calling me a dead ringer, and the first glimmer of fear began to clutch at my intestines. But I was determined not to show it.

We got off the main highway at the ramp just before the "Phoenix next five exits" sign and switched to small roads, the kinds that go straight from pavement to gravel without a shoulder. The kinds favored by organized serial killers for burying their victims because they're accessible but not obvious and don't retain tire marks.

The rain had slowed to a misty drizzle. The silver-blue of the Porsche's headlights polished the wet asphalt into an ebony ribbon.

Traffic was light on the other side, so we bet on how many cars would pass us between each mile marker, a dollar a marker. I won the first and second miles (three cars each); he won the third (six). The fourth was still a draw when he swerved without slowing into the gravel-covered parking lot of a medium-sized general store, spraying a cascade of grey pebbles with the back tires. He braked into a parking space in front of the door, said, "Wait here," and was out of the car, letting in a wave of cool air before I could protest. Through the window I watched him shake hands with the man behind the counter, exchange a few words, take a toothpick, and come back out.

He had the toothpick in the side of his mouth, rolling it around when he got back into the car. "Bridgette already stopped in for supplies, and she's at the cabin waiting for us," he said, his arm extended across the back of my seat as he made a reverse arc out of the parking spot.

"You're scared of her," I said.

The toothpick stopped moving. His head was twisted to look over his right shoulder, which meant it was facing me straight on, and he

21

stopped in the middle of backing up to move his eyes to mine. "No, I'm not. Why would I be afraid of my baby sister?" he challenged.

I couldn't answer, but I knew I was right. You learn to sense things like that when you've lived like I had.

We sat like that, his eyes on my face, toothpick clenched between his lips, for the space of three heartbeats. Long enough to become aware of not blinking. Long enough so that the challenge drained from his expression and was replaced with something else, something intense that could have been longing or hate or anything in between.

His tone unreadable, he said, "Seeing you makes me miss my cousin."

"Were you two close?"

"We were family." He was suddenly avoiding my gaze. Turning his head from me, he punched the car into third gear. He kept his foot on the break, revved the engine until it whined like it was begging for mercy, and exploded onto the road doing sixty.

We drove in silence for the next ten minutes, the headlights flashing from side to side as we sped up a curly road, first picking up cream-colored rocks, then grey boulders, and finally trees, taller and taller ones. We passed a silver mailbox, and Bain swung into a gap between the trees, slowed, and rolled the car to a stop in front of a triple-bayed garage. It was set into a wide stone two-story building with a square tower on one side that had vines growing up it. There was a warm yellow light spilling from the windows above the garage doors and the tower, but otherwise the entire area was dark.

"We're here," he said, opening his door and starting to get out. "Welcome to the family cabin."

I climbed out too. "I'm pretty sure most people would call this a castle."

Bridgette's voice came to us across the gravel drive saying, "As you're finding out, we're not most people."

She was standing inside a wide door at the base of the tower. She'd changed into grey leggings and a light blue baggy sweater, but she still had on the driving moccasins. Her arms were crossed over her chest. "For one thing, we're more careful. Before you take another step, tell me your name. And don't say Eve Brightman. Eve Brightman died eleven years ago; I checked. You're not even on Facebook. Who are you *really*?"

I didn't know how to answer that. Nothing about my life had ever really fit into birthday party invitation categories like *Who, What, Where, When, Dress to Impress*. But I couldn't tell Bridgette that. Instead I put some challenge in my voice and said, "Why does it matter?"

"That's not an answer. I want an answer."

I watched a moth flutter around the buttery light next to the well-kept, solid-looking door, and it made me think of the cocoon I'd seen earlier.

I decided to go with the truth.

CHAPTER 5

"I'm on the run," I said. "I've been hiding."

Bridgette's eyes narrowed slightly, and I got the feeling that wasn't what she was expecting. "From who?"

"Someone who thinks I have something they want."

"Are the police looking for you?"

"No." I was pretty sure that was true but not positive.

"So it's just this—individual. Who is he?"

"That's none of your business."

Bain was next to me then. "You didn't tell me you were a criminal. You played me."

"I'm not a criminal. And you didn't ask."

He said, "What's your real name?"

I considered it, truly, then said, "I don't think I want to tell you that."

Dark indentations appeared beneath his cheekbones as he clenched his jaw. "Forget it. The whole thing is off."

Bridgette looked at him curiously. "It was your idea."

"Well, I changed my mind. It's a bad bet. And as I'm sure you're dying to remind me, not the first." He shifted his eyes to me. "I'll drive you back to Tucson. Unless you'd rather ride with Bridgette."

"Either way."

Out of the corner of my eye I saw Bridgette watching us, and I sensed she was amused. "Bain, may I speak to you for a moment?"

He dragged his eyes from me and glowered at her. "What?"

"Let's go upstairs. You might as well stay for dinner. I made *macaroni au gratin avec lardon*," Bridgette said, with a hint of challenge.

Even though I had no idea what that was, I was suddenly ravenous. I'd skipped breakfast and lunch, and my dinner the night before had been a day-old scone. "That's a favorite of mine," I told her, like I ate it every day.

Her eyes narrowed again, but she turned and led the way up the staircase. They led up one floor into a wide open space with the windows I'd seen from below on one side, and a wall of French doors on another. There was a fancy-looking kitchen with an island surrounded by six tall stools with backs. An immense overstuffed couch and chairs were grouped around a huge sheepskin rug, facing a fireplace. The furniture was all white or cream and modern but comfortable looking. Three places were set at the kitchen island with plates and napkins and glasses and forks and spoons that looked like they could be real silver, and the smell of something delicious baking came from the oven. The kitchen area alone would take an hour and a half to clean properly.

But what drew my eye was the piano. A baby grand made of a rare dark wood gleaming like a beacon off in a corner by the French doors. It was a beautiful instrument.

Bridgette pushed Bain through one of the French doors onto the balcony that ran the length of the building, said to me, "Help yourself to whatever you want. We'll just be a second," and closed it behind her.

I took a bottle of Perrier from the refrigerator and moved toward the piano, which would give me a good vantage point to watch Bridgette and Bain. Lines of photos in matching hammered silver frames marched down the length of it like officers in the Army of Memory.

I picked up the largest one, a smiling group overlooking a tennis court. Unlike the others, it had a dark matte around the edges as though it had been cropped, and the center seemed shifted. A woman with striking silver hair sat in the front near the left edge, with an athletic-looking man in a yellow polo shirt and seersucker shorts leaning against the balcony edge behind her. There were enough physical similarities to make me think he might be Bain and Bridgette's father. The man was smiling, but he wasn't looking at the camera. He was looking intently to the left, off the side of the photo. On the other side of the old woman stood Bain and Bridgette, slightly younger, both dressed for tennis.

Every detail, from the glint of the double strand of pearls the old woman was wearing with her tennis dress to Bridgette's unscuffed tennis shoes to the watch tan line on Bain's wrist above the red handle of the racket combined to make the picture look like an advertisement for How the Rich Live. They were all smiling and appeared to be a complete happy family with everything in the world they could want. But it had a careful, curated feeling that seemed sinister. What was the man looking at so intently just outside the frame?

Suddenly I felt cold. I moved my eyes from the photo to the real thing outside. Bridgette and Bain walked up and down the balcony, so I could only catch snippets of their conversation. At first they went in jerks, a few steps forward, then a stop to argue, then a few more steps. Bain seemed angry and shrugged Bridgette's hand off, but then his posture changed, got straighter. I made out the words "fool us" and "leverage," before they moved on and the conversation got indistinct. Bridgette was clearly in charge. Soon they were strolling up and back in sync, heads close, him nodding at her. I caught something about "makes her dependable," before they wheeled away again. Watching them was like watching two predatory fish in a tank swimming slowly back and forth. Circling.

"What if they don't know they're in a tank?" I could hear Nina asking in my mind. I pictured her sitting on top of the washing machine, leaning out as far as she could to look through the door of the laundry room across the kitchen to the massive fish tank that separated it from the dining table at the Dockwood place.

I had been working for a cleaning service. No benefits, no questions asked about my age or ID or why I wasn't in school. $7.25 an hour plus tips. Although, despite spending my days inside houses with inlaid marble floors and walls of books that had never been read and built-in safes and ornamental bowls casually used to throw all the remote controls into, there were rarely tips.

Nina was fascinated by the fish, and I felt bad making her stay in the laundry room. But she wasn't supposed to be there, even though the Dockwoods weren't home. I knew they had security cameras, and I couldn't risk her being seen. "You mean, what if we're the ones in the tank and they're watching us?" I asked.

"Yes!" she squealed.

"How do you know we're not?" I asked her.

I knew the question would keep her for awhile. She liked to work things out and come up with concrete answers and often got exasperated by my high tolerance, maybe even preference, for not knowing. I was upstairs polishing the handles on the his and hers vanities—vanity indeed—in the master bedroom when I heard the patter of Nina's footsteps behind me.

"I figured it out," she said, sounding so excited I couldn't chastise her for coming to find me. "If we were in the tank, we wouldn't have to worry about what we were going to eat for dinner. We'd never be hungry. So we're not in the tank."

"No," I agreed, and the polish cloth in my hand started to tremble. I kept my head down, working the cloth in smooth circles and avoiding looking at her so she wouldn't see my struggle to hold back tears. "We're not." I was trying so hard, but it wasn't enough. I took a deep breath, put a smile on my face, and raised my eyes to hers in the mirror.

And froze.

There was a trickle of blood running from her nose down her face. "Sweetheart," I said, turning to wipe it, but it kept coming. "What happened?"

"What?" she looked at me blankly. Then she saw the blood. "I don't know. It just started."

"Has this happened before?" I asked.

She looked away. "No."

"How often?"

She shrugged. "When we were still with Mrs. Cleary, it was maybe once every week or two?"

"And now?"

Her eyes met mine and filled with tears. "Mostly maybe every day." She started to cry. "I'm so scared."

I got on my knees and hugged her, and that's where we were when Mrs. Dockwood came in and saw us and the two spots blooming like bloodred flowers on the edge of her white hand-loomed carpet.

"Not only does she have a girl with her, she has a *sick* girl," she screamed into her phone at my boss. "This is completely unacceptable.

Bringing something like this into my house. The carpet is ruined. *Ruined,*" Mrs. Dockwood moaned. "We're going to have to replace the whole thing, and it will cost a fortune. I hope you have good insurance."

I stared at the floor, squeezing Nina's trembling hand to reassure her.

"I'm very sorry," she said to Mrs. Dockwood, and to her credit, Mrs. Dockwood smiled at her and said, "It's not your fault, dear." Her eyes came to me. "It's hers. What was she doing here? This isn't a day care."

"I'm sorry," I told Mrs. Dockwood.

"I'm sorry," I told my boss when he fired me.

"I'm sorry," I whispered to Nina as she lay asleep in my arms in the emergency room waiting for someone to see us.

And when they did—

I shook myself out of the memory and realized I was gripping the silver picture frame so hard the edges bit into my palms.

I set it down carefully, in the exact spot I'd taken it from on the top of the piano, the way I would have if I'd been cleaning this house and not been a guest in it. Over my shoulder I checked on Bain and Bridgette and saw they were now leaning side by side against the railing. I raised the lacquered cover of the piano keyboard on its hinges, and my fingers tapped lightly across the cool smoothness of the keys.

"Do you play?" Bridgette's voice startled me. The cover fell with a sharp crack as I stepped away from the instrument.

I hadn't heard her—heard them—come in, but now she was standing right next to me. "A little. One of my foster parents . . ." I said.

"*One* of your foster parents?" Bridgette asked, her interest obviously quickening.

"It doesn't matter," I said, poorly concealing that her interest unnerved me. "I don't play much. It's just this piano is so—pretty."

"Yes," Bridgette agreed. "It used to be in our grandmother's house, but she decided she didn't want to see it anymore. So we moved it up here." She was watching me with an intensity and curiosity that made me feel like I was an insect pinned on a microscope slide.

I tried to strike a casual pose, moving to put my hands into my back pockets but remembering too late that one of them had been ripped off by Roman that afternoon.

Only that afternoon. It felt like a lifetime ago.

Instead I twined them behind me. "Do either of you play?" I asked to shift her attention.

"Bridgette is an accomplished pianist," Bain said.

Her eyes didn't leave me. "You don't play at all? What about tennis?"

I frowned. "Tennis? Nope."

"Horses? Do you ride?"

I couldn't help but laugh. "Sure. There are a lot of foster homes with stables." I tilted my head toward the balcony. "What did you decide out there?"

Bain and Bridgette exchanged a look, as though they were having a conversation without words. She said, "Let's discuss it over dinner. I'm starving."

CHAPTER 6

My most recent definition of dinner had been eating things that came out of cans off of paper plates with a plastic spoon.

Bain and Bridgette's version of dinner was a little different. As we sat down, Bain informed me that Bridgette had gone to Paris to attend culinary school the summer after her senior year of high school. She downplayed it—"It was mostly just basic sauces and knife skills"—but she was a really good cook.

Macaroni au gratin avec lardon, I learned, was a fancy way of saying macaroni and cheese with bacon in it, but this wasn't like any mac and cheese I'd ever had. Bridgette baked it in the oven, so it had a golden bread-crumb crust, and the saucy part managed to be delicate and smoky and cheesy all at once. I ate two plates of it, and Bain kept up. Despite saying she was hungry, Bridgette mostly pushed the pasta around with her fork while shooting furtive glances at me.

Finally I couldn't take it. I stopped mid-bite and let my fork fall into my plate. It made a sharp noise, and Bridgette jumped slightly. "Why do you keep staring at me like that?" I demanded.

To her credit she didn't deny it. She said, "I'm wondering how you digest your food hunched over, gulping it like that."

I was eating like the people I knew ate, face close to my plate, left arm curved around it to protect it, fingers of my right hand wrapped around the handle of my fork. "What's wrong with how I eat?"

"It's not that something is wrong. It's just—" She laid her fork down carefully, pushed her plate forward and crossed her arms in front of her. "I was just thinking about how much work this is going to take. Every detail is going to matter—how you use utensils, how you sit, how you talk. I hadn't realized how many little things there were until I was watching you right now."

I sat up straight and took my arm off the table. "Is this some kind of *My Fair Lady* thing where you win a prize by turning a guttersnipe into a countess?"

She smiled. "I love that movie."

Of course she did. Girls like Bridgette always loved that movie because it made the world seem pretty and made them believe that even though they were rich and clean, they didn't have to be morally bankrupt.

It was, in my opinion, a piece of shit. No one ever handed you a fairy tale.

"I guess you could say it's a little like that," Bridgette went on. She started twisting the triple gold ring she wore on her pointer finger. "We want you to pretend to be someone else, and if you pull it off there will be a lot of money in it."

I think I had known all along, somewhere in the back of my mind, where this was heading, but I let myself say it aloud for the first time now. "You want me to be your cousin Aurora."

Bridgette sat up straight, and her perfectly shaped brows snapped together. "How do you know about Aurora?"

"Bain told me. He said she loved thunderstorms like the one we drove through. Because she was like them."

She shot him a confused look, then came back to me. "Yes. I guess—" she stopped. "That doesn't matter. Three years ago Aurora ran away and disappeared. We want you to impersonate her for a few weeks."

"A few weeks?"

"A month or two."

"Why?"

"Our grandmother is very ill, and it would make her last days—" Bain started to say, but Bridgette interrupted.

"Don't be an idiot. She'll never believe that." She looked at me. "For money. On her eighteenth birthday, Aurora was supposed to inherit a lot of money. We want you to impersonate her until then, stay around long enough to get the money, and then give it to us. We'll give you one hundred thousand dollars, and you'll be free to do whatever you want for the rest of your life."

One hundred thousand dollars to walk in someone else's shoes for three months. Mrs. Cleary, my foster mother, would have been so proud of me. I glanced toward the photo I'd been looking at on the piano. I bet they were nice shoes too.

"Why wouldn't you do it?" Bain said when he thought I was hesitating.

"Because it's stealing?" I said.

"Not really." Bridgette shook her head. "In her will, Aurora left the money to Bain and me, so technically it's ours. But if she's not there, we have to wait another four years until she can be declared dead."

"Is she dead?"

"She's either dead or uninterested in the money because otherwise she would have been back by now," Bain explained. He spread his hands wide. "See, no one will get hurt. All you have to do is spend a few weeks playing dress-up and living like a princess, and at the end you get a fortune. Most people would jump at this chance. Or are you worried it will interfere with your career advancement up the Starbucks ladder?"

If I had seen then what this single-minded focus on money was really about, I would never have agreed to their offer. But at the time, everything they said made sense. And it all led to one conclusion. I said, "I'll do it." Bain started to smile, but Bridgette's face remained impassive. "For two hundred and fifty thousand dollars."

The smile froze on Bain's face. "You're crazy."

Bridgette's arm came up in front of him, like a mother protecting her child, and she stared at me. Her gaze was precise and appraising, and I wondered if I'd blown it. I really hoped not—"The best hiding place is in plain sight" was the advice a friend had given me once, and this seemed like the plainest possible. I forced myself to keep meeting Bridgette's eyes.

The tiniest hint of a smile appeared on Bridgette's lips. She said, "Okay. Two hundred and fifty thousand dollars."

In a distant corner near the back of my mind, a warning whistle shrilled that this had been too easy. That "dependable" sounded a lot like "expendable." And that I was missing something crucial.

Then my eyes went back to the photo. From a distance, it looked like just a nice family, the tensions I'd seen at closer range invisible. *Family*. That word was so foreign to me, and yet, suddenly, dangerously desirable.

I said, "How do we start?"

CHAPTER 7

t took less than an hour for them to explain what they had in mind. Fifty-three minutes to outline what would change my life and the lives of a dozen people irrevocably.

The plan was well-thought-out—Bridgette was an excellent organizer. Each piece clicked against the next with the precision of well-set-up dominoes. But the problem of being a good organizer is it gives you the illusion you know what is going on everywhere. It's the periphery that will get you every time.

It was simple: I would spend the next month living there in "the cabin" and learning everything they could teach me about Aurora. A month before Aurora's birthday, I would move to Tucson and take my place in the family. Once I had the money, they figured it would take me three weeks to get my affairs in order, and then I'd disappear. The way they made it sound, it was like being Cinderella: Girl goes from pauper to princess, only in this modern version she doesn't even have to tie herself up with a dubious prince at the end.

"The fact that Aurora took off once will make it easy for people to believe she'd do it again," Bridgette said.

"But everyone will think she just came back for the money. That she's opportunistic," I said.

"Exactly." Bridgette sat forward. "And that's precisely why it would be credible, her coming back right now after all this time. Otherwise we'd need some elaborate story."

"People like to believe the worst, especially about families like ours," Bain said. But his voice held no bitterness—he almost sounded proud. Bridgette, though, didn't feel the same way. Her neck went pink, and she fiddled with her ring.

I tried to think of the right questions to ask in the right order.

"Why would your grandmother still let her have the money? Wouldn't she get mad and cut Aurora out of her will?"

"It's not a will," Bain said. "It's an estate." Bragging again. It struck me that he was trying to impress me.

"She can't," Bridgette said, ignoring him. "The money Aurora inherits when she's eighteen is from her parents. They're both dead."

"What was Aurora like?" I asked.

Bain frowned. "Why does that matter?"

"I want to know if I'm going to like being her."

"She was nice," Bain started to say, but Bridgette cut him off.

"She was spoiled, conceited, and wild. She never thought about anything except pleasing herself and having a good time."

"She doesn't sound anything like me."

"All you have to do is ask yourself, 'What should I do to be the center of attention?' And then do it. I'm pretty sure that was Aurora's only guide to her behavior," Bridgette said.

"It sounds like you weren't exactly friends."

"Just because I'm frank doesn't mean I wasn't fond of her," Bridgette said. "She was careless, but she could be a lot of fun. And she was my cousin. Family. I loved her."

Wow. I wondered what Bridgette said about people she only *liked*.

"What about DNA?" I asked. "Won't it be easy to show I'm not your cousin?"

"They tried to take DNA samples when she disappeared. But there wasn't anything to take, so there's nothing to match it to. Her toothbrush and hairbrush were gone, and our grandmother has a very efficient cleaning staff. In terms of the rest of the family, her father was adopted by our grandparents, so she wouldn't match any of us. There were a few fingerprints, but we have a solution for that."

"A *solution*?" I echoed, curling my fingers into balls. "If you want me to burn the tips of my fingers off, it will cost extra."

Bridgette laughed. It was the first time I'd seen her laugh, and it seemed to surprise her almost as much as it surprised me. "We're not thugs," she said.

"It's simple," Bain told me. "If someone wants to check your identity, they're not going to look up your name; they're going to run your prints against the police database. So if your prints are already in the computer as Aurora Silverton, that's what will show as a match when the cops check. The fact that there's another Aurora Silverton with completely different prints never comes up."

"Okay," I nodded slowly. "How do you get my prints into the police database as Aurora's?"

Bridgette got up and started to clear the table as she spoke. "The Silverton Child Safety Project is sponsoring a tent at Old Phoenix Days next week where parents can bring their kids to have them fingerprinted and the prints stored in the police database. I'm running the event. It will be no problem for me to slip a card with your prints into the pile to be scanned."

Bain and I moved to help her clean up. As I rinsed the plates, I said, "You two have really thought of everything."

"I'm the big picture man, the brains of the operation," Bain explained, taking a plate from me and putting it into the dishwasher. "Bridgette takes over the details."

"You have got to be kidding," Bridgette said, throwing a handful of soap suds at him.

"You can't spell BRAINS without BAIN," he told her solemnly.

"You have been using that joke since junior high school." She leaned toward me. "Sadly he is the only one who ever found it funny."

"At least I know how to load a dishwasher. If you put the pot in like that, it will block the water flow to the rest of the dishes." He tapped his nose and said to me, "See? Big picture."

I rinsed, and they argued about putting knife points up or down, crystal yes or no, the right place for the spatula; making fun of one another. I found myself getting pulled into the easy rhythm of their back and forth, of their banter. *This is what it's like to be part of a family*, I thought. *To belong to people who care about you.* As we laughed together, some part of me that had been inert suddenly flamed into life, filling me with the joy and wonder of a child reaching through a crowd for a favorite toy she thought was lost forever.

I made myself let go of the dish I was washing, and it shattered in the sink, ending the banter. "Sorry," I said, not even trying to sound like I meant it. "We don't learn a lot about fine china on the streets."

That feeling of belonging was gorgeous, like a mirage, tantalizing, false, and dangerously out of reach. It wasn't a good idea for me to get close to these two. I didn't want them to like me, and I didn't want to like them. We would all be safer if they stayed wary.

Expendable, I reminded myself. *This was an act, and you are expendable.*

"I'm exhausted," I announced. "I want to go to bed."

Bridgette managed to look genuinely confused. She said, "of

course," and showed me to my room, two flights up at the top of the tower. "Wear anything in the drawers. There should be pajamas and a robe."

"Great," I said, my back to her, my palms cupping my elbows.

The concern in her voice even sounded real. "If you need anything—"

"I just need to go to sleep."

"Sure, okay." I sensed her hesitating, maybe going to say something, but it was only, "Well, goodnight," followed by the door clicking closed.

I listened for her footsteps to retreat before I risked turning around. I was biting my lip, and my hands were shaking so it took me two tries to lock the door. I barely made it to the bed and covered my head with a pillow before I started to sob.

CHAPTER 8

'm sitting at a wide polished table in a big room. I've never been there before, but it's familiar to me, the kind of room you find in institutions everywhere: a few round tables with chairs clustered around them, windows with bars on them, some easy chairs in the corner, a desk for the guard or nurse, depending.

There's a girl across from me. Like the room, I don't know her, but she's familiar. Somewhere outside a phone begins to ring.

"Who are you?" I ask the girl.

"Who are you?" she repeats back.

The phone rings again.

"I don't like games," I tell her.

"I don't like games," she says to me.

Ring-a-ling, says the phone.

"Why are you doing this?" I demand.

"Why are you doing this?"

"Stop it," I yell at her.

The ring-a-linging gets louder. "Stop it," she says calmly.

I know instinctively it's the phone she's talking about. That it's for me; it's *important, a matter of life and death. Just like I know I don't want to answer it.*

I get up from the table and move to the door. Why didn't I think of this before? I can just get up and leave; I don't have to talk to this crazy person. I'm not a prisoner.

The door to the room is locked. Behind me, the girl laughs, a silvery, amused laugh that sends a chill up my spine. I reach for the doorknob again but my palm is sweating and my hand slips off. I can't get out, I'm trapped.

I woke up clutching blankets and wondering where the hell I was. I could still faintly hear the sound of her laughing.

For a long time the line between my awake and asleep lives had been blurred or even inverted. My dreams were mundane—sharing all the pizza we could eat and frosted cans of Diet Coke in a mall food court with Nina or waking up in an airy room with politely floral wallpaper in a bed with sheets—while my reality bristled with grim faces calling me mean names and threats that lurked in shadows. Finding myself in a massive bed with a wrought iron headboard and crisp white sheets and puffy duvet, I really wasn't sure if I was dreaming or awake.

I hadn't registered much of the room the night before, just the presence of a bed and a bathroom. Now I had a chance to look around. Light tilted over me through a full wall of windows that made it feel like a Parisian garret. There was a little couch and chair with light purple and blue-and-white plaid cushions and a small table.

I climbed out of the bed and walked around, running my fingers over the fine fabrics—soft velvet, smooth silk, and a curling wool that was how I imagined lambs felt. None of the synthetic bedspreads, with crude sunflower patterns designed to hide the puckered cigarette burns and awkward stains, that had been the closest I'd been to clean sheets in a long time.

I made my way to the bathroom, and I felt a bubble of laughter burst from me.

It was magnificent. Two and a half hours to clean, easily. There were piles of pristine white puffy towels scented with lavender and a massive white tiled steam shower and a huge crystal and iron chandelier hanging from the ceiling. But the best part was the claw-footed tub. It stood in front of an arched window through which I could see a garden and a swimming pool and another gigantic house because, of course, where I was standing was just the guest house.

I slid into the empty tub, resting my cheek against the cool porcelain and hugged myself to make sure I was truly awake. I couldn't believe where I was. It was perfect, a fairy tale good enough to banish the yawning chasm of emptiness and longing that had threatened to completely swallow me the night before. It was impossible not to feel happy and secure and content surrounded by such beauty.

I pulled off the T-shirt I'd slept in, turned on the water, and ran a bath for myself. There were three kinds of bath salts on a table next to the tub, and I chose some that smelled like grapefruit. The water crept up the sides of the tub, washing away the dirt of the past day, but it felt more like the dirt of the past year.

I washed my hair with shampoo that smelled like rosemary and mint; used a conditioner that said it had harnessed the power of red orchids and smelled like a bouquet of wild flowers; and found a razor, shaving my legs and arms and bikini line with attention I hadn't paid in a long time. I slathered myself with Lime Basil lotion and felt clean. Completely clean.

That, I decided, was one of the perks of being rich: the idea that you could always just wash whatever you'd done away with a scented soap. When I got my money, the first thing I was going to buy would be bath products.

The mouthwatering smell of bacon cooking in the kitchen twined itself around the smell of everything I'd used and made my stomach growl, urging me to hurry up. In one of the drawers I found a tank top and leggings and in another a long cable-knit grey cashmere sweater. I put them on, and the sensation of the fine fabrics sliding along my smooth, clean skin made me aware of my body in a way I hadn't been in a long time. I felt simultaneously cosseted and nearly naked. It was heavenly.

Even as I enjoyed the sensual softness, a chill swept over me. I realized there was something I needed to ask, something crucial. It was a major oversight because it should have been my very first question:

What could possibly have happened to make Aurora leave all this behind?

CHAPTER 9

According to Bain, there was an easy answer for that and a more complicated one. Aurora ran away the same night her best friend Elizabeth "Liza" Lawson died. Liza had committed suicide, jumping to her death from the top of Three Lovers Point into the steep shadowy canyon below.

"You can read about it online," he said.

"But what about your cousin?"

He shook his head and looked down at his plate. "We assume Aurora ran away because she felt so awful about Liza's death. But our grandmother offered rewards and put private detectives on the roads into and out of Tucson, and no one could trace her. "

"Would her friend killing herself really make her run away?" I asked, licking raspberry jam off the end of the knife I'd been using to spread it across my toast.

"You're lucky Bridgette isn't here. She wouldn't like that," Bain told me, nodding at the knife that was poised halfway back to the jam jar. She'd been gone when I got downstairs, which was a relief. There was something about her that made me edgy.

I put the knife down and folded my hands like a good student.

Bain rubbed his wrist, his eyes fixed on the doors beyond me like he was looking into the past. "The two of them were nearly inseparable, like a little unit themselves. They didn't really hang out with other kids in their class, or Ro didn't anyway. I think Liza was more popular. And even though Ro always came off as so confident and in control, Liza was really the dominant one. Ro needed Liza, her approval, her guidance. At least, that's how it seemed to me," he added, half-undercutting his observation. I wondered if he was able to see the fissures in Ro's confidence because they were the same as his own. "So yeah, Liza's death would have hit Ro hard. Really hard."

I took a polite bite of toast. The butter said "Imported" on it, and the jam was some special kind with a typewriter-typed label. The two of them together tasted how I imagined fresh picked raspberries exploding on my tongue would taste. With the crunchy texture of the sourdough toast, it was incredible, distracting despite what we were talking about.

"So the idea is that Aurora was so freaked out she ran away? Sounds cowardly."

He didn't like me saying that. He got tense. "You didn't know her. I'm sure something must have happened."

"Like what? What do you think happened?"

He stared down at his plate. "I don't know. There are tons of different theories—coyotes, kidnappers." He pushed his chair away from the counter and stood, moving like a rangy animal who felt trapped. "The only thing I'm sure of is that either she died or she was seriously traumatized and ran away." He carried his dishes to the sink. "Which is why you can say you have no memory of what happened. That it was completely obliterated by trauma. But you still need to learn all of *those*."

"Those" were five file boxes full of everything I needed to know about Aurora.

The next weeks passed in a pine-and-lavender-scented cocoon. Being Aurora didn't just mean memorizing facts about her; it meant learning to use forks the way she did, how to dismantle a whole broiled fish, when to use finger bowls. It meant remembering that Aurora was afraid of heights and devising an excuse for why, unlike her, I didn't play the piano or tennis or get along with wild horses.

Aurora was a girl made up of the memories of other people, and I lurched into her life like a figurative Frankenstein. That was what girls like Bridgette forgot—the *My Fair Lady* story of a girl being constructed by a master was basically the same story as the making of a monster.

It started off with flash cards with a photo of a friend or family member on the front and their vital statistics—Alive or Dead, relationship to Aurora, notable facts, size of bank account—typed on the back. Dozens of lives, years of pain and agony and carefully tuned emotions, reduced (by Bridgette) to three lines on a card.

There was something both reassuring and sinister about the way everything was brought to the same level: "collects fossils," no different from "fought with brother at Father's Day dinner," or "committed suicide." It was like looking at the underdrawing of a massive altarpiece, the saints in the process of being marked out in the periphery, just vague outlines in charcoal to start with, Mary Magdalene indistinguishable from St. Jerome, until the shading kicked in.

Bain and Bridgette took turns visiting me. I was not allowed out of the house, and I was never seen with either of them.

Once I'd mastered the cards, I graduated to DVDs. Bridgette and Bain had compiled footage of important people, generally at incredibly dull-looking parties in one of the three reception rooms—Goldenrod, Heliotrope, and Lilac—at the country club, or at the dining room of the golf course. I watched them during the evening with a bowl of butterscotch ice cream (Aurora's favorite flavor).

I ate crustless mozzarella and ripe red tomato sandwiches (Aurora didn't like crusts) as I memorized the plans of Silverton House, the house where Aurora lived. The house belonged to her grandmother, **Althea Bridger Silverton** [Alive, 81 years old, matriarch of family, $60,000,000+]. Althea became Ro's guardian after the death of her parents, **Nellis Silverton** [Died when Aurora was three, during rock climbing accident. Ro asleep, wife saw him fall to death but could offer no assistance, $15,000,000] and **Sadie Silverton** [Died when Aurora was twelve, boating accident. Had shown signs of mental instability after death of husband; when Aurora was ten she took her and they disappeared for six months. Estate to Aurora]. The housekeeper at Silverton House, **Maureen March** [Alive, 63, loves Aurora, plays video poker, $76,000], was practically considered a member of the family.

"Why does it matter how much everyone has in their savings account?" I asked Bain one day.

"So you know who they are," he said, as though that made sense.

I ate sticky buns without pecans (Aurora didn't like nuts) as I practiced navigating the corridors and back stairs of Silverton House in my mind so I wouldn't hesitate if someone told me to go get something because Bridgette said, "Grandma is tricky that way. She'll want to believe you, but she'll be watching for little signs."

I ate cheese-covered popcorn as I studied the photos on top of the piano. There were a lot of pictures of Bain and Bridgette, which allowed me to see that they had outfits for every sport from golf to boating, sometimes just the two of them, sometimes with their parents, Bridger and Genette. I gorged myself on Aurora's facts, her family, her favorite food, but what I really wanted—what I was starving for, I realized—was a photo of Aurora.

There weren't any. Not one.

I kept returning to the picture that had captured my attention the first night. I couldn't help thinking there was something hidden in it, a message, a clue. One afternoon while I was eating a tofu corn dog (Aurora had unfortunately decided to become a vegetarian before she left; I was planning to change that), I realized what felt off about it. It was the only photo with a matte around it. And unless I was mistaken, the matte had been used to crop something—or someone—out. I had it facedown in my lap, trying to remove the back when Bridgette came in.

"What are you doing?" she demanded, nearly dropping the groceries she had in her arms.

"I want to see who else is in this picture."

She snatched it from me and put it back on the piano. "What makes you think there's anyone else in it?"

"You can see the tip of a shoe next to Althea. And your father," I pointed at the man in the polo shirt, "is looking in that direction. Who is standing there? Is it Aurora?"

Bridgette kept her eyes and one hand on the photo. She nodded, with her back to me. "This picture was taken the weekend before she disappeared. There'd been a tennis tournament at the club and—" She shook her head.

"Why did you cut her out? And why aren't there any pictures of her?"

"After she disappeared it just upset everyone to see pictures of her. So we got rid of them. Why are you so interested?"

"I wanted to see what she looked like."

She rounded on me. "She looks like you. Exactly. Like. You." With each word she took a step toward me. Her posture was tense, angry.

I put up my hands. "She may look like me, but she's not me. Whatever was between the two of you, it has nothing to do with me."

She stopped moving and stared at me, twisting the ring on her finger for a moment like she was calming herself down. When she spoke again, her voice was normal. "You're right. It doesn't. Some-times it—you just startle me."

Bridgette was there for the next twenty-four hours, so I stayed away from the photo.

I learned the names and identifying characteristics of the ten dogs Aurora had had in the course of her life (all dead) while devour-ing red velvet cupcakes with extra buttercream frosting (Aurora's favorite). Everything I memorized about Aurora, every new fact, made me more eager to see a picture of her. Would people accept me as Aurora? Would this really work?

There were no cards for Bain and Bridgette, but I made them up myself in my head. **Bain Silverton** [Alive, 23, working in the family real estate development business, capable but lazy, net worth unknown]. **Bridgette Silverton** [ostensibly Alive but only visible evidence of a pulse was twisting Cartier ring, 21, taking time off from University of Arizona to work on fa-ther's campaign for Congress, only uses fake sugar, net worth unknown but apparently inadequate or wouldn't be doing this because Bridgette didn't do anything without a good reason].

On my seventh night there, when I was eating frozen pizza (with pepperoni—Bain had slipped it to me when I'd begged for meat a few days earlier and it was our secret), a Sonora Heights Academy year-book dropped onto the counter in front of me. "This is Bridgette's from senior year," Bain explained, taking a beer from the refrigerator and sitting on the stool next to mine. "She told me you wanted to see a picture of Ro. Ro was a freshman, so her class is in there too."

My heart began to pound faster. I flipped through, looking for the freshman class, missing it the first time and having to fan the thick pages back. "Aurora would have been a senior this year," I said, half-babbling to cover my excitement.

"That's why you really only need to get an idea of who her class-mates are, in case they come up in conversation." Bain gulped the beer down fast. "They're graduating on June 14, and most of them will be taking off for the summer right after. So if you don't come to Tucson until a week later, you won't run into them."

"Clever. Bridgette's idea?"

I saw him start to frown then stop. "You just made a joke."

"Are you sure?"

"And another one. No more meat for you."

I don't know what I expected, but when I found Aurora's class picture, it wasn't like looking in the mirror or meeting an old friend. It was generic, long dark hair parted on the side, headband, cardigan. She was smiling but not really, her expression as blank and hollow as a tribal mask.

Bain took the yearbook from me, flipped a few pages to a spread of candid photos titled "Community Activities" and pushed it back in my direction. His finger tapped a picture of two girls with bikes, side by side under a banner that said, "Be a Hero Bikeathon."

One of them was dressed as Catwoman in an all-black bodysuit with cat ears, a cat collar, and a looped tail dangling off the back of her bike seat. The other was dressed as Wonder Woman in blue boy shorts with a white trim, a red T-shirt that had two yellow sequin W's glued on, and a yellow headband. She'd wrapped the hand grips of her bike in yellow tape to go with the Wonder Woman theme, and there was a red crystal star glued between handlebars.

"Aurora," Bain said, his finger resting on the one dressed like Catwoman. It was almost a shock to see her here. She looked so different from the sedate class photo. Here her hair was wild under the cat ears. She wore thick black eyeliner and was smiling in a confident, almost mocking way that was echoed in her posture, as though the costume fit not just her body but also her personality like a glove.

With all that confidence, the challenging smile, I would have expected her to be looking at the camera, but instead she was gazing at the girl next to her. That girl was lovely, with a golden mass of hair that framed her face like a corona, porcelain skin, and huge blue eyes. She seemed mild, and, unlike Aurora, her costume didn't seem to suit her at all. She looked like a doll someone had dressed up in another doll's outfit, but her smile was friendly and candid. I could imagine having lunch with her, talking for hours, lying on a picnic blanket and staring up at clouds and cracking stupid jokes. "That's Liza," Bain said, and I couldn't quite tell from his tone what he thought of her. "The one who committed suicide."

I stared at the photo for a long time, but the more I looked, the more it seemed to disassemble before my eyes. Liza came into sharper focus—sweet, funny, nice, pretty, kind—while Aurora became more of a blur. For the first time I began to see Aurora's resemblance to me. But it wasn't in her face; it was her eyes. I recognized the expression there from my own—the expression of someone who is keeping a secret.

Who are you? I asked myself. *What happened to you?*

I didn't realize, then, that I had been staring at half the answer since I arrived.

CHAPTER 10

There is noise coming from somewhere, like a television, a man's voice saying, "Come on." I'm standing in an unfamiliar room.

My heart begins to pound, and I hear a ring-a-linging in my ears. Then I realize it's the phone in the room. You have to answer it, I think. It's life and death.

"It's time," the voice on the TV says, getting louder, like it's trying to distract me from the ring-a-linging. I back toward the night table ("Let's go!" says the voice), toward the phone, groping behind me to answer it. I keep thinking I'm nearly there, but it keeps receding. Glancing down, I see a notepad with the name TOM YAW written across the top. Is that who is on the phone?

"Gotta go," the voice on the television says, and I realize something about it is familiar. My pulse begins to race, and an alarm goes off in my head. I grasp desperately for the phone, and my fingertips graze it. The receiver flies off and falls to the floor, and as I reach and catch it in my hand, my mind flashes Watch out! and I turn and see—

Bain was standing by the side of the bed when I opened my eyes.

"Did you know you talk in your sleep?" he said.

I was breathing fast, and my heart was pounding. "What are you doing here?" I got up on one elbow and glanced at the clock next to the bed. It read eight A.M. "It's the crack of dawn," I complained as though for years I hadn't been used to getting up hours earlier. Then I noticed his white shorts and white shirt. "Why are you dressed like a hospital orderly?"

"Tennis," he said, tossing the red-and-white-handled racquet I'd seen in the photo on the piano in the air and catching it. "Bridgette thinks it's important that you at least know the basics of tennis even if you say you won't play. The caretakers at the big house go to church Sunday mornings, so we have a few hours when they're not around. Come on."

I pulled the covers up to my chin. "I don't know what to wear."

"I put some of Bridgette's tennis stuff on the couch," he said. "Come on, we don't have a lot of time."

I was still slightly rattled as I jimmied myself into Bridgette's clothes, picked up the tennis racket, and stumbled downstairs. I hadn't heard Bridgette arrive, but she was sitting at the counter with one leg tucked up under her, sipping her fake-sweetened coffee, touching a piece of toast as though she might eat it, and reading the paper. She gave me a quick look, said, "Bain is already down on the court," and went back to her breakfast.

No coffee for me, I gathered.

Between the lack of caffeine and the fact that Bridgette's shoes were two sizes too big, I wasn't my most graceful as I went down the tower stairs to the front door, but as soon as I stepped out into the morning air I felt energized. The guest house was beautiful, but to avoid being seen, I'd been inside for the entire past week. I felt free, like I'd been liberated from some kind of prison. The kind with the eight-hundred-count Egyptian cotton sheets.

The tennis courts were between the main house and the guest house. You could see them from the French windows so I knew where I was going, but on the ground they were shielded behind a series of tall hedges. Even before I caught sight of them, I could hear the satisfying *thwop thwop thwop* of tennis balls being hit by a racket as a ball machine spewed balls at Bain. When I reached the fence, I stopped to watch him play. He moved with the kind of confidence and ease that come from natural skill, not practice. Which didn't surprise me—it was hard to imagine Bain practicing anything. He was the kind of person who did what he wanted but didn't work very hard at it.

He saw me standing there, hit a remote control, and the ball machine went quiet. "Just warming up."

"I think you meant showing off."

"Trust me, you'll know when I'm showing off. Let's see what you can do."

The next ninety minutes were an endless study in what I *couldn't* do. Which included: hold the racket properly, hit the ball forehand, hit the ball backhand, hit the ball over the net, serve, volley, and keep score.

At one point I saw Bain glance in the direction of the guest house hopefully, but apparently whatever he was looking for was absent. So he returned his attention, dejectedly, to me.

It was excruciating, him lobbing balls to me, me somehow managing to always be in exactly the wrong place and missing them. Once when I wasn't paying attention, I accidentally hit a ball, and Bain's face lit up. After that I tried harder, which guaranteed it wouldn't happen again. The times I did manage to connect the balls were either too long or too short, except for the one I smashed into Bain's shoulder so hard he yelped. Concentrating as intensely as I could, I got the ball across the net only three times, and either that was the magic number or Bain was running out of patience because after the last time he said, "I think that's enough," and shepherded me back toward the guest house.

When we got back, Bridgette was there, sitting at the counter nibbling toast and sipping coffee. "Good game?" she asked, looking up and giving me a big smile.

That was odd. "I'm a natural," I told her. "Ask Bain's shoulder."

I continued upstairs to my room and paused in the doorway. I'd been in a rush that morning so I hadn't made the bed and I'd just flung the T-shirt I slept in on the couch. Everything was how I'd left it, slightly untidy.

But not quite as untidy. The T-shirt looked like it had been folded out of habit, then unfolded and left in a slightly different spot. The hairs had been cleaned out of my brush before it was set back down parallel to the side of the dresser. It was as though someone had searched the room and tried to put everything back but just couldn't tolerate the disorder. Someone who wasn't good with messes.

I smiled to myself as I noticed the corner on the top sheet of the mattress had been squared off. Running my hand along the side of the mattress pad, I felt the bulge of my wallet and pulled it out. My Eve Brightman ID was gone. As my mind raced through the best way to handle that, I checked my other hiding place. That one, at least, was untouched.

I peeled off my clothes and got into the shower. My ID was probably safer with Bridgette than it would be with me once I got to Silverton House. But without it, it would be nearly impossible for me to leave. I couldn't think of any other reason Bridgette would have taken it.

As I was to learn, my imagination was pretty stunted.

One week down. Seven to go, I told myself as I stood under the warm spray of the shower.

If you live that long, a voice inside my head whispered.

After that, Bridgette got friendlier, and the days got more monotonous.

There were only four books in the guest house: *To Kill a Mockingbird, Northern Arizona Critters and Creepers, The Junior League of Scottsdale Favorite Recipes Cookbook,* and the yellow pages. I did spend some time reading over the messages people left in Bridgette's yearbook, but unsurprisingly those were as arid as Bridgette herself.

There were magazines, all with titles like *Arizona Today* or *Arizona Home* or *Home, Arizona.* I read every one, spotting people who appeared in my notecards at dismal-looking parties, and learned a lot about things like desert gardening and the *New* New Arizona Cuisine (Get out that grill!).

At the beginning of the second week, Bridgette and I had been at work all day, and we were getting on each other's nerves. I felt like the more I came to understand Aurora, the more she seemed to distrust me. We had dinner in silence, and I went to bed right after.

The clock said 11:09 when a line of silver light raked over the windows and I heard a car pull into the driveway. I assumed it was Bain, but when the door to the guest house didn't open, I went to the window to check who had arrived. I saw an old silver VW bug and caught the sound of footsteps on gravel as someone moved quickly through the shadows toward the main house.

Giving myself the excuse that I was making sure the person wasn't a prowler, I tiptoed down the stairs, out the door, and followed the same path he'd followed. As I rounded a corner, I saw light coming from the ground floor of the main house. Maybe the live-in couple who looked after the place were entertaining, I thought, but then I saw Bridgette.

The room I was looking into through the curtains was a library, with floor-to-ceiling shelves lined with the kind of unopened books I had spent hours dusting in other similar houses. Even though it was a warm night, there was a fire burning in a fireplace, as though to set the mood. Bridgette was standing in front of it talking to someone I couldn't see. She was smiling and looked—not like herself. Mischievous and happy. She was also naked. I quickly ducked down and out of sight.

Based on the card for Bridgette's boyfriend, **Stuart Carlton** [25, financial consultant, collects rare baseball cards, $5,000,000 (plus trust fund at 30)], he didn't strike me as the VW Bug type. Of course his car could have been in the shop, and he could have borrowed his housekeeper's. Or it could have been someone else. Whoever he was, I hoped he'd show her a really good time because with her out of the house I saw my first chance since getting there to get online. I hadn't been allowed near a computer, but with Bridgette busy I could use hers.

Backing away from the window, I sprinted back to the guest house. I found Bridgette's computer in the bottom of a drawer in her room and woke it up. It was password protected, but I'd seen her type it enough times to know where the keys were, and it only took me two tries to get it—CHLOE. Her password was her favorite designer. Ugh.

I got the browser open and searched "Aurora Silverton." There were news links in the context of the Silverton family's involvement in various charities for missing children, including the Aurora Silverton Foundation, one record of her winning a junior-level tennis tournament in seventh grade, and a link to a piece by the gossip columnist of *Tucson Today* about the preparations for Coralee Gold's graduation party, which would include "a special memorial moment for absent classmates Elizabeth Lawson and Aurora Silverton."

"They were a part of our class, and they should be a part of our celebration," Coralee Gold told the columnist during a hush-hush planning session for what promises to be the party of the season. "I can't tell you exactly what we have in mind, but I can say no one has ever done anything like it at a graduation party." Coralee is the daughter of nationally famous Domestic Diva Gina "Good as Gold" Gold and her adorable husband Bernie.

Among the comments from people who loved Gina Gold and thought Bernie really was adorable, one jumped out at me that sent an icy chill down my neck.

AzAngry: "It makes me sick every time I see the Silverton name. How many more problems will they be allowed to bury the way they buried Elizabeth Lawson?"

Problems? Bury?
Before I could search the site for more, I heard the sound of voices and the crunch of feet on gravel outside. Apparently Bridgette's boyfriend was not the sleepover—or even the stay-very-long—type. I closed the browser, shut the laptop, tucked it under the sweaters, and had just made it back into my bed when the front door opened. My heart was pounding so loud that when I heard footsteps padding slowly down the hall and Bridgette peered into my room, I was afraid she'd be able to hear it even from under the covers.

AzAngry was probably just a nutcase, or a disgruntled employee, I thought. Hadn't Bain said that people liked to think the worst of the family? Liza had committed suicide. Surely no matter how powerful the Silvertons were, they couldn't have orchestrated that.

Right?

A few evenings later, Bain, Bridgette, and I were together, sitting on the porch eating chips and salsa and discussing the plan for my return to Tucson. It was going to be the Friday a week after Aurora's high school class would have graduated. It had to be on a Friday, Bridgette explained—

"—because Grandmother always has tea at four o'clock on Fridays and all the grandchildren are required to attend," I interrupted. "This isn't a bee; you don't have to spell it all out."

Bain laughed and said, "That was creepily like Aurora," but Bridgette just stared at me and said, "Yes, it was."

I grinned at her. After an uncomfortable moment, she picked up where she'd left off. "You'll take the train from Phoenix and then a taxi from the station in Tucson," she said. "When you get there, you'll ring the doorbell. Mrs. March will answer, and you'll tell her to pay the taxi. It's the kind of thing Aurora would have done, and it will shock everyone enough they won't think of not letting you in."

Bain took the empty chip bowl and dumped the crumbs into his mouth. "And the fingerprints," Bain said. "We need to get them to check them right away because once they've done it you're clear. But we think if you suggest it, it could look suspicious, so I'm going to bring it up. As though I think I'm challenging you. Once Grandmother accepts you, everyone else in the Family will go along with it."

I noticed that both he and Bridgette always pronounced the Family the same way, as though it had capital letters and was somehow different from every other family in the world.

"Is the Family some kind of cult?" I joked.

But Bain didn't laugh. "The Family is the most important thing. You do whatever you must to protect it."

"Yes," Bridgette agreed, looking at him hard. "You do." She turned back to me. "That only leaves the hug."

"The hug?"

"Grandmother insists we hug her at tea, but Aurora hated it and wouldn't do it. If you come in and don't hug her, it could look like you don't know the ritual. On the other hand, if you do, it would be out of character for Aurora."

"Huh," I said.

"We'll just have to play it by ear," Bridgette said, twisting the triple bands on her pointer finger. Leaving things unplanned clearly made her nervous.

"Maybe one of us could make an issue of it," Bain suggested. He turned to me. "We figure if Bridgette and I doubt you the most vociferously, we'll be able to control the opposition."

"Vociferously. Fancy word," I said.

He winked at me. "I've got a library card."

Despite not trusting them and not wanting to like them, a strange kind of closeness had grown up between us during the past three weeks. A closeness I couldn't risk.

I determined I would destroy it.

The next day was Friday, exactly a week before I was supposed to go back. Bridgette drove me into Phoenix to have my hair cut, so that it parted on the same side that Aurora's had, and colored to resemble her slightly lighter brown.

She also gave me money to buy an outfit to wear back to Tucson, since the clothes I'd come in were a mess and I couldn't show up in something from the Silvertons' guest house.

I went to the mall and bought a shapeless nubby gray jacket with three-quarter-length sleeves that looked like something someone's grandma would wear, a midnight-blue sequin miniskirt that absolutely did not, a sleeveless pearl grey silk shirt, black peep-toe pumps with an ankle strap, over-the-elbow black gloves, two thick bangles, and a pair of Ray Ban knockoffs. The jacket just kissed the bottom hem of the miniskirt. It was definitely *not* the kind of outfit you'd wear to tea.

But it was perfect for a party.

Because I wasn't going to be making my rendezvous with Bridgette. I had somewhere else in mind.

I was passing one of those kiosks that line the walkways of all malls when I saw a pendant that looked like a shimmering orange-and-black butterfly. The price was high, but I couldn't pull my eyes away from it.

"That's a monarch butterfly," the kiosk guy told me as he stood a little too close to fasten it around my neck. He was young with dark hair and eyes, a few days' growth of beard, and a slow, confident smile that said he was used to his advances being welcome.

He spoke English with a slight accent, and when I'd walked up I heard him talking into his phone in a language that sounded like Hebrew. Now he said, "They are special because they migrate." He stood back and pretended to examine it while looking at my boobs. "For my people, the Native Americans, the monarch butterfly is a symbol of change. Of adventure."

He was no more Native American than I was a liger. "Really?" I asked, wide-eyed.

He nodded. "You look like a girl who could use some adventure."

My initial response was to turn around and walk away. I, Eve Brightman, couldn't afford to draw attention to myself, to play games with people. I'd spent the past few years trying to be invisible.

But you're Aurora now, I thought. *And the rich can afford to play all the games they want.*

I gave the kiosk man Aurora's cocky smile and said, "Who couldn't use some adventure? Any chance of a discount?"

Incredibly, it worked. His eyes widened slightly, and his hand went to my forearm. "That depends. Any chance of a date tonight, butterfly?"

"Sure," I lied. I took the 20 percent off and didn't mention that butterflies don't come out at night.

At the hair place I quizzed the woman who did my color about how to get to the Amtrak station and even made her write out the directions so she would be sure to tell anyone who asked that's where I'd gone. It was amazing how nice people were when you seemed to have money. I pretended to go to the bathroom, snuck out the back of the shop without paying, climbed a fence, and used the map I'd ripped out of the yellow pages at the cabin to make my way to the bus station.

I hesitated outside it. My mother had loved buses. When I was little, we spent a month taking buses, and whenever I would ask her where we were going, she would just say "farther." Looking at the station my fingertips tingled, as though searching for a hand to hold, and my chest felt tight.

But I couldn't think about my mother now. I needed to get ready, to stop being Eve and to really start to be Aurora.

What would Aurora do? I asked myself, and as the question lingered I spotted a bar across the street from the station. It was cool and dim inside, a long counter with mushroom topped bar-stools that rotated. The bartender wasn't sure he wanted to serve me, but a man three stools down said, "Just give the lady her beer, Art." So Art did.

"I'm Jerry," the man on the stool introduced himself. "What are we drinking to?"

"Eve," I told him.

"Friend of yours?"

"She was for a long time."

"Something happen to her?"

"It was her time to go."

"Well, then, to Eve," Jerry said.

"To Eve." We clicked bottles.

"Nice necklace. Monarch right?" he asked, then went on without me answering. "Interesting creatures. They're poisonous, you know."

"I didn't."

He winked. "'Course only to their enemies."

The sun was getting low two hours later, as the bus lumbered out of Phoenix. I stared out the window past Eve's reflection—now Aurora's—into the yawning darkness beyond.

PART II
HAUNTED

It's not like waking up. It's like breaking the surface of the indoor pool at the Country Club, *she thinks,* going from murky silence to the humid, slightly mildew scented air that hangs heavily over you.

Only this isn't the pool, isn't the Country Club at all. Her half-open eyes focus slowly on different objects, the thin grey light of evening trickling in through the partially closed curtains to her right, intermittent headlights across the ceiling above her, her toes in a pair of high heels so far away at the foot of the bed, the hazy outline of the dresser beyond that, a mirror atop it.

The sound of steady traffic makes a low buzz from outside; from somewhere closer comes the stuttering drone of a tired air conditioner.

She is incredibly thirsty. Her throat is dry and scratchy, and her tongue feels like it's twelve times too big for her mouth.

Memories slip in and out of her mind like the rake of headlights across the ceiling—looking for someone, falling, red brake lights by the side of the road, the whine of a powerful engine reversing toward her.

Only then does she feel the first stirring of fear. Remembering the car makes her heart beat faster; she feels something tighten in her chest. Get up, *a voice in her head says, suddenly urgent.* You have to get up and get out of here before he comes back.

He? He who? *she asks herself, but there is no answer, just abruptly, this sense that she must flee. Now.*

She sits up fast—too fast—sending a wave of pain and nausea crashing over her. Collapsing backward on the sweat-soaked bedspread, she takes three shallow, gasping breaths, then three deeper, more measured ones.

She swallows hard—God, she is thirsty—and tries sitting again, this time moving toward the edge of the bed and getting up more slowly.

There's another dizzying moment. But this time it passes and when her eyes refocus she is facing a girl in the mirror. Herself, it must be herself, because there is no one else in the room. But there is nothing familiar about the girl she sees, the girl in the dirt-streaked sleeveless blouse and the pale peach miniskirt with the bloody lip and the cut over her eye. She has no memory of her. She has no idea what her name is.

Panic overtakes fear, and she starts to tremble. Breathe, she orders herself, as she feels around and finds a pocket in her skirt. There's a twenty-dollar bill and a piece of broken chain but no ID, nothing to tell her who she is.

Her eyes slew to the reflection of the window behind her. The curtains are half-closed, but the space between them is lit by the artificial brightness of a clot of neon signs. She stares at them without consciously seeing them, forcing herself to keep breathing. She lets her gaze linger, unfocused, around the room, until it rests on her hands. They're badly cut and filthy. A handful of dust, she thinks, and then shivers. Something about the phrase makes her uncomfortable, but she's not sure why, or where she's heard it before. Maybe if she closes her eyes and lies down.

Go! the voice in her head orders, knocking her out of her thoughts. You have to get out of here!

This time it works. Stumbling to her feet, she makes for the door. She pauses on the threshold, caught by the dim sense that she's forgetting something—should she have a coat?—but it's fleeting, overpowered by the urge to get away and her thirst, almost unbearable now. She'd kill for a Diet Coke.

Wrenching open the door, she stumbles into the warm night air.

CHAPTER 11

FRIDAY

I fell asleep on the bus and dreamed of laughing girls and orange butterflies landing near my cheek and only woke up when the driver's voice announced our arrival in Tucson.

From the station I spent the last of my money on a taxi up into Ventana Canyon. It was the road that led to the Silverton compound, but that wasn't where I was going. Not yet anyway.

If everything went as I'd planned, though, it was where I would end up.

The size of the houses increased as the road rose, and so did my nervousness. My fingers tapped against the black vinyl seat next to me, and I pressed my forehead, suddenly warm, to the glass of the window hoping for cool relief. There was none.

As the taxi pulled up in front of the address I'd given the driver, I was seized with a jolt of apprehension so strong it nearly left me dizzy. *Why are you doing this?* a voice in my head asked. There was nothing wrong with Bain and Bridgette's approach; it would have worked. *So why are you rushing things, why this way, why tonight . . . ?*

I knew the answer, even if I hadn't been ready to admit it to myself until that moment. When I'd come up with the idea, I'd told myself I wasn't going along with Bain and Bridgette's plan because I wanted to appear in Tucson with a bang, not just stroll up at tea time. Tea time is languorous, that in-between moment in the day when all the shadows are slanted obliquely and reality can slip easily from one thing to another. People do things they regret mildly at tea time.

Night, though—if you do something you regret then, it won't be mild. At tea time "what if?" is a kid's game, something to keep conversation going; at night it's a beckoning whisper from behind a barely open door of your psyche. Night is the darkness of a theater before the curtain goes up, full of strangers' coughs and bodies shifting and unknowns that can be wonderful or terrifying or both. It is elusive, intriguing, and, fundamentally, lonely. It fit Aurora, this new Aurora, perfectly. She had to come home at night.

But sitting in the back of the idling taxi, staring at the mansion in front of me, I realized I'd also done it precisely because I was scared. Because if I'd shown up at tea with the Family, I could still have backed out somehow. Appearing this way, though—there would be no running away. I would be committed.

I'd copied the address out of the Sonora Heights Academy alumni directory, but for a moment I thought I might have gotten it wrong: The house was massive and apparently fancy, but the entire front yard was ripped up, a construction zone. And there were no lights in the windows.

The cab driver appeared to share my apprehension. "You sure this is what you want?" he asked, eyeing me speculatively in the rearview mirror.

He meant the address, but his question echoed in my mind. "You sure this is what you want?" I could still turn around, still go back to Phoneix, call Bain or Bridgette and have them come get me, arrive the way they'd planned—

I spotted a billowing purple silk pagoda on the far side of the construction zone, apparently spanning a path. That must be the entrance. "Yes," I said. "I'm sure." I paid him, took a deep breath, whispered, "Here we go, Aurora," and walked beneath the pagoda, along the tea-candle-lit path, into Coralee Gold's graduation party.

It was like walking onto a stage set. The swimming pool was filled with floating candles, the entire area around it covered with oriental rugs. Brightly colored silk cushions were grouped around low octagonal tables with hookahs on them, and iron candelabra twisted in exotic shapes taller than me hoisted thick white candles all around the yard. Shirtless serving men with well-oiled chests and puffy harem pants stood behind tables of drinks and food with their arms crossed, statue-still. There was a faint breeze that rustled through the leaves and made the candles flicker slightly, stirring a wind chime somewhere in the distance. Other than that there was no movement, no sound. It was like the moment before the director yells action.

I knew the party had started more than an hour earlier, but at first I didn't see any guests. Then my eyes moved to the terrace beyond the pool where a massive pink-and-white striped canopy had been erected over a dance floor. The floor was ringed with people, all of them staring solemnly toward the center. I couldn't tell what they were looking at, so I moved closer and stood on my tiptoes at the edge of the crowd to get a better view.

The crowd formed a U-shape, open at the far end, where a woman was sitting on a chair. "Chair" is the wrong word; it was more like a throne with ornately carved gold sides and plush red velvet cushions.

It was large and seemed larger because the woman inside it was tiny, almost birdlike. She could have been anywhere from thirty to sixty years old. She had long, unnaturally black hair and was wearing a lapis blue silk robe edged in gold. Her eyes were closed, her head was tipped back, and her lips were moving.

That's when I figured it out. Coralee Gold had hired a spiritual medium for her party. I had to stifle a laugh. This was either the best thing that could happen to me or the very worst.

Straining my ears, I made out the words, "Which one of you is there? I see two of you but I can only hear one. Which one are you?"

There was a moment of the kind of silence that comes only from one hundred people all holding their breath, the kind of silence that clings to you, turning a group into a single yearning organism. I had good reasons for not believing in ghosts or mediums, but as the silence stretched, I felt myself getting caught up in it. Wanting to believe, anxious about what was going to happen.

The tension wound itself tighter among us until it was nearly suffocating. At that moment, the woman with the dark hair opened her mouth and in a thin, reedy voice completely different from the one she'd been using said, "I am Aurora."

A shudder convulsed the crowd. Everyone craned closer to listen. But the next words were indistinct, jibberish.

Speaking in her own voice, the medium said, "Can you repeat that? We couldn't quite hear you Aurora."

Silence.

"I had her, but I feel her slipping away," the medium said with a small shake of her head, eyes still closed as though she were talking to herself as much as to us. Taking a deep breath, she raised her fingers to her temples and intoned, "Aurora or Elizabeth, if either of you is still there, can you ring the bell?"

More sticky, lengthening silence. And then, faintly, the bell began to ring.

Everyone around me straightened abruptly, as though they were all feeling the same chill I felt, and a whisper went through the crowd. I said to the person next to me, "That's cool."

He turned and looked at me. And gasped.

It was fascinating the way it happened—just the slightest murmur, the sound of bodies shifting as they moved to elbow their neighbor or point, like ripples begun by a leaf hitting the surface of a pond, until someone said aloud, "Oh my God, that's Aurora Silverton."

Then the medium woman's eyes flipped open, and she stared at me, shrieked, and began to writhe. The crowd parted to make way for her, and she jerked across the floor toward me, as though she were a marionette whose arms and legs were being controlled by an invisible giant. She stopped in front of me, swaying. Her eyes rolled, and her long, blood-red nails curled in my direction. "You—you dare to mock the work of our sister Madam Cruz," she said in a low, booming baritone completely different than the voice she had been using before.

"I didn't mock, I was just—"

"Silence!" Her head tilted to the side, and her face moved up and down next to me, as though she were an animal of prey sniffing meat. "You are a cursed thing only half-alive. Be careful that evil does not claim the half that still lives. You come from a world of lies and shadows, and they cling to you like ivy. You reek of the fetid stench of death."

"I'm really sorry, I—"

A strange growling noise came from deep in her throat. "Your punishment awaits you already. The spirits will have their revenge. Go! Leave! If you have any sense, you will fly from here forever." And then she passed out.

It got a bit hectic then. iPhones began popping out everywhere, and I was swarmed by people. From what Bain had said, I got the impression that Aurora and Liza were a bit aloof from the other students in their class, and that probably explains why most people drew closer to me but didn't address me, watching me instead through the cameras on their phones. There were a handful of girls, who came forward to hug me, but they seemed more wary than glad to see me.

As though Aurora was nice enough, but not really nice. Or as though they wanted a picture with me to post on their Facebook pages.

I wasn't disappointed. I'd only really had a chance to study Aurora's friends in a yearbook from three years earlier, so I wasn't going to be able to recognize most people, not easily anyway. Which meant this part was the most dangerous part of my arrival—and I would need to cut short.

That had been part of my plan from the beginning. Except it's not as easy as you'd think to start a fight at a fancy graduation party. Actually getting someone to stop tweeting and take a swing at me was a challenge. I had to goad three guys, including one whose iPhone I threw in the pool when he wouldn't stop filming me, before anything happened. Even then it was only because they summoned one of Coralee's mother's bodyguards, and after bruising my knuckles on his chin, I kicked him in the nuts.

The police arrived almost immediately—someone must have called them as soon as I started the fight.

The officer who brought me in was surprisingly young. He wasn't good-looking, not in the traditional sense anyway, but he had the kind of face you wanted to keep looking at. His mouth was too big, his nose looked like it had been sculpted in a bar fight, and he was scowling. His face was made for it.

He was the kind of guy you'd never see at a country club, but who would have no trouble getting past the velvet rope at a night club. The name tag pinned perfectly straight on his blue patrolman's uniform said "N. Martinez."

He approached me cautiously, but I could have told him he didn't have to worry. I only fight when it's unavoidable, and I'd already called all the attention to myself that I needed.

He cuffed me, then steered me into the backseat of a waiting cruiser. Neither of us spoke during the twenty-two-minute drive to the police station, and the scowl didn't change. When we got there, he scraped a chair out from next to a desk and pushed me into it. "Where's Ainslie?" he said to the only other person in the place, a white man with graying hair in a tweed coat and a tie, a detective. "This one's for her."

"What is it?" the detective asked, wincing a little as he looked at me. Clearly somewhere between the fight and getting thrown into the pool, my looks had lost a bit of their luster.

"She was that domestic disturbance at the Gold residence," N. Martinez said. I could tell he didn't like the detective and that he was not the kind of person who was good at hiding that. "Crashed Coralee Gold's graduation party. Looks a lot like Aurora Silverton, doesn't she? That case was Ainslie's."

I felt, rather than saw, the other man's eyes get huge as I sucked on the cut on my lip that I'd gotten from the Golds' security guard's right hook.

The detective came around to take a look at me. He had an urban road system of veins on his nose, and there were teddy bears on his tie. I gave him a smile, apparently a bloody one because he pulled back. He turned to N. Martinez and said, "You had better get her tidied up. This gets out, we're going to have flashbulbs lurking outside."

"That's not standard procedure," N. Martinez objected. The scowl hadn't wavered, but it might have deepened. "The evidence—"

"Get her cleaned up before Ainslie sees her if you want your job."

N. Martinez grabbed my arm with no pretense of trying to be gentle and led me out into the hall. He stopped to pick up a first aid kit, then dragged me to the men's room. "I'm a girl," I pointed out to him. You'd think someone with an interest in standard procedures would care about that.

"But I'm not, and I'm coming in with you." I knew from experience that police get very testy and overprotective when they hear you've kneed someone in the balls. He followed me in, put the first aid kit on one of the white porcelain sinks, and unlocked the handcuffs. "Wash yourself."

You reek of the fetid stench of death. Madam Cruz's voice echoed in my ears as I watched him watch me.

There were two sinks beneath a mirror. Behind me were two dingy green painted stalls, and alongside them was a urinal. There was a sign on the door with a time stamp that indicated the cleaning crew had been through that morning, but I didn't believe it. The place could have used a full five hours of scrubbing.

"Could you turn your back?" I said. "I'd like some privacy."

He ignored me and took up a position leaning against the wall with his arms crossed over his chest, still scowling. There was something familiar about him, I thought, but then realized it was probably just the expression in his eyes, the cold cop stare. I'd seen it before.

I wondered what the N stood for. "Nosey," maybe.

My left hand looked bad, the knuckles covered with blood— mine, I noticed, as I rinsed it off—and starting to swell. It would be useless for at least a few days, depending on how long I kept it wrapped in a bandage. And that was the idea: No one could expect me to play the piano or tennis with a bandaged hand.

Everything was going just how I'd intended. It was all—

Cursed thing, only half-alive.

I shivered. *Stop it,* I told myself. I reached around with my right hand to lift off my shirt, and it was only then that I realized I was shaking. Not just my hands but all of me, trembling uncontrollably. It was all going how I'd intended, but what was I really doing? Up until now it had been a game, pretend, an idea. Like a play, a character whose attributes you put on for a few hours and then later you get to go home and lie on the couch eating cheesy popcorn and watching movies and being yourself. But not anymore. Now it was irrevocably for real.

Crashing Coralee Gold's party was like plunging into a freezing cold lake, committing to it—it left no exit. I'd been seen. I'd been filmed. By tomorrow I'd be all over the YouTube feeds of Aurora's former friends and classmates. There was no running away now. I felt trapped in the worst kind of trap—one I'd set for myself. Apparently even *I* knew I was unreliable.

The floor seemed to roll under me, and my head swam. But I was damned if I was going to faint in front of Officer Sort-Of-Ugly. I leaned my hips against the sink and put my right palm on the mirror. I watched mascara trace lines down my cheeks. *I should have worn waterproof* I thought, and started to laugh the way you do when something isn't funny, the way you do right before you begin to sob.

"Hurry up," N. Martinez said.

If at that moment he had come over and asked if I were all right, if he had said anything nice, anything even the slightest bit reassuring or kind or thoughtful, I think I would have broken down. But the impersonal brusqueness of his command snapped me out of my panic. All my fear turned to anger.

"I would hate to do anything to inconvenience you," I said, grabbing a handful of paper towels and leaning toward the mirror to swipe the mascara from my face.

"I doubt that."

His tone stopped me—it was almost like he was making a joke. But that seemed . . . unlikely. I resisted the urge to glance at him, concentrating on rifling through the first aid kit instead. I found an ace bandage and wrapped it around my left hand. I ran the fingers of my right hand through my hair and was turning from the mirror when I realized I'd parted it on the wrong side. Eve's side. I quickly shifted it, then faced him and said, "I'm ready." I held out my wrists for the cuffs.

He let me stand there like that for a moment, the cuffs dangling from his right index finger, clearly enjoying himself. I could tell he was working up to something, probably some kind of unsavory proposal.

He said, "I don't know what you're up to, but whatever it is, do it between eight A.M. and ten P.M. weekdays."

That surprised me, so instead of saying what I should have, I asked, "Why?"

"I'm not on duty then. I don't like dealing with spoiled girls or cowards."

"How do you know I'm a coward?"

"You ran away, didn't you?"

I shook my head. "Someone has abandonment issues." That got no reaction, not even a deepened scowl. "Besides, I'm not up to anything."

"I have five younger sisters. I know when someone is up to something." He clicked the cuffs onto my wrists. "Come."

When we got back to the squad room, there was a woman

detective in trousers and a blue button-down shirt at the desk. To her left was a slight, dark-haired man in khakis and a sweater. He looked like a well-dressed math teacher, but thanks to the flashcards I recognized him as **Thomas Trident** [38, Silverton family lawyer, newly married to Aunt Claire, likes antique cars and cooking, doesn't like Uncle Tom jokes, estate depends on terms of prenup].

Standing beside him, her posture so straight she looked like she had steel in her spine, was the woman I'd come to meet.

Althea Bridger Silverton's hair was a surprisingly chic helmet of silver. Even though it had to be nearly midnight and she must have been roused from bed, she was wearing a silver pendant over her rose ruffle-front blouse, and her beige trousers had a perfect sharp crease running down the front. She had the wan thinness and rigid posture of someone who was ill, but somehow on Althea it came off as glamorous. Maybe it was the large framed glasses, the tint partially concealing her eyes, but I had a fleeting image of her sitting at a white clothed table at a chic bistro in Paris, moving small pieces of lettuce around on her plate, sipping Chablis and smiling as men with thin cigars said witty things to court her favor like an elegantly aging French film star. The only sign that she was anything but calm were her knuckles, taut from gripping the chain of her Chanel shoulder bag so tightly.

Would she believe I was her granddaughter, or wouldn't she? The female detective was saying, "We're still running her prints against—" But Althea silenced her by raising one perfectly manicured finger.

She crossed the room toward me, taking her time. The air seemed to get more densely packed with each step, heavy and with the scent of gardenias. She stopped a foot from me and stared long and hard through the tinted glasses.

My mouth went dry. My heart was racing. Her face was an unreadable mask. Without any change in her expression, her hand snaked out and slapped me hard across the face. "How dare you come back like this?"

Welcome home, Aurora.

"Althea, we should at least wait for the fingerprint—"

"Shut up, Thomas," she barked. "It's her. No one else would have the gumption to behave this way. Come on," she said, moving toward the door. "We'll deal with you in private." There was fury in her voice, but beneath it I could have sworn I heard an undertone of excitement.

Her nails dug hard into the skin of my arm as we left the station.

CHAPTER 12

We walked down the steps of the police station like that, with me pinned next to her, and toward a large dark blue Mercedes parked at the curb. When she was still a dozen steps away, a man got out of the driver's side and opened the door for her.

In all the photos I'd seen of **Arthur Redmond** [Silverton's chauffer since before Aurora was born, drove because he loved it, net worth more than $3,000,000], he had wrapped his large, mahogany bulk in a navy-blue uniform with two rows of gold buttons marching down the front. Now he was wearing khakis, a pink-and-white-striped button-down open at the neck, a brown belt with a sterling silver buckle, and slippers with playful-looking terriers embroidered on them. Apparently even chauffeurs got to go casual when dragged out of bed at midnight.

Althea turned to him and said with a sigh, "I'm afraid you will have to come back later for Thom." As though that were the big inconvenience of the night.

"Of course, ma'am," he told her. Turning to me, he added, "And if I may, it is nice to see you again, Miss."

"Thank you, Arthur," I said. I hadn't even realized I'd used his name until I caught the flash of a look pass between him and Althea, and was glad I'd done it.

But Althea's tone was still devoid of warmth as she pointed to the door and said, "Come along, Aurora. There is no reason for us to stand gabbing like parrots in the street. Get in the car." She let go of my arm, and I saw her savor the sight of the red gashes her nails had left.

Bridgette, Bain, and I had spent dozens of hours rehearsing this first conversation alone with Aurora's grandmother, plotting out answers to the inevitable questions—where have you been, why did you leave, why are you back, what happened that night?

"Don't tell her too much about where you've been," Bain had cautioned. "Just say that for a long time you didn't remember anything, and when you did you felt guilty for being gone."

"I think dirty is better than guilty," I'd suggested.

Bridgette had looked at me, cocking her head like a curious bird, and then nodded. "You're right. Dirty. Althea will understand that, but she won't want to hear too many details."

"And let her start the conversation," Bain plowed on. "Wait for her to ask."

I slid across the wide camel leather expanse of the backseat, and Althea got in after me. The door clicked solidly closed on us, and I got ready for my first private performance.

"Well, that makes a change from a normal Friday night," Althea said as her sedan pulled smoothly from the curb.

"Yes, it does," Arthur agreed.

Althea said, "Gin or Fish?"

I wasn't sure if she was talking to Arthur or to me. She wasn't looking at either of us. Was this a test? She was busy flipping down the armrest in the backseat and extracting from it a deck of gold monogrammed playing cards. It had been specially outfitted with a teak top and two little leaves that flipped out to make a card table. She held the cards toward me and repeated, impatiently now, "Gin or Fish?" Her eyes met mine.

"You want to play cards?"

"We always played cards before. Why not now?"

I considered for a moment, trying to mask the beating of my heart by tapping a fingernail against the teak table. Was it gin or Fish? Bain and Bridgette hadn't said anything about playing cards. "Gin," I said.

Althea smiled, but I wasn't sure if it was the right answer. "A penny a point," she announced. "It's not fun unless there is something on the line."

"I don't play for money."

"Everyone always says that. It's never true." She pushed the cards toward me. "Cut."

As I watched her even up the cards, I realized her cold reception had done me a favor—any lingering concerns I had that what Bain, Bridgette, and I were doing might hurt her had completely vanished. Althea Silverton was invulnerable.

She dealt with the quick competence of someone who did it regularly. We played in silence, broken only by the sound of cards being picked up and put down and once by her saying, "You're playing well."

She was a shrewd player, but I wasn't that far behind her, even with my attention divided between the game and watching where we were going. With the kind of life I'd been living, being able to gauge both people and their cards came in handy.

I knew from Bain's tutorials—the family real estate holdings were one of his favorite themes—that the Silverton compound was built on a massive property amassed over time by Aurora's grand-father, Sargeant Silverton, and Althea. As Sargeant developed his real estate empire, they bought more and more of the parcels around them until they owned nearly an entire hilltop that backed onto Ventana Canyon. They'd built their house, which was officially Sil-verton House but was referred to simply as the House, and then houses for their children when they married. Immediately next door to the House was Silverton Manse, the house Bridgette and Bain lived in with their father, and beyond that was Weathervane, Aunt Claire and Uncle Thom's house. When I'd asked why it was called Weathervane, Bain said I'd understand when I got there.

Now as we wound up into the hills I saw a glass and steel build-ing cantilevered out over the canyon like an eagle straining forward to take flight. Or, I realized, like a weathervane pointing due north.

We drew up in front of a set of massive iron gates with inter-locking S's on them, and the car came to a stop waiting for them to open.

Althea announced, "Gin," laid down her cards, pointed her tinted lenses at me, and said, "Are you on drugs?"

In the surface of her glasses I saw my eyes widen in surprise. "No."

"Do you have any diseases?"

"No."

Silence. She nodded once toward the rearview mirror, and the gates began to swing open. The big car slid between them and up the drive to the House. I had an anxious feeling that the real action was about to start.

She raised a thin fist to her mouth and cleared her throat. "When we get to the House, you will go straight to your room and wait until you are summoned tomorrow morning. The staff needs to be

informed of your return, but they will be told my way, not by you."
Her voice was hard and cold, without a shred of kindness. "I will
think nothing of throwing you out, young lady, so if you want to
stay, you had better show more cooperation than . . . in the past."

I nodded. *In the past. What was the real Aurora like?* I wondered.

The car swept around the massive stone fountain in the middle
of the circular drive and stopped in front of an entrance with three
flagstone steps. Small lights cast golden halos around the stone-
framed windows. The front door was a massive hunk of oak, hand-
carved, I knew, by Aurora's father for her mother as a wedding present with the story of Apollo and Daphne. It was set into a façade
that was supposed to look like a Tuscan Villa, but on a scale not even
a Medici could have conceived. Three stories built around an open
courtyard in the center, it seemed even more massive than in the
photos I'd seen.

As the car pulled up, she said, "Do you know why you lost, just
now, at gin?"

"Because you outplayed me."

"No. It was because you were careless." She spoke quickly, and
if I'd thought she was intense before, it was nothing compared to
the way she spoke now. "I could see your entire hand reflected in
the window. I knew every move you were going to make before you
made it. A stupid mistake." She looked at me over the tinted glasses.
"You should take care to protect yourself."

I had the impression she wasn't just talking about cards, and I
wasn't sure I was either when I told her, "Or maybe you shouldn't
palm the aces."

There was a startled intake of breath, and then she said, almost
wonderingly, "You've changed."

"I will take that as a compliment, Grandmother."

She seemed on the verge of saying something, but then Arthur was there, holding her door open for her. When she was out of the car, he came around to open mine. I stood for a moment breathing in the warm night air, sweet with the scent of honeysuckle, and looked up at Silverton House.

Althea had said everyone was asleep, but staring at the rows of glinting windows, I had the sense that someone was watching. *The House*, I realized. It was as if the House were watching. Waiting for me.

Something isn't right, a voice said in my head. *No good will come to you here. Leave now while you still can.*

Althea's hand gripped my arm like a talon, and she led me inside.

CHAPTER 13

As I walked next to Althea, I reviewed the layout of the House in my mind, preparing for the next test.

Althea cleared her throat. "Your room," she prompted. I felt her gaze burning into me. Aurora's room was on the third floor in the southwest corner. From the front door there were two ways to go.

I could either turn right . . .

"Where are you going?" Althea demanded. I turned to look at her. Behind her tinted sunglasses, her eyes were challenging.

"To my room," I said.

"You're not going to take the stairs?" she asked.

"The shortest way is to cut across the courtyard and take the middle stairs." I watched her expression change. "You said to go there directly," I said, working not to sound smug.

Standing, I was six inches taller than she was, which made it easier to see through her tinted lenses. I caught something between surprise and confusion flicker across her face.

"Indeed. I just didn't expect you to be so very obedient."

"As you've said, I've changed." I bent to kiss her cheek and said, "Goodnight, Grandmother."

She pulled away like I'd scorched her. "Don't call me that. After what you have done, you have no right to be so familiar. If you must call me anything, call me Althea." Her tone held the keen tang of an icicle in the moonlight. "Go to bed."

I bowed my head and crossed the courtyard. A wind blew, and the door that opened onto the hallway tugged at my hand as though being pulled from the other side. From somewhere above me came a faint wailing noise. A tingling started at the base of my spine and wove itself up my back, through my ribs.

The House doesn't want me here, I thought. It came to me with crisp clarity, as though it were a perfectly natural thing to think. *The House wants me to leave.*

But I had no choice. I'd made a deal with Bain and Bridgette. This was my chance at a new life. A new start. And I had to take it.

I climbed the two flights of stairs slowly, feeling with each breath like my chest was constricting. *Go! Get out!* that voice in my mind screamed. *Turn back.*

At the top, the corridor was completely still, and the air was cool and heavy and perfumed. *Like a tomb*, I thought.

I stood there, staring at Aurora's door, third on the right, both fascinated and repelled. Moving like a sleepwalker, I took one heavy step, than another, until I was standing outside it. I inhaled a deep breath and reached for the knob. There was a low keening as the door began to open. With trembling fingers I reached along the in-side wall and flipped on the light.

And laughed out loud with relief.

The room was beautiful. A warm glow spilled over the bed from a star-shaped lantern hanging from the top of a tall birch wood canopy. Everything looked exactly the way it had in the photos Bridgette and Bain had shown me: the modern bed made out of four solid pieces of birch wood brought back by Aurora's parents from the forest in Bavaria where they'd conceived her; the dozens of pillows piled atop it in shams of white lace or eyelet; the massive white (faux, I hoped) fur rug that stretched over the polished wooden plank floor; the nubby oatmeal floor cushions around a low white lacquer table. It was chic and comfortable and clearly designed by a decorator. There was nothing sinister, nothing scary at all.

Beyond the bedroom I could see a bathroom bigger than I'd seen in many city bus stations, but much cleaner and done in slabs of grey-green marble that would have blown any municipal budget.

I took a step forward and then another. I felt like I was sneaking around, intruding into someone else's space. Like I could be caught at any moment. *This is your room*, I told myself. *Yours*. All three-and-a-half-hours-to-clean of it.

And just like that the strangeness and apprehension vanished, and joy surged through me. It was gorgeous! It was mine! I flopped back into the white cushions on the bed and hugged myself. This bed, this room, this—

I got up and crossed to the closet. Dresses, pants, shirts, jackets all hung there neatly, more clothes than I'd had in years. I ran my fingers over them, turning up labels with names I'd seen in the closets of homes I'd cleaned, and in cast-off copies of *Elle*. Price tags poked out at me—one of the jackets, four of the shirts, and three of the dresses had never been *worn*. There were skin-tight minidresses and slouchy jumpers and fake leather pants and a long prairie skirt, a jangle of styles.

Everything that Bain and Bridgette had told me about Aurora made her sound brash and confident like a party girl, always in the middle of a crowd. But the confusion of her closet told a different story. It made me think of loneliness and insecurity. I could picture Aurora standing right where I was standing, flipping through different outfits, trying them on as though if she just found the right look she'd know who she was, or who she wanted to be. Suddenly she wasn't simply a spoiled girl with too much time and money on her hands, but someone who shopped just to do something, to feel something.

I thought about the coolness of my reception from her "friends" earlier that night at Coralee's, as though none of them had really known her either. *Who were you hiding from?* I wished I could ask her. If what Bain and Bridgette said was true, I realized that Aurora's relationship with Liza had been not only her closest, but in some ways her only real one. Running my fingers over the fringes and leather and silk in her closet, I wished I could go back and give that Aurora a hug, and tell her she didn't have to be alone, that everything would be okay.

Except, of course, that everything hadn't been, I reminded myself. *Stop it.*

I opened the second closet, and my knees went out from under me. It was lined, floor to ceiling, with shelves. I reached for a pair of black ballet flats with a supple rubber bottom that looked like they'd barely been walked in. I bent my foot behind me to slip one on, a do-it-yourself Cinderella. It fit perfectly.

Some of the shoes were boring and some were ugly—the Crocs went directly in the trash—but there was a pair of silver Prada wedges and a pair of platform Gucci sandals with crisscross straps over the ankle and a pair of motorcycle boots with rivets up the front. And all of them, every pair, was exactly my size.

Oh, Aurora, I thought, *how could you have run away from this?*

My mind flashed back in time to a rural bus station, linoleum floors, fluorescent lights that hummed, the sweet, fake pine scent of the industrial cleaner the grey overalled janitor was slopping back and forth as he swayed to the music in his ear buds. The clock said eleven thirty, and my mother and I were the only ones there. We'd been travelling by bus for weeks at that point, moving in sprawling loop de loops across the map as though driven by a crazy Spirograph.

I was using the nail of my pinkie finger with its chipped red polish to pick at the old resin on the wood benches while my mother sat next to me, her head slightly turned away, listening to conversations only she could hear.

"Are we running away from home?" I asked, giving voice to the question that had been on my mind for two days, ever since the lady at the Wok On restaurant asked where we were from and my mother lied.

My mother had laughed. I couldn't see her face, but her laugh I could always conjure—rich, ringing, like bells calling you to a wedding. "No, silly goose. You can't run away from home. It's not *home* if you want to run away from it." She paused to brush a strand of hair from my face. "You can only run away from a house. Home is something you run toward."

Home. Looking around the room now, I realized how sterile everything was. Sterile in a way that went beyond its neatness. It was more like a stage set of a room than a place someone had actually lived in over time. There were no photos in frames, no little notes or stupid toy surprises from crackerjack boxes, no rocks with faces in them you'd picked up on a walk, no once-loved-but-now-relegated-to-a-corner games or dolls, no pieces of sea glass or cards from a friend or pencils gnawed at the ends or half-used raspberry-scented erasers. No computer. It looked like the room of someone who had tried to erase their real identity. Or perhaps her identity had been erased after she disappeared.

My energy level flagged suddenly, like a sail when the wind dies. There were a dozen things I should do before going to sleep, but I decided that all but hiding the original note from Bain offering me one hundred thousand dollars could wait for the morning. I slid it between the mattress and box spring, figuring that with me on top of it, it should be safe enough until morning.

I pulled open the top two drawers of the dresser and found a frothing pile of underwear in one and socks neatly rolled into balls in the other. Below those was a big drawer with stacks of T-shirts, and below that sweatpants and shorts. I pulled out a pair of boy shorts and a T-shirt and reached for a pair of socks. A strip of photos came out with them.

It was the kind you get from a photo booth at an arcade or fair, four down, different poses. They all showed a guy with floppy dark hair and a girl, sitting close together to fit into the frame. In the first one they were smiling at the camera, the second one they were forehead to forehead, the third he was cradling her cheek with a very large hand, and in the bottom one they were kissing.

The girl was Aurora, but it could have been me. We really did look exactly alike, and the realization pierced me. She looked happy. No, more than that—blissful.

I couldn't tell what the guy looked like because his face had been scratched out with a black ballpoint pen. I could only tell his hair was dark because she'd missed a place on one of them.

I took the strip of pictures to the bed and sank back into the pillows to study them. My finger rubbed over the texture of the pen that had been used to obliterate his face. The cross hatching was deep, done with real feeling, back and forth over and over. I could feel the pain that had gone into it, the anger, the shattering of a dream. On the back of the photo strip the machine had printed a date. One week before Aurora disappeared. The same day as the tennis tournament in the photo on the piano at the guest house. The one Aurora had been cut out of.

She had gone from being in love, to being so angry that I could feel it in her pen marks, during the course of that week. What had happened? Did it have something to do with her disappearance?

And why hadn't Bridgette and Bain ever mentioned that their cousin had a boyfriend? Why didn't this guy have his own flash-card? Bridgette wouldn't have made an oversight that big.

Unless it wasn't an oversight. Unless it was intentional. I couldn't shake the feeling that they were up to something, something beyond our imposter scheme, something that I was unwittingly part of. As though it wasn't necessary, maybe even wasn't desirable, for me to get Aurora completely right. I didn't like it. *Expendable*, I could still hear Bridgette's voice saying that first day.

Of course, I hadn't exactly been fully honest with them about my plans either.

And I'd already put mine in motion. I yawned and realized again how tired I was. Everything else could wait until tomorrow. I set the photo strip down on the night table and snuggled under the covers.

I don't remember turning off the lights. But the only illumination was coming from the moon when I awoke to a faint scratching sound and saw the knob on the door to my room begin to turn slowly by itself.

CHAPTER 14

I came instantly awake, mind racing. I'd turned the lock, hadn't I? *Hadn't I?*

Fear crept up my shoulder blades with prickling fingers. I groped with my unbandaged hand around the surface of the night table next to the bed for anything I could use to defend myself. How had I been so stupid? I knew better than to let down my guard.

I was making a list of all the things I should have done—jammed a chair beneath the knob, got my knife out of my purse before putting it under the mattress, never agreed to have done this in the first place—when the handle stopped moving. The door jiggled, like someone was trying to get in from the other side. My fingers closed on a flashlight on the bottom shelf of the night table. I slid it into my palm.

The handle jiggled again. "Who's there?" I asked, struggling to keep the quiver out of my voice.

The handle stopped moving for a moment. I was in the middle of taking a breath when fingers began to scratch at the edge of the door once more, as though looking for another way in.

"Who are you?" I demanded, trying to swallow and finding my mouth dry. "What do you want?"

I had to lean forward and strain to hear, but when I did, it was unmistakable. "Aurora," a voice said. It was part whisper, part wail. The handle began to jiggle again.

I wasn't going to sit there terrified. I was going to face whoever was out there. In one motion I leaped out of bed, bolted to the door, and flung it open.

And was standing face-to-face with . . . nothing.

There was no one there. There was no sign that anyone had been there. The wide, dark corridor was silent, still. Empty.

Completely empty.

But the handle on my door had moved, there had been whispering, I'd seen—

The spirits will have their revenge, I heard the medium's voice.

This was not spirits, I told myself. *There are no ghosts.* My fingers trembled, and I could feel my heartbeat through my whole body. This had to be someone. I would find them. Probably this was some prank Bain and Bridgette were pulling. Maybe this was part of their plan, to scare me, drive me nuts, make me think—

What?

That didn't matter, I wouldn't let them.

Trailing my hand against the wood paneling, I began walking to the end of the corridor opposite the way I'd come up. I went slowly, the beam of the flashlight chiseling into the empty shadows. I paused after each step, listening, but the only sound I could hear was my breathing. Four steps in, a chill wrapped around me, as though I'd passed through a cooler patch of air, and I sniffed the faint smell of jasmine. I stepped forward, and the air was warm. I stepped back, and the chill settled around me. Embraced me.

Every ghost story I'd ever read came back to me, and my skin started to prickle. "Hello," I whispered. "Is there anyone there?"

Nothing answered.

I knew, rationally, there couldn't be anyone there. That this was just a place where the air pooled, an architectural peculiarity. *There are no ghosts*, a voice chanted in my head.

Alongside me, I heard a sound. It was distinct. The sound of footsteps shuffling.

There must *be someone else there.* Only I was unmistakably alone.

I swung the flashlight around, sending the beam bouncing off the walls. The corridor was empty. But even as I stood there, watching, seeing there was no one, I heard the footsteps again, now slightly in front of me. And beneath them a low, irregular sound. At first I thought it was someone sobbing. But then I realized it was . . . giggling. A horrible, manic giggling.

The flashlight arced wildly in my trembling hands as I ran back through the cold place in the corridor, back to the open doorway of my room and slammed it shut.

My fingers stumbled over the lock, and it took me three tries to turn it. I stood there thinking, *The footsteps sounded like they were next to me. But the corridor was empty, so that is impossible.* Thinking it as though it were rational, as though I could somehow see tunnel-like through my fear. Thinking all that as I furiously rubbed my arms to make the goose bumps go away, as my teeth chattered so loudly I couldn't hear my heartbeat.

There are no ghosts, I repeated to myself again and again. *There are no ghosts.*

My breathing was just starting to come back to normal when one of the shadows near the bookshelf peeled itself away from the others and, assuming a hazy shape, came looming toward me.

"Hello, Aurora," it whispered, reaching for me.

CHAPTER 15

In the split second before I screamed, the shadow resolved itself into a figure in black cashmere and laser whitened teeth. Bain.

"What were you doing out there?" he asked.

My terror evaporated, leaving behind a granular mixture of fury and relief. "What the hell were you thinking?" I whispered angrily, punching him in the bicep. "Was that some kind of joke?"

"*Ouch*," He stood back, rubbing his arm. "Was what some kind of joke?"

He did a good job sounding innocent, but I wasn't believing it. "Jiggling the door handle. Pretending to be a ghost. Why didn't you just knock and say who you were?"

Even in the darkness I could see him frown. "Because the door was open when I got here. What are you talking about?"

I realized the grooves of the flashlight were digging into my hand where my fingers were gripping it. "You weren't the person trying to open my door? Jiggling the handle?"

"No. I didn't have to. Like I said, the door was open. What happened?"

"Nothing. Just that. I woke up, and the door handle was turning. Or at least I thought it was. But when I opened the door there wasn't anyone there." I willed my fingers to uncurl from the flashlight. "I thought I'd locked the door. Where did you come from? Did you see a person in the hall?"

"I took the back stairs from the kitchen. Had the place to myself."

I pictured the layout of the house. There were the front stairs I'd come up and another set originally built for servants that connected to the kitchens. I'd forgotten about those, but if Bain had been on them, no one could have gone that way. I said, "I must have dreamed it."

"Probably," he agreed, losing interest. "Especially after what that medium said at Coralee's party. That was really something." He started moving around Aurora's room—my room—picking up and putting down her things. "Appearing at the party and having them haul you in was a smart play. You got them to run your prints without us having to ask. Once they got over being stunned by you being conjured from the dead. Made for some great YouTube viewing."

"I didn't know she'd hire a medium. That hadn't been part of my plan."

He sat in the desk chair and pivoted right, then left, balancing the tip of his index finger on the top of the desk. "Yeah. Tell me about that. Your *plan*. How did you come up with the idea to show up like that instead of doing it the way we talked about?"

"It seemed more like something your cousin would do." I shrugged. "Make a big entrance. Plus people are always more likely to believe something that has to be coerced rather than volunteered."

As I spoke the words I realized I'd said too much, revealed too much of my actual approach. If I'd been talking to Bridgette, it could have been a crucial mistake, reraised questions in her mind

I'd worked hard to put to rest, but Bain didn't seem to recognize it. He nodded toward my bandaged left hand, which was on top of the covers. "You got hurt."

I held it up. "No one can ask me to play tennis or the piano with this thing," I said.

He let out a low whistle. "Nice." He got thoughtful again. "The only thing I don't get is, why not tell Bridgette and me? We would have gone along with it."

"This way you won't have to pretend to be surprised."

He gave a little bark of laughter. "I think you wanted to show us who had the power."

"I think you must have me confused with your sister. I'm not nearly that clever."

He gave me a quick, sharp look. "Sure." He got busy opening desk drawers, poking around them with one finger. "Just remember that we're all on the same team here. Working together. Right?"

"Right."

Another sharp look. He picked up a piggy bank in the shape of a cat, shook it, and put it back down. "Of course Bridgette is livid. She spent something like six hours at the train station trying to figure out where you'd gone. She doesn't like it when people don't follow her plans."

The adrenaline must have been leaving my body. I felt spent, exhausted again. I yawned. "I got that."

"She'll come around. Now that you're here, the pressure's off. Since Grandmother brought you home, everyone else has to believe in you too. Tonight was a triumph. Only two more hurdles to go." He lifted a finger. "One, meet the Family. That shouldn't be too bad. And two, answer the cop's questions about what happened and where you've been."

"I'm sorry, Officer, I don't remember anything," I chirped, then went back to my regular voice. "I know what to say."

"Don't get cocky. The last thing in the world we want is for you to attract their attention for any reason." The word "we" seemed to hang in the air, emphasizing our complicity. He'd finished with the desk and was gazing in my direction, but I had the sense that what he was seeing was in his head.

"Look, I'm tired. Can I go to bed?"

"Oh, sure, of course." He didn't move. He just sat there staring at me.

"What?" I demanded. "Why are you looking at me like that?"

He shook his head slowly. His expression was the same one he'd had at Starbucks three weeks earlier, before this started. "It's just seeing you here, in her room—it's so *real*. So possible." He got up, but instead of going to the door he took a step toward me.

"Good. That's the point, isn't it?" I asked. I felt the cool metal of the flashlight handle against my thigh beneath the comforter, and I let my fingertips rest on it.

"Yes. Ro home again. Home, alive, in the flesh," he said. His fingers flexed, then straightened. "Irrefutable."

Something was going on inside him, something I didn't—and didn't want to—understand. He took another step toward me. My uninjured hand wrapped around the bottom of the flashlight beneath my comforter.

I wanted to snap him out of it. My eye fell on the photo strip on my night table, and I pulled the flashlight out and turned it on, pointing to the row of pictures. "Do you know who that is? Or why Ro would have scratched out his face?"

It worked. The faraway expression left his face. He took another step in my direction but this time focused on the photostrip. The beam of the flashlight was on the photo strip, not him as he bent to look at it, so I couldn't see his face. But I thought his forehead might have wrinkled in a frown. "Where did you find this?"

"In her sock drawer."

"Was there anything else?"

"Socks?" I said. "Why? Does it mean something?"

He stood up, shaking his head. "Beats me. I have no idea why Aurora would have scratched this guy's face out." The way he said it I believed him.

"She kept the photo though. So he must have been someone important to her. Any idea who it is?"

"I already said I didn't know," he told me, even though he hadn't. He seemed agitated and suddenly in a hurry to go. Glancing through my window in the direction of his house, he said, "I'd better get back. I don't want to ruin everything by getting caught in your room."

He made the door in two easy strides, paused, and turned back to face me. "I'd keep that picture you found out of sight. Somewhere safe where no one can get to it."

"Why?"

"People might ask who the guy is. It would blow the whole thing if you couldn't tell them, right?"

"Sure," I agreed. It was a good point. But I had the sense it wasn't the real reason.

As I moved to lock the door behind him, I replayed Bain's reaction to the photo strip. He'd been genuinely surprised by it, but not by the guy *in* it. I could have sworn that despite the face being scratched out, he knew exactly who that was.

Which meant something happened to Aurora the week before she disappeared that made her go from adoring the guy in the photo to hating him. Something Bain didn't want me asking questions about.

I decided I'd take his advice and keep the photo safe, but I doubted that his idea of safe and mine were the same.

CHAPTER 16

SATURDAY

*T*he lights are long silver dashes in the wet pavement, and the tires of the cars make squelching noises. Across the road a payphone is ring-a-linging. Every time I try to reach it, a car goes by, splashing me with more mud. I have to answer it, *I think*. It's a matter of life and death. When I finally get there, I see the numbers have been scratched out and the receiver is missing. I stand there, staring at it, while it goes on ring-a-linging. There's nothing I can do; I'm helpless. I must answer it, must answer for it—

I woke up in a cold sweat, heart racing, blankets twisted around my legs, thinking, *Answer for* what? The sun was blazing through the windows, bouncing rainbows off the faceted sides of the star lantern.

The brightness was like a rebuke to the racing of my heart, the fear-clenched tightness in my chest. *What could be sinister here?* the room seemed to say, mocking me. Looking through the window, I saw a luxurious carpet of perfectly manicured green grass, with hills and a blue sky beyond it. *See, it's paradise,* the room seemed to say. *Nothing to be afraid of.*

On my way to the bathroom I unlocked the door of the room, feeling stupid for having locked it in the first place, and was washing my face amid the green-and-white tiled splendor when I heard the sound of it opening. I turned around in time to see the woman enter, take in my empty bed, stop dead, then turn and see me.

She stood frozen, a tall, lean, woman with a face like an upside-down Anjou pear, smooth and golden brown with high cheekbones and a little round chin. Her dark hair was pulled back into a tight bun and had more silver in it than I remembered from the photos. But the face was the same, and the smart, miss-nothing eyes behind the rhinestone cat-eye frames of her glasses were the same. She looked like the best kind of high school librarian, and I would never have guessed she was past sixty if I hadn't known. She was wearing dark blue slacks, a crisp white blouse rolled up at the sleeves, and a silver and turquoise cuff bracelet that I imagined she'd gotten during a visit to her relatives on the Maricopa Reservation.

She was carrying a breakfast tray. I walked toward her and took the tray from her hand.

"Hello, Mrs. March," I said.

"You are a very naughty girl," she said. There were tears in her eyes.

"I'm sorry," I told her.

"You leave like that with no word, and we worry and worry. And now look at you. All grown-up and far too skinny. I knew you couldn't look after yourself on the streets. I fussed and fretted, and I was right." Now she burst into tears.

I went to put my arms around her, but she shook her head. I let my hands fall to my sides. "But here I am. Back. You know the only reason I came back was to see you and eat your cooking."

She sniffled. "Bah." She pulled away and took an ironed handkerchief out of her pocket to wipe her eyes. When she was done, she stood and looked at me. "I can't believe it."

"I'm sorry I left," I told her. It seemed like the right thing to say. And standing there, facing the only person who really seemed to have been moved by Aurora's disappearance, I found I meant it.

"She's sorry she left," she repeated, hands on her hips, looking even more like a high school librarian. "Do you know what I should do to you?" Without pausing, she went on. "Neither do I, and I'm going to think about it, but right now you should eat these and be quiet." She began smoothing her hair back into her bun.

"You brought me doughnuts."

"I did, and I don't know why because you don't deserve them. Mind you eat all of them. The Family is waiting to greet you downstairs, and then your Uncle Thom is going to take you to the police for an interrogation. If you survive that, you have the added terror of going shopping with your cousin Bridgette, so you have something to wear to the Country Club. I'm not sure which activity should frighten you more, but you're going to need your strength."

"Thank you."

She nodded to herself and turned toward the bed. Before she'd done anything, she froze and, as though giving in to something she couldn't check, turned, crossed to me, and wrapped me in her arms. "Welcome home, Aurora," she said. There was nothing frightening in the way she spoke the words, or in her touch. She was the first person to touch me on purpose with kindness.

Pulling away, she said, "I couldn't be happier today if you were my own granddaughter."

"I wish I were."

She shook her head at me. "Don't start with that kind of talk again. You know your grandmother. Hard on the outside but sweet inside. I could name someone else like that. Now get dressed."

"I'm not like her," I protested instinctively.

She laughed. Then her face took on a serious expression. "She needs you now. More than ever. You've come back just in time. Good girl."

"What do you mean?" I asked.

"She's aging—aren't we all?" she said, moving back to the bed and adeptly stacking the pillows on the low table next to it. She worked with the smooth precision of someone who has done this a lot, and I wondered if she enjoyed it. I hadn't loved my time working for Maid-for-You, but maybe it was different in a place like this. "Soon we'll all be as crotchety as this old house."

I saw the photo strip on the desk where Bain had left it and slipped it into a drawer. I said, "It's strange not remembering anything that happened. I know it was a long time ago, but did you notice anything unusual about me before I left?"

She froze. "Why are you asking that?"

I sensed the question upset her, but I didn't know why. "It's just—it's hard not to know. Like being dizzy. I'm hoping I can piece it back together."

She let out a long breath. "The morning before you and Liza disappeared, you didn't eat any breakfast." She turned to face me, clutching a pillow in front of her. "That was so unlike you that I came up to check on you, and you were crying. You told me you wanted to be alone."

"Do you know why?"

"Girl cries like that for only one reason. Boy troubles." She tilted her head to one side, and her eyes got distant like she was pulling something from her memory. "I knew you'd been up to something; I just didn't know with who. I tried to get you to tell me, but you wouldn't. And then—" She let out a breath. "And then you vanished.

I kept thinking maybe if I had done something, maybe if I had made you tell me, you wouldn't have run off. You wouldn't have—" Her hand went to her mouth.

I took a step closer to her. "There's nothing you could have done," I said. The words felt bare, common, but I hoped they worked. I liked Mrs. March. She gave a tight, trembling smile and nodded. Trying to figure out the right way to play it, I said, "I didn't realize you knew my secret."

Now she laughed. "Who do you think saw the tell-tale tracks of dirt up the back stairs first thing in the morning after you'd snuck in at night? Never a tidy one, you weren't." She looked down at the tangle of sheets and blankets on the bed and shook her head. "Still a tosser and turner, I see."

"I had trouble falling asleep," I said. Before I could remind myself that the door-knob-turning incident had just been a dream, I said, "We haven't added a crazy relative in the attic or anything?"

"I don't think your grandmother's quite gotten to that yet, though I won't deny some of your relatives could deserve it." She carefully folded the top of the flat sheet over the comforter and turned to reach for the stack of pillows. "Why?"

"I thought someone tried to get into my room last night. Turned the door handle. I just wondered if there was anyone else up here."

She had been leaning across the bed holding a square pillow with little silver beads on it. But as I spoke I heard a sharp intake of breath, and the pillow fell out of her hand and tumbled to the floor. I bent to get it. When I handed it to her, she didn't meet my eyes, instead turning to carefully position it among the others.

"I'm sure that was just the wind through an accidentally open window," she said, half-facing away from me. "This old house is as creaky as my back on a December morning." She gave a laugh that almost sounded genuine. I laughed with her, and for a moment I felt better.

But as she turned to go I caught sight of her reflection in the mirror next to the door, and there was no sign of laughter there. Her eyes flashed to the door handle, and her face was creased deeply with worry.

CHAPTER 17

I wasn't sure how to dress for both a police interrogation and an excursion to the mall with Bridgette, let alone how the old Aurora would have dressed, so I went with a mid-thigh-length navy blue dress with ruffles up the front and cap sleeves that reeked of innocence on top, and the studded motorcycle boots on the bottom in case Bridgette needed to be taught a lesson.

The edge of the photo strip poked out of the drawer, and I opened it and took it out. This must have been the secret boyfriend Aurora was crying over the night before she left. I tucked it into the pocket of the dress and went out the door.

I hadn't really been worried about the family reunion because from what Bridgette and Bain had told me all that really mattered was that Althea accepted me. But suddenly I realized I had no idea how Aurora would behave in this situation. What would it be like to see your family after a long absence?

Without warning my mind flashed to an image of walking into a large, elegant room.

There's a woman standing in front of a tall window looking out, and as I enter she turns toward me. The sun is behind her, so I can't see her face. But I know it's my mother, and I know she's smiling. She opens her arms and pulls me toward her, and I can feel her warmth as she holds me to her, rocking me softly. I say, "I'm so sorry, Mommy," and she says—

"What's keeping her?" Althea's voice, rising from somewhere beyond the base of the wide staircase, sliced through my thoughts, leaving me hanging somewhere between disappointment and relief.

You don't have time for this, I told myself sternly. It's time for you to play Aurora, the Aurora everyone expects to see. My knees trembled a little as I descended the rest of the stairs. I was scared, I realized, but also . . . excited.

Walking into the large parlor was a little like walking into one of those dreams in which the mannequins in a store all come to life after it's closed. I heard voices when I approached the door. But as I entered everyone froze, so the room seemed to be filled with very lifelike sculptures caught in self-consciously characteristic postures. **Bridger Silverton**—Bain and Bridgette's father [55, property developer, now running for U.S. Congress, widowed and remarried, $26,000,000]—half-rising out of the leather seat; **Margie Silverton** [35, Bridger's second wife, no money of her own. A former waitress and Bridger's mistress since his first wife died, she'd "somehow convinced" him to marry her right after Aurora left; "ambitious, carefully conniving, manipulative, and dangerous," according to Bridgette; Bain described her as "trailer trash with flair"], perched on its arm with her ankles crossed.

There weren't enough chairs in the room, as though it was designed on purpose to make people uncomfortable. Bridgette stood near the wall behind her father and stepmother with her hands in fists, and Bain lounged alongside her, his face in a sort of gleeful smirk. On the other side of the room Uncle Thom looked like he was wearing a suit even though he wasn't. He was standing, his hand dangling over the back of the upholstered chair occupied by **Aunt Claire** [44 but tells people she's 35, youngest of Althea and Sargeant's children, ethereal beauty, dabbled in all the arts, "nice" according to Bain, "ruthless" according to Bridgette, older than her husband but worked very hard to look younger. She claimed assets of $14,000,000, although there was a rumor she'd lost most of it to a cult and was living on loans based on her future inheritance]. She had been Aurora's mother's best friend, so I looked at her with interest. But her pale alabaster face with its slightly too wide eyes and careful contours was disconcerting. She had a large Irish setter at her feet. She looked relaxed, but I had the impression she was watching me more closely than anyone else.

Althea sat in the middle of them all, perched in a burgundy leather wingback chair with large brass studs like an Elizabethan monarch. "Come," she said, motioning me forward with one hand. The command shattered the tableau, and everyone started to talk and move and gather around me at once. After exactly two minutes of insincere hugs and wondering backslaps, Althea said, "Enough! We have work to do," and everyone resumed their positions, well-rehearsed actors taking up their marks.

A young woman with tightly curled hair pulled into a puffy ponytail and skin the color of caffe mocha had entered but stood discretely off to one side in the middle of the meet and greet. I recognized her from the cards—**Jordan North** [23, friend of Bain and Bridgette's from high school so had known Aurora socially; now Althea's social secretary while applying to graduate school for psychology, net worth negligible]—but she was far prettier in real life. She was beautiful, like a model, but didn't seem self-conscious about it. She wore a caramel fitted skirt and sleeveless sweater and was by far the most formally dressed person in the room. In her arms she held a well-worn leather folder. As she entered her eyes moved briefly toward the corner of the room where Bain was standing next to his sister, and it made me wonder if they were a couple.

Althea started to say, "This is my social secretary—" but I interrupted her.

"Hi Jordan," I said. "It's nice to see you again."

I could have sworn Aunt Claire sat up a little straighter.

Jordan said, "You too, Aurora." She was smiling at me, but for a fleeting moment I thought I saw something flicker at the back of her eyes, something that suggested seeing Aurora again wasn't really a pleasure. Then it vanished, and I couldn't be sure I'd seen it at all.

Althea cleared her throat. "As I was saying, Jordan is my secretary, and all bookings will go through her."

"Bookings?" I asked.

"We've been putting together the program for your launch," Jordan explained, opening the folder. It had all been worked out already, apparently, and would begin the next night, Sunday, at the Country Club Member's Dinner, which we would attend as a family. It would continue on Monday at the round-robin tennis tournament—it really was too bad about my hand, everyone agreed. A mixed doubles match with Bain would have been ideal—followed by the Country Club Dance that night to mark the beginning of the summer season. Wednesday morning we'd swing into the official portion with interviews, during which I would stay quiet on where I'd been and just talk about how happy I was to be home. Until then I'd make spontaneous "discrete local appearances."

I felt like I was watching the entire event as a spectator, not only because they were talking about someone else but because it really didn't seem to matter if I was there or not. No one consulted me or asked my opinion. Apparently the business of being Aurora Silverton ran on its own steam, and I just sat there and got pulled along behind it like a crop being hauled to market.

"Mother, I really must object," Bridger said. "Shouldn't the Family vet her first before unleashing the press on the story? If we take two or three months, like that girl in Utah who—"

"I have told you so often about using words precisely, Bridger. There is no *must* about your objection. You would like to object. You think it's objectionable but must object? No. You're thinking of the well-being of your campaign, not your niece," Althea accused him. Which seemed accurate but a bit unfair since I was pretty sure no one was thinking of my well-being.

"What did you mean by discrete local appearances?" I asked.

Jordan nodded, like I was a new, possibly slow student she wanted to encourage. "Well, for example, this morning you have a meeting at the police station to answer some questions, and we've been try-ing to contact Elizabeth Lawson's family to have them come from Tempe for a joint appearance—"

"Good luck," Bridger interrupted. "I tried to have the father come for the dedication of the new children's center we named after Eliza-beth Lawson, and he declined. Said he had his own way of honoring his daughter. Smarmy bastard."

Margie patted his leg with a perfectly manicured hand. "There's the Boys and Girls Club Day at the Tucson Days Fair on Tuesday," she said. Her red sweater strained over her cleavage as she sat up, and her blond head bobbed with enthusiasm. "It would only be natu-ral for Ro to go to that, and since Gina Gold arranged it, there's bound to be plenty of press there."

I could see what Bridgette meant by carefully conniving.

Althea scowled at Margie. "Where are those diamond stud earrings I bought you?" she demanded.

It seemed like a non sequitur to me, but no one else was surprised. "I wore them to the museum party last night, you silly goose," she said. "You can see the photos in *Arizona* magazine next month."

"Rather see the stones in your ears. I paid enough for them. Want to make sure you haven't traded them for paste."

"Mother, there is no such thing as paste anymore," Aunt Claire said. "It's all cubic zirconium."

"I'm sure you know," Althea shot at her. "And what did they use to make those fake pearls?"

Aunt Claire touched the pearls at her neck. "They're real, Mother, just as they were the day you gave them to me." Her eyes came back to me. "But since you are so concerned with authenticity, how can you be so sure that this young woman is really Aurora?"

Althea said, "Because I say she is, and I won't take any more questions." She settled back into her chair, and the machinery of being Aurora clicked on around me. I'd begun to lose interest when Mrs. March entered and bent to whisper something to Althea. Althea's bright eyes rested on me, and she smiled. It wasn't a smile I could easily read. She rose to her feet. "I have an appointment. You can show yourselves out."

Bridger, who had been straining his neck to see the new arrival through the open door, said, "Mother, why is Chester Mac here?"

"Why does anyone invite their estate lawyer over? To make a new will." Now her eyes definitely looked amused. "With Aurora back, obviously, some things will have to change. I'm sure none of you have anything to worry about. To each according to his merits." She let loose a laugh that sounded like dry leaves crackling. "I'll expect to see you all for supper at the golf club tomorrow night."

Then she looked directly at me, mirth and malice vying for the upper hand in her smile, and I wondered if this was why Althea let me into the family so easily—to use as a lever against the others. Or maybe this was her version of revenge against the granddaughter who had stayed away. Either way it seemed deliberately cold and cruel.

The air turned oppressive, almost sultry, as though we'd been shut into a greenhouse. Uncle Thom appeared next to me, making me jump. "We should go. Our appointment at Tucson PD is in half an hour."

I said goodbye to everyone, and we'd reached the door when Aunt Claire called out, "Oh, Ro. You know your grandmother got rid of all the horses, but Thom and I have a lovely new yearling. A bit feisty. Feel free to come over anytime and ride."

It was a test, I knew. "Aurora had a way with wild things," Bridgette had said. "Maybe because she was so wild herself."

"So she was a horse whisperer?" I'd asked. And maybe my tone had been a bit incredulous, but Bridgette had responded vehemently.

"This isn't a joke. Aurora had—a special gift. She didn't tame wild things; it was more like calming them. She could harness their energy. Especially horses. She could do things no one else could. And she loved them. She'd *never* say no to the chance to ride."

By offering me her yearling, Aunt Claire was challenging me to prove I was Aurora by showing I could ride a challenging horse.

Of course, I couldn't do that. But I also couldn't say no without raising any red flags. From what Bain and Bridgette had said, even a hurt hand wouldn't have stopped her.

Against the wall I sensed rather than saw Bridgette and Bain tense. Studiously avoiding looking at them, I gave Aunt Claire a small, sad smile. "Thank you but I—I'm not *comfortable* on horses anymore," I said falling back on a technique I'd used successfully in the past, injecting enough hesitation into it to imply that something really horrible had happened so no one would ask for details. It might not satisfy her, but it would at least not inflame doubts about my authenticity.

It worked. Aunt Claire's eyes widened as much as the Botox would allow, and her hand went to her throat. "I see. Say no more."

I chanced a look in Bain and Bridgette's direction. Bridgette was studying her nails, but Bain glanced at me. I hadn't realized, until Bain shot me a wink, that I'd been holding my breath.

CHAPTER 18

Despite that success, my nerves were rattled, and I had to work to pay attention to Uncle Thom as we rolled away from the House in his 1962 red Jaguar.

He coaxed it into gear gently, the way you'd calm a jittery horse and said with a sigh, "Your grandmother should have gone into the theater. She loves staging plays."

"You don't seem concerned."

He laughed. "It's just money." He said it the way only someone with plenty of it could. Maybe the rumors about Aunt Claire losing her fortune weren't true. "So you really don't remember anything?" he asked.

"I really don't."

He grinned. "Must be strange."

"It is."

As we descended down the winding road from the Silverton compound, we passed other large houses, masses of steel and rock and glass jutting out of flat ground. They didn't look like places to live, more like places of worship, monoliths from some strange religion, being carefully tended by acolytes in cargo shorts, wraparound sunglasses, and pastel polo shirts with words like Bob's Pool and Sonoran Landscape Specialists and Hollywood Home Theaters embroidered over their hearts. I imagined Aurora being friends with girls who lived in houses like that, imagined walking down corridors with lights that automatically sensed our presence to home theaters with black leather-covered chairs where we'd watch movies and eat Pop-Tarts and drink vodka.

Uncle Thom was humming a little to himself, tapping the wheel with one finger, like he was enjoying the ride. "I tried to get the police to put this questioning off, but they wanted to take your statement right away."

"It's okay, I'd rather get it over with." I had been telling stories all my life; I knew what I was doing. And yet as we got closer to the police station, I began to feel nervous.

For some reason everything I said seemed to amuse Uncle Thom. "I'm sure you would." He gave a little laugh. "By the way, if they try to introduce any extraneous matters, I will object, but you can also just refuse to answer."

That got my attention. "What kind of extraneous matters?"

"Family things. Especially now with Bridger running for office, there are plenty of people who would like to muckrake."

"Is there muck to rake?" I asked.

He laughed some more and downshifted into second gear. "You're funnier than the old Aurora," he said, adding, with a wink, "You might want to watch that. Could make people suspicious."

I felt frozen. He had as good as told me he thought I was an imposter. I wanted to open the door of the car and run away.

Don't be a moron, a voice inside my head said, one that sounded more like Aurora than me. *He doesn't know anything or he would have blown this for you already. Press him on it. He'll back down.*

I said, "What do you mean?"

His amusement wavered for an instant. "Only that, uh, cops don't always understand humor," he said stumbling over the words a little. "You'll want to keep it straightforward with them."

Before I could respond, we turned into the parking lot of the police station. The only other cars in the lot were patrol cars, and the tiled foyer of the station was empty when we stepped inside. The space had a lazy feeling, and I wondered if that was because it was Saturday or because there wasn't much crime in Tucson.

Detective Ainslie, wearing a pair of pinstriped pants and a rust-colored short-sleeved blouse, offered us coffee in Styrofoam cups printed with an Aztec motif and led us to a conference room. There was someone already seated there, a quiet-looking African American woman with close-cropped dark curly hair. From the sensible haircut to the brooch in the shape of a scarab and the grey sweater set she wore, she oozed Mental Health Professional, so I wasn't surprised when she was introduced as Dr. Ellen Jackson.

Uncle Thom seemed surprised, or at least something about Dr. Jackson's presence made him uneasy. "I didn't realize my niece's mental state is under scrutiny. This isn't part of what we discussed last night."

"I'm just here in an advisory capacity," Dr. Jackson said, not in the fake soothing therapist voice I expected but in a normal one which made me kind of like her. "I've had extensive experience with amnesia cases, and Detective Ainslie thought I might be helpful. Unless you object?" She looked at me as she asked the question.

I shook my head. "Anything that will help," I said, trying to sound eager but not too eager.

Uncle Thom still wasn't happy. "We'll agree, with the provision that we can change our mind at any point." I was surprised by his reaction—if he thought I was a fake, what better way to break me down than by submitting me to the scrutiny of a professional? I wondered what he thought he was protecting me from.

When we were all seated, Detective Ainslie said, "Why don't you walk us through what happened the night of your disappearance?"

"I can't," I told her, leaning into the table to indicate openness and injecting a note of apology into my voice. "I don't remember anything."

Dr. Jackson touched the detective on the sleeve and said, "May I?" Then looked at me. "What is the *first* thing you remember, Aurora?" There was something about her, the way her arms on the table were in the same position as mine maybe, that made her seem trustworthy. Like someone you could confide in.

Be careful.

I looked at my hands in front of me. "About a month ago, I was in Houston brushing my teeth, and suddenly I knew." I quickly glanced up, giving Dr. Jackson my most earnest gaze. "I can't describe it. It was just—my name was Aurora Silverton, and I was from Tucson."

She studied me a moment. "What did you do then?

The hardest thing about lying isn't making eye contact. It is remembering to blink. I blinked. "I went to the library and did a search for . . . myself. It was really strange. That's when I found out what had happened, the disappearance and everything."

"Why didn't you get in touch with your family right away?"

I looked back down at my hands. "At first I wasn't sure. I was afraid. You—you can't know what it's like to not remember anything about yourself. I hoped more memories would come back. Some did, distant ones. Not complete. I kept thinking if I waited a little longer there would be more. I was scared. I didn't know what had happened. The newspapers—they all gave such different stories. Some of them suggested that someone had tried to *murder* me." I put feeling into it, glancing around with the shocked expression I had practiced for this moment.

Detective Ainslie pounced. "And you thought that someone might be a member of your family?"

"What? No," I said, my voice rising sharply.

At the same time, Uncle Thom half-rose from his chair, declaring, "She didn't say that."

Dr. Jackson put a hand out in front of Ainslie as though to ease the detective back and kept her eyes on mine. "You were confused, unsure. Shaken. Of course."

"Right," I agreed, giving her a grateful smile. "Shaken."

Detective Ainslie said, "Why did you go to a graduation party instead of coming home to see your family? Were you afraid of a family member?"

"Should I have been?" I asked.

But it hardly mattered because before it was out of my mouth Uncle Thom had risen and was saying, "If this is the line you're taking, my client and I will be going."

"Please sit down, Mr. Silverton," Detective Ainslie said. "It is a legitimate question."

Uncle Thom subsided.

I said, "I'm not sure why I went. I mean, it was my graduation party, wasn't it? And I guess it was kind of like a test. To see if people recognized me, to make sure I really was Aurora. I was sure, but not—*sure*. It's hard to explain. And to see if I recognized them." I felt relieved, back on firm ground. I'd gone over this in my mind.

"Did you?" Dr. Jackson asked.

"Some. Not everyone. With some people it was more like a hazy feeling."

"Your grandmother? Your home? Your uncle?"

"Them, yes. My room. Not my clothes. Those seemed very three years ago," I said, trying to make a joke.

No one laughed.

Detective Ainslie looked at Dr. Jackson. She was watching me, not unkindly, but with intense concentration. She said, "And the night of your disappearance. What do you remember about that? Any scrap, any detail could be helpful."

I shook my head. "That's exactly what I don't remember. That and the—years I guess—after that."

"You said you'd have flashes of memories sometimes," Dr. Jackson coaxed. "Like what?"

I realized it had been a mistake to say that. "They're hard to describe." I racked my mind for what to say. "A pay phone," I said, seizing on my own dreams. "Night. Um, tires on wet pavement. Someone laughing." They were eating it up, so I decided to give them more. "And a name. Tom Yaw? I don't know what it means."

They loved that. Cops love proper nouns; anything that starts with a capital letter makes them happy. And I have to admit I was sort of curious to see what they'd come up with. Detective Ainslie wrote the name, then looked at it. "Tom Yaw. Is that someone you were with? The person who took you?"

I shook my head. "I don't picture a face with it, just the name. The letters. Like I said, I can't remember anything from that night."

Detective Ainslie had opened the file folder she had in front of her and was consulting something. "You said tires on wet pavement?" I nodded, encouragingly. "It didn't rain the night you disappeared or for weeks after that."

"Maybe it's a memory from another time. I'm just giving you everything I have." My heart rate began to pick up a little, and I suddenly felt less in control of the interview.

As though she sensed my confidence flagging, Dr. Jackson reached her arm slightly across the table toward me and said, "You're doing very well, Aurora."

Detective Ainslie cut in. "You don't remember anything about the party? Or the mall?"

"Party?" I repeated. Bain and Bridgette hadn't mentioned a party. Was this some kind of trap? The sense I'd had of losing control of the interview doubled. I felt my heart rate accelerate again, and next to me, Uncle Thom seemed to become fractionally more alert.

"The last place you were seen was at a party in a model home in one of the developments your family owns," she said. "Sunset Canyon Estates. Do you remember that?"

I shook my head and knit my fingers together to keep them from shaking. What was going on? First them asking about being afraid of my family and now this. "Who was at the party?" I asked, hoping my voice sounded less nervous to them than it did to me.

"Your cousin Bain was the host," the detective said. "His sister Bridgette was there, and a bunch of their friends. Stuart Carlton, Xandra Michaels, Grant Villa, Roscoe Kim, Jordan North. Do you remember any of them?" She pulled a series of Xeroxes from her folder and arranged them in a line in front of me. None of them, I noted, could have been the guy with the scratched-out face in the photo.

I mentally flipped through the flash cards I'd been drilled on, pulling out names to match the faces. I put my finger on the first photo. "That's Stuart Carlton, Bridgette's boyfriend," I said. I moved to the next, "And that's Jordan North. I saw her this morning."

The next photo showed a shaggy white guy with light brown hair I recognized as **Grant Villa** [20, friends with Bridgette, captain of the swim team, lifeguard at Country Club. Open secret that Aurora had had a crush on him since she was eleven. Net worth: none (attended school on scholarship). Now lived with his older brother in a trailer on the outskirts of Tucson]. After that was a dapper Asian guy, **Roscoe Kim** [20, two years ahead of Aurora in school, gay, $18,000,000 (or more)]. The only one I didn't recognize was the statuesque white girl with the thick dark hair, which meant she had to be Xandra Michaels. I wondered why there hadn't been a card for her. But that was secondary to the more major question of why Bain and Bridgette hadn't mentioned that any of these people had been with Aurora the night she disappeared. Or that they themselves had been among the last people to see her alive.

For the second time, I got the queasy feeling that there was more to the story of Aurora's disappearance—much more. And that Bain and Bridgette were hiding it.

I ran through all the names and photos, then pushed them away. I put on an apologetic expression. "I'm afraid I don't remember seeing any of them the night I—that last night. And there wasn't a party mentioned in any of the news stories I read. Are you sure?"

Detective Ainslie nodded. "That party is the last place you and Liza were seen. We kept that from the press as a courtesy to the Silverton family." Her eyes went to Uncle Thom, and they were not friendly.

"And because Liza was found five miles away, she'd left hours before it was over, and there was no way to link what happened to her to the party," Uncle Thom countered. "Everyone there cooperated fully."

"Can you explain why you and Liza would have been at a party where everyone was at least a year or two older than you?" asked Detective Ainslie.

"As we discussed three years ago," Uncle Thom jumped in before

I could speak, "that was not unusual. Aurora often spent time with her cousins. The Family is close-knit that way."

Detective Ainslie ignored him and kept her eyes instead on me. "Is that why you two were there? Because your cousins were throwing it?"

I shrugged. "I don't know. What—what do the others say?"

"Grant Villa was the first to leave, at around nine thirty, and you two were still there. At about ten Liza approached you and Roscoe Kim and said she wanted to leave. Roscoe offered to drive you two, but by the time he returned from retrieving his coat, you'd disappeared. He figured you left with someone else, so he took off as well. An hour later, a little after eleven, Xandra Michaels, Bain's girlfriend, went outside for a cigarette and saw you and Liza. She talked to you for a moment, but the two of you seemed to be in the middle of a heated discussion. So she wandered off in search of Bain."

Uncle Thom cleared his throat genteelly. "I believe if you consult the transcript of her statement she just said 'discussion.' Not heated."

Detective Ainslie gave him a tight smile. "Thank you. I'll keep that in mind."

I didn't understand what was going on between the two of them, not then, or what the stakes were, but the sense of unease that had begun in my stomach was winding its way through my rib cage.

It didn't diminish as Detective Ainslie's keen eyes came back to me. "No one saw you after that," she said. "The party ended less than an hour later when Bain and Bridgette had an argument about whether Bain should be driving. Bain got angry and stormed off, leaving Bridgette to ride with her boyfriend, Stuart, and Xandra to get a ride with Jordan North."

I willed myself not to look away from her. "So none of them

could have had anything to do with what happened to Liza and, er— me."

"Unless they all did it together," Detective Ainslie said in a mild voice.

"Oh, of course." Uncle Thom's tone was laced with sarcasm. "What would the motive have been? A thrill killing? Murder Orgy at Model House? I bet you'd like to make that stick to the Family." He shook his head. "Do you have questions to ask my client or are you just going to tell stories?"

"I was hoping by recounting the timeline of the party that something might jog Aurora's memory."

I shrugged. "I'm afraid not. I don't remember anything about the party. Is that—do you think that's where we were—where whatever happened to us happened?"

"This is what happened," Detective Ainslie said and held up a photo.

CHAPTER 19

A broken heap, a voice whispered in my mind as I looked at the photo, like the first line of a song, only not quite right.

It described the image though. In the photo it is a sunny day in early summer. It must not be too late because the first tiny shadows hang like dewdrops from the tips of rust-colored rock out-croppings. A bee alights from a white flower, captured midflight by the camera, suspended in time. A girl in a white dress lies next to it, head tilted, eyes closed, a slight smile on her lips like she's in the middle of a pleasant dream. On her shoulder there is a ladybug. One hand lies next to her nose in the incandescent halo of her hair, and the other arm is extended behind her, hand open. Her legs, beneath the hem of her dress, make a number four.

When people talk about dying, they say, "She just drifted off," or "She went quietly," but it's not like that. I know this from personal experience. No matter what, at the end there is a rattle, like wind making a door shutter against its hinges as someone tries desperately to hold it closed. There is no such thing as resting in peace.

If there were, though, it would look like the girl in this picture.

The way she was lying she could have just finished a picnic and snuggled back for a little nap except there was no picnic basket. And the bent part of the 4 was made by her leg being bent backward at an impossible angle, the knee shattered, so that the toe of her dusty white Keds lay along her calf, not the sole.

A heap of broken images, the voice whispered in my head, and I thought, *Aha, yes, that's it. But what?* Words, phrases began to drift into my mind. *Where the sun beats, and the dead tree gives no shelter.* The words, though not completely unfamiliar, weren't mine. They had to be from a song or a poem, long buried in my memory, but I had no idea what it was.

I couldn't quite believe that the girl in the picture was dead. She looked as if she was just waiting for the kiss of the right prince or princess to wake her up, waiting to turn and smile and open her eyes—smile first, you could tell she was that kind of person. To blow the ladybug off her shoulder and say, "Make a wish."

I shuddered. Detective Ainslie said, "Did you remember something?"

I shook my head. "It's just . . . she looks so—not dead."

Detective Ainslie gave a curt nod. She took another photo from the folder, this one showing more of the surrounding landscape, and went on. "Three Lovers Point is eight miles from the building site where the party was held. We think she jumped from here." She pointed to a spot on the side of the cliff. "She seems to have hit the wall here"—her finger rested on a large boulder—"bounced off and rolled the rest of the way down." She waited a beat, then said, "Does anything about this look familiar to you?"

There is a shadow under this red rock, my mind burbled, the stream of memory—it had to be memory, but memory of what?—rushing on. "No," I said.

"What about this?" She pushed a piece of paper across the table toward me, and I saw it was a receipt from a department store. "Do you recognize it?"

At the bottom of the receipt, on the line marked, "I have read and understand the return policy," *Aurora Silverton* was written in the overflowing, blowsy script I'd been practicing forging for weeks. I shook my head. "No. But unless someone faked my name it must be mine. Where is it from?"

"It's from your last Friday here, when you and Liza ditched summer school to go to the mall. And the cashier is certain it was you who signed it. Among the items on it are a pair of "Emma" three-inch high heels in green. What size shoes do you wear?"

"Eight," I answered, remembering the closet full of shoes I tried on the night before.

Detective Ainslie made a note on a pad, then said, "The shoes you bought were a size 10. Liza's size. Would you have bought her shoes?"

"I—I guess. Yes. Why?" I was finding myself increasingly distracted by the photo. It wasn't just that the girl didn't look dead, I realized. It was *wrong* somehow.

"Were you trying to cheer her up? Was she depressed?"

"I don't remember." I stared at the photo. Was it the dress? Was that what was jarring?

"You two had originally become friends on the tennis team right? And after that you were very close."

Bridgette told me that Liza and Aurora had become friends during eighth grade on the tennis team. It had been a few months after Aurora's mother had died, and maybe that was why they were so close, Bridgette had speculated. I thought about how Bain had said they were nearly inseparable. "I—I guess so," I answered the detective.

It wasn't the dress that was wrong, I decided. It looked new, but it wasn't unheard of for people to wear new clothes when they committed suicide. But it was something related to the dress.

Detective Ainslie went on. "She left the team after Christmas. Do you know why?"

I shook my head slowly from side to side, increasingly aware of all the things Bain and Bridgette had failed to mention. "I suppose she just didn't want to play tennis anymore." I had the sensation that the room was growing close, as though something was crowding me.

"Wasn't there an altercation with another girl on the team? Coralee Gold?"

"Maybe. I don't remember."

"Her mother had passed when she was in seventh grade. I believe your mother passed around the same time. Was that something you talked about?"

I shrugged. "Sometimes."

Detective Ainslie leaned forward, as though she was getting impatient, but Dr. Jackson quelled her with a gesture.

"She had two sisters, I believe," Dr. Jackson said, consulting her notepad. "Victoria, the eldest who attended boarding school out of state, and Eleanor, younger, who was living at home. All three of them were named after English queens. Her mother had been an English teacher. Your mother was a teacher too, wasn't she?"

"Why do you keep asking about my mother?" I demanded. I was too sharp, too abrupt. "I mean, what does that have to do with this?"

I expected Dr. Jackson to give me a long look, maybe a smile, show me she'd won by shaking me, but she didn't. She said, "I'm sorry, I didn't mean to upset you." Not in a counselor way—in a way that made me think she meant it. "I was hoping that asking questions about your relationship, its foundations, might trigger your memory. It's a common technique. It didn't work. But would you mind answering a few more questions?"

"No." I agreed. But somehow her admitting that, and treating me like I was human, was more disconcerting than if she'd just acted like a shrink. The air seemed to be growing denser, like it was surrounding me.

Stop, I told myself. *That's all in your head. You need to focus. None of this is your business,* I reminded myself. The girl in the photo committed suicide, and that is too bad but has nothing to do with you. I took a deep breath and thought I smelled jasmine. The words *Come in under the shadow of this red rock and I will show you something* rushed into my mind like a river bursting through a dam.

"Are you okay?" Dr. Jackson asked, staring at the edge of the table in front of me.

Following her eyes, I saw I was gripping the table with my good hand, hard. I pulled it away. "Yes. Fine. I'm sorry, I—it's just a lot to take in. What were you saying?"

She hesitated, but went on. "Behavioral changes like resigning from the team could be signs of trouble at home. Did she ever mention anything like that to you? Did she fight with her father or her sisters?"

"No," I answered. "Not that I know about."

"You left your phone at the party, and when it was found, all the messages had been erased. Did you often do that?"

"Maybe." I thought about how sterile Aurora's room was—and the photo strip hidden in her drawer—and I suddenly realized why. I said, "I didn't want my grandmother to read them."

"Was that the kind of thing she did?"

"I guess I thought it was."

"During your day at the mall you spent more than"—Detective Ainslie consulted a piece of paper in her file—"seven hundred fifty dollars total. You'd withdrawn it over the course of the previous week, leaving only twenty-three dollars in your bank account. Was that a normal thing for you to do?"

"I don't remember." I took a deep breath and thought I smelled jasmine again, and I began to tense up until I realized it was probably Uncle Thom's aftershave.

"Where did you and Liza go after you left the party?"

"I don't remember."

"Was it your idea or her idea to go to Three Lovers Point?"

Uncle Thom cleared his throat. "Excuse me. You have a witness who saw a girl—one girl—getting into a white car heading in that direction. Which means—"

Detective Ainslie interjected, "He saw a girl. He wasn't sure whether there was more than one."

"—Which means," Uncle Thom resumed with what I'm sure he thought of as a glower, "there is nothing to suggest my niece was there."

"Actually," Detective Ainslie said, reaching into a box next to her on the floor and bringing up an object in her hand, "there is. This button was found in the place where Liza jumped." She slid a small plastic evidence bag toward me. "It comes from your niece's trench coat. But as you can see from the crime scene photos, there was no trench coat there."

I looked at her, not the button. "How do you know it was my trench coat?"

The detective pointed to the receipt she'd shown me before, the one with my signature on the "no returns" line. "You bought it at the mall that day."

Uncle Thom threw up his hands. "Two years ago it was a watch. Now it's a button. Really, this is absurd. There must be dozens of identical trench coats like that out there."

A watch? I wanted to ask what that meant, but a confusing jumble of words seeped into my mind, distracting me. *Something different . . . striding behind.* It was like a bad phone connection, a radio station only half-tuned in. Like someone was speaking in my mind.

"They'd just gotten them in that day," Detective Ainslie said. "And your niece is the only person who bought one. They hadn't even been put on the floor yet."

"There are other stores, in other states. That isn't conclusive. Besides the body wasn't found until the next day. That button could have belonged to someone else who went to the Point. Or someone could have put it there to implicate the Family."

I noticed he said "the Family" the same way Bain and Bridgette did, and wondered how long the indoctrination took. Would I be saying it soon too?

"Are you sure you weren't there?" Detective Ainslie asked me.

I fingered the button in its plastic bag. It was antique gold and faceted to look like the setting for a gem. In the center was a crystal heart. It was ugly, but it was also distinctive. "No. I'm not sure about anything."

I realized that Detective Ainslie and Dr. Jackson were watching me, not like they were curious about what I remembered, but like they thought I was guilty and lying to them. "I don't understand. She committed suicide. Why are you asking me about this?"

Detective Ainslie flipped her hand over, showing the palm. "Leaving your phone behind. Erasing all the messages. Emptying out your bank account. We have to wonder: Was it some kind of suicide pact? She went through with it and you didn't?"

"Oh my God," I said, jerking my hand back from the button. "I—no, it couldn't have been."

"You're sure? That is more positive than not remembering."

I wasn't sure. How could I say I was sure? But I wanted to. The idea of it froze me from the inside. I felt like the walls were closing in around me. "I'm—that just doesn't feel right."

"I don't like this," Uncle Thom said.

Detective Ainslie ignored him and kept her eyes on me. "Were you aware of the legal battle between your family and Liza Lawson's father?"

"What?" The chill intensified, and with it the idea that whatever Bain and Bridgette had been planning was not what they'd told me. I was starting to feel like an animal who has walked into a cunning hunter's trap and stands there docilely as it tightens around her.

Next to me, Uncle Thom was flapping his arms. "Okay, enough. We sat through the rest, but that is outside the scope of this meeting. We discussed this last night."

Detective Ainslie said, "Look, Thom. There are people who think it is quite a coincidence that Liza Lawson would kill herself in the very valley her father was currently suing the Silverton family to protect. It would be remiss of me and bad for you if I did not at least ask these questions."

"Is that true?" I looked at Uncle Thom. "That Liza's father was suing"—I paused, then made myself do it—"the Family."

Uncle Thom's lips were set in a thin line. "Not exactly."

"Which parts of it are true?" I demanded, half dreading the answer.

"The Family is just one party to that lawsuit, and her father represented a bunch of environmental groups. It is needlessly reductive to pretend it was some kind of battle between two families. This wasn't *Romeo and Juliet."*

Detective Ainslie glanced at me with raised eyebrows. "Or Juliet and Juliet."

Before I could ask if Liza and Ro—if she thought Liza and I— had been lovers, Dr. Jackson's pleasant voice said, "The week before Liza killed herself, Mr. Lawson said in the press that he was out to destroy your family. That had to be upsetting for you, Aurora."

Uncle Thom leaned back in his seat. "Or maybe what was upsetting to Liza was her father's single-minded interest in his lawsuit rather than his family. Surely that could be the significance of her committing suicide in that particular place." He draped his elbow along the top of the chair, obviously feeling like he'd scored a point.

Detective Ainslie shrugged. She bent forward, across the table toward me, tepeeing her fingers. "All we know for sure is two girls went to Three Lovers Point alive—".

"Two girls *might* have gone," Uncle Thom interrupted. "You cannot place my client there."

"—And only one came back."

"But it was ruled a suicide," I said. My tone sounded desperate, but I didn't care.

"The family pressed for that," Detective Ainslie said.

I turned to gape at Uncle Thom. "Not our family," he said emphatically, shaking his head. "Hers. We just want the truth. That's why we helped then, that's why we came today, that's why we've been sitting through these inane questions." Beside me, Uncle Thom got busy collecting up papers. "But that's enough. We have been more than generous. Aurora, we're going."

I was just pushing my chair back when the door of the room burst open. A man with sandy brown hair came in, took one step, and stopped. "I'm sorry, detective," N. Martinez said, trailing after the man. "I tried, but I couldn't—"

The man stood staring down at me. His eyes were light blue and watery, and his jeans and yellow polo shirt looked tousled, like he'd slept in them. "My God," he said. He rubbed his hand over his chin, which was covered in light stubble. "I—when I heard last night, I drove right down from Tempe. It's true. It's—" His mouth worked for a moment, but no sound came out. He turned to look at Uncle Thom. "I congratulate your family on getting Aurora back, Thomas."

"Thank you, Leo," Thom said. He glanced at me uncertainly. "You remember Leo Lawson?" he prompted. "Liza's father?"

"Mr. Lawson," I said. I stood up, seized with an overwhelming urge to hug him, but at my slightest gesture he pulled back. A sharp chill wrapped itself around me, and my hands dropped to my sides. I said, "I'm so sorry for your loss." It sounded ridiculous.

His eyes roamed my face, the most intense scrutiny I'd gotten since I'd been in Tucson, like he was looking for something.

Something I couldn't give him. In a cracked voice he said, "Why are you doing this?"

"Doing what?" The pain on his face was awful. I wanted to turn, run away. This wasn't what I had agreed to when I told Bain and Bridgette I'd impersonate Aurora. I had no idea what I'd be doing to these people.

"Reopening it. Reopening this whole mess." His eyes moved from me to the photos on the table of Liza. I wished someone had covered them up.

I felt worthless, mean. "That wasn't my intention, Mr. Lawson. I—the police just wanted to—"

His gaze returned to me, and now it was different. Composed, determined. Cold. I had the sense he'd made a decision. His hands came up and rested on my shoulders. "My daughter committed suicide. I have to live with that. But I will not live with having it dredged back up. She died by herself. All alone, my sweet girl. You left her alone then. Why can't you just leave her alone now?" Mr. Lawson's feverish eyes sought and held mine. "Don't do this. Leave her be. If anything else happens, it will be on your head. Your head. *Do you understand?*" His grip was furious, his tone almost menacing.

But his gaze was—scared. He was *afraid* of something.

"That's a threat," Uncle Thom declared. "I want it noted for the record that he laid his hands on my—"

"Fear in a handful of dust," I said, the words coming out of my mouth before I'd even realized it, and I felt the relief you feel when you remember the lyrics to a song that's been eluding you.

Then I looked in Mr. Lawson's face. The color had drained from it, and he was a pale, sickly white. "What did you say?" His fingers dug into my shoulders as though if he let go he would fall, and his voice was jagged like it had to be dragged out of him. "What—why did you say that?"

"I said, 'Fear in a handful of dust.' I—I don't know why. It's a poem, I guess, that I've been trying to figure out. Do you know what it means?"

"It was Liza's favorite poem. *The Wasteland* by T.S. Eliot. You knew that. You must have known she had that stanza written down and tacked on her wall."

Liza's favorite poem? Why would that have been what I was trying to remember? How?

The terror I'd felt the night before when I saw the door handle moving by itself flooded back over me. I stared at Mr. Lawson.

The agony of his expression was almost unendurable. His fingers gripped my shoulders. I didn't know if I wanted to hug him or flee.

I stood there, shaking, my mind reeling. "I'm so sorry," I said, falling back on my prepared script as my mind staggered around like a drunk unable to cope with reality. "I didn't remember. I didn't know."

"He's hurting my client," Uncle Thom squawked somewhere in the distant background.

N. Martinez stepped forward, and Mr. Lawson's hands dropped from my shoulders. "I'm going. It's done." He kept his agitated gaze on mine, repeated, "Please, just stop," and stalked out.

There was silence for three beats. Uncle Thom stood up. "We're done here."

He and Detective Ainslie did some jockeying about would we or wouldn't we be hearing from one another, and she handed me her card and told me to call if I remembered anything. I said the things I needed to say, but I wasn't paying attention. My eyes were glued to the close-up picture of Liza in the middle of the conference table, to the way she was half-smiling up at me. As though she and I shared a secret.

It had to have been a coincidence, me thinking of that poem. It was the photos, the dust on the rocks in the desert. Just a coincidence and not worth thinking about anymore.

I felt myself being propelled toward the door, and when I came out of my haze I realized Dr. Jackson was speaking to me. "It was nice meeting you, Aurora," she said. "Good luck." She held out her hand.

We shook, a strangely formal gesture, but it momentarily made my lethargy evaporate because when I got to the door I remembered something. I half-turned, my hand on the lintel, and said, "It's uncommon, isn't it? For people to commit suicide by jumping?"

Dr. Jackson nodded. "It is. Despite what you see on TV and in the movies, less than 10 percent of suicides happen that way."

"Although Three Lovers has become a popular spot for it," Detective Ainslie said. "There was another suicide there after your friend's. A man named James Jakes."

"You already tried to pin that on the Family without success," Uncle Thom said. "You couldn't link anything to Bain then, and you won't be able to link anything to Aurora now." He put a hand on the small of my back and pushed me the rest of the way out the door.

As he and I stepped out of the police station, the dazzling sunshine and warmth hit me, and I stood there for a moment breathing them in. The wind had picked up slightly, tinged with the faint smell of smoke.

"Wildfire season," Uncle Thom said. "They're predicting a bad one this year." He spoke casually, as though we hadn't just endured something strange and uncanny. Because, I realized, he hadn't.

How had I known that poem?

I shivered, suddenly cold despite the heat.

There was a knot of people at the bottom of the stairs, some of them holding signs that said, "Send Silvertons to Jail Not Senate." They spotted Uncle Thom and me and started booing. A woman in a blue baseball cap shouted, "Murderers!" as we went by, and several others joined in.

I looked at them and heard them, but it was as though they were behind glass. Like I was observing from a great distance, with someone else's eyes, someone else's body. I kept feeling the tickling of that other voice in my head and picturing the girl lying at the bottom of the rust red ravine. I wondered if that was what it felt like to be haunted.

Haunted. I shivered again. *There is nothing to be afraid of,* I told myself. *You just thought of a poem because the images matched the photo. There is no such thing as being haunted. There is no such thing as ghosts.*

And for the next forty-three minutes, I believed it.

CHAPTER 20

It took eleven minutes to drive from the police station to the mall where I was supposed to meet Bridgette. After Uncle Thom had told me that I'd done a great job and I'd mumbled something appropriate, we spent them in silence.

I tried to concentrate on the scenery to blot out the image of the girl lying at the bottom of the canyon. There was a geological quality to Tucson, moving from the flats upward, as though it had been developed in layers. I watched the buildings go by with exaggerated interest, first the old adobes, newly gentrified: a turquoise one with a green door, a red building with a red door and a massive cacti peering over a tall fence, and a yellow house with an electric blue door flanked by bright fuchsia bougainvillea on either side.

This didn't look like Aurora's world—but I could imagine living in the house with the blue door, doing homework at a carved desk and waiting for my mother to come in from painting in her studio. I'd make us *macaroni au gratin avec lardon* for dinner, and we'd eat off of plates with brightly colored horses or camels painted on them. And later we'd sip tea from wide mugs and watch television together on an old oversized green couch covered with mismatched pillows.

Then we were past the houses and into the next layer, low-slung strip malls whose tenant lists could be the template for a game of suburban American Mad Libs, [dry cleaner], [nail place], [smoke shop], [pet spa], with the occasional Native American Gallery or Gem Depot to remind you that you were in Tucson. From there, closer to the mall, we moved into a realm of stucco-covered townhouses that somehow managed to look dirty despite being painted the color of the dirt.

Uncle Thom dropped me in front of Macy's. It took me seven minutes to find Bridgette in the back corner of the designer section. I was sure she'd been saving up a barrage of fury for me, and there were a lot of things I wanted to ask her, like about the party she hadn't mentioned to me, and the boy in the photo strip with his face scratched out. But when I found her, she was deep in conversation on her phone. She was, of course, perfectly put together, each reddish brown hair perfectly in place, her blue eyes subtly outlined with brown shadow, her high-waisted wide-leg jeans and cream eyelet top creaseless, her brown undoubtedly designer sandals unscuffed.

Without pausing in her conversation, she motioned me over, pointed toward a bottle blonde salesgirl whose name tag said "Maisie," and turned her back.

"Your cousin started a dressing room for you," Maisie told me. Her quietly chic off-white skirt and top looked like they aspired to grow up to be Bridgette's wardrobe one day. Her tone was close to worship, but she seemed a little shell-shocked. "She's very energetic."

At least I wasn't the only person Bridgette had that effect on. "Yeah."

The dressing rooms were separated from the sales floor by a wide cream-colored arch. It led into a subdued hallway with dark burgundy flocked velvet walls and thick carpeting that looked like you'd have to vacuum three times to really get it clean. A row of star-shaped lanterns that seemed to create more shadows than they eased hung from hooks along the wall. It felt like a boudoir, not a corner of a department store.

There were four curtained alcoves off the hallway, and Maisie led me to the first one, nearest the arch. "She put you in No. 1," she said, pulling aside a heavy velvet curtain as though she were unveiling a new home spa on a game show. "It's our nicest changing suite."

The "changing suite" was large—large enough for an overstuffed chaise lounge and small table near the entrance, a console table against one wall, and a kind of dais in the front where the three-way mirror stood. The corners were in shadow, but the part of the room with the mirror was well-lit. The console table held a velvet jewelry case with necklaces, earrings, and bracelets, and next to it stood six pairs of shoes and three purses. There were four sets of bars to hang clothes on, and they were all full. I'd never seen so many beautiful clothes in one place before.

"She has day wear on this side," Maisie explained, pointing to what looked like ten outfits, arranged by color. "Going-out clothes over here." Another ten outfits, also arranged by color from light to dark. "And the gowns are back here, although she said you might just have to have some made."

That sounded like gowns plural. "Did she say where I would be wearing gowns?" I emphasized the last syllable.

"Many of our ladies have black tie affairs to go to, and there are the dances at the club. But I think she mentioned something about your eighteenth birthday party."

"Oh. Of course," I said. And for some reason that both delighted and relaxed me. After everything I was learning, it was reassuring to have some evidence that Bain and Bridgette intended to stick to at least some part of their original proposal.

"She said to start over here"—she pointed to her left—"and then go around, so you are moving clockwise."

Bridgette couldn't even let me try on clothes in my own order. I was increasingly glad that I'd decided to ignore her plan and come a week early. How incredibly annoying for her that must have been. "I'll be sure to consider that," I said.

"Oh, and she said to tell you that your phone is in that bag by the chair." I glanced at the brand new iPhone and wondered why Bridgette had bothered. It wasn't like I had anyone to call—or who would call me. "It's your old number; she just got a new handset. If you need anything, I'll be right nearby. Although"—she looked around with clear admiration—"I doubt you will."

"Thanks," I said, feeling a bit disoriented.

She pulled the heavy velvet curtain back into place with a discrete clicking of the large wooden rings it hung from. With it closed, the sound from outside was muffled, and it was like being in a little cocoon. I fingered an inky indigo silk dress with a row of pearl buttons that was in the middle of the "night" section and toyed with starting there. But since I was still a little afraid of how Bridgette would react to my show at Coralee's party now that we were alone, I decided to follow her instructions.

I was on the second of the "day" outfits when I heard a phone ringing. It was coming from the bag on the chair. With a jolt, I realized it was mine.

Slowly, I walked to the chair, opened the bag, and pulled out the handset. "UNKNOWN NUMBER" blinked up at me from the screen. My heart beat faster.

Who would be calling me? I thought again. *Bain? Althea?* Who else had this number or would know it had been reactivated?

"Hello?" I said, trying to keep the trembling out of my voice.

There was silence on the other end.

At first I thought I had been dialed by mistake from the bottom of a purse.

Then I heard, very faintly, the sound of breathing. Someone was there.

"Hello?" I repeated.

It was soft, faint breathing, as though coming from very far away. It reminded me of how my mother, my real mother, sounded when she'd call me from pay phones. The tinny, crackling sound of her voice making it seem surreal, inhuman.

"Who is this?" I demanded.

The breathing stopped. The line went dead.

Super, I thought, setting the phone down. *I'm not even here for twenty-four hours, and I'm already getting prank calls.*

I tried to laugh it off, but as I slid into a short-sleeved cashmere sweater, I had to admit there was something unnerving about the call. If the breathing had been heavy and perverted, that would have been one thing. But it wasn't. It felt like the breathing of someone asleep on the other side of the world.

It took me ten minutes to work through the first three "day" outfits, and at that rate I figured I was going to be there until Aurora's birthday. To speed things up, I decided to forgo fastenings, which is how I found myself trapped half in and half out of the silver grey blouse when I felt the air behind me move and something brush against my leg.

I couldn't see, and I couldn't move my arms. I started to say, "Who—"

A hand closed over my mouth, an arm locked around my chest, and a voice said, "Don't scream."

CHAPTER 21

No one who has lived the life I've lived would follow that order.

I'd managed to keep my motorcycle boots on through all the trying, and now I kicked backward with one of them, making contact with a shin.

"Stop it," a girl's voice said. "Ouch."

Scrambling my head out of the top of the blouse and plowing my arms into the sleeves, I turned around. I was face-to-face with Coralee Gold.

"You are so violent," she complained, massaging her shin.

My heart was pounding, and my mind flipped from the fact that this was the girl whose graduation party I had ruined the night before, to what the police had said about her and Liza being enemies.

She pushed clothes I'd discarded on the chaise aside, sat down, planted her arms behind her, and leaned back. She was wearing tight jeans, a billowing yellow top with gold-wrapped tassels at the sleeves—which was sheer and open enough to make it obvious she wasn't wearing a bra—and one long beaded earring.

My mind flashed to the picture of her parents—Gina "Domes-tic Diva" Gold, tall and Japanese; and the "adorable Bernie," short and white—that showed up in every issue of *Tucson* magazine, and I realized Coralee's looks were a perfect blend of the two. With her mother's thick dark hair and features and her father's piercing green eyes and cleft chin, she was more beautiful than pretty. I imagined that had been challenging when she was younger. Now she was a knockout, and the way she carried herself suggested she knew it. A little too much maybe, like she was making up for lost time. Or had an axe to grind.

She looked me up and down. "I never would have thought of pairing motorcycle boots and flowers. Sort of a 'naughty grandma' look. Not everyone could pull that off."

It took me a moment to realize that the flowers she was referring to were my—Aurora's—panties. I found the black suede shorts that were supposed to go with the silver blouse and tugged them on.

"I'm sorry I scared you," she said, crossing one leg over the other. "I didn't know how else we could meet in secret."

I didn't like people seeing me in my underwear. I felt off-kilter and at a disadvantage, so I made my voice as unfriendly as possible when I asked, "And that was important?"

But if she noticed, she wasn't bothered by it. Coralee laughed for exactly two point five seconds. Then the laugh vanished, and she was all business. "We don't have long, so I'll get right to it." She typed on her iPhone as she spoke.

"If this is about last night—"

"It is in fact. Do you know how many hits we got?" She sat up and held her iPhone to my face. The screen was open to YouTube, and whatever the video was it had been viewed 10,093 times. "At this rate, it will be past twenty thousand by tonight. That's good. No,

I won't lie to you—that's great. It's not 'Relapsed Celebrity Throwing Furniture into the Pool,' sure, but we're certainly building at a solid 'Kitten vs. Kitten' rate."

"What are you talking about?"

She stood up, put her arm through mine, and pulled me out of the dressing room toward the arch that led to the sales floor. She pointed across it. "See?" I followed the tip of her emerald green lacquered fingernail and saw two guys sitting on an upholstered bench. One of them had a retro-looking set of big puffy headphones on over his closely cropped black hair and was leaning back with his eyes closed and tapping his foot to the beat of whatever was playing on his iPod. The other had brown hair that could use a trim and tortoiseshell glasses and was hunched forward intently reading a hardcover book.

"You're being stalked by slackers?" I asked. "Should we call security?"

"Slacker stalkers, L-O-Love it," Coralee said, typing something into her iPhone. "No, that's my camera crew. Today they're using their discrete rig—the iPod is a mic and the book has a hidden camera—but they follow me everywhere, to get footage for the webisodes."

"Webisodes?"

I went to peer out again, but she put an arm in front of me. "Don't lean too far. They're filming, and I don't want them to catch you."

"Why are they filming if you're not there?"

"They're rolling for when I come out. Or in case you and I have a fight in the middle of the store. That's one of my core promises to my viewers, nothing is staged. One life, one take. Catchy right?"

"No."

She smiled. "I love your energy. That's why I'm here. Let's talk."

She motioned me back into my dressing room, holding the curtain open as though it were her office.

"I know what you're thinking," she said, preempting anything I could say. "'We weren't friends before; in fact we were pretty much enemies. So why would Coralee Gold suddenly embrace me now?'"

Since I had only a faint idea what their past history was, I decided to limit my response to nodding and "mm-hmm."

"But if you think about it, it makes perfect sense. I want to be an investigative journalist," she explained, moving toward the outfits Bridgette had selected and flipping through them. She shook a hanger in my direction. "Try this on. Anyway, investigative journalism isn't that easy to break into these days; you need an edge."

What she gave me was a poncho-like sweater in yellow, knitted to look like a ruler. It made me look like I was going to a teacher's rodeo.

"No, not like that," Coralee huffed, standing up and adjusting it so it hung off one shoulder. "Better. So, I'm going the Paris Hilton route—only instead of hotels, my family is big in housewares. A whole new direction for the Good as Gold line. Perfect, right? That's what my publicist Blaze White says. Yes, *that* Blaze White, the legend. Let me tell you, he is so worth his rate plan. Before he agreed to take me on, I was doing that thing where you talk about yourself by your first name? Horror face! Blaze completely saved me from me."

I stopped halfway out of the yellow sweater to gape at her. "Did you just narrate an emoticon?"

"I'm testing out catchphrases." She thrust a purple sweater dress at me, and I got the message I was supposed to try it next, even though technically I still had six outfits to go in the day-wear section. "The thing is," Coralee went on, "it's not as easy as you think. It used to be one sex tape, and you were golden. But now you need to build, and TMZ won't come to Tucson for hardly anything."

I was fumbling with the zipper on the dress—certain things are hard to do with only one good hand—when Coralee stepped toward me and took over, talking the whole time.

"That's why you are such a godsend. Blaze kept saying that I needed a feud, but all my girls are too nice. You're perfect, though—former enemy and wild girl, now with a mysterious past. Smirk." She stepped back and eyed the dress. "Very nice but it needs a necklace. You'll do it right? Will you do it?"

I tried to sort through all the different parts of what she'd just said while she bent over the console table holding one velvet tray of jewelry. "Your goal is to be a reality Internet star? Don't you think that's a little—" I hesitated. I didn't want to be mean, but there was really only one word I could think of. "Pathetic?"

She got still for a moment, and her head cocked to one side. Slowly she straightened up and faced me. "Not quite," she said. Her eyes were looking slightly above me, and she was biting the inside of her cheek. "I mean it was okay, but you need to—how should I put this—*own* it. Don't be so tentative. Say it like you mean it. Go on, try again."

"Try what again?"

"Your line. Say it not like a question, but like you really want to hurt my feelings. *That's a little pathetic.* The way you would have before you disappeared. You would have really lain into me. Now you seem—I don't know, different." She looked me up and down. "I can't quite put my finger on it but—"

That was something I couldn't risk. If Coralee Gold figured out my secret, this would all be over. She'd webisode it in three point five seconds. I cut her off. "This is ridiculous."

"Yes!" Coralee declared, pumping her fist in the air like I'd just scored a point. "That's exactly the right tone. I'll set up your Twitter account and tweet for you. And you only have to fight with me in public. In private we can be friends. Phone." She held out her hand, and I realized that was a command. When I hesitated, she made an impatient little come-hither gesture. "At some point, probably in a few months depending on how things go, we'll have a public apology and be best friends and reveal that we've been pals all along. So it's totally okay for you to e-mail me and text me and stuff. I just called myself from your phone, so now I have your number and you have mine." She put the phone down and picked up a string of clear round stones ending in a mirrored pendant. "Here, put this on."

She stood back, studying me, then shook her head. "That's not right. Hang on." She went back to the accessories table. "Turn around."

I did, and she slipped a choker made of a tangle of silver chains and crystals around my neck. Her fingertips softly grazed my skin, and I felt the breath catch in my throat. She didn't move when I turned back. We were facing each other, nearly nose-to-nose, only a hand's width apart.

I could smell her expensive conditioner and her lip gloss and the cinnamon gum she'd been chewing earlier. She looked at me, right at me with a directness most people avoided, and something about her being so close sent a tingling ripple through me that could have been expectation or fear or both. I'd never stood this close, this *way*, with a girl before. Her thick lashes tilted down as her glance moved to my lips, then came back to my eyes.

She reached out and touched my cheek with her fingertip. "I'm a very good kisser."

I gave her a smile and tried to seem nonchalant, not letting on how strange her proximity was making me feel. Or that I had no idea if I was a good kisser or not. "Is that a proposition?"

"It's a fact," she said. "It would be great for ratings." Her fingertip rested on the corner of my mouth. "And it would be fun. Maybe next week when we've built a fan base a bit."

I swallowed. "No."

She leaned closer and cocked her head slightly to whisper in my ear. "The old Aurora would have done it."

Her breath against my ear was soft and warm, and the tingling inside of me had turned to a fizzy, slightly demanding heat. I felt my pulse beating in my knees as she moved her hand to my upper arm, and the knit fabric of the dress suddenly felt electric against my skin. It had been a very long time since someone kissed me.

I stepped back a little. "I wasn't saying no to kissing you. I was saying no to all of it. The show, everything. Your idea is really— something—but I can't be part of it. My grandmother wouldn't let me, and I don't want to do it without her approval. "

"Oh, of course," Coralee said, laughing like I'd made a hilarious joke.

"I'm serious."

"Says the girl who once rode a horse wearing nothing but a thong and a pair of cowboy boots across the Ventana Country Club golf course on a dare. In the middle of her grandmother's charity golf tournament. You *live* to disobey."

"That—I was a different person then," I said truthfully. "I've turned over a new leaf."

Coralee brushed that aside. "You say that now, but wait until you have your own spin-off."

"Were you just listening to me?"

She rolled her eyes. "I was My-Profile-Picture-Is-Grumpy-the-Grouch, but I'm single-minded. Blaze says that's what is going to take me to the top. Well, that and God. You'll change your mind."

She flicked across several screens on her iPhone, stopped, and held one up for me. "Look, you already have your own fan page."

"AURORA SILVERTON IS A HOTTIE. I'D PSANK HER ANY-TIME," I read. "Great. Someone wants to p-sank me."

"It's a typo for spank."

"It's a synonym for stupid."

"Retweet! I am so posting that from your account. You're a natural!" She tapped me on the tip of my nose. "Oh, and I'd want an exclusive on your story."

"I'm not sure—"

"Listen, everyone will be trying to go the interview route, but I was thinking what if instead . . . we did a reenactment of the night you disappeared?"

"No," I said emphatically, maybe a little too emphatically, because she frowned at me. My head swam at the idea. Even hiding behind the amnesia excuse, there were too many ways a reenactment could go wrong for me to risk it. But almost as bad would be arousing the suspicion of an aspiring investigative journalist with a large YouTube following. "That—that isn't possible," I stammered. "All interviews have to be run through Jordan North," I said. "Besides I don't remember what happened that night. I don't remember anything. So that's not—"

She put up her hand to silence me. "O-M-Genius. Listen to this: We'll do a séance. Madam Cruz wanted to see you again anyway; this will be ideal."

"Coralee that is—"

"Don't say anything. I'll take care of it all. Good talk. Hugsbye."

With a whoosh she was through the curtain. But the wooden rings clattered again a moment later, and she poked her head back in. "My wardrobe tends to be Roy G, so it will look best on camera if you focus on Biv. Like what you have on is perfect." The expression on my face must have told her I had no idea what she was talking about because without waiting she said, "The rainbow? Roy G. Biv? Blue, indigo, and violet for you."

And she was gone.

I was confident that no part of Coralee's plan went with Althea's "roll out," and that in any contest Althea would win, so I decided I didn't need to worry about it.

I turned to examine what I still had left to try. There were six more outfits in the day-wear section, but my eye was drawn to the dark blue silk gown with a long row of pearl buttons up the front. I decided to put it on next.

It was a mermaid cut with a narrow skirt and a train, and the fabric felt cool and exotic against my skin. It's not easy to do up buttons with only one good hand, and I was bent over concentrating on them when I had the feeling of being watched. It started slowly, just a pricking on the edge of my consciousness. But then the hair on my arms stood up, and the back of my neck felt warm.

"Go away, Coralee," I said. "It's Biv, see?" But Coralee didn't answer. I felt a shiver run through me.

I knew I was being silly, but I glanced quickly at my reflection in the mirror in front of me just to check and looked back down at the buttons. Then I registered what I'd seen, and my eyes snapped to the mirror again.

She'd been standing behind me, in the gap of the curtain Coralee had left open. A girl with long blond hair and a slight smile on her face. The girl in the photo from the police station. The dead girl.

Only her eyes were open. And staring right at me.

CHAPTER 22

When I looked back up, there was no one there. She'd vanished like a ghost.

There are no ghosts.

I lunged out of the seat toward the curtains and tripped over the narrow bottom of the gown. Clawing the air, I managed to catch myself on the wall before I went down entirely and was moving forward when I plummeted into Bridgette.

She helped me back up, horror-struck—a look that changed when she caught what I was wearing. "Oh, thank God you're already on evening wear," she said. "It's taking—"

"Did you see her?"

"Who? Wait, where are you going?"

I pushed past Bridgette, ducked under the curtain, and caught sight of the girl at the end of the dim hallway. "Wait," I called. "Stop."

She stopped. I teetered toward her, my heart pounding. "Hello?"

She turned around and gave me a bright smile. "Yes?"

"You're not—" I staggered back. It was Maisie, the salesgirl. "How did you get here?" I asked stupidly.

"Through the door?" She was regarding me like she thought I might be more in the market for a straitjacket than a bomber jacket. "Did you need a size? That gown looks amazing on you, by the way."

"What happened to the girl who was just here?"

"What girl?"

I felt like someone was playing a trick on me. "Blonde? Hazel eyes?"

Maisie shook her head. "You and Coralee Gold and your cousin are the only people who have been back here. The only ones all day."

"That's impossible. I just saw—" My pulse was roaring in my ears. There had been a girl, hadn't there? I steadied myself with my palms against the purple flocked wallpaper. I could tell from how Maisie was looking at me that I sounded crazy. I made myself laugh. "Sorry, I thought I saw a friend." I rubbed my head. "Big night last night."

Maisie nodded enthusiastically. "I know. I saw the video on You-Tube. That was nuts."

Apparently, Coralee wasn't kidding about—

The video! That was it. Saying "thank you" over my shoulder, I ran-tottered down the hallway and through the cream arch in pursuit of Coralee. I spotted her standing with the two guys she'd pointed out as her crew. The one with the headphones was looping a cord around his hand, and it looked like they were packing up to leave. I rushed over, nearly diving headfirst into them when I tripped over my train again.

"Hang on," I said. "Wait."

Coralee turned and frowned. "Not here, not now. We're enemies, remember?"

I ignored her and talked to the brown-haired guy with the tortoiseshell glasses who was bent over the book that was a camera. "Excuse me, did you film—" I cut myself off as he looked up.

"Grant?" I said hesitantly. I was nearly positive it was the same Grant Villa the police had shown me photos of, but I didn't want to be wrong.

He gave me a wry smile. "I was starting to think you'd forgotten all your old friends."

I stiffened slightly, then relaxed realizing that was a joke, not a test.

Grant Villa, who had been at the party the night Aurora disappeared. Grant Villa, who had been Aurora's longtime crush—but not the guy in the photos. How would she react to seeing him?

"Well, I didn't want you to think I was throwing myself at you." I paused. "Right away."

He laughed, then reached out and wrapped me in a bear hug. He smelled really good, and I could see why Aurora had a crush on him.

"It's nice to see you back, " he said as he pulled away. The hug had been just friendly, but there was something in the way he was looking at me now that made me a little tongue-tied.

Fortunately before I had to sort out lucid response, Coralee was standing between us. "What are you doing out here?" she hissed.

My eyes went from her back to Grant. "Were you filming the dressing room the whole time?"

He nodded. "Of course. Captain's orders." He tipped his head toward Coralee. "Unfortunately we just stopped, so we didn't capture your brave attempt at setting the floor-to-face speed record. I'm sure there would have been bonus points for the formal wear."

"Could I see the video you were shooting?"

Coralee, who had been trying not very successfully to interrupt, now came and stood between Grant and me. "If you want to watch the footage, you have to agree to be *in* the footage," she said, as though reciting the rules of *Fight Club*. "That means you do my show."

I nodded. "Okay."

She looked a little taken aback. "And my exclusive interview."

"That's fine too," I said. "Can I see it now?"

"Yes. Sure," she agreed, like she was not quite buying what had just happened but couldn't figure out why.

She gave Grant a thumbs-up, and he flipped open the Dickens novel to a place near the middle where there was an iPad. "The camera is in the spine, and it feeds to this," he explained as he tapped the screen to cue up the footage. "Ready?"

"Yeah."

He pressed *play*.

It started with Coralee going into the dressing room, then nothing for so long that I asked him to put it on fast-forward. Around minute three Coralee's head poked out and went back in as she'd shown me her camera crew, and then there were seven more minutes of nothing until Maisie went in and Coralee came out. She walked over and talked to the camera for a moment, and you could just see Bridgette in the background going into the dressing room as Coralee gave the "cut" sign.

"I didn't see anything," Coralee announced.

I hadn't either.

My mind ran through excuses: The girl had been an illusion. I was seeing things. It was my imagination. I was tired. I was spooked by the pictures Detective Ainslie had shown me.

I was desperate to assure myself this had nothing to do with the voice that seemed capable of whispering not in my ear but right into my mind at the police station, of taking possession of me, like—

Like a spirit. Like a ghost.

There are no ghosts!

Grant was watching me closely. "Are you okay? You look like you need to sit down."

I shook my head.

He said, "Did you find what you wanted to?"

"I don't know. I thought I saw—"

"What?" Coralee asked.

"Liza," I told her.

She went completely still for a long beat, as though someone had turned off the power to her. Then suddenly she was back, pulling out her phone. "That's it," she said. "I'm calling Madam Cruz. We're doing the séance tonight." She made what she would have described as a "winking smiley face." "It's short notice, but they don't say Good as Gold for nothing."

In my mind I heard Madam Cruz's voice saying, *The spirits will have their revenge. Go! Leave! If you have any sense you will fly from here forever.*

"I don't really think—" I began to say, but Coralee cut me off, saying breezily, "Don't worry, you don't have to do anything but show up."

Coralee got busy on the phone, and Grant and the sound guy— who introduced himself as Huck Chin—were starting to stash their gear when Bridgette stalked up. She gave Grant a cool smile and a nod of recognition, ignored Coralee and Huck, and demanded of me, "What are you doing out here?"

"Coralee was helping me with the buttons," I said, indicating the front of the dress.

"We're here to get you clothes, not make a music video. The dressing room is back there." She pointed behind her.

I hadn't been aware that Coralee was listening, but she hung up the phone and leaned toward Bridgette to say, "It's a webisode not a music video, and you really should have edited that room better." Before Bridgette could recover, Coralee said to Grant and Huck, "Pack it in boys," and to me, "See you two tonight. I'll text you the info."

Bridgette watched her go with a stiff, unreadable expression. "What did that mean? And why were you talking to her anyway? She and Aurora weren't exactly friends."

"So she said. Of course that's the kind of thing you might have told me."

"It's the kind of thing you wouldn't have had to know if you hadn't decided to show up early and go to her party," Bridgette shot back. "By doing that you got yourself unnecessarily tangled up with all these people Aurora had relationships with."

"Wouldn't that have happened anyway?" I shot back.

"Not if I could help it."

I had been ready for her recriminations earlier, but I really wasn't in the mood for them now. "Why don't you like her?"

"That's none of your business."

"I think we're past 'none of your business.' You should assume that everything is my business. Like the party Liza and Aurora went to the night she disappeared. You know, the one where you and Bain were the last two people to see your cousin alive?"

Bridgette's glance now was swift and furious. "Who told you that?"

"The police." I gave her a condescending smile. "You can imagine how interested I was to hear it."

She began to twist the triple-band ring she wore on her finger. "Finish getting dressed," she said stonily. "We'll talk about it in the car."

CHAPTER 23

"So, the party," I said when we'd crammed my six shopping bags and Bridgette's four into the trunk of her white BMW convertible. "Why didn't you tell me that you and Bain were probably the last people to see your cousin alive?"

"Stop saying that," she said, adjusting her sunglasses. We pulled out of the lot and into the sunshine. "First, because that is completely not true. There were ten people there—"

"Nine," I said, remembering the photos at the police station.

"Whatever, nine. And second because you two—I mean Liza and Aurora—left the party by themselves before any of the rest of us. Not to mention Liza died miles away."

For some reason I decided not to tell Bridgette about hearing the poem in my head in the police station or seeing—whatever I had seen—in the dressing room. Instead I said, "What about Ro's secret boyfriend?"

She nearly swerved into the red Honda next to us. "What are you talking about?"

"The one with the floppy brown hair and the big hands?"

The color left her face. "How did you find out about Aurora and Colin? The police couldn't have told you about that."

"No, you did. Just now." I looked up. "Light!"

She slammed on the brakes, bringing the car to a shuddering stop in the crosswalk, and turned to me. "I don't like these games you're playing."

"And I don't like yours. If you won't tell me things, I'm going to have to dig them out. How do you expect me to be your cousin if you leave out crucial things like whom she was dating?"

"I didn't know they were dating. I'd heard rumors, but I didn't believe it. I'm still not sure I do."

"It's true." I pulled the photo strip out of my pocket and held it toward her. "This was taken the week before she disappeared." She glanced at it, then pulled up her sunglasses to glance at it again. The light changed. Cars honked behind us.

She flipped them off, dropped her glasses back over her eyes, and, still looking at the photo strip, stepped on the gas. We'd gone about a block at sixty miles per hour when she leaned on the horn and veered across three lanes of traffic and into the parking lot of a strip mall. She threw the car into a space in front of a dollar store and turned it off.

I peeled my fingers off the door handle. Given everything I knew about Bridgette I'd expected her to be a strict speed-limit-traffic-signal-inside-the-lines kind of motor vehicle operator. "Do you drive that way all the time?"

"I learned one summer from a taxi driver when we were in Greece," she said like that was an explanation. She made no move to get out of the car. She pushed her glasses up onto her head again and held the photo strip close to her face as though she were trying to see through the hash marks. She let it drop, leaned back in her seat, and closed her eyes. "So it was true."

If her driving had surprised me, her reaction to the photo sur-prised me even more. She seemed genuinely upset, like my showing her the picture had depressed her.

"You really didn't know about it?" I asked.

She shook her head, her eyes still closed. "We—Aurora and I—we weren't that close. When Bain told me—" She let out a deep breath and opened her eyes, and I was shocked to see tears there. "Poor Aurora." She shook her head and cleared her throat. "And poor Colin."

"Who *is* Colin?"

"Colin Vega. He—he was my year in school. A basketball star. Headed to Dartmouth." She tapped the photo. "Where did you get this?"

"It was in Ro's sock drawer. Kind of hidden but not very hidden. You said their relationship was super secret, but Bain knew."

"What makes you say that?" she demanded, suddenly on the de-fensive. *She feels guilty about something*, I thought. That was where the sadness had come from, or at least part of it, I was sure.

"You just said Bain told you," I explained evenly.

She relaxed a little and made her voice deliberately casual. "That was after Aurora disappeared."

It didn't add up. There was something she wasn't telling me. I decided to push. "Even if he didn't know about them dating, he knew Colin."

"Of course."

"Then how come when I showed this picture to him he said he had no idea who it was?"

She closed her eyes for a moment, and her brow tensed like she'd suddenly gotten a bad headache. "The face is pretty scratched off. And he probably figured there was no reason for you to know."

She opened her eyes, but she wasn't meeting mine. "That it wasn't likely to come up. Since no one knew, and Colin's not around anymore."

"Why would Aurora have kept this secret?"

"The Vega family and ours have this longstanding—thing."

"Like a feud?"

She nodded. "Something happened when Colin's mom and my dad were in high school, and the families have been at odds since then. We talk about how the Vegas have a terrible temper, and they talk about how the Silvertons are unethical schemers."

"Wow, that's hard to believe," I said.

"No, the Vega temper really is notorious," she assured me, apparently oblivious to my sarcasm. "I had to stop being a cheerleader when Colin made the basketball team because my parents didn't want to run into his at games. It has eased a bit recently. We're members of the same country club, but restaurants in town still try not to take reservations from both families on the same night. And all of Grandmother's lawyers and bankers know if she hears they are working with the Vegas, she'll fire them."

"That sounds tough." I made no attempt to sound like I meant it.

"It is," Bridgette said, again ignoring, or not detecting, the sarcasm in my voice. "Very Montague and Capulet. That's why it was so hard to believe they might be going out. And why they wouldn't have risked letting anyone know. On the other hand, it probably made him more appealing to Aurora. Another way to flout the Family."

It dawned on me now that Bridgette had been using the past tense to talk about him. I felt an uneasy knot in my chest as I asked, "Did he die too?"

"N-no," she answered slowly. "He's alive. He just moved away." She was gazing at the photo strip pensively. "He left right after

Aurora disappeared." Still thoughtful, she said, "From what you can see of Aurora's face, they look happy, don't they?"

"Yeah," I said. "They do."

She ran her finger over the pen marks. "I wonder what changed."

"It can be hard when you have to keep a big part of your life secret," I offered.

"Yes," she agreed. She seemed withdrawn into her own head for a moment, and then she said brightly, like she was reciting something she'd read in a waiting room, "But secrets can also keep things precious. Private. That's what can be hard for people to understand. It can be nice to have something you don't share with the world."

It was so odd being with her. Sometimes she was likable, and other times she was—Bridgette. "Sure."

"Who are you to judge anything?" she demanded, angry and defensive. She shoved the photo back at me. "I'd keep this somewhere no one can find."

"Your brother said the same thing."

"Did he? That's one thing we agree on then."

"Why?"

She looked at me sharply. "If you start flashing pictures around, people are bound to start asking questions. Remember, you're only here temporarily. The more inquisitive people become, the more likely they are to uncover what we're doing. And the last thing we need is for you to attract the attention of the police."

"Right," I said. I believed what she was saying, but I was still certain there was more to it. Unfortunately, I wasn't completely successful at keeping the skepticism out of my voice.

She eyed me closely. "I don't know what *inspired* you to show up here a week before we'd planned, but I would suggest that from now on, you do what I say. I would hate for things to get messy for you."

The threat was a deliberate undertone in her voice, for some reason I wanted to make her spell it out. "How exactly would they get messy?"

She reached into her purse and pulled out a Prada wallet. "Like if I were to turn this in to the police." From behind a black American Express card, she pulled my Eve Brightman ID.

I'd been waiting for this moment, I realized, ever since I'd come back from playing tennis with Bain and found it gone. It was almost a relief to have it out now. "If you did that, I would be forced to tell everyone about my deal with you and Bain."

"Of course," she said, nodding. "But I doubt they would believe it. Besides, even if people did believe your crazy story, you don't really think that piece of paper you've got hidden beneath your mattress with the note on it about paying you one hundred thousand dollars would hold up, do you? When obviously you must have fished it out of the garbage from the Starbucks you were working at?"

The night Bain had been in my room—he had been looking for the note to see where I'd put it. My face must have registered my surprise because she laughed. "Oh, you did think the note would work. That's sweet. Anyway, even if people did believe your story, you're still the only one of us breaking the law. And the only one liable to be punished." She slipped the Eve Brightman ID back behind the black credit card. "But there's no reason for any of that, is there? Just do what I tell you to do, and this will all work out fine."

Fine for who? a voice in the back of my mind asked.

Just like that, her personality flipped again. As though we'd gotten something nicely settled, she popped off her seatbelt and gave me a conspiratorial smile. "Come on." she pushed her door open. "I'm going to introduce you to one of the best things in Tucson."

I gazed around the strip mall. One of the stores was closed, one of them was a Middle Eastern café and hookah lounge, one was the dollar store, and one was a holistic bookstore. Before I had a chance to guess which one hid the best thing in Tucson, she'd dragged me toward the dollar store and said, "Treasure hunt. The goal is to find the choicest item in the store. The winner pays."

I raised my eyebrow. "You've been in the dollar store?"

"Everyone needs to let off steam somehow." She smiled. "See what I mean about keeping some things private? It's my guilty secret."

"What if we don't agree on what the *choicest* is?"

"The cashier will break the tie."

It sounded fair. It also sounded like she'd done it before. I stopped her as she'd set the door chime tinkling. "You haven't bribed the cashier, have you?"

She laughed aloud. "If I didn't know better, I'd think you were a real Silverton."

I thought I had it locked with a wind-up chicken that pooped candy eggs and came in a box labeled Watch Chicks Get Laid with Authentic Motion®, but the Fur You™ fake fur beard to keep your face warm while you skied NOW FOR TODDLERS OR PETS that Bridgette uncovered was the clear winner.

If you had told me that I could enjoy spending time with Bridgette, or that she had a sense of humor, I wouldn't have believed it. But she surprised me. Away from the Family, she was fun. Normal.

It never occurred to me that this could all be part of a larger, and more dangerous, scheme.

I was paying with money she gave me, since I had none, when my phone buzzed with a message from Coralee, saying that the séance would take place that night at nine P.M. at the same model house that had hosted the party three years earlier.

When I told Bridgette about it, she said, "A séance. No thank you."

"Why?"

"Three reasons: one, ghosts do not exist," she said. "But bad press does, and a séance is like a magnet for it in this town. Two, there is no way Althea will possibly consent to you going. And three, even if you go, there is no guarantee everyone else will."

As it turned out, she was right about one of those things.

CHAPTER 24

"I've never been to a séance," Bain said, steering his Porsche up the hill toward the Sunset Canyon Estates where the Event (as Coralee was calling it) was going to be held. "I doubt it can top what's already happened. I'm not sure which is more remarkable, Althea agreeing to let you go or Bridgette agreeing to go to an event planned by Coralee."

By the time Bridgette and I had gotten back from the mall, Coralee had not only e-mailed Jordan North asking for Althea's permission for the séance, but had also managed to get the matriarch to agree to a whole schedule of events, including a spa day with some of Aurora's classmates the next day and a joint appearance at Tucson Days Fair on Tuesday.

"I'll be glad not to have you around the house," Althea said at dinner that night, her tone suggesting that the mere sight of me was upsetting to her.

It was worse when Althea reached her hand across to take Bridgette's wrist and said, "At least I have one good granddaughter."

Bridgette momentarily looked shocked, but she recovered

quickly. "Of course you do, Grandmother," she said. "I'll never leave you."

Bridgette, Bain, and their parents had joined Althea and me for dinner in the massive dining room of Silverton House. The long table that ran down its middle could easily have seated thirty, but the six of us were huddled at one end.

The room itself was extraordinary with a coffered ceiling and blond wood panels I knew had been imported from a monastery in France by Sargeant after the First World War. Evening sunlight filtered through a pair of tall stained glass windows he'd taken from the same place, turning the walls into a jewel-tone tableau of saints and angels. Given what I'd seen of the Family, it made sense that the Silvertons would turn something others held sacred into a place to satisfy their appetites.

I focused on the reflections on the walls, the way that the breeze through the leaves of a tree outside seemed to fan the Virgin Mary, rather than on the unexpected stab Althea's words had given me.

Why did I care? Why did it matter to me that this woman didn't like me? Everything I'd been learning told me she and Aurora had lived in a state of uneasy détente, their only interaction sparky, never sweet. But it confused me—how could people who had so much, and spent so much time talking about the Family, be so cold to one another?

Mrs. March entered then, wheeling a trolley that contained a covered china soup tureen with woodland nymphs frolicking on it, and a covered silver platter. She lifted the lids off of both and revealed tomato soup and grilled cheese sandwiches.

"Is this some kind of a joke, Mother?" Bridger asked.

"You want fancy food, spend your own money and eat at your own house," Althea snapped at him, reaching for a sandwich.

The rest of dinner was silent against a soundtrack of spoons clinking against china bowls and knives and forks being carefully picked up and set down and throats being cleared. Finally Althea wiped her mouth with her napkin, dropped it on the table, and pushed her chair back. "Dismissed," she said, and everyone scattered as quickly as they could. It had seemed endless but had only lasted twenty-two minutes.

As we were leaving, Bain offered to drive me to the séance, since Bridgette was riding with her boyfriend, Stuart. Everyone who had been present the night of the party was going to be there, except Xandra Michaels, who turned out to be Bain's ex-girlfriend. She was at school in London, and even the force of Coralee Gold couldn't bend time to get her there tonight.

"Why doesn't Bridgette like Coralee?" I asked Bain. His driving style was pretty much the opposite of Bridgette's. He drove like a senior citizen who could see—staying inside the lines and obeying all the signs.

"Because they're too much alike," he said. "At least that's what I think." I was again struck by how he did that, said something astute and then backpedaled from it, as though he only had part-time use of a backbone. It suddenly made me wonder how much of this plan was his idea—and how much of it was Bridgette's.

I absentmindedly registered that there seemed to be a lot of traffic traveling away from Sunset Canyon Estates, a development that, according to Bain, had only forty-five premium luxury residences, of which ten were occupied. "They don't seem alike to me," I said.

"Not on the surface, but below it. They both like secrets, they both like to be in charge, and they're both good at it. There was one time—"

I didn't get to hear what happened one time because we rounded a bend then, right into stopped traffic. The road had been narrowed to a single lane by a row of cars and news vans parked along the slope of the hill. Ahead of us was a wooden police barricade with an officer standing in front of it. If Bridgette had been driving, either the officer or I would have ended up as a hood ornament, but Bain had no trouble slowing to a gentle stop. The officer walked around to Bain's side of the car and tapped on the window. When Bain opened it, the man gave a big smile. "Silverton. Thought that was my grandma driving." He and Bain did one of those handclasp-fist-bump-patty-cake kind of handshakes before his eyes came to me. "You must be the long lost cousin. Welcome back."

"What's going on?" Bain asked.

"What did you expect? Everyone wants to see the returning heiress. Got all the news networks, plus the amatuer paparazzi. Your little gig tonight got a lot of attention. We've been holding back crowds the last two hours. Residents and guests only from here, but that's not stopping the lookie loos from parking below and taking the scenic way in." He nodded his head toward the side of the road, where a steady stream of shadows was making its way up.

We passed through the barricade. As Bain's headlights swiveled around curves, the figures of people walking along the shoulder of the road seemed to pop out of the darkness like monster cutouts on a carnival horror ride. "Why would anyone hike up here for this?"

"Aurora's return is big news." Bain was concentrating on driving, taking the curves slowly. "Rich girl who's been missing for three years and just wanders back into town? It would be a good story on its own, but add the Silverton name and it's a great story."

"Why? Why do these people care about the Silvertons?"

"Because they want to be us," Bain said matter-of-factly.

As we pulled up to the address, I saw another cluster of people being held back by more uniformed officers. Bain's car edged slowly forward. Someone pointed at me and said, "It's her!" and suddenly there were cameras lighting up like a fireworks display outside our car.

My stomach contracted as though I'd been punched, and I covered my face with my hand.

"Stop it," Bain's voice lashed out at me. "Aurora would be loving this. Smile and wave to your fans. *Now.*"

His tone was brutal, but when I looked at him, he was grinning— a grin I could tell he'd practiced for the cameras. I copied him, waving and smiling, and as we went by, I saw that one of the officers on crowd-control duty was N. Martinez. I caught his eye and gave him an Aurora wave-and-smile, which made his frown deepen.

A different officer directed Bain to a quiet spot behind the house, then explained that Coralee had requested all guests walk around back up the front, where the news cameras had been set up.

"Of course," Bain told the cop affably. He draped his arm over my shoulder and pushed me forward. "This is what we're here for. I don't know how else we're going to sell these houses."

"You agreed to this as an advertising stunt?" I asked as he pulled me toward the front of the house. "Bridgette said this would be bad press."

"Bridgette doesn't understand. Press you don't pay for is never bad," Bain said, gesturing with the hand that was over my shoulder. "For the development or for Dad, free press is great press. The more ink we get, the better our bottom line looks."

The reporters surged forward like a porcupine with microphones for spines as Bain and I came into view. Acting like he hadn't expected them to be there, he said, "No questions," hid my face against his chest, and pulled me through the crowds as though we were fleeing shrapnel.

"I thought you wanted to talk to the press," I said when we were inside and he'd closed the door behind us.

He laughed. "Be *seen* by them, not talk to them. Never let them think you want to talk to them. That way they make up their own stories, and we have complete deniability." Then he shed his jacket, looked around like he owned the place—which, I guess, he did—and said, "How about a séance? I am feeling ghoul tonight."

Every woman in the room giggled.

I rolled my eyes. "How long did you work on that?"

"Modified it from a Dixie cup." He winked, moving on to check out the female members of the catering staff Coralee had brought in. It took Bain two minutes to survey the selection, pick out the hottest girl, ask her name, and tell her that if she took care of him all night he could promise she'd be well-rewarded.

"Her name is Scarlet but she goes by Scar," I overheard him telling Bridgette's boyfriend, Stuart. "How hot is that?"

"Searing," Stuart said. I felt Stuart looking at me, so I smiled and he shot me a little nod-smile back. He and Bain both gave off the "he knows how handsome he is" vibe, but otherwise they were nearly opposites.

While Bain seemed like he could have stepped off the cover of next month's *Men's Journal*, Stuart's looks were more classic. With his curling light brown hair, olive skin, wide-spaced tawny eyes and a mouth just firm enough to avoid being pretty, Stuart looked like something a Greek sculptor would have swooned over. He had a lazy, laid-back way of looking at people from beneath partially closed lids. I bet a lot of girls found it sexy, but to me it was strangely repellant. He was listening to Bain, but his eyes were surveying the room. He wore a vague smile on his face as though he were amused at something that no one else knew.

We were in the main room of what Bain had told me to call the "Model *Property*," because it sounded more upmarket than "Model *Home*." This particular one was sleek and modern, which meant the living area was a large open space with stark white and grey surfaces and a wall of glass that opened onto a pool area. There had only been nine people, counting Liza and Aurora, at the party that night three years ago. But with the bartenders and the caterers, there were easily two dozen people there tonight, and the space still felt nearly empty. One person working all day might have been able to get it clean.

I turned and looked out the plate glass window. The house was nestled in the middle of a series of hills. As the darkness set in, the hills assumed deep blue outlines against the purple sky. Bright white stars began to appear, first a handful of dots, then more. The properties that were inhabited had discrete outdoor lighting, so the blanket of stars seemed to go on forever, and the darkness turned the window into a mirror.

I looked past the reflection of myself—in my new grey leopard print cardigan, cuffed skinny jeans, and silver wedges—to the people behind me. It was like gazing at a group portrait come to life. Coralee was on one side conferring with Huck and Grant, Jordan was talking to Scar, and Bridgette had perched herself on the arm of the chair Stuart was occupying next to Bain. But it was the details of the scene that I found fascinating. Bain trying to catch Coralee's eye. Jordan deliberately avoiding Stuart's. Bridgette jumping when Stuart's arm brushed the leg of her jeans. She looked even more on edge than usual.

I tried to imagine what the party had been like for Liza and Aurora. Earlier that afternoon I'd decided to clear out all of Aurora's clothes to make places for the new things I'd just gotten, and I'd discovered a false bottom in her sock drawer. Lifting it out, I found a romance novel with all the sex scenes marked and a picture of Liza and Aurora.

I could figure out why Aurora had hidden the book but was less sure why she was hiding the picture. It showed the two girls somewhere that looked like a mall, each wearing Santa hats and a necklace. The pendants on the necklaces, which they were holding out for the camera, were two halves of the same heart. Aurora's half had the letter B stamped on it, and Liza's half had FF. *Best Friends Forever*. Two of the fingers Liza was using to hold the pendant were wrapped together in surgical tape, as though they were broken.

Aurora's smile at the camera was carefree and happier than she'd looked in the yearbook photo Bridgette had shown me. Liza was smiling too, but instead of looking at the camera, she was looking at Ro. There was something in her eyes I hadn't seen before, something I couldn't quite describe that reminded me of how I'd seen parents look at their children, part satisfied, part protective.

With a shudder, I realized it was exactly the way the girl I'd seen in the mirror at the mall had looked at me.

But there had been no girl at the mall, I reminded myself. There couldn't have been. And even if there *had* been, it couldn't have been Liza. Because Liza was dead.

My gaze moved back to the people reflected in the window and caught Bridgette's eye. She frowned and made a little spiral gesture with one finger, as if telling me to circulate. I realized with a start that I hadn't been acting like Aurora at all. I turned, looking for the easiest person to launch myself on, when Coralee broke away from her crew and moved to the center of the room. She clapped her hands for quiet and a hush fell.

"Roscoe Kim's plane from L.A. got delayed, so he can't make it," she said. There was a hint of blame in her voice, as though she thought he'd done it just to inconvenience her. "We're going to go ahead and get started anyway. Madam Cruz has been meditating all afternoon, and she is ready to welcome the spirits. Unlike other mediums, she does not mind doubters, but she does ask that you don't give voice to your doubts until the session is over. Is that acceptable?"

Everyone nodded. A tiny knot of fear began to tighten in my stomach. Not for the first time, I wondered what I'd gotten myself into.

"Great. We've got two cameras set up in the corner to record whatever happens. But just act natural, you know, don't perform or anything. I've got waivers for you to sign on the way out. This is going to be the most rocking séance ever. We've set it all up in the music room, so if everyone could go in there—"

She pointed to a passage off the side of the main room, and, suddenly subdued, the group stood and started to file in.

"Aren't you coming?" I asked her.

She shook her head. "I wasn't there that night, and we don't want to do anything that might disrupt the spirits. But don't worry, I'll watch the whole thing on monitors out here."

The music room was essentially a soundproof glass box cantilevered over the edge of a hill. Seven stools had been set up in a circle on the hardwood floor, centered around a large stone board with the letters of the alphabet on it—like a large, stone Ouija board. There were candles placed around the edge, and they flickered as we shuffled in. Coralee closed the door that communicated with the rest of the house behind us, and the noise of the caterers vanished.

No one spoke. The only sound was the spluttering of the candles and a quiet, almost inaudible chanting coming from Madam Cruz. She was sitting on a straight-backed chair on one side of the circle of stools, wearing a bright red dress with red ribbons braided into her hair. Her eyes were closed, and her eyelids were caked with black kohl. She rocked back and forth, making strange, low humming noises.

There was something about the atmosphere of the room that made everyone somber, and we all took seats without speaking.

As if that were a cue, Madam Cruz began rocking faster, and her eyelids lifted slightly, showing a glimpse of the whites beneath them. She made a wheezing noise, and her tongue moved around her mouth like she was soundlessly speaking ten languages at once. Her breathing got labored, coming in gasps until she was panting like an animal. She bared her teeth, and a growling noise came from her throat. The lids of her eyes sprang open, and her pupils had disappeared, her eyes rolled hideously back into her head to show only the whites. She leered around at us that way and, in a voice somewhere between a bellow and a growl, said, "Silverton, you goddamn bastard."

"Jay," Bain whispered. He'd gone completely white. Bridgette, next to him, rolled her eyes.

Madam Cruz's head started to flop around, and she made indistinct noises, some of them that sounded like words, and some gibberish. "That night . . . tried to cheat me . . . bastard."

Stuart started a slow clap, saying, "She nailed Jay," and several other people laughed, but Bain ignored them.

"Jay, can you hear me?" Bain was leaning forward with an intensity that was almost comical. "That wasn't me. I would never cheat you."

"Did it," Madam Cruz hissed. She pointed a finger at Bain. "Changed the plan . . . set me up."

"Jay, J.J., man, I swear. Listen about that other thing—"

Madam Cruz lunged from her seat, arms extended, and wrapped her hands around Bain's neck. "Bastard," she roared. Her eyes were rolling in their sockets and spit was running out of the corner of her mouth. The mood in the room had shifted abruptly. No one was laughing now, and Stuart had gone pale. "I was there. I kept my mouth shut. But now . . ." Her hands were squeezing Bain's throat so hard his face was red and he was gasping, struggling to peel her fingers off. "I never told—"

She was strangling him in front of us before our eyes, and we were all frozen, watching in horror, unable to move.

Except Grant. He leapt to his feet and moved to crouch next to Madam Cruz. He put a hand on her shoulder and one on her arm and said, "It's okay, Jay." His voice was friendly but soothing. "You can go now. He knows. He understands. Leave in peace. It's okay, Jay, leave in peace."

And as if Grant were some kind of ghost wrangler, Madam Cruz's hands fell from Bain's neck, her face relaxed, and her head slumped against her chest. Grant maneuvered her hulk back to her chair. Bain rolled sideways off the stool and lay in a fetal position on the floor.

He was still coughing and spluttering and clutching his neck a moment later when Madam's eyes opened and she looked around curiously. Our faces must have told her something happened. "Did we have a visitor?" she asked.

"Someone called Bain a bastard and tried to strangle him," Bridgette said dryly. She studied her fingers. "But we don't have to go all the way to the afterlife to find people who want—"

"Shut up," Bain snarled, climbing to his feet. His face was stormy, and his fists were clenched. He turned to where Grant was sitting and towered over him. "Why did you get in the middle of it?"

Grant frowned at him. "Because it looked like you couldn't breathe."

"Damn you, Villa, why can't you ever mind your own business? I can handle myself."

Grant said, "Sorry. I—I thought I was doing you a favor."

Bain leaned anxiously toward Madam Cruz. "Can you get him back? I need to ask him something."

"I—I don't know," she said. The strangling grunting creature of a minute earlier was gone, replaced by a friendly-looking lady with watery blue eyes. Some of the kohl had run down her face, and she looked a bit spent. "With the spirits, we are on their time, not them on ours." She looked around the room. "Welcome to you all," she said with a cheery smile. "That was something, wasn't it?"

We all agreed.

"You never know what will happen. Sometimes the spirits arrive without our asking, and sometimes they must be invited. Shall we try again?"

"I'd really like to get Jay back here," Bain urged.

Madam Cruz smiled up at him placidly. "You've made that clear, Mr. Silverton. And we will do what we can." Her eyes came back to the group. "I ask that you all stand and hold hands."

We did. I had Bridgette on one side and Grant on the other. He was taller than I'd realized earlier. He smiled down at me as he took my hand. It was warm, and suddenly I was glad he was there.

"Repeat after me," Madam Cruz said, closing her eyes. "Powers beyond, powers who are near."

"Powers beyond, powers who are near," we repeated.

"Please let our loved ones kindly appear."

"Please let our loved ones kindly appear."

It was a foolish rhyme, and yet saying, hearing us all say it, gave it a strange kind of resonance.

"Again," she commanded.

"Powers beyond, powers who are near. Please let our loved ones kindly appear."

"Again," she ordered.

"Powers beyond, powers who are near. Please let our loved ones kindly appear."

"More," Madam nearly shouted, and we matched her volume, getting louder and louder with each repetition.

"Powers beyond, powers who are near, please let our loved ones kindly appear. Powers beyond, powers who are near, please let our loved ones kindly appear. Powers beyond, powers who are near, please let our loved ones kindly appear."

"Stop!"

Silence dropped like a trapdoor, sudden, fast, absolute. Madam Cruz's eyes shot open.

My phone rang.

CHAPTER 25

"Answer it," Madam Cruz commanded.

It said, "UNKNOWN NUMBER." My hand was shaking as I brought it to my ear. "Hello?"

I heard breathing.

"Hello?" I repeated. "Who's there?"

A weak, raspy voice said, "Ro-ro."

My hand began to shake. "What?"

"Ro-ro," the voice repeated, sounding plaintive over the static.

"Who is this? Who's there?" I repeated. "Tell me your name right now or I hang up."

"No!" The sound was plaintive, a wail. "Please don't . . . so lonely . . . I've missed you. I . . . I forgive you, Ro-ro."

The words froze me. "I'm hanging up," I said.

"Liza," the voice said, the whisper urgent. "Who else? It's Liza, Ro-ro."

In my mind I saw the girl with her eyes closed, closed forever, in the photo.

In my mind I saw the girl that afternoon in the dressing room, staring at me in the mirror.

I groped behind me for my stool and sat down, hard. *There are no such things as ghosts,* my mind repeated. "That isn't possible. You can't be Liza. Liza is dead."

"Best friend for . . . *ever*," the voice said. "You know. You . . . saw me. At the mall . . . in the mirror."

"No. I imagined that."

"I was . . . there . . . with you . . . need you . . ."

The sound trailed away. "Hello?"

There was a whisper like wind brushing over the mouthpiece. I pressed the phone to my ear to hear better. The voice said, "They . . . must be stopped . . . before . . ."

"Before what?"

"Help me . . . find . . . the truth. Find the . . . coat."

I wasn't sure about the last word. "Coat?"

"*Be careful!*" The voice became higher pitched and urgent. "I feel . . . they're . . . there. Someone . . . from that night. Someone . . . with you . . . *Now*."

I looked around the room. Everyone was staring at me. "I don't understand. What do you want me to do?"

"The coat . . . If you—"

Bridgette's hand wrenched the phone from mine. "This isn't a funny joke," she shouted. "No one is amused. Leave my family alone or you will be—"

There was a rush of cool air like something leaving the room, and all the candles went out at once, plunging us into complete darkness.

We sat in silence. I couldn't move. I was freezing, but my heart was racing as though I'd just sprinted a mile.

Bridgette crossed the room, found a light switch, and flipped it on.

It felt like waking up in an unknown bed in bright daylight. Everyone seemed uncomfortable and shifted to avoid one another's eyes.

Still holding my phone, Bridgette planted herself in front of the medium, who had sunk back into her chair. "Where is your assistant? Where is the person on the other end of this phone? Are they close by? Someone on the catering staff? I will find them and you will pay."

With her words, the tension in the room dissipated. It was such an obvious, easy stunt, I felt stupid for having been taken in by it. I had the sense that everyone else did too.

Madam Cruz looked at Bridgette with an expression that could have been pity. "I have no assistant. I had nothing to do with that. That—was the spirits."

"I have a hard time believing the spirits have a calling plan," Bridgette said. I don't think I'd ever liked her as much as I did then.

"I cannot help what you believe or don't believe. Spirits communicate in many ways, whatever is at hand." Madam Cruz wiped her forehead with her palm, and I realized that she was sweating. She gazed around at all of us intensely. "I have never experienced anything like that before." She swallowed, and it struck me that she was as disconcerted by what had happened as we were. "Never."

"I'm sure," Bridgette said, sounding unconvinced.

But her objections felt hollow in the face of Madam Cruz's very real agitation. The medium's eyes went to my face. She leaned toward me at an angle, half in and half out of her seat like she was afraid of approaching too near me. "You have been given a gift," she said. "That—never before. Perhaps this shows the strength of your love for this girl, or hers for you. Extraordinary. Most extraordinary. Use it wisely."

Her eyes were regarding me with a mixture of wonder and fear. Bridgette moved in front of her to hand me my phone back. "Use it wisely," she mimicked.

"Can't you let it rest?" Bain burst out. "Just because you don't believe doesn't mean the rest of us can't."

Bridgette's posture became rigid. She turned slowly toward him. "I'm sorry if I am undercutting your experience of the occult," she said stiffly. She leaned over my head to whisper to him, "You'd better start hoping ghosts can't come back and talk. For all our sakes, you'd better hope that."

Then she turned and headed for the door.

I looked around to see if anyone but me heard what she'd whispered to Bain, but Bridgette's opening the door had broken the spell of the room. And as the noises from outside filtered in, the taut bond that had seemed to hold us all together vanished. Suddenly, everyone was an unreadable stranger.

This has nothing to do with you, I told myself, but my heart wouldn't stop racing.

Coralee breezed through the door headed right for me. "That was amazing. Totally gnarly. You should see your face in the footage."

"Pass."

Her head tilted to one side, and she studied me. "You look a little pale."

"I think I just need a second. I'll be right back," I said and threaded my way out of the music room.

I reminded myself that this had nothing to do with me. And even if it did, there was no such thing as a ghost—

You saw me.

—Liza had jumped off a ridge—

Find the coat.

—and there was absolutely no proof—

Find the truth.

—to the contrary.

Please just leave her alone, her father's voice screamed into my mind.

Liza was dead. She had committed suicide. This was some kind of prank to scare me—

Someone . . . there. That night. Someone with you.

—and it was working.

Involuntarily my mind flashed over the guest list from that night, first past the faces of the people there tonight—Jordan, Grant, Bain, Bridgette, Stuart, then what I remembered from photos of Roscoe Kim and Xandra Michaels. They were beautiful, polished, spoiled, perfect. None of them looked like killers.

But any of them could be one.

I forgive you.

There was a powder room between the music room and the main area, but I passed it and ran up the stairs to the second floor. I wanted to be alone, and as far from the others as I could get. I turned into the master suite, crossed several miles of Siberian white carpet, slipped into the master bathroom, and let the solid wood door slide closed.

A strong hand caught it two inches before it hit the wall, and my heart froze. Slowly, the door was pushed back open. Stuart Carlton stepped in, closed the door, and clicked its lock into place.

He leaned back against it and grinned.

CHAPTER 26

Stuart let his hooded eyes rest on me and whispered, "I've been waiting for this moment for so long." I stepped away, but he followed and trapped me against the wall.

I pushed against him, hard, but he was stronger than me. "What are you doing?"

Stuart laughed. "This is a re-creation of the party that night, isn't it? I'm re-creating all of the events."

I braced my arms against his chest and kept my elbows locked. "I don't remember what happened that night. Any of it."

"I'm a little surprised you don't remember our part," he said. "But that's okay, just follow my lead." He leaned down and nipped at my neck.

"Ouch," I said, pulling away.

"Very good. That's what you said that night."

I felt like a caged animal. No one downstairs would hear me scream up here, and he was between me and the door. My mind raced in panicked circles: *I'm trapped . . . get him away . . . I'm trapped.*

He seemed to sense my fear and smiled slowly. "That's just how you looked that night. You were scared then too, weren't you?"

Breathe, I told myself. *Think.* "Why don't you tell me what we did first?" I blurted, trying to buy myself some time. "You know, to, um, get me into the mood."

I saw his Adam's apple go up and down as he swallowed hard. "Well, I was leaning against the counter, and I held you pressed up against me. Like this," he said, gathering me to him.

I struggled to keep as much space between us as I could. "And?" I swallowed.

"I had my hands on your shoulders like this, and I told you to grab a towel to kneel on, so that you could—"

"What I was wearing," I interrupted, trying to steer the narrative in a different direction. *Distract him.* "Do you remember?"

"Yeah. That's how it all started. I came in here for obvious reasons, and you were in the bathtub taking a little nap. No water in it, just you, sitting up in that coat you were running around in." He gazed fondly at the bathtub. "When I came in, you sort of woke up, and I said, 'Let's see what you have on underneath that coat.' And I undid it, and—"

"I was wearing a *coat*?" I repeated. "In June?"

"Yeah. A trench coat. Very sexy. And it wasn't like you had much on beneath it." The way he said it made him sound like a panting dog.

I was staring at myself in the mirror over his shoulder. And then something shifted, and I could picture it—

Aurora standing by the sink, staring into the mirror. Her mascara running down her face, Stuart behind her. His hands stripping the coat from her shoulders, his mouth on her neck, his fingers closing on her breasts, squeezing them through the fine fabric of a summer dress. Her eyes widen then, realizing what's about to happen. She reaches up to pry his fingers off of her, but he turns her around, toward him, and starts pushing her to her knees with one hand, the other going to the waist band of his jeans—

My mind flipped to another man, another girl. A shadowy bed-room, the only illumination from the streetlight outside and the Winnie the Pooh digital clock next to the bed. The man is holding the girl pinned against a wall. She is wriggling and crying and beg-ging him to stop. Pleading. She promises she won't tell anyone what he's done if he just leaves now.

The man laughs. "Who you going to tell, little one? Who would believe a little whore like you?"

Her eyes widen as she realizes what is about to happen—

"Things were getting good," Stuart said, his voice, his breath-ing hot and fast against my ear, wrenching me back to the present. "Then things were getting *really* good." His eyes were glassy, and his hips pressed against mine.

"Then what happened?" I asked, trying to move away slightly.

His eyes refocused on me. "Then your little bitch friend came in and dragged you out."

"Coralee?"

"No, the dead one. Liza. She said you'd hate yourself in the morn-ing if you went any farther with me. Like she was your mother. Snotty bitch."

"Do you remember if I was wearing my coat then?"

"I think you put it back on. I left before the two of you came out. I'm not into that girl-on-girl lezzy shit," he sneered.

Charming, I was thinking when something occurred to me.

"Do you remember if I was dating anyone?" I asked casually.

"Not that night you weren't." He took a big handful of my leopard print cardigan and pulled me up against his chest. "So, now that you know the script," he said, rolling one of the silver buttons around in his fingers, "why don't we rehearse?"

"You're my cousin's boyfriend," I objected.

"Bridgette and I have an agreement. Besides, that didn't bother you before."

"You're lying," I said. I couldn't explain how, but I knew I was right.

The way his sneer wavered confirmed it for me. "You know you wanted it. You were just afraid to admit it. I could see it in your eyes, no matter what you were saying."

"No," I said, and my voice sounded small, almost childlike. "You're wrong." I cleared my throat. "Besides, I'm different now."

"Yes, you are," he said. "You're all grown-up." He tugged at the neck of the cardigan, popping one of the buttons.

I pulled back and covered my chest with one hand and tried to push him away with the other. "Stop it. I don't want to do this."

His eyes weren't lazy anymore. Now they looked hungry. "That's what you said that night too. But you didn't mean it." One of his hands plunged down the front of my sweater to grab my bra, and the other grabbed my ass. "I can't tell you how much I regretted having to leave this untapped," he said, giving it a squeeze. "Tonight could be the night." I tried to wrench away, and another button flew off the cardigan.

"Let me go!" I pushed against him with my fists.

He grabbed both wrists in one surprisingly strong hand and held them to the side, staring at my bra as he said, "That's right, baby. Fight me harder."

"No!" I said, trying to twist my arms free. "Let me go!"

His eyes looked wild with pleasure. He licked his lips. "Make me."

I brought my knee up into his groin hard.

"Aww man," he moaned, recoiling in on himself. "You filthy little slut, what the hell did you do?" He was rocking back and forth, clutching his crotch with both hands.

I moved away from him. "I told you to stop."

"Dirty tease," he said, crab walking to the door. He shot the lock and threw the door open. He paused on the threshold to shout, "Stay away from me, you filthy slut," and disappeared around the corner.

For a moment I stood frozen where I was, his parting words ricocheting from wall to wall. I could picture him saying the exact same thing in that exact same room three years earlier, picture it all with a clarity that knotted up my stomach.

Dirty tease! You filthy slut!

I slid the door closed and locked it, then went and sat in the bathtub shivering and rubbing my arms and wondering what you had to do to clean a fireplace like the one in the wall.

After awhile there was a knock at the door.

"Aurora?" Coralee's voice said. "Can I come in?"

"I'm fine, I'll be out in a second."

"Okay."

More time passed. I lay back in the bathtub and thought maybe I could just stay there forever. There was another knock. "It's me," Bridgette's voice said. "Let me in."

"I'm okay," I said.

"Let me in. Bain will kill me if I break this door down before he sells the house, but I will if you force me to."

I got out of the bathtub and unlocked the door, then climbed back in. She came in and stood with her back to the sinks. I braced for her to yell at me.

She twisted the ring on her finger and looked near—but not *at*—me. "That was unfortunate."

"Unfortunate?" I repeated.

"It shouldn't have happened."

"That's for sure," I agreed. I was glad she wasn't screaming at me, but this was even stranger.

"I'll talk to him," she said, nodding to herself. "It won't happen again. Just—whatever he says, go along with it?" Her eyes were on me now. "He's a pain when he's angry."

"What are you talking about?"

She bit her lip. "He's out there now saying you made a pass at him and got angry when he rebuffed you."

I felt like I was in a nightmare. This couldn't be real. This wasn't how people acted. "Are you crazy? Why would I—"

She put up her hand. "I know. It's what he needs to do. Just let it go, okay?"

"What does he have on you?" I asked.

Her eyes flashed with surprise, and she snapped, "You don't know what you're talking about." When I just stared at her, she said, "I don't think you understand. It doesn't matter if you don't like it. You're going to do it because I told you to." She tapped her clutch. "And I have an ID in here that says you agree."

She opened her clutch, took out a lip gloss and a travel brush, and began carefully applying it. "Besides, Stuart saying you acted like a bitch is more in keeping with what people would expect of Aurora anyway."

"She always sounds so charming when you talk about her," I said.

Bridgette faced me. She was perfectly made up, every hair, every eyelash in place. "As I was saying, it doesn't matter if you like it, or if people like you. It just matters that they believe in you. This séance was your idea. You need to stop whining and get out there and play your part."

She's right. I realized. *This is just a job. Like cleaning houses. Just a way to make money.* "Okay," I said.

But that didn't mean I was going to make it completely easy for her.

She was turning to go when I spoke again. "He said he got together with Aurora the night she disappeared. Something about her kneeling right where you're standing."

Bridgette winced but regained her composure quickly. "Why are you bringing that up?"

"He said she told him no the first time and fought him, but he was sure that she liked it."

"Stop," Bridgette said. "This is absurd." Her voice was calm, but her eyes had begun darting around like she was looking for a way to escape. "Whatever happened, it happened to Aurora not you. It's none of your business."

"He grabbed my ass and said maybe this time we'd get around to that."

"Stop talking," she said. She was still smiling, but her back was pressed against the door, hard.

"She was just a girl," I said to her, unable to keep the horror out of my voice. "Your cousin was only fourteen. And he just stood here and told me he used her against her will, and you not only don't seem to see anything wrong with that, you're trying to cover it up."

Her fingers had gone to the clasp on the door, and they were shaking too hard to work it properly. Yet her voice was still even. "Stop," she said breathlessly. "Aurora was no innocent girl. You don't know what you're talking about. You have to stop."

"Or what? You'll send him back in here? Maybe this time you'll watch."

"Shut up!" she said, finally raising her voice.

As she got more agitated, I got calmer. "How many more girls are you going to let him get away with hurting?" I asked, my voice level, cold. "How many more, Bridgette?"

Bridgette stood sideways against the door, her face away from me. "I didn't know about him and Ro, okay? I would have warned you. Her. Whatever."

"But you know now. Are you still going to date him?"

"It's not that simple," she said.

"When was the last time you saw your cousin alive?"

She frowned. "I already told you. I saw her and Liza leave together a little after the party started. Why do you care?"

"What was she wearing?"

"I don't know. This is—"

"Does he like it when you fight too?" I asked.

For one moment I saw such a portrait of bleakness and despair on her face, I wanted to hug her. And then before my eyes, the pieces of Bridgette, the careful puzzle pieces of her identity, slipped back into place, and she looked exactly how she always looked. Perfect. Varnished.

"She was wearing a trench coat," she said finally. Her voice quavered in the middle despite her efforts to control it. She straightened her shoulders and smoothed the front of her jeans. "This conversation is over. I'll expect to see you downstairs in no more than five minutes, and I'll expect you to act like nothing happened." She clutched her purse and slid out the door, shutting it with a click behind her.

I stared after her a moment and realized I felt better. I hoped it wasn't because I'd made her feel worse, but I couldn't be sure. And, as she pointed out to me, I shouldn't care.

I climbed out of the bathtub, decided the new less-buttoned cleavage on my cardigan was not completely obscene, and left the bathroom. Maybe it was a defense mechanism, but I wasn't thinking about what Stuart had done to me as I left. I was thinking about how badly Stuart reacted to having his pride injured.

And about the fury in his voice when he'd called Liza a "snotty bitch." It had been, well . . . murderous.

CHAPTER 27

Coralee was sitting on the bed in the master bedroom outside when I came out. She sprang up and rushed toward me.

"You're sure you're fine?" she said.

"Yes."

She held me at arm's length and examined my outfit. She straightened the necklace I was wearing—a silver chain with the heart and the arrow dangling from either end—frowned at the missing buttons on my sweater, nodded, then stepped back. "Do you have anything to say about the incident?"

"Only that Stuart needs to watch where he puts his hands." I stopped. "Are you filming this?"

She smiled and tapped the big floral broach she was wearing.

I held an open palm in front of my face. "I'm done for the day."

"We'll talk more at the spa tomorrow," she said. "Steamy confidences in the steam room."

I moved past her and descended the stairs back to the main floor. The big room got quiet for a moment as I came in, and then everyone started talking again, with a little too much animation.

Stuart was leaning against the bar talking to one of the caterers, and every now and then he'd cast a mean glance in my direction. Huck had managed to corner Bain and, based on his hand language was trying to sell him on either a huge night club concept or a new kind of shammy.

From the snippets I could overhear, the room was divided into two factions. Those, like Coralee, who thought the séance had been *gnarly* (apparently another catchword contender) and that Madam Cruz was amazing, and those, led by Bridgette, who thought it was a scam and the medium was a fake.

The only thing I knew was that I wanted to leave. As though sensing it, Bridgette came over and moved to steer me into conversation with Jordan, but we'd only gone two steps when she smiled brightly and said, "Grant. Hey. What did you think of that?"

Grant looked from her to me, then back to her. "We sure had some *spirited* fun," he said, keeping it deadpan.

Bridgette gave a tepid smile. "Clever."

Grant turned to me. "Do I stand a *ghost* of a chance of making you laugh?"

I tried to look skeptical. "Maybe if you keep trying."

Bridgette detached herself from my arm. "I'll leave you two." She gave me a discrete nod of encouragement, as though indicating that Grant was someone Aurora would have spoken to.

We watched her cross the room toward Jordan and Scar. When she was out of earshot, Grant said, "How are you doing?"

How would Aurora be doing? "Okay," I said. "That was weird. Kind of cool."

"Yeah it was," he agreed. "Do you think it was Liza?"

"How could it be?" I asked. "She's dead."

He looked intrigued. "So you don't believe in ghosts?"

I shook my head. "Do you?"

He pressed his lips together and nodded once. "Yes and no." Then, like he was making up his mind, he said, "Want to get out of here and go have some fun?"

My first impulse was to thank him and then go home, but before the words were out of my mouth, I knew that was wrong. That was an Eve answer. I took a deep breath and gave the right—the Aurora—answer. "Depends what you have in mind," I said.

"I was thinking we could go do some ghost busting."

I felt myself stiffen. "Not another séance."

He snickered. "No way. Hands on. With gear."

"What kind of gear?"

"Really? That's going to be the deciding factor for you? You get the opportunity to ride along with a ghost-busting legend, as well as a prime chance at coaxing out the long version of my life story since you've been gone, and you want to know what you get to play with? Forget it." He sighed dramatically. "I remember when my company would have been enough."

I chuckled, and I realized that for the first time, my laugh was genuine. I could see what had drawn Aurora to him. "No wait, please. I'd love to go. I mean, since you're a legend."

"You won't be sorry," he assured me. "I'll get the car and bring it around the back. Unless you want to make an appearance for the four major news networks and two gossip shows camped on the lawn."

I shook my head.

"Give me ten minutes. And if it's okay with you, keep it under your hat. I don't want the others to get jealous."

"You mean you don't want Coralee to know you're leaving early."

"You always did put such a sinister spin on my actions," he said with mock exasperation.

I grabbed my jacket from the back of the chair where I'd left it when I came in, stole a second of Bain's attention from Scar's cleavage to wave goodbye, and slid out the back door of the house.

It was warm out there and quiet. I stood on a flagstone patio that was separated from the road by a low mound where the scrub brush had been left to grow, so that the patio seemed to melt into the landscape. There was a sleek-lined table with four chairs and three oversized pots of glossy-leafed lemon plants. A half moon hung low in the sky, and a warm, dry wind slipped by me, making a noise like rattling paper. I took a deep breath and smelled wood smoke.

I remembered Uncle Thom talking about wildfires, but it made me think of a different fire. A different city, the smoke of chimneys lit for the first time in the fall, and I heard Nina's voice asking, "How do you know which way they're going?"

The leaves on the tree we're sitting beneath are startlingly bright yellow. Occasionally one of them will drift down in front of us, or on the front lawn of the house we're looking at. Its chimney is puffing out wood smoke, and Nina is sitting next to me in the new purple parka I'd found for her, the sleeves rolled up because it was too big.

We liked this house especially because they never closed the blinds and they had a big TV and they tended to watch things with a lot of kissing. Tonight, though, it was an action movie, with people going back and forth across the screen, sometimes running, sometimes on horseback. The game was to make up a story to fit whatever we were watching, so tonight's story was about some people who were running away from the bad guys who wanted to turn them into dainty handbags.

But Nina had been moody all day, and when she got like that, she was full of objections. "They could be going home. How do you know they're running away from something and not to it? They both look the same on the outside. It's all running."

"The theme music," I'd told her, feeling pretty clever. "That's how you can tell."

She'd looked at me somberly for longer than I expected and finally said, "You are going to need a better answer than that."

The memory brought back the timbre of her voice and the tickle of her hair on my chin as I put her to bed that night and the feeling of belonging to someone, mattering to someone, having someone whose first smile in the morning was for you. Someone who slipped their hand into yours when they were scared and trusted you to make them feel better. Someone who knew you, the important things about you, and loved you anyway.

Maybe it was the effort of having to play Aurora all day, or maybe it was the memory, but without warning I began to cry.

"Is it possible to feel homesick if you have no home?" I could hear Nina asking.

Yes, I wanted to tell her. It was. I missed her so much. I ground my fingers into my palms to get myself to stop crying, but I couldn't.

I would rather have been me, with her and nothing else, than Aurora and all the money in the world. Standing under the stars, with a house full of people behind me and a crowd on the lawn clamoring for even a glimpse of me, I felt more alone than I ever had in my life. More alone than when my mother left me. More alone than when I'd first ended up on my own. And more scared.

What had I done by agreeing to this? What could I have been thinking?

"Here," a hand roughly shoved a pack of Kleenex at me, and I recognized the shadowy form of N. Martinez in front of me.

I took it, slid a tissue out, and mopped my eyes and nose. "Thank you."

I turned to face where he was, but it was so dark I couldn't see him, only his outline. He seemed so compact, contained, that I had pegged him as being wiry, but now in the moonlight I was struck by how broad his shoulders were, how powerful and well-muscled his arms.

He said, "Have you ever considered reevaluating your life choices?"

Just like that. Boom. Not one for small talk, N. Martinez. I took a step forward, so we were standing side by side, but not looking at one another. "Just because you don't like me doesn't mean there's something wrong with my life."

He shifted slightly as though my proximity made him uneasy. "I was more thinking about you. About how I've had to watch you cry in secret twice in two days."

Talking to him was like catching a glimpse of yourself in a magnifying mirror, all imperfections and blemishes. "Sorry if it bothered you. No one said you had to stick around here."

He ignored that and said instead, "If you were my sister, I'd be concerned." The authentic feeling in his voice touched something deep inside me. Something unfamiliar and scared—and suddenly eager to get out.

No, I told myself. *Stop.* My voice sounded haughty, harsh to my ears. "I'm not your sister, am I? I'm no one's sister. I don't have anyone to be concerned about me. And I don't need anyone. I don't want anyone."

There was a pause. "Okay."

"I'm fine," I said coldly.

He brought his hand to his mouth and cleared his throat. "You bet."

I turned to face his outline. "Stop acting like you know me or my life. You don't know anything."

There was a long silence. When he spoke, it was so quiet I had to lean in to hear it. "I know you aren't used to people being nice to you. But you were, once. And despite whatever secrets you're carrying around that tarnish your vision of who you are, there's a part of you that knows you still deserve kindness."

I felt like I'd been punched.

For a moment my mind reeled with absurdities. I saw myself at a state fair eating things on skewers with him, saw us walking together through an arch of trees whose leaves were changing colors, pictured picnics near a mountain stream, watching the sunset from a deck overlooking a pond, watching it rise over the red tile roof of a European town. I wanted to tell him things, tell him how I didn't speak for a year when I first got into foster care, tell him about Miss Melanie and the Durlings and who Eve Brightman really is. Was. I felt a wave of longing roll out of me, but not the way it usually did, diffuse and sad. This was hopeful, as though it had been coaxed out by a whispered promise.

Don't do this, a voice in my head screamed. *Don't even think it. You're making it up. This man wants nothing to do with you. He's a police officer; he's trying to win your trust so he can learn things about you. Things you can't afford for him to learn. If he finds out the truth about you, who knows what will happen? Even if it was different, you know what you are doing here, and no one, especially no cop, has a place in that. Aurora would never have had anything to do with him. And you can't afford to have anything to do with him either.*

I drove my finger nails into my palm, forced a hard laugh, and said in my most brittle voice, "I can't imagine why you'd think I care about your cheap cop psychology."

He went very still.

"Wait," I said, wanting to take it back. I reached out and laid my hand on his forearm, and as my fingers touched the solid muscle there, I felt something like an electric shock ricochet through me. "I didn't—"

He moved his arm away. "Your ride," he said, nodding toward the street where Grant sat in the driver's seat of an idling white Ford Bronco. I hadn't even heard it pull up. "You should go."

I hesitated a moment longer than I should have before walking down the hill toward Grant's car. Right before I got in, for some insane reason I turned to wave goodbye. N. Martinez was standing where I'd left him, his hand over his arm where I'd touched it, rubbing it as though to erase any trace of me.

Of Aurora, I corrected myself. But that didn't matter. I could never be anyone but Aurora Silverton to him.

I felt like a hand was closing over my heart. *Damn him. Damn N. Martinez.*

CHAPTER 28

"What was that?" Grant asked as I slid into the passenger seat of his car. There was a slightly petulant curl to his lip.

"Nothing," I shook my head. "Just a police officer giving me some advice. He suggested I rethink my life choices."

"You're not tied up with him or anything, are you?" he asked, cruising toward the police barricade.

I noticed the silver VW I'd seen in Phoenix parked behind Bain's Porsche. I must have been wrong about it not being Stuart's style. "Tied up?"

"Enamored of the law. The thing is, what we're about to do? It's a tiny bit illegal. Is that going to be a problem for you?"

"Have we met? I'm Aurora Silverton. The only problem with what you just said is the 'tiny bit' part."

"I'm serious. You can't tell anyone about it. If you squeal, the whole squad will get in trouble. It's all for one and one for all. If you're friends with cops, that's okay, but you can't be part of the ghost-busting team."

I thought about the way N. Martinez had looked at my hand on his arm, like it was somehow sullying him. "I am not friends with cops," I told him definitively.

He gave me a suspicious glance in one direction, then in the other. "I believe it," he said. He held out his hand. "Welcome to the team. Now buckle up because we're going to take back the night, one ghost at a time."

As we drove down to the flats, I said, "You mentioned something about your life story?"

"That was an idle threat."

"No, I want to know." I touched his arm. He looked down at my hand, differently than the way N. Martinez had, then back at me. He looked intrigued.

"We'll see," he said. He handed me a camera. "Take that and start spotting."

The image on the camera's screen showed up in different shades of green, like in a leaked sex tape or army video. "Spotting what?"

He glanced at me. "Ghosts, of course."

"What do ghosts look like?"

"You'll know one when you see it."

"You're just trying to distract me from your story. "

"Is it going to work?"

I shook my head.

He puffed out his cheeks with air and then exhaled. "There's really not much since you left. Graduated, started at the U in cinematography part-time, moved in with my brother in a trailer on the Kim family ranch. And now of course I am part of the fledgling Coralee Gold media empire."

"Your fortune's made," I said. I was watching the scenery we were passing flash by on the green screen of the camera, but I didn't see anything even slightly spectral.

"Yeah. Fortune and my reputation. I can't wait to be the king of the webisode." He hugged the steering wheel with his left arm and leaned over, peering from the road to the screen on the back of the camera. "Ghosts can be tricky, especially on pavement and—there, look!" He swerved manically to the curb. "We got one!"

He was grinning from ear to ear and pointing at what appeared to me to be a completely blank cinderblock wall.

"Where?"

He nudged me with the camera, and when I looked at the wall through it, I could suddenly see something that looked like a gum drop with two round eyes and a scalloped bottom painted about a foot from the ground. "No way!"

"That's a ghost," Grant explained. "The designated Haunters paint the ghosts on in light sensitive paint, and then the Hunters—that's us—have to find them and eradicate them."

"Eradicate how?"

"Watch and learn." He hopped out of the truck and went around behind it. When he reappeared on the sidewalk, he was holding a bucket, a roller, and a tube of paper. He dipped the roller into the bucket, smoothed the piece of paper over the wall, and turned to me. "Is it over the ghost?"

I laughed. The paper had a large yellow PAC-MAN printed on it. "About four inches to the left," I told him. When it was right, he rolled over it, applying paste so it stuck to the wall.

"Now we take a picture and submit it to the game master and—ta da. One point for us. We got a late start, but I'm feeling lucky."

We hunted ghosts all around the flats of Tucson. While we were pasting our fifth one, a sneaky partial on the side of a bus bench, I asked, "Who taught you to talk to ghosts the way you did at the séance?"

"That is all because of crazy Aunt Rosalie." He chuckled to himself as he added more paste to the roller. "She was a gypsy, or anyway that's what she said, and my dad confirmed it every time he was mad at my mom by calling her a gypsy bitch. So it must have been true, right?" I was kneeling to hold the poster on, and he was bent over so his face was upside down to my face. He glanced over and gave me a little smile that made my heart rate pick up slightly, and I was struck by how easy it was to be Aurora around Grant. He brought out the Aurora in me.

He stood up and went on. "Aunt Rosie used to take me on her rounds. She was kind of a spiritual doctor to a lot of people. I guess I learned from watching her. She said I had a good way with troubled spirits. The *tocco luces* she called it, the touch of light. I think she made it up just for me, to make me feel important, but I don't care. I like the phrase."

"You certainly had it tonight."

"I don't know what that was tonight. Weird."

"Do you know who Jay was? The guy talking to Bain?"

"No idea. There wasn't anyone named Jay at the party three years—" He stopped talking and got a confused look on his face.

"What is it? What do you remember?"

"Did Bain say 'J.J.' at one point?"

I searched my memory. "I think he might have. Why?"

"There was a guy named Jimmy. He was a handyman at the country club. Everyone called him J or J.J. But he wasn't at the party." He looked thoughtful for a moment then, like he was shaking something off, and smiled at me. "Probably unrelated. Anyway that's what it is, the *tocco luces*. You saw it in action tonight. It's also the title of my first movie."

"How many movies have you made?"

"That's—" he began, then looked up with alarm and whispered,

"It's the law." Without another word, he took my arm and dragged me behind the bench.

We crouched there, waiting, listening for the sound of tires or sirens, but there was nothing. No police car went by either. I looked at him kneeling next to me. "Did you just do that to avoid answering my questions?"

His face was very close to mine. "Yes," he said, grinning. "Come on, we're not even contenders yet."

After that we saw more and more PAC-MEN already up, so our work became more focused. We had to race another team for our eighth one and almost lost our roller hanging off the side of an overpass on No. 10. I didn't get to ask him about his movies again until we were driving around looking for No. 11.

"Did I say first movie? I should have said only. It was a student film I did at the university."

"What's it about?

"What everyone's first movie is about: myself. It's kind of autobiographical, except to be subtle I changed all the male roles, me and my brother, to be played by girls. Xandra, Bain's ex-girlfriend, was in it. And so was Victoria Lawson, Liza's older sister. Liza even had a cameo, although that was pretty much by accident."

"What do you mean?"

"Victoria and Liza got in a fight while we were shooting, and I caught it on tape and edited it into the movie."

This was a chance for me to see Liza alive. The real Liza. "Can I see it?" I asked.

"Uh, no." He glanced at me. "Why would you want to do a crazy thing like that?"

"Because I want to see what Liza was like," I blurted before I realized what I'd said.

"She was your best friend. You know what she was like." His tone was a little sharper than I would have expected.

"Yes, but—" I stammered. "I mean, it might help me remember, watching her move and hearing her voice and everything. And—I miss her."

He shook his head a little and said, "The answer is still no."

"Please?"

"Maybe. Never."

"Why?"

"It's embarrassing."

I decided I'd try a more roundabout approach. "What's Vicky like? Liza's sister?"

"It's Vic-TORY-a," he said, giving each syllable its own breath. "She hates nicknames."

"Right. I think I remember Liza telling me that," I lied.

"You mean E-LIZ-abeth." He pronounced her name with a slightly sing-songy British accent.

"She sounds like Bridgette."

"I guess she is a little. Very strong views on what was right and wrong. But fair. She demanded more of herself than of others. Good to work with. I haven't seen her in ages since . . . well . . . since Liza. Now more hunting and less chatting," he said, tapping the camera.

I propped it on my knee and watched predawn Tucson go by. "How do you think they got along with their dad?"

"Victoria and Liza? I know Victoria worried about Liza a lot. She felt like Liza was her responsibility, since she was the oldest and their mother was dead." He glanced over at me quickly. "I don't know if it's appropriate to say this, but the fight I caught? It was about you."

My throat went dry. "What about me?"

"Victoria told Liza she didn't think you were a good influence on her. That she should spend less time with you."

"Why?"

He looked at me incredulously. "Maybe she didn't want her sister sneaking out in the middle of the night to go to fraternity parties?"

Had Aurora done that? It sounded possible. I tried to keep my tone neutral. "Oh. Sure."

I think he misunderstood my not knowing for being upset because he said, "Look, I shouldn't have said it. I'm sure you weren't a bad influence. Whatever Liza did, it was her choice. She wasn't the innocent—" He stepped suddenly on the gas, pointing wildly. "A block up. On the left."

We swerved across the street, and Grant brought us to a stop at the same moment another team pulled up.

Ghost No.12 was my introduction to paste wars and also the end of the game for me. By the time we were done, we were filthy, and it was starting to get light.

"I'd better get you home," he said. He gave me a quick, sheepish glance. "We should probably not mention that we were out doing this together. Coralee doesn't like the crew mixing with the talent."

"I'm not sure I qualify as either."

"You're on the call sheet for nine A.M., tomorrow, but she thinks it would be fun to wake you up before that."

"Kind of hint to her that you've heard I sleep with a shotgun."

"I am afraid that won't daunt her."

As I typed in the security code for the big gates with the double S's, I asked him the question I'd meant to ask first.

"What do you remember about the party the night Liza died?"

"I don't remember much," he said, pulling through. "I left pretty early. You were still there when I took off."

"You're sure?"

"Positive. I only showed up because your texts sounded so hysterical, but when I saw you were okay, I—"

"My texts?" I asked. "I invited you to the party?"

"Sort of. It was more like some combination of begging and ordering. By the thirteenth one you were threatening that if I didn't come, you couldn't be responsible for your actions."

"I'm so embarrassed."

"What? It's not like that was the first time you'd done that. You must remember."

I kept my head in my hands. "It's still embarrassing," I said, not answering.

"Don't be. I thought it was cute, most of the time."

I made a face at him. "Did I mention why I was so miserable this time?"

"I didn't really get to talk to you. You were pretty drunk, so you slurred on me for a while and then wandered off. I had a date, so I took off too."

"A date? Are you still seeing her?" I asked quickly, and I realized I was feeling a pinprick of envy.

He laughed. "For awhile there with all the contrition and the fact that you weren't trying to kiss me every half hour, I had started to doubt you were Aurora Silverton. But you've restored my faith."

"That's not an answer."

"No, I'm not still seeing her. She moved."

"Oh." We rode in silence then, and I watched his profile as he navigated the long driveway. When he pulled up in front of the steps of Silverton House, I said, "That was really fun tonight. If only all ghosts were that easy to eradicate. Some paper and wheat paste."

"They are. You just have to figure out what they want, and they'll go away."

"You don't believe that, do you?"

"That's what my aunt used to say. It could be true. Of course she also said that writing a bully's name on an egg and cracking it into the sink would rid them of their power, and as a late bloomer I can tell you that was not the most effective use of eggs."

I glanced at his broad shoulders and square jaw. "Well, you look more athlete than mathlete to me now," I said. "So maybe it just took some time to kick in."

He laughed. "Could be. Anyway, it's worth a try. And as a fellow ghost buster, I pledge to help you in whatever way I can."

"Thank you," I said, meaning it.

"I had a really good time with you, Aurora."

"I had a really good time with you too."

I tilted my head to one side to look at him. Aurora would have tried to kiss him, and he knew it. And if he let her, I would have been okay with that. I leaned forward slightly, and my eyes began to close.

"Well, goodnight," he said abruptly, hitting the button to unlock the doors.

The sound jolted me. Beneath it I heard Stuart's voice hissing, "filthy slut," and I realized there had been no way he'd kiss me. Not after what he must think of me. What everyone at the party must have thought of me.

"Yeah, sure," I said, fumbling for the door.

The house was quiet when I got inside. I ran to my room, stripped off my clothes, and got into the shower. I made it as hot as

I could bear and stood under it, letting the water scald me. No matter how high I turned it on, I couldn't get it to drown out the sound of Stuart's voice—*filthy slut*—and get it to stop pinging around my mind like a silver pinball, bouncing off of unimagined markers—*dirty tease*—in the missing parts of my memory—*Tom Yaw*—that sent it careening back to me as though telling me—*who would believe a little whore like you*—hinting that I had done so much worse. Been so much worse.

Just let it go, I heard Bridgette say.

I washed my hair three times and scrubbed my skin until it was red and raw, and shaved my legs twice each. When I was done, I took the towels and mopped down the inside of the shower, wiping away any last trace, any last particle of me that had touched him. It still didn't feel clean, so I got out the Q-tips and used them on the grout and around the drain. I took them and the towels and the cardigan I'd been wearing and carried them downstairs to the trash.

When I got back to my room, my phone was ringing. My heartbeat quickened as I looked down to see: "UNKNOWN NUMBER." I stared at it, not sure what to do. Then, just like that, it stopped.

I slept.

CHAPTER 29

SUNDAY

I'm standing in the middle of a maze of payphones, hundreds of them in neat, orderly rows. As I glance around in search of the exit, one of the phones begins to ring.

I know instinctively I have to answer it; it's a matter of life or death. I hold my breath to try and gauge which phone it is, or at least which direction. I think I've got it and start moving that way, but stop, unsure. I turn around, retrace my steps.

Ring-a-ling.

Now it sounds like it's to the left, now to the right.

Ring-a-ling.

I'm starting to panic. A matter of life and death, *my mind repeats, the words matching themselves almost playfully to the ringing, life and death, ring-a-ling, lifeanddeath, lizasdeath, Liza's death.*

It's a matter of Liza's death.

The breath catches in my throat and my pulse accelerates with new urgency. I race down one row and up the next, always convinced the right phone is just up ahead. Or behind me. To the left. Diagonally down. The ring keeps going, unrelenting, becoming more like a tapping, a summons. I'm going to be too late, *I think as I move from phone to phone.*

"Coming," I try to shout, but discover my mouth won't work. The words are like boulders having to be heaved from the rigidly locked interior of my jaw. "Trying," I grunt, my jaw aching from the effort. "Won't . . . let them hurt . . . Will find . . . I'll—

My eyes opened, and I realized the tapping wasn't in the dream. It was real. And it wasn't exactly tapping. It was more like the sound of doors opening and closing. Doors along the corridor outside my bedroom.

A tendril of fear began to skitter crab-like up and down my spine as the sound got closer. This wasn't the wind. This wasn't my imagination.

The sound approached, now the door two down from mine. Hoping to stop it, I yelled, "Who is that? Who's there?"

Silence fell, full and heavy for a moment. *Had I done it? Scared them aw—*

My door began to shake wildly, straining against the lock and the hinges.

I was frozen in bed, my breathing coming in huge gasps, tears stinging my eyes. I heard grunting, as though whatever was shaking it was exerting a lot of effort. And then, beneath the shaking, I heard a voice whisper "Aurora."

Tears pricked at my eyes, and my stomach flopped. "Who are you?" I cried.

"Aurora," the voice whispered again. "Want . . . Aurora."

"Go away!" I shouted. "You can't get in here."

"Can't get in," the voice chanted softly, and let out a thin giggle. "Get in, get in!"

There was a scraping noise along the side of the door near the lock, like it was clawing at the wood looking for a point of weakness.

You should have answered the phone, I thought. *She is coming for you because you didn't answer the phone.*

"I'm sorry," I said to the door. "I'm sorry I didn't answer."

Abruptly the noise stopped. *Was that it? Was that all I'd had to—*

The scraping started up again, this time along the bottom of the door, as though whatever was out there was going to burrow its way in.

I sat in bed transfixed, taking in strange details, the sky turning from black to blue outside my window as dawn approached, the pain in my palm from my fingernails digging into it, the gaping shadowy space at the bottom of the door. It was going to come through at any moment. Every muscle in my body was rigid, and I could barely breathe.

And then from one moment to the next, in the span of a finger snap, it was over. The door went still, the noises vanished, and silence fell like a heavy blanket. It was as though nothing had ever happened.

But it had. *It had.*

With my knees tucked beneath my chin under the blankets, I found it harder and harder to believe. *It wasn't possible. There are no ghosts. It wasn't possible.*

I must have dozed off because I woke up to a room flooded with daylight and the sound of my phone on the night table ringing.

I grabbed for it as quickly as I could. "Hello?"

"Did you have a nice time with Grant?" Bridgette's voice asked. She sounded perky, like she had been awake for hours, and also tense.

"I did have a nice time with Grant," I told her, copying her phrasing. "Is that okay? Why?"

"Yes, Grant is okay. Can you hear me clearly?"

"Yes," I said hesitantly, wondering what she was getting at.

"Good. Because this time I don't want there to be any confusion. You are not supposed to be talking to cops unless it's unavoidable."

"I know that."

"So why were you having a secret conversation with one outside last night? What did you tell him?"

She'd seen me with N. Martinez. That explained the careful control in her voice—she probably thought I was telling him about Stuart. "It was nothing. It's none of your business."

"I thought we'd discussed this. Everything you do, everything you say, is Bain's and my business."

"It wasn't a secret conversation. And I didn't tell him anything."

"Then how do you explain that he spent the rest of the night quizzing everyone about what had happened to trouble you, and then he started asking questions about the party three years earlier. We wasted a lot of time carefully answering those questions. No one wants to have to do it again."

I was struck by the word "carefully." I said, "Everyone knew I was upset. I didn't mention anything about the séance or Stuart," I added. "And you don't have to worry about me talking to him. I'm pretty sure that won't happen again."

"Not pretty sure. Completely sure."

Her insistence seemed a bit extreme, but at the time I didn't think to question it. "Fine, completely sure."

"Good. Bain and I have discussed this ghost thing, and we think it can be a great distraction from the story of your return. As long as people are talking about the ghost, they won't question you. The right attitude is for you to be casual about the phone call and treat it and any subsequent calls you get like a joke. That's what Aurora would have done."

"Okay," I said. I decided not to tell her about the hands clawing at the door. Somehow in the bright light of day it all seemed so . . . improbable. Like a strange dream. But it had been real, hadn't it? I glanced at the clock and saw it was after eight thirty. "But I have to go."

"Where?"

"Coralee is taking me to the spa."

"I didn't approve that."

"Althea did," I told her brightly.

I pulled on some clothes and was halfway down the stairs when my phone buzzed again. The screen flashed "Coralee Gold."

"Hell—" I began, but she didn't even let me get it all the way out.

"Question: Where are you when you're not with me?"

"Are you the Riddler now?"

"Answer: not where you are supposed to be. What's keeping you?"

Before I could think of an answer, I could hear stomping up the stairs toward me. Coralee must have been waiting in the courtyard below. She was wearing an orange tube top jumpsuit with a gold-and-green necklace that looked like she'd lifted it from some maharaja's stash and a gold bracelet on her upper arm. "It's nice that you're practicing for your Madame Tussauds wax figure audition, but we have footage to shoot." She ran her eyes over my outfit, made a "turn around" gesture with one orange-and-gold-tipped fingernail, and marched me back into my room.

"Wha—" I tried to ask, but she held up her hand like a maestro demanding silence and stalked to my closet. She pulled out an electric blue tube dress and red platform sandals. "This dress, those shoes. And your jacket from last night," she said, lifting the black fitted motorcycle jacket from the back of the chair where I'd left it. "Or maybe this one," she said, pulling a cropped brown leather jacket out of my closet.

"I don't need a jacket. The weather report says it's ninety."

"Yeah, here's the thing. I know it's called YouTube, but it's actually MeTube. You do what I say."

I put on the dress and shoes and took the jacket.

"Hot," she said, smiling. "Very. You're lucky I'm not worried about being upstaged. Come on, we're late."

I took a second to make sure you couldn't see the note from Bain in the thesaurus where I'd moved it after Bridgette's mention of the mattress or the photo strip I'd put in there with it. Coralee leaned around the side of the door, made a typing motion with one finger, and said, "Question: What does caps lock sound like?"

I stared at her.

"Answer: ANY DAY NOW. Come *on*."

CHAPTER 30

"Is that your new tagline?" I asked Coralee as we walked across the courtyard and out the front door. There was a white Range Rover parked in front of Silverton House with a chrome CG set into the grill that I assumed was hers.

"I'm trying it out." She glided a lip gloss wand around her lips and made a *swack* sound. "It's a little cumbersome, but the uniqueness might compensate in terms of retention."

I watched her use her phone camera to check her makeup. "You're so smart. Why are you purposely acting dumb?"

She said, "I think if you reverse those sentences you'll find the answer."

Huck was in the driver's seat of the Range Rover, and Grant was in the front passenger seat. When he turned to say hi, I felt myself blush. He was wearing a greenish-grey T-shirt that hugged his body and brought out the gold flecks in his grey eyes. There was a faint shading of light brown stubble on his cheeks, and his eyes had the slightly bruised look of someone who hadn't gotten much sleep. He looked cute, really really cute, and I couldn't help but think about how I had acted the night before, thinking he wanted to kiss me when it was so obvious he didn't—and wouldn't.

Dumb slut, Stuart's voice said in my mind. *Dirty little*—

"So there's been a change of plans," Coralee said as Huck steered the car down the driveway. Grant was twisted around from the front passenger seat, shooting Coralee with a handheld camera. "The footage from the séance already has twenty thousand hits."

"Twenty-two thousand," Huck said from the driver's seat.

Coralee held her wince long enough for the camera to get back to her and capture it. "Huck, what have I told you about talking off camera?"

"But I thought given your new concept—"

Coralee thought about that. "You have a point."

"What new concept?" I asked, and the camera swung toward me. "Whiplash filming?"

"Not one of your best," Coralee told me objectively. "I've decided we should shelve the feud and do more of a *Blair Witch* kind of thing." She was pretending to be looking at me but was really looking at the camera in this strange three-quarter profile way. "We're going in search of the ghost. We're going to solve the mystery of what really happened to Liza."

My mind flashed to the scrabbling around my door the night before. I didn't want to get any closer to Liza than I already had. I stared directly at her. "We know what happened to Liza. She committed suicide. There is no ghost. The phone call last night was just a joke."

"If you really believe that, then you won't mind participating in a little experiment."

Her tone and her expression—what I could see of it from the weird way she was facing me—made me nervous. "What does your experiment entail?"

"You just show up and look photogenic."

"Huck, would you please stop the car?" I said.

Coralee rolled her eyes. "Fine. We're going to shoot at the one place the ghost is nearly guaranteed to try to make contact with you. Three Lovers Point. Where Liza's body was found." Coralee's orange-and-gold-tipped pinkie was gesturing frenetically below the sight line of the camera, urging me to look at it rather than her.

"But anyone could go there and pretend to be a ghost or call me while we're there."

"They could. Except no one but the people in this car know that's where we're headed."

"Coralee tweeted that we were having breakfast at Maria's," Huck supplied with a hint of admiration in his voice.

"I said I was getting the corn cakes and you were getting the waffles," Coralee informed me.

"Why does it matter what we're not having for fake breakfast?"

"Later we'll see if one or the other has a sales spike, and we can use that to assess our relative popularity. Market research." Before I could even begin to imagine what to say about that, she kept going. "Since no one knows we're going to be at Three Lovers Point, if the ghost shows up, that proves she's real. And she is really haunting you."

"And if she doesn't?" I asked.

Coralee shrugged. "Then it's probably a prank, and we shift from *Blair Witch* format to a *Law and Order* and find the culprit. Either way, it's must see YT."

"YT stands for YouTube," Grant supplied for me from behind the camera.

Our eyes met for the first time that morning, and my heart leapt a little. Then he looked away, fast, and the knot in my stomach tightened.

Stop being an idiot, I told myself. *He's not interested in you at all. How could he be? You're a—*

"Anyway, I have a feeling she'll appear," Coralee said, breaking into my thoughts.

"Who—I mean, why?" I asked.

"You'll see," she said with a sly, almost dangerous smile.

Coralee spent the rest of the ride discussing camera angles and approaches with her crew, and my mind flipped between the nervousness growing in the pit of my stomach and what a fool I'd made of myself with Grant.

The parking lot for the trail to Three Lovers Point was empty when we pulled in, so Huck decided to mic us there. While he was busy with Coralee, I leaned against the side of the Range Rover, arms crossed over my chest, and watched as the light breeze kicked the red dust of the path into eddies that blurred the edge of the parking lot, like the ocean coming to meet the shore. Grant came around the car and leaned against it next to me.

I tipped my head and glanced toward him sideways. He gave me a nice, sort of shy smile and said, "Are you okay with this?"

I moved my eyes back to the ground, studying the lines of rust-colored dust already creeping over my feet and the toes of his navy PF Flyers. "Sure, I'm fine. What could be more fun than visiting the place where your best friend leaped to her death?" The words were out of my mouth before I'd really thought about them. I realized it was getting easier for me to be Aurora.

Grant crossed his arms over his chest, giving me a chance to admire the lean tendons of his forearms beneath the sleeves of his grey T-shirt. "Gee, when you put it that way, it does sound great."

There was a beat of silence. We both leaped into it at the same time. He said, "So I wanted to apologize, last night, at the end, I—" right as I said, "I'm so sorry about last night, I—"

We both stopped and started to laugh. Our eyes met, and it was like that moment the previous night when the air was so full of possibilities, when I thought he'd kiss me. My breath caught in my chest, and my knees tingled.

"Is this a joke we're going to want to get on video?" Coralee asked, coming over. She seemed keyed up, tense but more excited than usual.

"No," we said in unison.

"Then go get mic'ed so we can start."

Once that was done, Huck ran ahead to set up his equipment, and Coralee and I started up with Grant shooting from behind. The path was covered in a combination of gravel and the fine red dust from the parking lot that swirled around our feet as we walked covering everything in a layer of red. It was an easy slope and would have been a cinch in sneakers, but the platform sandals Coralee had picked out for me weren't ideal. At least staying upright gave me something to concentrate on other than the growing sense that I should not be doing this.

There were no such thing as ghosts, I knew. This experiment of Coralee's was going to end in nothing.

Wasn't it?

Coralee had been talking nonstop, almost a parody version of herself. But as we climbed higher, she got more somber and quiet, and she only spoke once in the last two minutes, to point out a shortcut. At first I thought it was an act for the cameras, but glancing behind me I couldn't even see Grant. Her preoccupation fed mine, and by the time we'd neared the crest of the trail my heart was racing.

The top of the hill came as a surprise as we rounded a corner.

One moment we were winding through a pair of red rocks that had been shaved to broaden the path. The next we were standing in open air on the edge of the point. Jagged, ochre-colored rocks jutted up all around, but Three Lovers Point itself was smooth and flat, extending like a plateau over the deep canyon below. It was windier up here than it had been below. Cool, still air seemed to rise from the canyon's mottled lavender shadows, untouched at this early hour by sunlight.

It looked just like it had in the police photos, only there was nobody there now. And where there had been just red rocks and boulders tracing the path of Liza's descent—I recalled Detective Ainslie's flat-accented comment, "She seems to have hit the wall here . . . . bounced off and rolled the rest of the way down"—there now were hundreds of fleshy white flowers. They cascaded like a frothing waterfall from where our feet stood all the way to the bottom of the valley. It was an extraordinary, otherworldly sight.

"They're called ghost flowers," Coralee said, as though reading my thoughts. Her voice sounded thin and somber up here. "No one knows why they grow where they do, but it's said that they mark the places where the souls of the dead are restless." Now she looked not at the camera but at me. "That's why I think she'll come. She's restless. She's been waiting."

CHAPTER 31

A chill looped itself around my spine with lithe, sticky fingers. I cleared my throat. "Waiting for what?"

Instead of answering, Coralee said, "Is your phone on?"

It was, but Huck had forgotten the phone mic, so he ran back for it while Coralee, Grant, and I stood there, staring into the canyon. I wasn't sure if it was something about the place or the errand that had brought us there, but the silence felt like something I could touch, or feel. Like it was full of potential.

"Are you here, Liza?" Coralee said unexpectedly, making me jump. "Can you hear me?" She spoke like a mother talking to a lost child. "I brought you Aurora. Ro-ro."

Silence, deep and profound, answered her.

"Liza, if you're out there, please give us a sign," Coralee said. Her tone was more heartfelt than I would have imagined, which surprised me. Didn't Bridgette say they hated each other? "Please, Liza. We want to help. We want to give you peace."

Silence.

"Check your phone," Coralee snapped at me.

"I just looked at it, it hasn't rung—" I started to say, but she cut me off.

"Just check it."

There was nothing.

"You try," Coralee said. "You try calling to her."

"Liza, it's me, Aurora," I said. "We spoke on the phone last night?"

From behind me, where Grant was standing, I heard a stifled laugh, and I had to admit it did sound ridiculous. But Coralee's expression was dead serious, so I went on. "I was hoping we could continue our conversation. There's so much I want to ask you. So much I want to know. If there is any way you can get in touch with me again, you have my number or—"

Or what? I thought. *You should feel free to haunt me?* Something about that struck me as funny, and I stifled a giggle too.

But I didn't catch it fast enough. "Is this a joke to you?" Coralee suddenly demanded. "Your best friend is dead, and you're treating it like some big joke?"

"Coralee, we're standing on a ledge, talking to the air, waiting for a *ghost* to appear. You have to admit, that's funny."

"It's not."

"There's no one here. No one is coming. There are no such thing as ghosts," I said gently.

She turned on me. "There are! There are too! She'll be here. She'll come. She'll come for you." Her eyes sparkled, almost feverish.

"Why do you care so much?" I asked. "I thought you weren't even friends."

The question, which seemed banal to me, seemed to jolt her. It was as though a mask was lifted off, or maybe put back on. The feverish, serious look disappeared from her face almost instantly, replaced by her careful, camera-ready slate of expressions. "I care for the show," she said, wide-eyed. "And of course I care for Liza. To find out the truth about what happened to her."

The change was so quick and so complete that it was *almost* convincing.

"What if we already know the truth? That she committed suicide?"

"I don't believe that," Coralee said. "Does being up here bring back any memories?"

"I wasn't up here."

"How do you know? I thought you didn't remember anything." Her tone had a slight bite to it.

"I don't," I said, working hard not to sound flustered. "But I'm— I'm just sure. It doesn't feel familiar."

"I think you're lying," Coralee said.

Aurora took over for me then. I laughed and said, "You're nuts. Look, this has been fun. But it's pretty clear there's no ghost coming, so I'm going to take off." I started for the path, and my phone rang.

Unknown number.

I stopped and turned back. Coralee stared at me. I stared at her. I'll admit, my heart had begun to race.

"Answer it," she whispered. There was a catch in her voice.

I took a breath. "Hello?"

"Where are you?" Bridgette's voice demanded. "You're not at the spa like you said, and you're not at Maria's having breakfast like you tweeted."

I suppose I shouldn't have been surprised that Bridgette was keeping such tight tabs on me, but I was. "How sweet of you to take an interest in my well-being. Before you say anything else, you should know that this call is being recorded."

I put my hand over the speaker and said to Coralee, "It's Bridgette.

I'll see you at the bottom," and started down the path before she could object.

"What are you talking about? How is this call being recorded?"

My balance in the platform sandals was abominable. I slid and teetered down the path, sending sprays of red pebbles and dust up all around me. "I'm at Three Lovers Point filming with Coralee. We were waiting to see if the ghost would appear."

There was a longer than natural silence. I could tell Bridgette was composing and discarding comment after comment. "Did the ghost appear?" she asked finally.

"No, there was no sign of a ghost." I wobbled from the slope toward the bottom end of the trail, which I remembered was mercifully flat all the way to the parking lot. What had been wind on top was a faint, soft breeze down here, barely enough to take the edge off the hot sun.

"Where are you going next and when will you be home?" Bridgette asked.

I felt like a marionette controlled by a jittery child—gangly knees and jerky elbows as I tried to pull off my jacket and walk upright while talking on the phone. In front of me I saw the sign that marked the entrance between the path and the still empty parking lot. "I don't know when I'll be back. I think—"

I forgot whatever I was going to say, and the phone dropped from my hand. On the back of the sign someone had written in six-inch-high dusty red letters, "BE CAREFUL, RORO."

I heard Bridgette's voice from the phone on the ground, but it seemed a long way away and unimportant. All I could focus on was the message. Like a scientist encountering a new species and wanting to make sure it was real, I reached out to touch the first R of *Ro-ro*. It brushed right off beneath my fingers, and disappeared into dust.

I will show you fear in a handful of dust.

If it was that delicate, the message couldn't have been there long, I thought. It wouldn't have lasted. Which meant someone had been there while we were at Three Lovers Point. Someone (but no one knew we were going there) had come and written this (we didn't hear any car pull up), and there was a reasonable explanation (Huck had come down and not seen it). It had to be a prank, a joke—

Right there, before my eyes, the R began to rewrite itself.

No, I thought. *This can't be happening.* I stared, mesmerized as centimeter by centimeter, the R that I'd brushed away rematerialized from nothing.

"Liza," I whispered. "Are you here?"

A breeze caressed my cheek, and I heard a low whimper, followed by an earsplitting scream.

CHAPTER 32

At first I thought I was the one who had screamed, but it was actually Coralee. I'd been so enthralled by the sign that I hadn't realized that she and her crew had joined me.

"Did you see that?" she asked them urgently. "Did you get that, the letter being written by an invisible hand?"

Grant shook his head. "We were too far away and it was too—"

"Do it again. We have to do it again," she said, frantic. She looked at me. "Make it happen again."

"I don't know—"

Not waiting for me to finish, Coralee reached out and erased the B with her hand, then stepped back.

Nothing happened. It stayed erased.

Then, as we watched, each of the letters began to disintegrate in turn, as though being brushed off by someone we couldn't see, until there was no sign of the message left.

"She must be gone. She was here, and now she's gone," Coralee said, her voice high-pitched and confused. She rounded on me and pointed a finger at my chest. "She did this for *you*." Her tone was half-accusation, half-disbelief. She was clearly upset.

"Maybe that was all she had time for," I said to soothe her. "Maybe she only has limited power."

"That's right," Coralee said, more to herself than anyone else. "That must be right. And the important thing is, now we have proof. Proof that this ghost exists." She stopped like she'd just realized what she'd said. "We did it. We have proof."

The sound of sirens approaching brightened her up even more. "This is the part where the authorities try to explain it away. Grant, make sure you get every word."

"I'm going to leave," I said.

"O-M-Good one," Coralee said, sounding like her old self. "You can't go anywhere. You're a prime witness. You were the first one down here to see it."

Coralee was right—there was no way I could get around it. At least a warning like this should make the police stop suspecting Aurora of having killed Liza.

Or so I thought.

Detective Ainslie, accompanied by N. Martinez, arrived on the scene first. They questioned Grant, Coralee, and Huck but not me. "I'll be questioning Aurora with her lawyer and the rest of the Silvertons at her home," Detective Ainslie explained. The look N. Martinez shot her made me think that there was more going on than simply asking me what I'd seen.

I stood by the burgundy unmarked Ford sedan and observed the forensics team swarming over the sign and the surrounding area. I knew it was hot because everyone was in short sleeves, but I was freezing. I kept replaying what I'd seen in my mind, first the letter R writing itself, then the way all the letters had vanished, leaving no trace, only moments later.

BE CAREFUL, RORO. *Of what?* I wanted to know. *Of whom?*

I watched Detective Ainslie talk to Huck while N. Martinez interviewed Coralee. I found myself wondering if he thought Coralee was pretty, if she was his type. She kept surreptitiously urging Grant to film, and N. Martinez kept openly telling him to turn the camera off. But he seemed more amused than annoyed, and at one point, when I saw him swallow an involuntary laugh, I felt a pang of pure, potent jealousy.

Idiot, I told myself.

I was trying to gauge his reaction to Coralee's resting a finger on his knee when I looked up and saw Grant approaching. "It's nice to know some things don't change," he said.

"What do you mean?"

"There was never a dull moment around you before, and there isn't one now. Of course, this is the first ghost."

"I like to keep things—"

Before I could finish what I was saying, he did the most remarkable thing. He reached for me and pulled me to him, and his mouth came over mine, soft, sweet, and warm.

I sighed.

He cupped the back of my head in his hand and tilted it back, kissing the corners of my lips, then gently slid his tongue between them. The tip of my tongue found his, and as he brought his mouth down harder on mine I nipped at his lower lip with my teeth.

He gave a low, throaty groan that made me shiver and gathered me to his chest, so my head was cradled under his chin, and said, "Man, I should have done that last night."

My cheek rested against a firm, round shoulder. "I thought you didn't want to. Because you thought I was—"

"Because I thought you were wonderful," he interrupted, tilting his neck to bring his lips to my ear. "I always have. And I've always been intimidated." He pulled away slightly, so he was looking into my eyes. "But I lost you once. I don't want to lose you again."

For a moment I wrapped myself in his eyes, his kiss, his words. Then I realized I wasn't the girl he was talking to, and I felt a sharp stab of guilt. It wasn't me he felt this way about; I wasn't really the one he thought was wonderful. Was it fair for me to let him think I was?

Especially since when he'd been kissing me, when I closed my eyes, he wasn't the person I'd been imagining kissing either.

"Your heart is racing," he said.

"Yeah. It's—it's been a long time since I've been kissed." Out of the corner of my eye I saw Detective Ainslie approaching. Which meant N. Martinez was probably close by as well.

I pulled out of Grant's arms. "I think my ride is coming," I said, tipping my chin toward the police.

"Yeah, I should get back to the boss." He kept his eyes on mine. "I'll call you later."

"That would be great," I said.

He gave me a little salute and turned and pivoted, and I turned and was looking right up at N. Martinez.

He didn't say a word, just opened the door of the car for me. I felt like I owed him an explanation for something, but I had no idea what. Or why. God, he was annoying.

"Thank you," I said, getting into the car.

"Since we're not supposed to talk to you without your lawyer present, it would be best if you didn't speak," he said.

"Sure, okay. It's just—"

He looked at me curiously as though wondering how I could fail to grasp simple rules. Gritting my teeth, I nodded and shut the car door.

When we arrived at Silverton House, we found the entire Family waiting for us in the dining room. Uncle Thom was at one end, with three empty seats beside him. Detective Ainslie and I took seats, but N. Martinez assumed a station behind me, beside the wall, where I couldn't see him.

The questions began sensibly. "What were you doing up at Three Lovers Point?"

"After the séance, Coralee became convinced that the ghost was real, and she wanted to see if we could make it come out."

"Did you believe the ghost was real?"

"I didn't then," I said.

Detective Ainslie cocked her head to one side. "And now?"

I spoke without thinking, being more honest than I'd meant to be. "I don't know what to think. I saw the message on the sign. There was no one around, and no one could have written it. And when I erased part of it, it came right back. Like—" I swallowed. "Like someone invisible was writing it. How could that happen?"

"Our lab will figure it out, of course, but it could be faster if you just told us what you did."

I stared at her silently, trying to make sense of what she'd said. Fortunately Uncle Thom stepped in, demanding, "What are you suggesting?"

"That your niece wrote the message herself, and then encouraged Coralee Gold to destroy it," Detective Ainslie said matter-of-factly.

"But I didn't write it," I protested, half-rising from my seat. "How could I have? *When* could I have?" I felt Uncle Thom's hand on my wrist, urging me back down. "And I definitely didn't encourage Coralee to destroy any evidence."

Detective Ainslie said, "On the video it shows her asking you to do it, and you shaking your head."

"I wasn't refusing; I was more—stunned. It happened so fast." I made a plaintive gesture with my hands. "And I never thought that what she was doing was destroying anything. When I rubbed the letter off the first time, it came back."

"The time when you were there by yourself," Detective Ainslie wanted to confirm.

I nodded. "Yes, but Coralee and Grant and Huck all saw it."

Detective Ainslie pressed her lips together. "They *think* they did. They aren't sure. It was far away." She consulted her notes. "How far ahead of the others would you say you were as you went down?"

I thought about it. "I was on the phone, so I'm not sure. Maybe two minutes."

"According to the footage shot by Mr. Villa, you were almost five minutes ahead of them."

"Okay," I shrugged. "Five minutes then."

"That would have been plenty of time for you to write that on the sign. As the first one down."

"I guess but—I still don't understand. Why would I do that? Warn *myself*?"

"To make it appear you're in danger."

"Maybe I really *am* in danger," I said, my voice sounding tight and high-pitched in my ears as the reality of it sank in for the first time.

Detective Ainslie smiled. "Of course, that's the other option. And that is why I'd like to offer you round-the-clock police protection."

The thought filled me with an immense sense of security. If I had round-the-clock protection, there would be no more fingers clawing at the door, no more pretend ghosts, no more—

I heard Bridgette's sharp intake of breath and realized it was impossible. Next to her, Althea barked with laughter. "Nonsense. She doesn't need police protection. That will only encourage this prankster. The Family will take care of her."

Detective Ainslie gave a tight smile and a nod of her head, but I had a feeling this reaction didn't surprise her. In fact, it seemed more to solidify something for her. "Of course. The Family always takes care of its own, doesn't it?"

"What's that supposed to mean?" Bridger growled. "Are you—" he began, but subsided at a look from Margie.

"I was simply saying that the Silvertons are a model of self-sufficiency and teamwork," Ainslie told him.

"I have to say I think you're making a mistake," Aunt Claire said. "If there is a madman out there targeting Aurora and we don't ask the police to protect her—" her voice trailed off slightly. I was surprised that it was Aunt Claire of all people who was advocating for my safety, until she added, "I mean, people might think the Family was quite cold."

Uncle Thom smiled at her. "I don't think we need to worry, dear," he said, then turned his attention to Detective Ainslie. "I'm sure if we stop poking around in all this old history, the 'ghost' will disappear."

Detective Ainslie gave him a sad smile. "That's why I wanted you together, actually. Three years ago I told you I didn't believe Elizabeth Lawson committed suicide, and I have not changed my mind. I wanted you all here, so I could tell you that I won't rest until I find the truth and bring her murderer to justice. No matter who it is, or how well they are protected. I won't tolerate obstructions or games." When she said "games," she looked at me. There was something in her expression that made me feel guilty even though I'd done nothing wrong.

"Naturally we could hardly expect you to set aside a high-profile case that will get your name in the papers," Althea sniped. She gave an exaggerated fake yawn. "It's time for my nap. I believe we're done here. Mrs. March, please show the police out."

As they left, N. Martinez moved into my line of sight. He gave me a swift, questioning glance that seemed to ask if this was really all right with me, but I pretended not to see it. Bridgette was staring at me; it was the only thing I could do.

I wondered if Althea was correct, if it was the police investigation that inspired the fake ghost.

But how did that explain the hands clawing my door the night before?

Althea dismissed the rest of the family after the police left, reminding them that we had dinner at the golf club that night, and went to her room for a nap. I went to mine to try to think about anything but ghosts.

CHAPTER 33

'd expected Althea to suggest cards again on the ride to the club, but instead she looked at the landscape and hummed quietly to herself. At one point she turned to me and said, "Why don't you ever wear the emerald bracelet I bought you?"

"I'm not sure," I answered. There hadn't been any classes about emerald bracelets at Aurora Academy.

Arthur cleared his throat. "The emerald bracelet was for Sadie," he said.

"I know that," Althea told him. "Of course I know that. And this is Aurora. Her daughter. I'm not crazy. I knew that. I thought perhaps Sadie had left it to her."

"My mistake," Arthur said.

"Yes. Stop putting your nose in," Althea snipped, very stern. But she looked slightly frightened, and she reached out and took my hand and held it as we rode the rest of the way in silence.

By the time we reached the golf club, Althea seemed completely in control again. The club house was a low-slung red stone building with a putting range on one side and a rolling green course behind it that stretched to the edge of the canyon. It was built into the hills, Tucson twinkling in the basin below us and rocks sloping up behind us.

It was modern on the outside but old-fashioned on the inside with dark green carpet flecked with peach paisleys and wood paneling. Althea immediately commandeered a large chair and a large Scotch and motioned me to stand beside her.

Cocktail hour could have been a study in different varieties of insincere greeting, I thought. There was the one-arm hug, the pat on the back, the too-tight squeeze, the double kiss, the polite fingertip shake, the "You seem to be doing a great job fitting back in," and the more reserved, "Your family must be so delighted to have you back, dear." I got a pat on the head from the attorney general, polite nods from a judge and the chief of police, and the governor's warmest greetings, conveyed by his secretary. People seemed unsure of whether to treat me like a returning pilgrim with an air of sanctity or as something soiled and slightly suspicious and dirty. I had the impression that none of these people had liked Aurora very much before she went away, and their interest in her return was more prurient than pure.

A tall beanpole of a guy in a white linen suit, madras button-down shirt, cream-colored loafers that looked Italian, and classic Ray-Bans sauntered in. Even if he hadn't been the best dressed and only nonwhite person in the room, Roscoe Kim would have stood out for the sheer popularity with which he was greeted. But when he spotted me, he broke away from the gaggle of apparently genuine hearty-pat-on-the-back friends, whipped off his glasses, said, "Kitten!" and rushed across the room to fold me in a long limbed hug.

Bridgette's flash card description of Roscoe Kim was so short— [20, two years ahead of Aurora at school, gay, $18,000,000 (or more)]—I'd assumed they weren't friends, but I realized now there was simply no way to put Roscoe on a card.

He draped a long arm over my shoulders, said, "Go on without us," to the bar at large, and guided me out the door onto the back patio of the golf course. The setting sun tinted everything slightly gold and made butter-colored puddles between the long bluish shadows cast by the hills. He had me stand three feet away and spin around so he could take me in. He took a breath like he was getting ready to deliver a good line, opened his mouth—

And started to cry.

"I had so many good remarks prepared, but all I want to do is say, 'Fuck you, Aurora' for leaving that way, and then hug you and tell you how much we missed you."

"Both fair," I said.

He took a handkerchief from the pocket of his suit and wiped his eyes on it, then held it toward me. "This was supposed to be decorative," he said before jamming it back into his pocket. "I'm sending you the dry-cleaning bill."

I laughed. "How have you been?"

"Oh, great, you know. Got disinherited by my parents when I came out, but re-inherited by them when my sister got married because they wanted to show the new in-laws our family was capable of breeding boys. The usual. What have you been up to?"

I had the insane urge to confide in him, tell him the truth about everything. I don't know if it was Roscoe, or the fact that the effort required to keep all my lives, all my lies, straight was getting too massive to bear on my own.

He spared me having to lie by saying, "Don't answer. I probably don't want to know." He leaned close. "Was it raunchy?"

I thought of some of the places I'd slept. "Definitely."

He wrapped an arm around me again and pulled me toward him, and we stood side by side looking out over the golf course. "Ah, nature," he said. He took his arm away to rifle in his pocket and pulled out a hand-rolled cigarette. "Smoke?" he asked.

I shook my head.

"You never did get into it." He lit up, and I realized it was a joint. He was smoking a joint right in the middle of the golf club with half of Tucson society behind us. He took a long hit, held it, then exhaled, waving the smoke away with a practiced gesture.

"Do you remember when we used to ride our bikes over the course at night? God, that was so insane. Pitch-black, and I'm on your handlebars, and you have no idea where you're going."

"Terrifying," I agreed because it sounded like it was.

"But exhilarating too." He took another hit, exhaled. "And you were a demon. You could ride anything." He exhaled a long stream of smoke. "Do you remember that crazy mare my parents bought right before you left?"

I shook my head.

"About a hundred hands tall and with a take-no-prisoners attitude toward people. They called her Medusa because she scared the trainers stiff. But when you came over, you walked up to her like it was no big deal, had a little chat, and climbed on. No one else could do that. We had to separate her out from the rest of the stock because she was so wild."

"I don't ride anymore."

He gave me a probing look. "Are you sure you're Aurora Silverton?"

"No," I said. Just speaking the word, saying something true, made me giddy.

He looked down at the half-finished joint between his fingers like he was seeing it for the first time, then put it out against his palm. He shook his head. "I guess we all have our own forms of self-destruction." I smelled burning flesh.

"Are you okay?"

"Me? Of course."

I saw him slip the rest of the joint into his pocket and caught a glimpse of a hand puckered with burn marks. He said, "So you must miss Liza."

I hedged. "I still have a hard time believing it."

"That she's dead or that she killed herself?" he asked sharply.

"Both, I guess. Why?"

He shook his head and gazed out over the golf course. "I couldn't decide if it made the most sense in the world or the least sense. Did you have any idea she was going to do it?"

I shook my head. "Did you?"

"No. I would have said it was impossible. Frankly"—he looked at me—"I would have thought you were more likely to be the one. Especially after what I saw that morning."

"That morning? Why?"

"Do you remember the guy I was dating then, Ox?"

"You did not date someone named Ox."

"It's a common name in Slavic countries," he protested. "Anyway he was Liza's next-door neighbor, and his room overlooked her backyard. That was one strange family. Well, you must know, you were her best friend."

"I wish I could remember," I said. "I just . . ."

"Liza was definitely the normal one. I didn't see the oldest sister much because she was away at school, but the little girl was like something from the Addams Family, pale and greasy and always with a book right in front of her face, even when she walked around the house. Her dad seemed harried and like he was in a bad mood all the time. And he always parked in the driveway, never in the garage. Ox and I talked about it a lot, you know, the way you speculate about your neighbors, coming up with different crazy theories. Especially when we realized that the garage was double-insulated, had its own cooling system, and was protected by a fancy alarm."

"You figured that out just from watching him out the window?"

He grinned. "We snooped."

"So what was in there?"

"We considered an S&M dungeon, a harem, a lab for making mutant species, a giant tarantula, the table where he dismembered his lust rage murder victims, wine cellar—all the obvious things. But the truth was way weirder."

I swallowed down my growing sense of apprehension, and the sound felt strangely loud out on the quiet patio. "What?"

"Records."

I let out a sharp, involuntary laugh. I'd been expecting something so much worse. "Records?"

"Vinyl. Like maybe ten thousand of them, all in original sleeves covered in plastic." He paused like he was trying to put together all the parts of the story. "It's about three A.M., and I am rolling a joint or something. And I hear this noise from next door. I look down, and there is Liza carrying case after case of her father's records outside from the garage, right?"

I nodded, and he went on. "When she's got about ten cartons of them in the yard, she takes a record out very carefully, places it on the ground, and smashes it with a hammer. She did it again and again, smashing them one by one. Not just hitting them once but pulverizing them. *Smash, smash, smash.*" He hit the palm of his hand with his fist. "At some point she must have gotten bored because she started going faster, making a less careful job of it."

He took the half-joint out of his pocket and relit it.

"And here's what's weird," he said, exhaling a cloud of purplish smoke. "Or, weird-*er*, I guess. I swear as she smashed them she was crying. Like she was sorry to be doing it. But the next morning when her father came out and saw it, her face was completely expressionless. She stood there in a sea of broken records and watched, totally impassive, as he collapsed. Her older sister had to catch him in her arms before he fell to the ground. Then Liza dropped the hammer, right there, and walked off. Curtain. I don't think she ever went back to her house. That night I saw you and her at the party and then . . . poof." A shiver ran down my back, though the air was warm.

"I—I had no idea," I stammered.

"That's why I was surprised when we heard what she did. I mean, she seemed so strong. Unflappable. Without even a hint of remorse when she saw how upset her father was. He must have done something really horrible to her to make her act that way."

"He must have," I murmured.

"Intense, right?"

I nodded. Cleared my throat. "I know this is weird, but do you remember what I was wearing that night?"

"Of course I do, cutie. A trench coat. I remember it because I asked you if you were having an assignation, and you said you thought you had. But then you got your heart broken, so now it was to become an adventuress. And then I had a smoke, and someone said they saw you with Stuart."

My mind was reeling with all this new information. Liza's fight with her father. Aurora's broken heart. It was like the clues kept coming, but none of them seemed to be adding up.

Uncle Thom poked his head out of the bar then and said, "Dinner, kids."

Roscoe said, "That's my cue. I just came to see you. I don't do dinner theater." There was a rumble of voices behind us, and he glanced over his shoulder. "Speaking of outrageous acting . . ."

CHAPTER 34

followed Roscoe's eyes and saw Coralee and her crew coming toward us. Roscoe leaned toward me, said, "I'll see you at tennis tomorrow," kissed my cheek and took off.

"Wait," Coralee called, running after him. Grant hung back to stand by me. He held his camera toward me. "Look at the screen, not at me, in case Coralee is watching."

I pretended to be very interested in the footage he was showing me, which was of Coralee doing some kind of dance in fast-forward. "I think I'd like to see this for real," I told him.

"Funny, I didn't peg you as a masochist. Coralee's dancing is not for the faint of heart. Anyway, the thing is, I can't stop thinking about kissing you. Don't look at me; look at the screen."

I kept my eyes on the screen and bit back my smile. "I liked it too."

"I have this idea that it could be really pleasant to make out with you for four, maybe five hours. Are you free tomorrow afternoon after the tennis tournament?"

"I have to check with Bridge—"

"So that's how I shoot a musical number," he announced, slightly too loud.

I looked up and saw that Coralee had rejoined us. "You're showing her my Sonoran Sunrise Festival clogging performance?" She rolled her eyes, but I could tell she was secretly proud.

"That was really great," I said, looking sideways at Grant.

She turned to Grant. "I'm going to run to the bathroom, then grab my date. You and Huck get into position in the dining room."

"As you wish, sir," he said.

She made a heart with her fingers and held it up to her chest. "Love him!" She grabbed me by the arm. "And you come with me."

"Clogging?" I whispered to Grant as she pulled me away.

"It begins and ends with her initials," he explained with a grin.

I was still digesting that as Coralee dragged me through the crowd toward a sign that said "RESTROOMS" in gilded serif letters more suitable for a bank than a bathroom.

There was an arrow pointing down a set of dark green carpeted stairs. "The stairs to the old pool are at the bottom to the left through the door that says 'AUTHORIZED PERSONNEL'. In case you 'forgot.'" She put "forgot" in air quotes.

I stared at her. "What are you talking about?"

She pulled me against the wall and whispered in my ear, "Look, I know your secret. So you can stop with the I-don't-remember-anything-about-anything act."

My stomach lurched with shock. Coralee knew I was an imposter. Coralee. Queen of tweeting. If she told anyone, it would all come out. The deal with Bain and Bridgette. Who I really was . . .

I couldn't let that happen. My heart started to pump in my ears. "You do?"

She nodded. "Of course. I figured it out ages ago. But don't worry,

I didn't tell then, and I won't tell now."

I suddenly had the feeling that she and I were not talking about the same secret. "Thanks," I said. "Who told you?"

"No one *told* me. I could just tell. I'm good at watching people. The way he always happened to pass by during tennis practice. And I saw him leaving notes for you at the Old Man."

"Notes? With an Old Man?" I repeated.

"The Old Man? That big cactus near school." She sighed with exasperation. "I told you, I *know* about it. You don't have to keep pretending. It was romantic the way you had to be secret and have Liza pick them up and deliver them for you." My heart foundered as she said, "But now you get a second chance."

"What do you mean?" I asked. Although, in that instant, I was fairly sure I knew.

"Hugsbyefornow," she said, pushing me excitedly in the direction of the stairs.

Turn and run, a voice in my head told me. *Go. This is one meeting you are completely unprepared for.*

But I couldn't. Like I was being urged forward by an invisible hand.

The face in the scratched-out picture.

I followed the short stairwell down until it ended at a door that said: "NO EXIT. AUTHORIZED PERSONNEL ONLY."

I paused, then pushed through it.

The smell hit me first, the clean smell of chlorine and the less clean smell of mildew. My footsteps echoed through the massive tiled room. The pool was empty, but in the dim light coming from the emergency exit signs, you could see it had once been fancy, with a wall of green-and-gold mosaics on one side and a wall of mirrors on the other.

Halfway down the length of the pool, I saw him. He was sitting on an abandoned lounge chair, legs straight in front of him, arms crossed over his plaid button-down cowboy shirt, leaning back with the kind of quiet patience of someone who could wait all day, all year for something. I could imagine him sitting there a dozen, two dozen, times before—same place, same posture. I could imagine Aurora walking toward him just like I did now.

He said her name out loud now, and the way he said it was enough. Even though his face had been scratched out in the photo, I knew immediately who he was.

Colin Vega.

CHAPTER 35

could see why Aurora had scratched his face off so completely because if she hadn't, it would have been hard to be angry with him.

He was the kind of good-looking that smacks you in the stomach, the kind you see a hundred miles away and only looks better
when it's up close, the kind that makes your stomach feel gooey and
all your joints seem to be less functional than they were the minute
before you saw him. He looked like Superman in the moment right
after he's done something death-defying but before he's put Clark
Kent's glasses back on—a little rough, not quite tame.

But maybe the Superman impression was wrong because there
was an edge to him, a tautness of his jaw. This was no good boy, but
he wasn't a simple bad boy either.

Given what I knew of Aurora, I could imagine the two of them
had been sparky together.

He had deep-set brown eyes ringed with thick lashes, high cheekbones that cut his face into plains, and a tight mouth that looked like
it could curl up in the corners, but didn't. His hair was shorter than in
the photo strip and kind of fuzzy, like it had been buzzed off. He had a

scar through his left eyebrow. His face looked older than I'd pictured it, or maybe just careworn. His eyes seemed like they were the kind that could dance with mischief or even laughter under the right circumstances, but there was no laughter in them now. There was nothing.

He didn't stand as I drew closer, just looked me up and down and said, "You cut your hair."

My heart caught in my throat. I said, "You too."

He ran his hand over his, front to back then back to front and nodded. "Occupational hazard."

I said, "You—you're not supposed to be here. I heard you moved."

"I heard you were back."

The coldness in his tone and his gaze was awful. He hated me, or who he thought I was.

"How's Dartmouth?" I asked.

"I didn't go. I enlisted instead."

"Enlisted?"

"Marines. Did a tour and a half in Afghanistan." He rubbed his thigh like it was really important for the fabric of his jeans to be smooth. Without warning he said, "You know I waited for you that night. And the next day. And the next night."

I didn't have to ask which night. I knew he meant the night Aurora disappeared. "I'm sorry."

"'I'm sorry'? That's all you have to say?"

"What else do you want me to say?"

He seemed genuinely at a loss for words. Silence spread through the vast tiled room. "Something about why you didn't come? Or call? Or show up? Why you ran away without me?" He shook his head and moved his eyes to stare at the middle distance. He said, "I thought you were dead."

"You sound disappointed I'm not."

His eyes came back to me, and now I would have given anything for the blankness that had been there before because the pain in them was terrible. "This is not a joke. Do you know what you did to me? Thinking you were dead? It destroyed my life. You were alive all this time, and you didn't once write? Or call? What happened to 'let's run away together'?" He swallowed. "What happened to 'I love you forever'?"

He stared at me waiting for answers I couldn't possibly give. "I—I didn't know," I said lamely.

I saw the inadequacy, the searing failure of that answer in his face. "You know why I enlisted?"

I shook my head.

"Because I didn't care if I lived or died anymore. If you were dead, the world wasn't worth living in. And the whole time there was a part of my mind that still kept wishing maybe you were alive. Maybe one day you would come back, and maybe, just maybe, you could tell me what happened." He was breathing hard. "And now here you are. I'm listening." The pain in his expression was lit with a flickering flame of hope.

Seeing it broke my heart. He deserved so much better than the half-lies and tawdry excuses I offered to everyone else like distracting toys. He deserved the truth.

I said, "I'm not who you think I am."

The pain, the shimmer of hope, didn't disappear, but it wavered. "What are you talking about?"

"I'm not the person you missed. I'm not that girl." This was hard. Too hard. I had to get him away from me, keep him far away.

He frowned. "Say that again."

"I'm not that girl."

He took a deep breath and said, "I am a fool."

I reached out a hand for him. "No, you're—"

He recoiled. "Don't touch me. Whoever you are, don't touch me." He sat up straighter, bending at the waist to lean toward me. "Are you telling me you're not Aurora Silverton?"

I hesitated. But I knew it was the only way. The only way to make this right. "Yes. I'm a fake. My name is Eve Brightman."

He let a long low breath and shook his head. "What are you here for? Why are you doing this?"

The agony in his voice made me hate myself. What could I say? What explanation could I possibly give? Suddenly the whole thing, the quarter of a million dollars, the not wanting to be lonely, the finding out the truth—everything felt squalid.

Like he was reading my thoughts, he said, "You're right. Don't say anything. There is no good reason."

"It was Bain and Bridgette's idea. They'll tell you," I said. For some reason it seemed important to think of anything that could make me seem less hideous in his eyes.

"No. This isn't possible. Why would they do that?"

"For money," I said. "Aurora got some money—"

"When she turned eighteen. So you get it and give it to them and then what?"

"I get a small amount and leave."

"But they didn't need you. They would have gotten it anyway from her will. If she wasn't alive, it went to them." He paused, and I could almost hear his mind working. "But no one knows for sure she's dead, do they? Of course. They just need the ID."

"What?" I didn't like the tone of his voice, the way his face looked mean, almost sinister.

"A dead Aurora is as good to them as a live one. Better, even. A charred Aurora would be especially good, so they wouldn't have to worry about DNA." He seemed to be relishing my growing discomfort. "You've probably noticed by now that Bain and Bridgette are resourceful. It's a dangerous game you're playing, Eve—that's what you said your name is, right?"

He had become cruel, and it made him ugly. I supposed after what the Silvertons, what Aurora's absence, had put him through, it was fair. "Eve. Brightman. If you want to alert the authorities."

"Why should I? I have no love for the Silverton family. Frankly you're in far more danger from them than they are from you. It's not just Bain and Bridgette who would benefit from having Aurora die in some highly visible, easily confirmed way. They all would, when the old lady kicks it. Which from what I hear could be soon."

"She's fine."

He shrugged. "Could be. I hope you realize that you become much more disposable after her death. God, and I was sitting here worrying about how I was going to tell you—" He barked with laughter and smoothed the leg of his pants some more. "My God. My God." Then, as fast as it had come, the laughter was gone, and his body tensed. He pressed his eyes together and rocked back and forth, hitting his head against the wall. "Not really her."

"I'm sorry," I said. "I'm so sorry." My mind flashed to the photos with the scratched-out face. "I'm sure there was a reason Aurora didn't call. A good reason."

He opened his eyes and leaned toward me. "Never say her name to me again. *Never*." His teeth were bared, and his eyes were dark with rage. "Go. Get away from me. Get out of my sight." His hands came toward me, twisting like claws. "Go. Before I do something I regret."

I staggered in the direction of the door I'd come through, unaware of where I was going. The ground was seesawing beneath my feet, and my eyes were swimming.

What had I done? What kind of horrible bargain had I entered into? There was nothing benign or innocent about the horror I'd seen on his face. There was nothing safe. He hadn't been at the party that night, so he wasn't Liza's killer. But the way he'd just looked at me made me think he might very well kill *me*. That look followed me out the door, through the one marked, "AUTHORIZED PERSONNEL," and into the corridor with the bathrooms off of it. I wasn't ready to face anyone yet, so I went into the lady's room and locked myself in the stall farthest from the door. Sitting on the toilet, I leaned my forehead against the green trellis wallpaper and fought back tears.

A dead Aurora is as good to them as a live one.

A dead ringer. That's what Bain had called me the first day. Perhaps he meant it more literally than I'd imagined. Perhaps that was the real impersonation they'd had in mind all along.

No. It was inconceivable.

I was shaking so hard, I didn't hear my phone right away. When I looked down at the screen, my heart pounded at the "UNKNOWN NUMBER." I answered it.

"Where have you been, Ro-ro?" the ghost said angrily. "I've been trying to call you all day. Trying . . . to warn you."

CHAPTER 36

felt like I'd spent twenty-four hours preparing for this call, but now I was tongue-tied.

"Liza?" I said.

"Of course. How . . . was your . . . visit with Colin?"

I had to grip the phone with both hands. "How did you know about that?"

"I . . . know everything. We're . . . best friends forever."

"Please. Stop this. Tell me what you want, and I'll try to see that you get it. But please stop pretending you're Liza Lawson."

"I'm . . . not pretending. What . . . have to do to . . . make you believe me?"

"Nothing. Stop. Please. Just stop it." I felt tears prick my eyes.

"After everything . . . done for you."

"You haven't done anything. You've just made things worse! Stop it!"

"Wait . . . tomorrow . . . you'll see."

"Don't. Please. Just make this be over." I was yelling now, shouting into the phone. "Please!"

"Never over. You're mine . . . my best friend . . . What . . . friends are for."

"If you want to be my friend, you should tell anything you know about Liza's death to the police."

"It's not about my . . . death, Ro-ro. It's about . . . you. . . . I'm trying to *warn* you."

I shook my head even though no one could see. "No. Stop."

"Trying . . . to help you."

"I'm done playing these games with you. Goodbye whoever—"

"*Listen.*" The voice was so urgent that it caught me off guard, and I paused. "You're . . . not safe until . . . you figure out what happened. What . . . happened to . . . *me.*"

My eyes narrowed, and I crossed one arm around my stomach. "That doesn't make any sense. You're just trying to scare me."

"It was . . . supposed to . . . be you. I died in your place. I died . . . for you."

My heart stood still.

Her words hung between us. I didn't want to believe them, but they made too much sense. That would be why Aurora left. Because someone had been trying to kill her.

No. There are no ghosts. Liza committed suicide, I reminded myself.

"No," I said. "That's not what happened."

"Find the coat," the voice said. "Find the truth. But be careful. They . . . need you dead."

"Who? Why?" I demanded despite myself.

"Must . . . pay attention . . ."

The line went dead. I stared at the phone, running back over the conversation. The impossible conversation.

Supposed to be . . . you. I died . . . for you.

The meaning of the words themselves would have been chilling enough even without the echo of Colin's. If Colin was right, I was in danger from Bain and Bridgette. But if that really was a ghost, Liza's killer had unfinished business to attend to. And now that I—Aurora—whoever—was back, it meant that they could finally finish the job.

Either way, I was a target.

I burst out of the women's bathroom and into the hard, wide chest of N. Martinez, who was standing right outside the door as though I'd conjured my own personal superhero.

He wasn't in uniform, but wore a very nice dress shirt that smelled like wood smoke and cinnamon and of something I'd like to bury my face in forever.

He quickly stepped backward, jolting me back to where we were. And who I was supposed to be.

"How did you find me?" I stammered.

"The way you flew out of the bathroom, it was more like you finding me."

I nodded and took a step backward myself, bashing into the wall. "I meant, um, how did you know I'd be down here?"

Instead of answering, he asked me, "Are you all right?" Then quickly added, "I'm not trying to be nice to you, don't worry. It's just—you look strange. Upset."

I knew the right thing to do was thank him and walk away. Bridgette had been unequivocal about talking to the police, and he was clearly there trying to get information from me. He was dangerous.

And he was looking at me like he could really see me. Not Aurora Silverton. Me. More of me than anyone had seen in a long time. And he wasn't leaving. It was terrifying and exhilarating, and I didn't want it to stop.

"The ghost just called again."

He acted like that was the most normal thing in the world. "What did she have to say?"

"That someone is trying to kill me. That it was supposed to be me dead on Three Lovers Point, not her. That I have to find who killed her before they come after me."

"I could see why that would be upsetting."

"The thing is," I said in a small voice, "that's not what scared me. It's that I'm starting to believe in her. That it really is Liza's ghost. Because I can't think of any other explanation. She asked me why I continued to doubt she was real, and I couldn't really answer."

"There's an explanation. We just haven't found it yet."

"Maybe. She also said I should expect a surprise tomorrow."

"We'll have to—"

"I was under the impression the police would be leaving the Family alone." Bridgette's voice buzzed between us like a crop-duster, cutting short whatever he had been about to say. She stepped from the stairs into the hallway and came and stood next to me.

"They are," N. Martinez said. "I'm here as Coralee Gold's guest. I was on my way to the bathroom when I ran into your cousin."

I wanted to melt into the floor and die. Of course. He hadn't been looking for me. He wasn't there to protect me secretly because he cared so much. He was Coralee's date, and he was going to the bathroom. He wasn't thinking about me at all.

"Don't let us keep you from your evening then," Bridgette said, taking my arm and leading me away.

"I thought you were done talking to the police," she hissed at me as we made our way toward the dining room.

"I ran into him by accident," I protested.

"That had better be all that happened," she said. I wasn't sure if I was imagining it now after talking to Colin, but her voice was laced with menace.

As we neared the center of the dining room, that menace was replaced by a warm smile. She seemed to be looking straight ahead, but I could tell she was aware of all the eyes on us. Leading me by the hand to an upholstered chair in the middle of a long table filled with the Family, she said sweetly, "I found the guest of honor. Now we can start."

CHAPTER 37

The first course was handmade pasta ribbons coated with bright green pesto. It was followed by grilled steak for everyone but Aurora the vegetarian, who had a grilled portabella mushroom, served with french fries made from purple potatoes. There were skinny green beans that crunched when I bit into them and onions roasted until they were caramel sweet. For dessert there were three kinds of gelato and tiny bite-sized lemon meringue cakes that melted on my tongue.

For all their discord and bickering in private, the Family worked like a well-rehearsed ensemble cast in public, making just the right number of clever remarks to keep just the right volume of conversation and laughter to make everyone else in the room watch and wonder. They were civil and charming and polite and interesting.

They would all benefit from my death.

It was someone who was there that night. Someone with you now.

Bridgette and Bain had been there that night. Had whatever they were planning now actually begun three years ago?

Pieces clicked into place, things I should have seen all along. Like looking back over a map of terrain you've covered, I saw the signs so clearly. Bridgette and Bain's too easy acquiescence when I asked for more money. Their lazy omissions of any facts having to do with anyone but the immediate family. The hair of mine that disappeared from my brush the day Bain took me to play tennis. Bridgette's almost hysterical desire to keep me from talking to the police more than was absolutely necessary. They didn't really need a live Aurora. Just the body of a dead one.

Maybe it wasn't even just Bain and Bridgette. Maybe they were all in it together. What if their plan hadn't been for me to actually pass as Aurora; it had been for me to pass as Aurora outside the Family, just long enough to die. It would explain everyone's easy acceptance, even Uncle Thom and Aunt Claire who were openly skeptical. It was devious and ruthless and, I had to admit, very smart. It had all the hallmarks of something The Family would figure out for its mutual benefit.

I couldn't help thinking that the only reason I was still alive was because I'd arrived early and they hadn't yet had a chance to figure out the most expedient way to get rid of me. They might wait until after Aurora's birthday, but there was no need to. After tonight, every-one who wielded any power at all in Tucson believed I was Aurora Silverton.

I had to leave Tucson. I only had thirty dollars and no ID. I could continue pretending for a few days and try to find a way to get the ID—and possibly more cash—out of Bridgette's wallet. But every day I stayed was a day my life was at risk.

I glanced around the table, at the Family, their perfect smiles and easily faked laughter. I'd lived on less than thirty dollars before. I could do it again. I would leave that night, I decided.

Arthur drove Althea and me home after dessert. We spent most of the ride looking out our own windows, but at one point she said casually, "You know I've disinherited you. Not leaving you a penny."

"I understand," I said.

"I hear how you can't control the fury in your voice. You'd like to rip me limb from limb, wouldn't you?"

"No, Althea. I wouldn't." I was surprised at how calm my voice sounded. "The money doesn't matter that much to me."

"Oh, yes it does," she said. She turned to me, and her eyes were blazing. "I know it does. Why did you come back if it wasn't for the money? You don't love me. You can't love them, any of them. We're a family of unlovable creatures. We're stunted, every one of us, like plants grown in rocky soil. Deformed and ugly." She was leaning toward me, and I backed away involuntarily.

"You sit there thinking you're different because you left, but you're not. You came back. You came back like a vulture scenting fresh meat. You came back to feed off of my dead body with the rest of them."

It was suddenly stultifying back there, as though her fury were another creature in the back seat with us, breathing up all the air. I was pressed against the door of the car, the handle digging into my lower back when the car rolled to a stop.

"We're home," Arthur said, and I wanted to correct him, remembering what my mother had said about running away from home. This was most definitely not a home.

My knees trembled, and I nearly fell getting out of the car. The next two and a half hours passed as though time had been frozen in amber. We got home at nine, but I knew it wouldn't be safe to leave too much before midnight. I stuffed the least easily identifiable change of clothes, my $30 in cash, and the original note Bain had handed me into a backpack. I debated leaving a note, but I couldn't figure out what to say. And I doubted it would matter anyway. Everyone makes up their own stories, I'd learned.

Finally the clock on my—not mine, I reminded myself—Aurora's bedside table showed ten minutes until midnight. I flipped off the light switch, opened the door, and listened.

The house was still.

I'd already decided the best way was to go out the front door. The back door sent me around by the garage over which Arthur had his apartment, and it posed a bigger risk of being seen.

I knew the main stairs creaked less than the back stairs, so carrying my shoes, I padded down the hallway in that direction. I glanced down at the courtyard below to make sure it was empty. It was still, stiller and friendlier than when I'd first come.

Once I got outside, there would be no pausing to look back, no one-last-glimpse, I told myself. Once outside, the clock started ticking, and I was on the run. Again.

I took each stair slowly, letting my weight settle a little at a time. I was four stairs from the bottom when one creaked. I held my breath.

"I can't believe you forgot about that stair," Mrs. March said, coming out from next to a potted palm. "That was the stair that always got you caught before. Nasty piece of work, always quiet by day but sounds like a shot going off at night."

I saw she was still dressed. "You knew I was going to sneak out," I said.

She nodded. "I hoped I was wrong. I've been waiting up, every night since you've been back. Just in case you tried. In case you really were a coward."

The word was like a slap. "How is leaving being a coward?" I asked. "No one here wants me. No one needs me. I thought I could come home, but this—it's not home. Anymore," I added.

Mrs. March's gaze didn't leave me, and it wasn't comforting. "You've been back three days, and you're moaning about not fitting in. That's quitting. The Aurora I remember was many things. Selfish. A pain in the ass. Stubborn. But she wasn't a quitter."

"That Aurora left," I said, compelled for some reason to defend myself. "If that isn't quitting what is?"

"Something happened to that Aurora," Mrs. March insisted. Her fists were clutched. "*That* Aurora wouldn't have snuck out in the night like this. She was hurt, and she was confused. And maybe she didn't pick the best way to handle it, but she felt like she had to go. I am as certain of that as I am of my own name."

My hands on the straps of my backpack were shaking.

"That Aurora, the Aurora who didn't know what else to do, that Aurora I can forgive," Mrs. March said. "But an Aurora who sneaks out in the night? I have no time for her."

Silence stretched between us. When I spoke, my voice sounded small, like a much younger girl's, and it trembled. "Why do you care? What do you want from me?"

She nodded to herself, like she was making a decision, and said, "Follow me. There's something you should see."

CHAPTER 38

I didn't know what to expect as she led me up the main stairs one flight to the room next to Althea's bedroom. On the plan of Silverton House I'd studied, it was called the junk room.

She opened the door and flipped on the light, and it seemed true enough to its name. There was an old chair in there, a table leaning against the wall, an empty bookshelf, and a massive old armoire. Mrs. March unlocked the armoire and opened one of its double doors.

Inside there was a jumble of objects, some in boxes, some jammed in haphazardly, some gift-wrapped, some in paper sacks. There was a hat with flowers on it and an electric guitar and a Barbie in a box and a baby doll and an unopened computer and a waffle iron and a pink plastic Christmas tree. I saw a set of pots and a set of Winnie the Pooh books, a sewing kit, a hairdryer, and a popcorn popper. There were other packages too that were wrapped, so I had no idea what they were, but some of them were strange sizes and shapes.

"What is this?"

"These are the presents your grandmother has bought for you since you've been gone," Mrs. March said. Her eyes dared me to look away from her. "She'll see something advertised and say, "Aurora would like that," and then go out and buy it. Or she'll stop someone on the street and ask where they've gotten something. The other day she made Arthur take her to Walmart because she felt you needed that." "That" was a giant inflatable NASCAR.

I stared.

"The idea was, if she found just the right present, you would come home." She lapsed into silence as I took it all in, her words, the objects. She stood watching me. Finally, in a voice so soft it was almost a whisper, she said, "Do you see? Do you understand?"

No, I wanted to say. "If she loved her granddaughter so much, why couldn't she just show it? Why all this and not—not something simple?"

"She knew she'd failed you before. She's a hard woman, and she has ghosts that dog her. But more than anything, the entire time you were away, the one sustaining thought of her life was that you were alive and would come back."

"Then why is she so determined to push me away now? Keep me at arm's length? Why can't she show it?"

"She's terrified of you."

"Of me? No. That makes no sense."

"Terrified of *losing* you. The way she lost your father and your mother. You're the best thing she has, and she knows it. But she only knows how to lock valuable things up, to protect them. That's what she was doing the other night. Your first night here."

An idea began to take shape in my mind, but it was hazy, abstract. "What do you mean?" I asked.

Now she opened the other door of the armoire. That side appeared to be empty until she touched a switch and a light came on, and I saw it had no back. It led to a hallway parallel to the one outside.

"The House is filled with secret passages you never discovered," Mrs. March said. "Your grandmother used this one to get to your room and make sure your door was locked. She was checking that you were safe. She's gotten a bit paranoid, and she's—she's constantly worrying about thieves now."

"Why?"

Mrs. March closed both armoire doors and stood very still, with her back to me, as though making a decision. "Her mind isn't as clear as it used to be," she said, turning around. "Recently, the last few months especially, she gets confused. It wanders, and when it does, it's always to you and your mother. I think—" she stopped herself with a little shake of her head. "Arthur told me it happened in the car on the way to dinner tonight." I nodded. She looked down at her hands, like she was frustrated they couldn't do anything to fix this. "She knows it's happening, and it scares her. She's asked Arthur and me to not mention it to the Family; they'd get her into a home faster than Bridgette could drive her there. But it's getting harder."

The backpack seemed to have become unbearably heavy on my shoulders.

Still looking at her hands, Mrs. March went on in a quiet voice. "She thinks people only care about her for her money. She's afraid that right after your birthday, you'll leave."

Suddenly I saw Althea not as a cold, conniving matriarch but as a very lonely old woman, desperate to exert her control the only way she knew how. Not out of cruelty but because she felt that control slipping away and otherwise no one would pay attention to her.

Now Mrs. March looked at me. Her gaze was direct and demanded complete honesty. She said, "Will you?"

"Will she what?" Althea demanded, appearing in the doorway.

"Why are you two gabbing practically in my bedroom in the middle of the night?"

"I was giving Aurora a tour of the House," Mrs. March answered smoothly.

Althea frowned. "At midnight?" Then she looked slightly confused. "It is midnight, isn't it?"

"It is," Mrs. March confirmed. "She couldn't sleep."

Althea's eyes came to mine. "I couldn't sleep either. I kept dreaming about thieves." I noticed she was rubbing her fingers together. "I liked it better when I kept a gun under my pillow." She looked at me. "Don't suppose you fancy a game of gin."

I said, "I don't know. Are you going to cheat?"

"Do you hear that?" she asked Mrs. March. "Calls her own grandmother a cheat."

"Well, you are one," Mrs. March said.

"Insolence. Everywhere." But she was happy. It was as though the entire scene in the car had never happened. "Well, come on. We don't have all night, and I want to win some money."

She led the way into her bedroom. It was old-fashioned with dark red wallpaper and a big mahogany four-poster bed and Persian rugs on the floor. There was a round card table near the heavily curtained windows. On one wall hung a tiger's head, a fox, a rabbit, and a deer, all slightly dusty. "Shot all of those myself," she told me proudly. "Sit. Penny a point. You shuffle."

There were only two chairs at the table, and I noticed Mrs. March had disappeared. A little while later she came in with milk and cookies. Forty minutes later she came up to take the plates away. Althea yawned and laid her cards down. "I'm sorry, my dear. I think I have to go to bed."

I tallied up the points. "You're just saying that because I'm winning."

Her eyes sparkled. "Untrue. To prove it, I propose we continue in the morning. Two pennies a point."

"You're on," I said before I'd even thought about it. It was as though I'd made the decision without realizing it. I would be staying. Even if everything else was wrong with the Silvertons, this one thing was right.

I helped Althea into bed. As I reached the door, she said, "It's such a pity you can't see her. She—your daughter looks just like you, Sadie. Same stubborn look in her eye. Same smile. You'd be proud of the kind of young woman she's become. You'd be so proud."

"Thank you," I whispered. I closed the door and ran back to my room.

There were four missed calls from an unknown number. I turned off my phone.

For the first time since I got to Tucson, I had a dreamless night.

CHAPTER 39

MONDAY

The yellow-and-white awning snapped back and forth in the breeze blowing across the upper balcony of the tennis club. It was a glorious day: blue sky, three perfectly placed cirrus clouds high up. Althea was next to me, her chair turned to face the awning, peering at the courts below through binoculars.

"I don't see Bridgette. I guess Stuart is standing her up for the doubles tournament," she reported, sounding gleeful. "Too bad you wouldn't take my bet."

"I would have," Bain's voice floated to us. I turned and saw him walking across the patio toward us, his arms tan and muscular in his white polo shirt but his calves strangely scrawny, as though he only worked out the parts of his body people saw the most.

"You'll take any bet. That's your problem," Althea said.

Bain didn't look as happy. "That's not true," he objected.

"A good man can make a joke," Althea intoned. "A great man can take one."

Althea had been in fine form picking on everyone all morning, and I was enjoying being with her. My phone had rung three times with an unknown number, but I had ignored it. After the previous night, everything seemed so clear: What I'd thought was a ghost trying to attack me at Silverton House had been my grandmother trying to check on me; whoever was making these calls was just a prankster trying to scare me. I wasn't going to let them.

Now Althea announced, "What time is it? I could use a lobster salad."

I looked at Bain who shrugged. He pointed to his wrist. "No watch."

"What happened to your watch?" Althea snapped at him. "The gold Rolex I bought you for graduation. Why don't you ever wear it?"

That made me think of the closet full of presents for Aurora, and I began to think this calling to account might be her way of asking people not to validate that they valued what she'd given them, but that they valued her. She reminded me of one of those Chinese boxes carved out of a single piece of jade that are wonders of intricate craftsmanship but delicate and impossible to completely see into.

"It's in the safety deposit box," Bain said. "I don't want anything to happen to it."

"Bosh, watches were meant to be looked at; that's why they're called watches. Otherwise they'd call them ignores." Her eyes went to me. "I feel a few more witty comments coming on. Go get me a lemonade. And put it on your tab. You'll be rich soon; you can pay."

I'd just picked up the lemonades from the sliding window at the snack bar when I heard a laugh behind me. It was a ringing peal, happy and joyful, and it struck a chord of memory. I swung around fast—too fast. I ran right into the woman who had laughed, spilling lemonade down her front.

I started apologizing without looking up, saying, "I'm so sorry, I hope I didn't—" But before I could finish, a voice snarled, "Watch where you're going." My eyes snapped up, and I was looking at Colin Vega.

He was standing next to the pretty brunette woman I'd walked into. She had a splash of lemonade on her blue-and-white argyle polo shirt. "Look what you did," he said to me, his eyes challenging, as though I'd done something much worse than spill lemonade.

"I'll clean it up," I offered.

"Don't bother, we're going," he growled. Taking the brunette by the arm, he said, "Come on, Reggie. This was a mistake," and turned to go.

That's when I saw it. The lemonade slipped from my hands, splashing down my front and all over the patio. "Your leg," I said. "You're missing part of your leg."

He was wearing shorts, and his left leg beneath the knee was a prosthesis.

The brunette he'd called Reggie smiled and squeezed his arm. "Isn't he amazing? His walk is so even now. You can barely tell when he wears pants. I'm Regina." She leaned forward to hold out her hand, but Colin batted it down.

"Don't talk to her," he said, wrapping an arm around her and pulling her away as though to shield her from me. He gave me a look of pure venom.

I stared at the ground, looking at where one of the paper cups I'd dropped rolled to a stop beneath a table. I said, "I'm sorry I upset you."

"Upset me?" He made a thin, mirthless sound. "I lost my leg fighting because of Aurora Silverton. I gave up my basketball career because of Aurora Silverton. I'm not going to give up another second of my life thinking about Aurora Silverton. You have no power to upset me."

Bain had come up to stand next to me. "Don't talk to my cousin that way."

"Your cousin," he snorted. "Like you care. Look at my leg. Look at it." I moved my eyes to it, and then to his face. "This is what the Silvertons did." His glazed-over eyes began to slowly focus on Regina, and as they did, he relaxed. "I'm sorry you had to see that, sweetheart," he said, kissing the top of her hair. "I shouldn't have brought you here." He pulled her, still wrapped in the protection of his arm, away.

It became very important to me then to collect up the two paper cups and flatten them and fold them and slide them one at a time into the trash. There were sounds, but they seemed to come from a long way off. And my ears were roaring and muffled at once, as though the entire ocean were in there, and it was too crowded for it to move much.

I watched a napkin flutter end over end toward the edge of the patio and thought it was the most beautiful thing I'd ever seen, so beautiful that it brought tears to my eyes, and I stood there with the sticky lemonade drying on my legs and my chest feeling like someone had punched it.

And just when I thought it couldn't get worse, it did.

I heard Althea say, "Oh my," and turned in time to see Stuart step onto the patio. He was followed by a small crowd of people, including Coralee and her crew. "You witch," he said to me holding up his hands. "Did you do this? Did you curse me?"

From the fingertips to just past his wrists, Stuart's hands were red and covered in sickly yellow-and-white crusty blisters that looked like they might have pus in them.

"Are you happy now?" Stuart demanded.

I was bewildered. I had no idea how to reply, and I looked around for Bain or Bridgette. But I didn't see either of them. Finally I said, "I had nothing to do with that. I haven't seen you in two days."

Stuart brushed that aside. "Some crazy magic you learned on the street? One minute my hands are fine, and the next they look like this. I know it was you. If you tell me how to reverse the spell, I'll drop the charges."

"What charges?"

"For assault."

"I think you have that backwards," I said, working to keep a tremor out of my voice. "*I didn't assault you.*"

He leaned close to me to growl, "You'll pay for this."

"All I said was that you should be careful where you put your hands," I told him, leaning as far from him as I could. "Frankly, it looks like I was right."

Someone laughed behind him, and he turned to scowl, then brought the scowl to me. "I know this was you," he repeated. "I'll figure out how you did it, and I'll get you. I've got protection if you try to do anything again." He pointed behind him with two grotesque thumbs, and I saw N. Martinez and another officer standing at the back of the crowd.

At least N. Martinez's low opinion of me could be confirmed.

Stuart hissed, "Keep your distance."

Over his words I heard the ghost's from the night before. *Wait until tomorrow . . . you'll see . . .* I had a sinking feeling this was what she'd meant.

But who could have done something like that? Since Stuart had told everyone that I attacked him, almost no one knew what had really happened. Coralee and Bridgette did, but I doubted either of them would have hurt him. And even if they'd wanted to, *how could they have done it? How could anyone?*

I was suddenly desperate to get out of there. I glanced around again, looking for Bain or Bridgette, but instead spotted Grant coming toward me. I'd forgotten that he and I were supposed to have a date. His mouth moved, but somehow I couldn't hear what he was saying, couldn't hear anything. Then, as though the ocean drained out, I heard him say, "Are you okay?" and sound came pouring back in dizzyingly.

"I'm fine. That was just a surprise," I told him, compressing horror, guilt, sadness, grief, sorrow, pity, momentary regret that I hadn't left the day before, and confusion into that one sentence.

He said, "Good," which was probably a compression as well.

Uncle Thom appeared and announced to Althea, "Arthur is waiting with the car."

Her face took on the expression of a petulant child. "We just got here," she said. When Uncle Thom looked unmoved, she sighed and stood up. "Very well." Her eyes moved around the group and rested on me. "Sa—you. You come with me," she said. I had the impression she wasn't sure of my name, but she covered it well.

I turned to Grant and said, "I know we talked about leaving together but—" And before I'd even finished he said, "I understand," and I was following Uncle Thom and Althea into the parking lot, grateful to be out of there.

As Arthur steered away from the tennis club, Althea announced we were playing gin and dealt the cards, but I had to work hard to concentrate. *Would it have been better,* I wondered, *if I hadn't told Colin I was Eve Brightman? If I'd let him go on thinking I was the same Aurora who had left him behind? If I'd made excuses, told him about the amnesia, the sickening doubt, the feeling of unworthiness? Of what I'd learned had happened with Stuart the day Aurora vanished?*

Who did that to Stuart's hands?

I glanced at Althea and found she was staring at me hard. Her face was a warren of concern. She pursed her lips together and said, "Sadie, I'm afraid I haven't been the best grandmother to Aurora."

I saw Arthur stiffen in the driver's seat. I flashed him a look to tell him it was okay and said to Althea, "I'm sure you've done your best."

She shook her head a little and pressed her lips together. "I've failed. She hated me. She hated me, and she ran away."

"She didn't hate you," I told her, setting aside her cards and taking one of her hands in both of mine. "She was probably just confused."

"It was because I lied to her. It was your fault though. You cheated us. All of us."

"How?" I asked.

"We got you all the help we could, put you in the best clinic." Her voice trailed off, and her expression got far away.

"I know you did. You did everything."

"Everything," Althea repeated. "Every year for your birthday and Christmas, I gave you a pocket watch the way you asked. Every year. Sixty-six pounds of watches."

"Quite a collection," I said noncommittally, unsure where this was going.

"Just enough," Althea murmured, her bony hand clenching in mine.

"Enough for what?"

Althea didn't answer, saying instead, "I told her you died in an accident on the way to come and see her." I waited for her to go on. "That's what I told Aurora because I thought it would be better for her. I thought it would be something she could understand, you coming to see her ring ceremony, wanting to see her so much, and then accidentally driving off the road. She missed you too."

"But that's not what happened," I said.

"Of course you know it isn't. Sixty-six pounds. Just enough to drag your body to the bottom of the lake and keep it there. You—you made me help you."

Now her eyes were on mine, seeing me, but not me and the sadness in them, the horror was nearly unbearable. "I did it to be kind. You understand, don't you? I thought it would be better than the truth, but it was worse. So much worse."

She shook her head. She seemed to have aged ten years during the car ride—her face sallow, her cheeks sunken. She took a long, shuddering breath and went on. "For some reason—for some reason Aurora blamed herself for the accident. And then when I finally told her the truth, she blamed me. She said I drove you away." Tears quietly slid down her cheeks from each eye, but she seemed unaware of them. "That I drove *you* away. When you were the one who left us. *You* ran away. I tried to tell her that I'd begged you to stay, that I'd gotten you all the help I could, but how could she believe me? She didn't know you were sick. She didn't know you were in that special hospital. I kept my promise to you not to tell her." She dabbed at her eyes with a Kleenex that Arthur held out from the front seat. "It was so hard to see her. See her beautiful and smart like you. Every time she smiled, it was like you smiling. It hurt me, here." She put a hand over her chest.

"So you made it hard for her to smile," I said, finally following. Finally seeing the life Althea and Aurora had led together, understanding it. The silences, the fights, the recriminations. Not because Althea had hated Aurora. Because she'd loved her and hadn't known how to express it.

Listening to the pain in her voice, I felt like the unwitting audience of a play I hadn't wanted to see, now unable to look away. I felt the chasm that had existed between Althea and Aurora, imagined them both groping toward one another, but somehow both were always stopped by their stubbornness, really a cover for their fear of rejection, before they could touch. Mrs. March had been right—grandmother and granddaughter were alike.

I could picture them sitting at the long dining table together night after night in silence filled with all the things they didn't know how to say to one another. Picture Aurora sneaking out, getting wilder and wilder because it was the only way to break the round of cool "goodnight, dears" and chilly "good mornings." Sneaking out not simply for attention, but because she wanted to feel, wanted to *be*—wanted. Needed. Worthwhile.

"I wanted to protect her. I wanted to keep her safe," Althea said, her voice pleading now. "The way I promised you I would after you brought her back. And then she ran away too. You both left me all alone." She took a deep, shuddering breath. "She is so like you. So beautiful and smart like you."

Two people sitting across from each other but never really seeing each other.

I saw Althea now, though. I saw agony etched into her features, into the lost expression in her eyes, into her white knuckled hands. I couldn't change what had gone before, but I realized I had the power to make her feel better now.

I told her, "I'm sure Aurora will forgive you if you ask her to."

Althea shook her head. "It's too late. I'm afraid it's far too late."

I took her hand. I said, "Maybe she feels bad about something too. You could try."

Her eyes rose from our clasped hands to my face. There was confusion at first, and then they cleared, as though she was seeing Aurora again, realizing that, yes, in fact, she could try. "I suppose—"

It occured so fast I had no idea what was happening. Out of the corner of my eye, I saw a flying streak of light. I turned to look, and there was a terrible screeching noise. I was thrown forward and then sideways, and then I was hanging upside down. The queen of hearts brushed my cheek as it went fluttering by, turning end over end, and the back of my mind echoed with a girl's laughter.

Everything went black.

CHAPTER 40

S*moke.*

I smelled smoke and felt heat. I opened my eyes, and the stinging made me close them again almost instantly. But I'd seen the orange tongue of flame shooting out from the hood, and the forms of both Arthur and my grandmother hanging unconscious in their seatbelts. The car was at an angle to the ground, but I didn't know which one, only that it was one that had me pinned beneath them both. I struggled to undo my seatbelt with my injured hand, then reached in Althea's direction. She gave a low moan but didn't open her eyes.

Colin's words—*a charred Aurora*—echoed in my mind.

I opened my eyes again. The flames around the front of the car were burning higher, and I heard a crackle that sounded like dry grass catching. My door was against the ground, so it was impossible to get out that way. I skirted Althea and pulled myself up to her door. Bracing myself against the seat, I pressed on it.

It didn't move.

No, I thought to myself. *It doesn't end like this, not another accident. There's still too much to do, too much to fix. I am not—*

My fingers fumbled along the door again, and I flipped the lock. This time when I tried the handle it worked. With a heaving push, I flung the door open.

The car was surrounded on three sides by fire, and although there was some licking at the rear tires, it hadn't reached Althea's door yet. Bracing my hands on the body of the car, I pulled myself out like I was pulling myself out of a swimming pool, and swung my legs outside so I was lying on my belly.

I reached in and grabbed Althea around the chest and tried to pull her out, but the seatbelt was holding tight. The crackle-hiss of the fire moved closer, and my eyes burned as I felt blindly for the seatbelt release.

My fingertips grazed it. Holding her with my right arm, I pushed the release with the left. She flopped loose against my one arm, and the weight of her pulled me down into the car too.

I felt a brush of flame against my calf. Taking a deep breath of the blazing air, I heaved as hard as I could and managed to get Althea halfway out of the car door, then with another breath, all the way. I fell backward with her head resting on my chest, my arms shaking from the exertion, my lungs aching for breath.

The fire, taller and hotter now, inched closer. I had to get her away from the car.

I hauled myself to my feet and got my arms under her shoulders and started drag-carrying her up the hill. The fire dogged our steps as if it could scent us. The smoke clogged my lungs, and my eyes were soot-caked slits. I could barely see where we were going. I'd hurt my ankle somehow, and the burn on my calf stung like it was being lanced every time I moved.

The flames began to dance in my eyes, and I started to see figures in them, first my mother, then Liza. Liza just stood there, watching me, her body surrounded by flames. She said, "Now do you understand, Ro? It was the shoes," and in that moment I think I did. *The shoes,* I repeated to myself. *Of course.*

Somewhere in the back of my mind I heard a wailing noise, and at first I thought it was coming from me. But then I realized it was sirens. We were near the road. We were saved. In front of my eyes the flames seemed to splinter into a cloud of dancing orange butterflies, and I heard someone laughing. I passed out.

I woke up with a bad burn on my calf, lacerations on my arms and legs, and the vague sense of having figured something out but no memory of what it was. The doctor said I'd be fine after a good night's sleep.

Like me, Arthur skated through with only cuts and bruises, but Althea's condition was more serious. The trauma brought on a heart attack in the ambulance on the way to the hospital, and she'd had to have emergency open heart surgery.

"In a way it was a blessing in disguise," the doctor told Bridger, Uncle Thom, and me as we huddled together in the waiting room of the hospital. "Her heart was in terrible shape. Did you notice her acting differently recently? Erratic or moody? Absentminded or maybe delusional?"

"The difference would have been if Mother *wasn't* erratic and moody," Bridger said, and the doctor said, "You know, I hear that a lot." They shared a good laugh. I seethed.

I thought about how neither Bridger nor Uncle Thom knew that in fact Althea had been different recently, that she'd been erratic, forgetful, delusional. About how they lived nearly on top of one another and knew so little about each other.

About how neither of them looked particularly happy when the doctor said, "If it weren't for the accident, she might have suffered a major heart attack too far away to get the help she'd need. This way, with any luck, she stands a good chance of making a full recovery."

Uncle Thom offered to drive me home, but I didn't want to leave Althea's side.

The accident was a weird one. It had been reported by the people in the car coming toward us. They'd seen a blue bicycle come careening down the hill on the side of the road directly into our car. The bike was found badly mangled, twenty yards from the site of the accident where it had fallen after impact. There was no sign of a rider. In fact, the witnesses swore there hadn't *been* a rider. Just a blue bike on its own, rushing down a hill on a collision course with our car. "A ghost bike," the witness called it.

When Detective Ainslie told us that, I started to shiver. I knew that was stupid. *There is no such thing as a ghost bike,* I told myself. *Those are just words.*

The air around me seemed to stir, and looking up, I saw N. Martinez coming down the corridor toward me. He was in uniform, but instead of making him indistinguishable from others, it seemed to set him apart. *He moves better than other men,* a voice in my head said. *As though the space around him respects him.*

I looked away.

"Don't worry, I'm not here to spy on you," he said. Before I could object, he added, "I just thought you would want to see these." He held out a manila folder.

I put the folder on my lap and opened it. It contained copies of the crime scene photos from the accident. The funny feeling in my knees got stronger. *He brought me a present,* they said. *He brought you crime scene photos,* my mind interposed. *Because he knew you'd want to see them.*

I felt myself starting to smile and bit it back. *What would Aurora do right now?* I asked myself. Looking for the answer was like groping in the dark through a cobweb-covered forest for the right path.

"Thank you," I said, keeping my voice as formal as possible. "These are very interesting." Then I blurted, "Did you enjoy your date with Coralee?"

It was clearly the wrong thing to say. He nodded stiffly. "It was very nice. Goodbye, Miss Silverton." And then he turned and stalked back down the corridor.

As he left, he took the air of safety and security with him. "Wait," I called after him, getting to my feet. I realized I didn't want him to go. I was sore and stiff and not moving well, but he didn't come toward me, just stood there, a solid mass. "Was there something strange about Liza's feet when she died?"

"Can I ask why you want to know?"

"I'm not sure. Not her feet, her shoes. They—they weren't the right shoes for the outfit." That wasn't quite right, I felt, but it was close.

"I'm not aware of anything strange about her shoes. I'll let you know if I hear anything," he glowered.

"I didn't have anything to do with what happened to Stuart's hands," I told him.

"I didn't think you did."

"Oh. Okay. Well, I—I just wanted you to know."

He gave me a curt nod and walked out. I watched him go and again had the mad, insane urge to tell him I wasn't what he thought I was. But even though he was the only person in the world I wanted to tell, he was the last person in the world I could.

I was going to have to work harder to stay away from him.

I filed that idea into the same drawer where I kept my better impulses, slid into the closest chair, and reopened the folder he'd brought me. Flipping past the pages detailing the accident, I went straight to the photos. I saw our car from various angles, and then the bike.

It was twisted but still recognizable, a blue girl's bike. The handgrips were white, but they looked like they'd been wrapped in yellow electrical tape. And on the metal bar between them someone had glued a red crystal star—

Liza's bike. I suddenly realized. *Liza's bike from the yearbook photo.* I felt unnaturally calm, like I was watching all this from outside, looking down on myself.

That's when I realized I wasn't even supposed to be in the car.

I'd thought the threat was from the family, from Bain and Bridgette, but what if I'd been wrong? Maybe it was, but our little deal had unleashed something else. Something much more dangerous. Something vengeful.

Mine . . . best friends **forever**, I heard Liza's voice saying, and I began to be afraid that I understood.

Pay attention.

My phone rang.

CHAPTER 41

An icy prickle skittered up my spine like it was a living thing. I reached for the phone with bloodless fingers.

It was Grant. "I heard about the accident. Are you okay? Where are you?"

"I'm at the hospital," I told him. The warmth of his voice, his genuine concern, shattered me. "I'm scared, Grant," I said. "I—I don't understand what's happening."

"I'm coming to get you," he said.

"I can't leave," I told him. "In case something happens to my grandmother."

"We'll meet downstairs. There's a coffee shop called I Heart Warm Beverages. I'll be there in ten minutes. You come whenever you can. You don't have to do this alone."

I had to swallow back a sob. "Thank you," I said, awash in relief. "Thank you. I'll—I'll see you there."

"You're not alone, Aurora," he said and hung up.

I tried not to think about the fact that it wasn't me he was coming to help; it was her. The other Aurora.

He wrapped me in a big warm hug as soon as he saw me and held me like that, safe, kind, for a full minute. He pulled away slightly and noticed the folder I was holding.

"What's that?" he asked.

"Photos from the accident. They—she—" I stopped myself, trying to figure out how to explain the inexplicable. I ended up with, "Can we sit down?"

He guided me to a green bench that wrapped around a yellow table and slid in after me. "Sometimes when you're trying to catch an image, an oblique angle is best, but I feel like for this we'd like to be more head on. Start at the top."

"There's something about shoes," I said.

He shook his head. "I'm afraid I can't help you there. I've been wearing the same kind of shoes since I was ten." He gestured under the table to his sneakers.

"Not like that, something—" I sighed and pushed the folder away across the table. His arm was next to mine on the bench, and I reached out and started playing with the cuff of his shirt. "Actually, I think what I want is not to think about it for a little while."

"There are a lot of things I'd like to do to help take your mind off of it. But for now, what can I get you to drink? I Heart Warm Beverages is known for their warm beverages."

"I'd love some tea."

"Black? Green? White? Bubble?"

"Black, I guess."

"With?"

"Milk."

"Skim, whole, almond, or soy?"

Despite everything, I laughed. He smiled and patted himself on the back.

I said, "You take this seriously."

"Warm beverages are not to be trifled with." He slid out of the booth. "Besides, if working for Coralee doesn't pan out, my food service skills may well be my livelihood one day. I'll be right back."

I followed him with my eyes. He had an easy way of moving, as though he were comfortable and relaxed in his body, and I had a flash image of what it would be like to lie next to him, stomach pressed against warm, smooth stomach, my head on his collarbone, his hand cradling my—

"Excuse me," a female voice said, and looking up I saw the girl Colin had called Reggie at the club. His girlfriend. "Aurora, right? We sort of met earlier at the club."

"I remember," I told her. It didn't come out exactly friendly, and she winced.

"I'm sorry. That's why when I saw you here, I—but I understand if you don't want—I mean—"

Grant came back then with my tea and the skim-milk jug. Reggie's eyes got huge, and she blushed. "I'm sorry, I didn't realize I was interrupting. I'll just—"

"No," Grant said. "Stay." He turned to me. "I got a call from Coralee. She's got some kind of emergency film need, so I have to go. I'm really sorry."

I nodded. "Okay, but you owe me."

"I do. Anything you want."

"I want to see your movie."

He said to me, "Anything but that."

"Coward."

"In this regard, yes." He looked at Regina. "Will you take my place? Aurora needs some cheering up. I'll bribe you with a warm beverage."

I protested. "No, don't—" To him I said, "She doesn't have to—" I turned back to her: "Really I don't need cheering up, I'm—"

Reggie slid onto the bench. "Tea," she told him.

He took away the skim milk I'd finished and headed back to the counter.

"You didn't want me to stay, did you?" she asked.

That's one of those questions you can't answer honestly. I said, "I didn't want you to feel obligated," which walked the line.

She pushed up her sleeves and tucked a stray hair behind her ear. "I'll go in a second. I came over because I wanted to apologize. For Colin today."

"You don't have to apologize." I blew on my tea. "He was angry."

"He's got a temper," she said, hunched over, hands in her lap, eyes staring into space. "He certainly does."

Grant came back with a tea for her, the soy-milk jug, and three brown sugars. He turned to me and said, "We'll pick up where we left off tomorrow? Lunch? Say one o'clock?"

I nodded. He bent, and we did an awkward kiss somewhere between the mouth and the cheek.

Reggie added some soy milk, then poured all three sugars into her tea. Real sugars, I noticed, not like Bridgette. She watched Grant leave. "He's cute. He obviously adores you."

"I'm not sure." I brushed it away. "You were saying. About Colin's temper?"

"He's working on it, but sometimes it gets out of hand."

I thought of the way he'd growled at me the night before, like a feral animal. "Does it ever scare you?"

She shook her head, swaying her glossy black ponytail from one side to the other. "My father had a temper when I was growing up. I know how to take care of myself." Unconsciously, she began to rub

289

her right wrist where there was a tattoo of an orange butterfly, like the one on the necklace I'd bought.

"I'm sorry," I said, feeling a kind of kinship with her.

She shrugged. "What are you going to do? Families are complicated."

I thought about the Silvertons. That was an understatement. I said, "I like your tattoo. Is that a monarch butterfly?"

She glanced at it, as though she'd forgotten it was there. "Yes." She smiled to herself. "When I got it, I was much younger, and I made up this whole thing about it being a symbol of rebirth. Now I just like it because it's pretty."

"Monarchs are poisonous, you know," I told her.

"No," she said sipping her tea. "I had no idea. Pretty and poisonous. Sounds like a lot of the girls I've met since I came here."

I laughed despite myself, then immediately regretted it as I realized it probably wasn't the kind of thing Aurora would have done.

It doesn't matter, a voice in my head reminded me. Reggie didn't know Aurora. Maybe it was that, the fact that I didn't have to worry about her, or the way we seemed to have so much in common, but I realized I liked her.

She put her tea down. "That's the other reason why I came over to your table. Not just to apologize but—I could use some cool friends. And you seem cool. I know it's weird with me dating your ex-boyfriend, but just, you know, think about it."

"I don't think Colin would like it," I said with real regret.

"That's okay. I'm not crazy about some of his friends."

"Okay," I nodded. "I will."

She glanced at her watch and put the lid on her cup. "I've got to go if I'm going to make my bus. It was nice running into you." She reached around in her purse and came out with a pen and a paper. "This is my number. Call me if you want to do anything. Really. Even grocery shopping. I don't want to sound desperate, but I'm desperate."

I took the paper she passed me, glanced at it long enough to see she'd written, "Good for one Warm Beverage. Call me!" and slipped it into my pocket. I doubted I would have time to call her, or that Bridgette would let me, but somehow the prospect of having a friend—a connection, a lifeline—who had nothing to do with the Silvertons or Liza or Coralee or any other part of that world was appealing. Safe.

The cinnamony scent of her tea was still lingering in the air when my phone rang. I didn't even look at the caller ID. As I answered, I realized I'd been waiting for this.

"Why . . . been ignoring me," Liza's voice said when I answered. She sounded plaintive. "Who is more . . . important?"

"I'm done playing games with you. Did you cause the accident today?"

"You didn't answer . . . I had to get . . . your attention somehow . . . no one hurt."

"Are you kidding? You almost killed three people."

"You . . . just have a Band-Aid . . . on . . . your calf."

I stared at the phone. "And Stuart's hands? Did you do that?"

Liza laughed. "Made him pay . . . what he did to you."

"I didn't want you to do that."

"What friends . . . are for."

"You can't pretend you did any of this to help me."

"Of course . . . I love you . . . RoRo. No one . . . will ever love you like . . . me."

"Stop it. Stop saying that, stop calling, stop trying to help me. If you know something, go to the police, otherwise—"

"For you, Ro-ro. For . . . your own . . . good. Everything I . . . do. "

"I don't want you to do that, and I don't need you."

"Why can't you . . . believe me? I'm . . . best friend."

"No, you're not. You're just someone making a cheap joke. I'm not answering the phone anymore for you."

"Don't say that . . . Ro-ro, don't . . . ignore me. You'll be sorry."

"Goodbye." I hung up. It was only as I was gathering up my cup and the folder that I remembered what she'd said at the beginning of the conversation. *You just have a Band-Aid on your calf.*

How could she know that?

CHAPTER 42

My phone buzzed again. Unknown number. "Are you here?" I demanded. "Can you see me?"

"No. Can you see me?" a female voice, not Liza's, asked.

"Who is this?"

"Who is this? I'm looking for Aurora Silverton. Is this the right number?"

"This is Aurora."

"It's Xandra, Xandra Michaels? Calling from London. You left a message for me a few days ago?"

She had the fake British accent and cadence that Americans with comfortable savings accounts get when they've been in England for more than five days. "Thanks for calling back. I'm trying to fill in the blanks in my memory about what happened the night of the party, and I was wondering if you could tell me what you remember."

"It was three years ago," she said.

"I know. Believe me. What would be great is if you remembered the last time you saw Liza or, um, me."

"It was when I let you out of that ridiculous wine cellar Bain excavated for the house. 'A Southwestern *Cave*,' he called it. Too absurd."

So that was where Liza and I had disappeared to when Roscoe went to get his jacket. A wine cellar. "Do you know how we got in there?"

"No, but you were a bit loopy when I found you. I got the impression there might have been something extra in your drinks. Or you'd been helping yourself to Bain's wine."

"How did you find us?"

"You were making quite a racket. I'm not sure what would have happened if I hadn't come along. You were at each other's throats."

"We were arguing?"

"I meant that literally. As in you tried to strangle Lizabeth."

"Why? What were we fighting about?"

"About a guy of course. Your boyfriend was texting Liza to come meet him. She said the texts were really for you, but you were livid. You asked me what I would do, and I said I would positively confront him. So you did. You marched out like a little soldier going off to battle." I heard her say, *"Oh, pardon,"* to someone in the background and then to me, "Does that help?"

"Do you remember what I was wearing?"

"A dress or something?"

"Could it have been a coat? A trench coat?"

"No no. Then you and your friend would have been twins."

"Liza was wearing a trench coat?"

"Yeah. Look, I've got to run. Send my love to everyone there."

After she hung up, I spent a moment putting this new piece into the puzzle of that night. Picturing it as though I'd been there. Being trapped in a dark cellar with Liza, the light of her phone illuminating her face. Jealousy, as I think that Colin is texting her. Fighting until the door opens and Xandra lets us out.

Marching off to meet Colin.

Marching off to meet Colin.

Colin who acted as though he and Ro had never broken up even though I knew, from the scratched-out face on the photo, from what Roscoe had said about a broken heart, that they had. Colin who tried to suggest that one of the Silvertons would try to kill me. Colin who didn't like it when things didn't go how he planned. Colin who had a temper.

Colin who felt so guilty about whatever happened that night that he threw away a basketball scholarship he'd worked years to get and enlisted in the Army. Colin who, according to Xandra, had actually been texting Liza. To come meet him. Because he was there.

It was someone who was there that night. Someone you know.

But the accident with Liza's bike. The rash on Stuart's hands. What was the explanation for those?

I started to shiver as I got up and walked back to the hospital. "You'll be fine after a good night's sleep," the doctor had said.

But where could I go that I would feel safe? Whom could I trust? I was nearly at the door to Althea's room when I saw the answer.

Or thought I did.

Coralee was coming down the corridor toward me as though it had better watch out for itself.

She said, "Your grandmother is sleeping, but we got some great footage of the doctors. I think *Ghost Bike* might be my hardest-hitting webisode yet." She sounded upbeat, but I noticed that there were dark smudges under her eyes.

I looked behind her. "Where's your crew?"

She waved a hand. "Off editing somewhere. It's a twenty-four-hour operation keeping CG on the A-I-R." When she said C-G, she made curves with her hands and interlocked them.

"You're lucky," I told her. "My initials wouldn't work for that."

She patted me on the shoulder. "We'll think of something."

"Smiley face. Could I come home with you tonight?"

She did a fake double take. "What? You actually want to hang *out?*"

"I just thought it could be nice," I said. Which was a good-sized piece of the truth but not the proverbial whole. Since she wasn't in Althea's will and hadn't been at the party the night Liza died, Coralee was one of the few people I could think of who wasn't possibly trying to kill me.

I saw an expression on her face I hadn't seen before, and for an instant she looked both younger and more mature, as though I was seeing the smart little girl she had built her entire brash exterior to protect. But also as though she wasn't sure she wanted me near her.

Sensing her hesitation, I said, "It's okay if this isn't a good night."

"It is." Her voice sounded smaller too. "Sure. Um, that would be, yeah, fun."

She was back to normal by the time we got to the Golden Mile, the Golds' massive estate. The front of it was a construction zone because it was always in the process of being renovated.

Given that her mother was a famed domestic diva, Coralee's room was a surprise. It had dark red walls and mahogany furniture and looked like the room of a little girl. The only grown-up thing was the queen-sized bed with the dark wood headboard, but even that had a floral quilt on it that looked girlish and slightly frayed.

I was thinking that maybe when everything around you changed all the time, it was nice to know something would always be the same, when I became aware of Coralee watching me intently.

She was standing with her back to the door, like she was blocking it. Our eyes met, and she said, "I can't believe I finally have you here," half-like she was talking to herself. "You just walked right in. You had no idea, did you?" She smiled, but not like her-self. Her face had completely changed. It now wore an expression of pure hate.

Without taking her eyes off me, she reached behind her, and I heard the door lock.

CHAPTER 42

"What—what's going on, Coralee?" I asked.

"It's time for us to have a little talk," she said.

"A talk?" I repeated. My palms were damp.

She nodded. "There are two things you should know."

She took a step toward me. I took a step back. "W-what?"

She held up a finger. "The first one is, I hate you. I've hated you for years."

I nodded. My back was pressed against her dresser. "But I thought—"

"Shut up," she hissed. She held up another finger. "The second one is, I was there that night. At the party."

I felt like my knees were going to go out from under me. It was only then, too late, when I saw what an idiot I'd been. Coralee was the one person who could have done everything—she could have made the phone call during the séance, she would have known when we were going to Three Lovers Point, she knew I was going to talk to Colin, she saw me leave the tennis tournament with my grandmother. "Are you saying that you're the one who killed Liza?"

Her hand snaked out, and she slapped me. "Don't you dare," she said.

Now I was really confused. My palm went to my cheek. "I don't—"

"Why don't you tell me what happened between the two of you on Three Lovers Point the night she died?"

"I wasn't there."

"Then how did a button from your coat get up there?"

I frowned. "How did you know about that? The police said—"

"I have connections. Stop stalling, how did it? If you weren't there?"

I shook my head. "I don't know."

She slapped me again, and I reeled back. "Stop lying!" she said, and she was almost hysterical now. "It's no use—I know what happened." Her voice quivered. "You and Liza went up to Three Lovers Point together. You made her come with you—you were always making her do things—and she didn't want to. I think you were joking about jumping, going over, and she tried to stop you. And when she did, she fell. She fell trying to save you, rescue you the way she always was. And you ran."

"What? Are you nuts?"

"I think you killed her," Coralee went on, sounding more rational even as her words sounded less. "It may have been an accident, but I think you killed Elizabeth Lawson. And you ran away like a coward."

I was frozen. The temptation to tell Coralee the truth about myself, to make her take back these horrible accusations, nearly overwhelmed me. But I couldn't.

"You don't really believe that, do you? Coralee?"

I thought her expression might have wavered. She said, "Why is she haunting you? Why you?"

"I don't—"

Her hands snaked out, this time to grab my shoulders. Her grip was firm and hard. "Why you and not me?" Her tone was demanding, but the anger seemed to have been replaced by something more feverish.

"What are you talking about?"

Her face crumpled. There was no other description for it. Her face crumpled, and she let go of my shoulders and stumbled backward, falling onto the bed and bursting into tears.

"Did I do—?" I started to say. She shook her head before I finished and pressed the heels of her palms into her eyes.

I sat down next to her and waited for her to stop crying. Her hands dropped from her eyes. She took a ragged breath and said, "I'm sorry. I didn't really think you killed her. I mean, I did, before you got back. But then when you returned." She shook her head, not meeting my eyes.

"Were you and Liza close?" I asked. Nothing I'd heard or studied suggested she and Liza had been especially good friends.

Coralee said, "Yes." She closed her eyes and took another deep breath. "Liza and I—we—we were in love." A tear trickled down her cheek. She opened her eyes and looked at me. "We loved each other, and it's been killing me that she's haunting you and not me." She laughed drily, but her body trembled with the effort of keeping back a sob. "I just wish I could see her again." The last words came out as though they had been mined by anguish deep inside of her.

I was stunned. I put my hand on her shoulder to comfort her, and she grabbed it and held it. "I'm so sorry," I said. "I—I had no idea. How long had you two been together?"

She flopped back onto her back with her head on one of the pillows. Her voice was scratchy from crying. "Almost six months.

It happened when she left the tennis team, after Christmas break. Remember, she'd come back with broken fingers? Coach said they were healing fine and she could just take a break, but Liza insisted on quitting completely. I went to talk to her and ask her why she was leaving because, no offense, I thought she was the best player on the team. She got mad at me and told me to mind my own business and—" She tilted her face toward mine. "Did she ever really yell at you? Like really?"

I lay on my side on the pillow next to her and shook my head.

Coralee let out a whistle. "She was incredibly hot when she was angry. There was so much she bottled up inside, and it almost never came out but—" She turned back to looking at the ceiling. "Anyway, she was yelling at me, and I just—I just kissed her. She was the first person I'd ever kissed. And she kissed me back. And that was that."

"You kept it so secret," I said.

"We were afraid. My family, her family, her older sister, you. Everyone at school. We didn't know how people would act. Now it would be different. But that was three years ago, and we were only freshmen . . . " She shrugged.

"I thought—the police thought—you two didn't get along."

"Ah." Her eyes went back to the ceiling. "We thought that would be good cover. Then no one would suspect. And no one did. Mostly we hung out here. That's why I haven't redone my room—because it still reminds me of her."

I said, "Why did you go to the party that night?"

She didn't answer, asking instead, "Do you remember Victoria, Liza's older sister? The one who went to boarding school?"

I thought about what Grant had said, about Victoria telling Liza I was a bad influence. "Not really."

"I think Liza idolized her, kind of. When Victoria was home from school, Liza dressed different and talked different, like a little version of her sister. She would barely answer my calls or texts, or else she'd let Victoria answer her phone and have her tell me that Liza was busy. And I'd hear laughing in the background. Like I wasn't good enough for her and her sister's friends. Like Liza was embarrassed about me." Coralee twisted a length of her glossy hair around her finger. Her voice was lower and sad when she went on. "It happened for the first time over spring break. I spent pretty much all of it right here, crying. But when we got back to school, everything went back to normal. I was so happy, I didn't even ask her why she'd been so mean. And then she did it again when her sister came home for the summer. Disappeared."

"So you came to the party to see her?"

Coralee nodded. "Yeah. She finally called me back that morning and said you were having some kind of nervous breakdown, so she couldn't leave you. Something about Colin and a breakup? That's how I knew about you and Colin, actually. Liza had told me about picking up his notes for you from the Old Man and leaving yours for him, so no one would know you were in a relationship. We weren't the only people in Tucson keeping things secret."

"I guess not."

"Anyway, I was desperate to talk to her. I hadn't seen her in two weeks, since Victoria got home, and when I heard she was out with you, I got jealous. So I went up to the party to just, you know, talk to her, but when I got there I couldn't find either of you. All I managed to see was your cousin, talking to J.J."

I remembered Grant mentioning a J.J. "The J.J. who worked at the golf club? He was at the party?"

"He was, but not *officially*. That was kind of J.J.'s thing, right? Sure, he worked at the golf club, but mostly he was kind of a thug of all trades. People like Bain love hanging out with people like J.J. because it makes them feel cool and edgy, and they like to imagine that J.J. wants to be them."

That sounded about right for Bain.

I sat up on one elbow. "Was that the J.J. that Madam Cruz channeled at the séance?"

She laughed. "Yes and no. It was that J.J., but I told her what to say. So she wasn't channeling him." She saw my expression and rushed to add, "She's a real medium; she could channel people. But she's also a friend of Mom's, so she agreed to pretend to get in touch with J.J. as a favor to me. She kept it separate from the rest of the séance because she didn't want to upset any real spirits."

"Why?"

Coralee yawned, as though this confession had tired her out. "I just wanted to see what Bain would do. It was delicious, with the strangling and then Grant coming over and ghost whispering. 'Vitamin Must-See TV.'" She turned serious. "Don't tell Grant he isn't a ghost whisperer, okay? He has so few pleasures. Besides you. But you're going to break his heart, aren't you?"

"I don't know what you are talking about."

"L-O—nevermind. I'm too tired." She yawned.

"But no one saw you at the party. Why didn't you go in?"

"And say what? That I was looking for my girlfriend? I don't think so." She yawned again. "I'm beat. Would you mind if we went to sleep now?"

"No."

She lent me a blue camisole and matching shorts to change into and slid into a nearly identical yellow set herself. We crawled under the covers, and she stretched to turn off the beside light. "Goodnight, Ro."

"Goodnight, Coralee."

I hadn't quite drifted off to sleep when she said, "You know, Liza wanted to tell you. About us. She thought you'd understand, and she also said you were starting to get mad because you knew she had a secret and it made you feel bad she wasn't telling you. I wasn't sure. I thought you were kind of a bitch, but Liza said I didn't understand you." I heard her let out a deep breath. "I guess she was right."

The next morning I was up before her. I tried to be as quiet as possible getting ready, but as I went to leave, she said, "Thank you. For letting me talk about Liza. I miss her, and it—it was great to be able to think about her again."

"You're welcome."

"Hugsbye," she mumbled sleepily.

"Hugsbye."

In the car on the way to the hospital, I checked my phone. When I saw the battery had died, my mouth went dry, and my chest got tight.

Don't ignore me, I heard Liza's voice. *Pay attention.*

You're being nuts, I told myself, taking slow deep breaths. *Nothing will happen.*

I was wrong.

Liza was standing at the foot of Althea's bed when I walked into her room.

CHAPTER 43

TUESStDAY

"Liza?" I breathed, rushing toward her.

She didn't smile, just looked at me somberly and shook her head. "No. I'm Ellie. Her little sister. You probably don't remember me."

"Ellie," I breathed, nearly collapsing. "You liked to walk around reading books all the time," I said, quoting what Roscoe had told me.

Her eyes got minimally less somber. "You do remember."

I glanced at Althea, who still seemed to be sleeping, and then back at Ellie. Close up, she only looked a little like Liza, with the same blue eyes and golden hair but slightly less generous features. Or maybe her mouth just got less practice smiling.

I looked around for Victoria or her father. "You live in Tempe now, don't you? How did you get here?"

"I took the bus. No one can know I was here, okay?"

My eyes widened. "Sure. Are you—are you okay? Is something wrong?"

Her fingers knit together, and she bit her lip. "I think—" she began. "I think I killed Liza."

For a moment I couldn't speak. She said, "Can we walk?"

I shook myself out of my shock. "Sure." We stepped out into the corridor. "Can you tell me how you—I mean—"

"I didn't mean that literally," she explained. "I don't think. I don't know. See, that's the problem. Do you understand?"

Her voice should have been pleading, but instead it was flat, like she was asking me if I understood algebra or checkers.

I said, "I'm not sure. Can you tell me more?"

"I just think I was *responsible* for her death." She reached into her pocket. "Because of this."

She held a piece of paper out to me. It was light blue with a darker blue star in each corner. It said, "I've got everything ready. We leave Friday. 9pm at the old Five and Dime. I love you."

I had to press my elbows into my waist to keep my hands from shaking as I read it.

"Where did you get this?" I asked.

"From their secret hiding place. Colin and Liza's. That big cactus called the Old Man," she said. "They left notes for each other there. It was romantic. "

It took me a moment to realize she'd called it Colin and *Liza's* secret hiding place. I remembered what Coralee had said, about Liza picking up and dropping off the notes. Ellie must have seen that and gotten it confused. She thought the note was for Liza.

But really it had been for Ro.

"I know it's wrong," Ellie was going on, "but sometimes I read the notes. Just to see. And I always put them back."

"Except this one?"

Ellie stopped walking. "She was going to *leave*." Her face was stricken. "She was going to leave me. She promised one day we would run away together, but she was going without me. I—I just didn't want her to."

"Oh, sweetheart." I wrapped my arms around her. "What did you do?"

"I showed the note to Victoria, and she told my dad. I figured they would stop her, you know? But instead—" She started to sob again. "I didn't think it would make her kill herself. I didn't think having to stay with us would make her kill herself. If I'd given her the note, she would still be alive."

"No," I told her, wiping the tears off her cheeks. She had to be thirteen now, but with the sadness on her face she looked about ten. "This note had nothing to do with what happened to her."

"It didn't? How do you know?"

"Because the note wasn't for your sister. It was for me."

"But—"

"She picked up notes and dropped them off for me. Because I didn't want anyone to know I was going out with Colin."

"That can't—"

"Trust me."

"You're sure?"

"Positive," I said. And then for reasons I couldn't explain even to myself at that moment, I added, "Don't tell anyone about giving me the note, okay? It's better if we keep this between us. I mean, it was supposed to be mine."

She nodded. "I guess that's true."

I smiled at her. "I bet you could use some breakfast."

"Um, I just—I'd rather get back home. If that's okay? I don't want to run into anyone and have them find out I was here."

She's afraid of something, I thought. *She's terrified. But not of me. And not of killing her sister. It was something else.* I remembered the photo of Liza with the broken fingers over Christmas, the broken leg over Easter. I said, "Is everything okay at home? With your father?"

She tensed. "Everything with Dad is fine. I'm just going to go."

"You're sure? Do you want me to get you a car to take you back?"

"No, the bus goes in half an hour."

She finally consented to letting me drop her at the bus station in a taxi and buy the ticket, but that was all.

I took the same taxi back to Silverton House. I kept my hand on the note she'd given me the whole way as though it were a magical object that might disappear. The writing on it looked familiar, and I realized I must have seen Colin's somewhere. It proved Colin hadn't been lying. He really hadn't thought he and Ro had broken it off. He'd been planning to run off with her.

So why did Ro get so angry she'd scratched his face off? And why had he texted *Liza* the night of the party?

I paid off the taxi and was walking around to the back door of Silverton House when I heard two people arguing. I spotted a silver VW Bug and next to it, Bridgette and Jordan North.

Bridgette was using wide, uncontrolled gestures I'd never seen her use before, and her hair was unbrushed. I thought I caught "out of control" on Jordan's side and "you don't understand" and "please" on Bridgette's, but those must not have worked because Jordan said something I couldn't hear and walked to her car.

She spotted me before I could move. I said, "I didn't mean to eavesdrop."

She was holding a pile of clothes in her arms, and she looked exhausted, like she'd been up all night crying. "Listen all you want. The entire fight was about the danger of secrets, so the more people who hear the better."

"I'm sorry," I said.

She opened the passenger side door of her car. The car I'd seen that night at the cabin when Bridgette had been with her lover.

I remembered Bridgette at the dollar store talking about how nice secrets could be.

"Can I help?"

Jordan's beautiful face was a picture of sadness and loss. She glanced back at the door Bridgette had been standing in, which was now closed. "No. No one can help. Unless you can convince her"— she tilted her head in Bridgette's direction—"that what her family thinks, and how much money her grandmother does or doesn't leave her, is unimportant."

So that was why Bridgette was doing this. "How long were you two going out?"

"A little more than three years. That night, the party? That was one of our first dates." She wiped her cheek on a blouse on top of the pile. "We spent the whole time together. Well, until the Silverton Show started."

"What's that?"

"Have you noticed how whenever Bain and Bridgette are together, they have to fight? It's like contractual?"

I laughed. "Yes."

"That night Bain and Bridgette had this huge fight. She'd found out about Bain locking you and Liza up in the wine cellar, and she was furious."

"It was Bain who locked us in there? Why?"

"I don't know. It had something to do with Jimmy Jakes—J.J.? Some scheme they'd been working on. But it didn't go according to plan, and when Bain got back there, only Liza was still there. You were gone, and he was mad."

"That's not what the police told me."

"We all agreed the police didn't need to know anything about that. Well, Bain and Bridgette agreed. The rest of us went along with it."

Naturally, I thought. I said, "So I left and Liza was still at the party. Do you know what happened next?"

"The last time I saw her, she was talking to him."

"Him as in Bain?"

She nodded. "That was the last time I saw him that night too." She glanced back toward Bridgette's room. "I have to go."

"Of course," I said, stepping back so she could get the door open. "I'm sorry about the fight."

"It was time." She sighed. "Things couldn't keep going the way they had been."

She had the car in reverse when I realized I'd forgotten to ask something. I stopped her, and she rolled down her window. "You said Jimmy Jakes. As in James Jakes. He's dead. isn't he?"

She nodded. "He committed suicide."

That's where I'd heard the name before. In the police station. He was the other person who had committed suicide off of Three Lovers Point.

CHAPTER 44

went into the house, plugged in my phone, and reached for the thesaurus, in which I had hidden the original paper ripped from Bridgette's Filofax with the note from Bain about the one hundred thousand dollars. I slid the note Ellie had given me in next to it and stepped into the shower.

There was something about it that bothered me. Something that sent my mind spinning back across everything I'd heard the past few days. As the water washed away the grime from the accident, my mind replayed a cacophony of voices—

Xandra saying that Liza had been getting texts from Colin.

Jordan talking about the Silverton Show.

Uncle Thom at the police station saying, "First a watch, now a button."

Suddenly, I gasped. I hopped out of the shower, wrapped a towel around me, and was reaching for the thesaurus when the phone rang.

Like a dog conditioned to come at a certain command, I grabbed for it. My pulse quickened when I saw N. Martinez's name on the screen. I told myself it was because he was the one person who could help me, but I knew that wasn't the real reason.

When I answered, he didn't bother with niceties. He said simply, "We have to talk."

"I know. I think—"

"Where are you?" he asked, cutting me off. I realized his voice sounded more taut and serious than I'd heard.

"At home."

"You need to get out of there. Meet me in the lobby of the hospital." My knees went soft. "What is going on?"

"Just get here," he said. "As soon as possible."

My hands started to tremble, and the thesaurus slid from my fingers to the ground. The original note from Bain fell out, as well as the note from Colin that Ellie had just given me.

I held the notes up side by side, not sure if what I was feeling was hope or dread. The writing on the note from Ellie was familiar not because I'd seen Colin's before—but because it was the *same as Bain's.*

The note from Colin was forgery. And yet he had acted like he and Ro were leaving together.

All of a sudden all the pieces clicked into my brain with painful precision. And each click echoed with the same name.

Bain. It was Bain's writing on the forged note. Bain who was missing his watch. Bain who was the last person to see Liza that night.

Bain, who was now standing in my bedroom doorway, slapping the flashlight against his palm.

"So you've been doing some investigating," he said.

I wrapped the towel tighter around myself and went to lean against the desk. I wanted to look unafraid, but I needed it to keep my knees from shaking.

"Not intentionally. You should have hidden your tracks better if you didn't want anyone to find out."

"And just what do you think you've found out?"

Stall for time, I told myself. "You knew your cousin and Colin were dating?"

"Colin told me. Told me all about how he was in love with Aurora, how you left notes to keep it secret from Grandmother. We were friends. Of course that all changed after Aurora disappeared."

"So you take Colin's real note and substitute one of your own, telling Ro to meet at the old Five and Dime, which is pretty deserted. How am I doing so far?"

He weighed the flashlight in his hand. "Not bad."

"Then you give your watch to James Jakes—J.J.—to get him to snatch your cousin from the Five and Dime while you enjoy a fail-safe alibi at the intimate party you're throwing miles away in your Model Property."

He sat forward, looking interested. "You're good at this."

"But for some reason, Aurora doesn't go where you want her to, messing up your plans, and shows up at the party instead. That doesn't stop you, though. You somehow manage to get Ro and Liza into the wine cellar, where you lock them up. Then you call J.J. and give him new directions to come and kidnap Ro while you are seen talking to her best friend."

He nodded slowly. "It sounds good when you say it."

"Which means, you were the last person to see Liza alive before she went off of Three Lovers Point."

He pulled himself up. "What? No."

"And a few months later, your other associate that night, J.J., dies the same way in the same place. Wearing your watch. That sounds a bit suspicious."

"Whoa." He put up a hand. "First of all, whatever happened to Liza, J.J. killed himself. Ask the cops. Secondly, as I told the cops when it happened, if I had been there, I would never have let him die with my watch on. Are you kidding? Grandmother drives me nuts about it."

I had to admit, that rang true. "Why did you want him to kidnap Ro?"

Bain relaxed again. He let the flashlight roll out of his hand and leaned back, palms flat on the bed. "I needed the money. I had a bad run of luck at some tribal casinos and in a few private games—stop looking at me like that; it reminds me of my sister." He sat forward, elbows on his knees, getting very earnest and trustworthy. "You're making a face like it sounds bad, but it was all going to be very professional. J.J. wasn't going to hurt her, just keep her for a few days, get the ransom from my grandmother, and return her."

I didn't change the expression on my face. "No wonder Aurora left."

He clenched his jaw. "It probably would have done her good. She was totally out of control, wild. It could have scared her straight."

I shook my head in wonder. "Yeah, *she* is the messed up one in the Family."

"Let me tell you, you don't know the first thing about my cousin. She was disobedient just for the sake of disobeying. There wasn't anything she wouldn't have done for attention. She would have loved my scheme. Lapped it up afterwards, all the press."

I stared at him as he spun lie after lie, justifying this to himself.

He lashed into my silence. "You're no better than I am. You're taking money from the Family for lying. How is that different than what I would have been doing?"

"I am nothing like you," I said.

He crossed one knee over the other and leaned back again, nodding genially. "Sure. You're worse. You're stealing from strangers. I'm just taking an advance on what's supposed to be mine."

His fingers toyed with the handle of the flashlight. "You're wrong about the other part too, about me being the last person to see Liza at the party. She and I were talking, and she got a text and took off." He seemed to get very interested in the flashlight's On/Off button.

"Who was the text from?" I asked.

He looked up. "From you." He shook his head. "I mean from Ro. Ro was the last person to see her alive."

I tried to put the chain together. Liza gets a text from Colin. Ro and Liza fight. Ro goes out to meet Colin. Then Ro sends Liza a text. And Liza winds up dead. I felt my eyes widen. "You think your cousin killed her best friend?"

Bain tried to sound casual. "All I know is she texted Liza."

I sat forward, leaning toward him. "This whole time. This whole time you thought I—she—was a murderer. That's why you were so confident Ro wasn't coming back. Because you thought she'd killed Liza."

"That's it," he said agreeably. Something about his enthusiasm pricked at me, as though he liked that answer a little too much.

What could he still be hiding?And why had Ro crossed out Colin's face in the photos? I was still missing something.

My phone rang, cutting through the silence between us. I answered it and had N. Martinez's voice in my ear.

"Are you on your way?"

"Not yet, I—"

"You need to leave. Now."

CHAPTER 45

got dressed, borrowed Mrs. March's car, and made it to the hospital in record time—twenty-two minutes. N. Martinez was standing in the middle of the lobby in a pair of jeans and a dark green T-shirt that, despite saying, "Kiss Me, I'm Irish" on it, looked like it had been custom-made to flatter him. It was the first time I'd seen him casually dressed, and it was not unappealing.

I said, "I think your shirt might be lying."

"It's my sister's birthday. Part of her present is she gets to choose what I wear." He started walking toward the door, and I had to move fast to keep up.

"Is my grandmother okay? Are we going somewhere?"

"For a walk. It will be better if you're not easily available when they get there."

"They?"

"The police."

"I thought you were the police?"

I glanced over and saw his jaw tighten, but he didn't answer me. *What was going on?*

We were at a crosswalk. He pushed the button repeatedly. Finally he said, "I checked Liza's file. The shoes she was found in were definitely hers. They had LAWSON written in them. The only strange thing is that they were a size 8, and she wore a 10. Is that what you were thinking of when you said they were off?"

"Maybe," I said. It didn't trigger any insights the way I had hoped it would. "That's not what you came to tell me, is it?"

His head went back and forth slowly. "Regina Boyd, Colin Vega's girlfriend, was attacked last night."

"My God." He stepped off the curb, and I stayed with him. "Is she okay?"

He shot me a quick glance, and I couldn't tell if I'd said the right or the wrong thing. Of course that wasn't at all unusual between us. I never seemed to know where I stood with him.

"She will be," he said. "It was mostly superficial. But her assailant did try to strangle her. Using the belt of a trench coat. The same kind of trench coat you bought three years ago."

I stopped walking without realizing we were in the middle of the street. "No."

He grabbed my arm and nudged me to the curb. "What I think you will find most interesting is that there was no sign of forced entry. All her doors and windows were locked from the inside, and the security cameras on her building didn't catch anyone going in or out."

I felt like the sounds around us were echoing loudly in my ears. *No sign of forced entry. No one in or out.* "Liza," I whispered. *I have to believe in her now. I have no choice.*

I hadn't realized I'd said the words aloud until N. Martinez countered, "I still think there must be a rational explanation. I'm just not sure my reason is up to it." He shook his head. "Nothing makes sense anymore."

There were benches laid out in a sort of serpentine pattern on a large reddish concrete courtyard. We sat down at one. Across from us two women dressed for office work poked at salads with white plastic forks. A University student jogged by.

I wondered if you asked them how many would say they believed in ghosts.

N. Martinez said, "Regina's assailant kept saying, 'Leave them alone.'"

"Them?" I repeated.

"Colin thinks she must be confused, and it was 'him.' But Regina is sure it was 'them.'"

I thought of my phone's dead battery. Of how angry Liza had been the day before when I was talking to Regina. How she'd said I'd never have another friend like her.

She was very good at keeping her promises, I thought, again amazed at my calmness.

"Colin found Reggie on the floor of her apartment, unconscious." N. Martinez's voice pierced my thoughts. "He called an ambulance, and on the way to the hospital she told him what had happened. Then he came to the station to give evidence." He paused. "I took his statement. He had a lot of interesting things to say. Mostly about you."

This was it. I'd known this was coming. If it hadn't been for what came before, I would have been almost relieved. I said, to be the one who put it out there, "He told you that I'm an imposter."

N. Martinez nodded. "So I ran your prints. By name as well as from the prints in the system."

He'd found one flaw in Bridgette's plan, the one vulnerability. And now he *knew*. Knew the truth. It was almost a relief, and I realized I'd been braced for this, half-hoping for it all along.

I wasn't ready for what he said next.

"I also checked your prints nationally."

My breath caught in my throat.

"I only got one hit. Someone named Edie Poe with fingerprints that match yours was arrested for shoplifting in Oregon. An ice cream cake. And the only reason she got caught was because she stayed long enough to write the name *Nina* on it."

I waited for what else he would say. What he was going to do.

"So who is Nina?" he asked.

"That doesn't matter."

"It does. Who is she to you?"

"She was my foster sister. She was eight." I saw him waiting for more, and I longed to spin a life story for him so interesting, I would wish it were mine.

"What happened?" he asked.

I didn't want to do this. I didn't want to talk about this. I closed my eyes, and there she was.

Tell me a story, I heard Nina's tiny voice in my mind. I remembered how I had to lean close to hear her, her request a faint whisper over the sound of the traffic nearby. Her voice was disappearing, but her skin was still as soft as a downy peach.

I was exhausted, spent. She was dying. There was nothing I could do to help her; she was beyond all help, the nurses at the mobile clinic told me. Assured me. As though that was supposed to make me feel better.

It did not. I couldn't give up.

Our days passed in a strange haze in the corner of the abandoned warehouse we were living in, the sound of traffic and birds nesting in the rafters and squatters at the other end like white noise. They'd once stored fruit here, and the air was always tinted with the faint scent of overripe melons.

Nina lay behind the pink-and-gold cotton tapestry I found in the dumpster next to some college dorms, alternating between wake and sleep, two-hour intervals of each. While she slept, I went out and tried to find, steal, or trade for things I thought she would like: a mango one day, a bottle of Horchata, rose-scented soap snatched from the bathroom of a fancy restaurant, a penguin that dispensed toothpicks from its beak, a Cadillac hood ornament, a crystal star on the end of a fishing wire. One day, cutting through the park, I found a toilet seat with a mirror glued to the inside of the lid and the words "Hello, Good-looking!" hand-painted around the edges. All these treasures sat on the ledge next to her, a museum of memory, along with a doll missing its arm and an ivory comb. Mostly, though, I stayed near her, telling her stories of princesses and adventures like a 99-cent store Scheherazade, hoping to save her life with my tales.

That day she'd surprised me. When her eyes opened, I'd said, "I have a new story. Princess."

But she shook her head. She got the little furrow between her brows she had whenever she was doing really deep thinking. "How do the princesses know? If they are sleeping, how do they know when the right prince kisses them so they can wake up?"

"They can just tell."

"But don't all kisses feel the same? Nice?"

"Not all kisses are nice," I told her.

"So you think there's a difference."

"There must be," I said, not wanting to admit I didn't have enough experience to know.

She closed her eyes, and I thought she was going to sleep. But instead she spoke. She said, "You have to go."

"Go where? What do you need? Juice?"

"Go," she said. "You know where."

"I have nowhere to go. Nowhere to be but right here."

"Yes," she insisted, opening her eyes. She tried to raise herself off the bed of green wide-wale corduroy couch cushions and snoopy blankets I'd gathered around her, to protect the frail bones and razor sharp elbows that threatened to shear through her skin. "We both do."

I wanted to pretend not to know what she was talking about.

"No," I said. Pleaded. Begged. "Not yet. You can't go yet. You don't know what happened to the princess."

Her head turned to me. She smiled. "I do," she said and closed her eyes.

In the park, sitting next to N. Martinez now, I opened mine. I told him, "She died. Nina died. I tried to save her, but I couldn't."

He sat next to me, being quiet in a way that was better than words.

"She was my sister in my third foster placement, with Mrs. Cleary. She came when I'd been there about six months. Mrs. Cleary was a widow who lived by herself except for me. She had a son who was older, maybe thirty. At first when he would come visit, I was nervous, but he never bothered me." I swallowed. "I only found out why when Nina arrived."

Who would believe a little whore like you? I heard echoed from memory.

As though he were reading my thoughts, N. Martinez said, "So you rescued Nina." It was a statement, not a question. But then he asked, "Why not go to the police?"

"He *was* the police." We were quiet again until I said, "Nina made me believe in family again," answering the question I knew he had to ask, why I would ever agree to a scheme like Bain and Bridgette's. "But family you *chose*. That's why I came here like this. As a fake

Aurora. I thought maybe this way I could, you know, choose my own family. And be chosen."

"And have you?"

"I don't know. That depends. Are you going to tell what you learned about me?"

He shook his head slowly. "I don't see any reason that anyone needs to know. Or at least needs to find out from me. Not right now anyway."

I turned to look at him. Right at him. I felt as though I were seeing him, and seeing him see me, for the first time. My heartbeat felt like a butterfly in my chest. "Thank you. Why?"

He took a deep breath. His eyes stayed on me. "Wildfires," he said. "That's why it smells so smoky. We had a dry winter, so the brush is like kindling."

My eyes couldn't look away from his face. "Are they different from regular fires?"

"They're more unpredictable. They leap from one object to another, so it's hard to guess at their path or limit their destruction. Outside the city, they can roll over the landscape like a wave and hit you before you know it."

I couldn't stop watching his mouth move. I wanted to touch it. "How do you stop them?"

"You can't. Once they start, they choose their own path. All you can do is try to contain them until they burn themselves out." His eyes held mine. "They're beautiful to watch, but they can be dangerous."

We sat next to each other in silence for a little while. I had the sense that he was building to something unpleasant, so when his jaw got tight, I braced myself. "Do you want to come to my sister's birthday party tomorrow afternoon?"

I touched my chest. "Me?"

He made a little growling noise and rolled his eyes. "Who else? Why do you have to be so difficult?"

"It's just a little out of the blue."

"Forget it."

"I'd love to." I reached out and touched his arm, and I felt the same electric jolt I'd felt the first time. "I would really love to."

He stared at my arm on his. Then his eyes came to my face.

"I just realized. I don't know your name," I said.

If it were possible for him to frown more, he did. "I usually reserve that for people I'm not going to see again. Clerks at the Department of Motor Vehicles. Court reporters. Insurance agents. Official business. My family calls me Leo."

"That doesn't begin with an "N.""

"No, it doesn't." He stood up, slipping away from my touch. "Tomorrow at six. There's a pool, so?" He shrugged. "Here's the address." He handed me a card with a pony on the front. Inside it said, "You are invited to come horse around for Josephine's birthday."

"How old is she turning?"

"Eight. Like Nina. That's what made me think of it."

I fell in love with him at that moment. It was like the pin being pulled out of a grenade, the tiny little ping that turns something inert into something dangerously combustible. I stared at him, willing him to kiss me. His eyes moved over my face, from my eyes to my lips and my chin. For a split second I saw something soft and yearning.

"What if you don't want to contain them? The wildfires?" I asked.

"People would get hurt."

"Not if they were careful."

"I don't think that would work." He shook his head, and I thought

I saw a whisper of sorrow in his frown. "See you tomorrow." He turned and left.

I watched him go, feeling confused and rejected and cherished and paid attention to at the same time. He knew all my secrets now, and he'd neither embraced me nor repudiated me. He'd just accepted me.

As a friend, I reminded myself. *A dangerous friend.*

Best . . . friends forever.

My phone rang, jolting me out of my thoughts, and I saw it was Grant. "Are we still on for lunch?"

I'd completely forgotten about our date. I said, "Of course. Sure. I—"

"Are you okay?"

"I'm—I'm fine. I just—"

"Where are you? I'll come and get you."

I described where I was, and he said he'd be there in five minutes. But my phone rang again almost immediately. "Are you having second thoughts?" I said, trying to joke.

"You're . . . in danger, Ro-Ro," Liza's voice said.

"What did you do to Regina?"

"Girl . . . no good. Distraction . . . They're coming for you."

Despite myself, I shivered. I thought of Reggie being attacked in her apartment with no sign of anyone coming in or out. "What do you want from me?"

"Pay attention . . . they are already . . ."

"Already what?" I demanded

"Turn around!"

I turned and saw Bridgette crossing the street toward me.

Before she reached me, Grant's car pulled up at the curb. I ran for the door and leaped in.

PART III
AWAKE

She's had this nightmare before.

She's running through an unfamiliar landscape, pursued by footsteps that get closer with each step, each breath. Tree branches slash at her, and her ankles wobble like buoys.

But this is no dream, no nightmare she can wake from. The footsteps she hears behind her now are real. Her neck aches for real, every muscle in her body burns, and each breath sears her windpipe. But she can't stop.

As she runs, flashes of what happened earlier in the night grab at her, trying to slow her down, trap her. Shopping at the mall. The party. The bathroom. The text messages. The fight.

Opening her eyes and seeing the girl, wide eyes nearly sightless, lying on the gravel next to her. The girl saying, "Go. It's me they want, not you."

Hearing herself promise to be right back. "I'll bring help. I won't leave you alone."

Her chest heaves with a sob, which catches in her throat as the beam of a flashlight scores the path in front of her. She's been found, they're closing in, they—

She veers away from the flashlight and is engulfed by complete darkness. Giving her eyes no chance to adjust, she heads blindly toward where she thinks the path should be. Before she reaches it, she stumbles over a rock and is flung headlong past the path and down a steep slope.

Hands out in a vain effort to slow herself, she tumbles over the dirt escarpment until her back thuds against some kind of ledge. Her eyes jolt open with pain and shock. Reaching out with one hand, she discovers she is lying on a ledge of dirt caught between the branches of a dry tree. Above her, she sees the edge of the flashlight beam.

The light zigzags down the wall she's just descended, getting closer with each pass. It stops inches from where she is, close enough that she can see it reflecting off her pinkie nail. Nothing happens. Could they not have seen her?

Above her a single set of footsteps paces along what must be the edge of whatever gully she's fallen into with a regular one-two gait, as the beam played in wide arcs around the whole area. A pebble trickles down and hits her in the face, and as she shifts to shunt it off, something cold slithers across her wrist.

She bites back a scream. She lies there petrified, her heart racing so fast she can't hear the footsteps above, until she realizes the thing on her wrist is just the chain from her BFF necklace. It must have broken as she fell and slid down her clothes. Soundlessly she closes her fingers around it and gropes for the pocket of her skirt. Finding it, she pushes the broken chain in next to the twenty dollars she always carries for emergencies.

Now the footsteps stop, and the beam of the flashlight remains stationary a few feet in front of her head, as though whoever has it is standing and listening. She holds her breath, listening, hearing nothing.

From above, a voice whispers her name, a voice she recognizes. "Come out, I just want to help you," it says. Its tone is genuine, nice. But she knows this is a lie. It's the same voice she heard right before everything went black. The voice that said, "You stupid moron, why did you change your clothes?"

The light makes another arc, grazing her arm this time, and she thinks, This is it. It's over. But then the beam of light returns to the side of the person holding the flashlight like a well-trained puppy. Illuminating his navy blue canvas sneakers for a few moments before he moves on.

"I have to get help; I promised," she thinks as the branch below her gives way, and she tumbles down, falling headlong into complete darkness.

CHAPTER 46

Grant looked a little taken aback at the enthusiasm with which I burst into his car.

"You okay?" he said.

"Yes. I'm just—happy to see you."

He eyed me. "I was thinking maybe we could go out to my place but—"

"Let's go," I said enthusiastically. Bridgette was waving at me frantically. "I'd love to see where you live."

The drive out to the trailer that Grant shared with his brother—"we like to call it a trailer estate, actually"—was only thirty-five minutes, but the landscape and the feeling of the air changed so dramatically, it might as well have been thirty-five hours. Tucson dropped away like the tide ebbing during the first ten minutes of the drive, and after that we were in flat, golden desert.

We exited the main highway, looped under it, and were on a smaller, secondary road that was headed right into the hills. After the second mile the pavement stopped, and we were driving on a rocky dirt track. I realized Grant drove his Bronco out of necessity, not vanity. Green pom poms of scrub desert blanketed the horizon on either side of us, and the hills in front looked flat and reddish brown in the midday sun. A handful of cows grazed on the rise next to the road.

"Yours?" I asked.

"They belong to the Kims, Roscoe's parents. They own the ranch; my brother oversees it," he said.

He glanced over at me and looked like he was going to say something, but instead reached out and tucked his hand over mine. I smiled at him. Without taking his eyes off the dirt track, he smiled back, and we drove the rest of the way like that.

We crested a rise between two hills and a valley spread out below us like a golden bowl. The only building you could see was a double-wide trailer.

"Home sweet home."

I felt like we were a reinterpretation of Adam and Eve, alone together in a secluded paradise. As we got closer to the trailer, I noticed a corral built from slats of wood off to one side. "You have horses?"

"A horse," he said. "A project of my brother's, trying to break her. She's a bit wild though."

As we pulled up, I saw what he meant. The massive horse eyed us, snorted, then reared on her hind legs and made a kind of shouting noise for fifteen solid seconds. Her landing made the earth shake, and she stood there, glaring at us, pawing the ground with one foot.

Grant's eyes got huge. "Never seen her do that before," he said. "Well, now that you've met the welcoming committee, let me give you the rest of the tour."

He pointed to a faded chair and table set up off to the side of the trailer with an old transistor radio on it. "The media room." His finger moved to a trough that looked recently dug—"the mud baths." He spun around and pointed to a dog house covered in peeling paint. "The guest house." He came back to me. "I know you're accustomed to something kind of luxe so—"

"Is that why you've been so nervous?" I asked.

He didn't look at me, just nodded and led the way up the stairs into the trailer. He held the door open for me to enter and let it shut with a clatter. Then he stood there, his arms at his sides, little bars of sunlight crossing his face from the slatted blinds, his eyes glued to the tips of his navy blue PF Flyers sneakers. "I really like you. And you're Aurora Silverton, and I'm—me."

"You're terrific," I said.

"No, you are." His face looked stricken, and he grew even more serious. "Which is why I'm really sorry for what I'm about to do to you."

My mouth went dry, and I felt my pulse in my neck. "What?"

"This," he said and held out a VHS tape with the words *Tocco Luces:* A Film by Grant Villa" typed on the label.

I laughed.

"But first, what can I get you to drink?" He pulled open the refrigerator. "I have lemonade and—looks like lemonade."

"That would be great."

He poured out two glasses and brought one to me as I was looking at a shelf crammed with books and tiny animals whittled out of corks.

"My brother's work," he said. "He's the artistic one."

We toasted and made small talk, but I realized how nervous he was when he was reaching to show me something and knocked his glass down my shirt.

He looked panicked, like he'd done something irredeemable. To show him it was okay, I said, "If you're trying to get me out of my clothes, all you had to do was ask."

He laughed and relaxed a little. "I'm so sorry. My closet is over there. Grab anything."

He turned and carried the glasses to the sink, and I went to his closet. It had two shirts, three pairs of pants, a trench coat missing both a belt and button, and a pair of green high heels in size 10.

One of the people who was there that night. Someone close to you.

Grant? But he had left. He left early. Everyone saw him.

That didn't mean he couldn't have come back, I realized.

There was a wide red stripe of dirt up the back of the trench coat and matching stripes of dirt on the backs of the green shoes.

That's what I'd realized during the fire as I tugged Althea to safety. That was the answer. Liza had been dragged up to Three Lovers Point.

I closed the closet and was fumbling in my pocket for my phone when he came up behind me and said, "What's taking so long, sexy?"

"I'm so sorry," I said, trying to keep my voice cool and level. I pointed to the phone in my hand. "Bain just called, and something happened to my grandmother. I—I've got to get back to the hospital. It's an emergency."

He smiled at me. "Are you sure?"

"Yes," I said, putting one hand on his chest and skirting around him through the door.

"It's not just because you're suddenly having second thoughts about my movie, is it?"

"No," I forced a laugh. "I really want to see it. Soon. It's just, my grandmother," I gestured with the phone again.

"I understand," he said, following me.

"Stay where you are, I can let myself out."

He was smiling as he reached the door and stood in front of it. "I can't let you do that."

"I thought chivalry was dead."

"That's not what I'm talking about. I think we both know you aren't going to be leaving here."

I swallowed. "I don't know—"

"There's no phone service out here. You didn't just get a call from Bain. You saw Liza's trench coat and shoes in my closet. And you realized the truth."

"That's ridiculous. Look if you just let me—"

"I killed her," he said, just like that.

My knees went out from under me.

Because I knew he was right. There was no way he could let me leave there. Not alive anyway.

"Why?" I asked.

"I didn't mean to, not at first. I only wanted to teach her a lesson. But you coming out first when it was supposed to be her—you made me so angry. I squeezed too hard."

"It was my fault?"

"I just wanted to teach her what it felt like to have someone hurt you. To be in someone else's power. She had everyone fooled. Even you. Everyone thought she was so sweet and nice and compassion-ate. But at home—you should see what she did. She manipulated them. Terrorized them."

This didn't sound like the Liza everyone described, but it abso-lutely sounded like the Liza I knew in her ghostly form. "What do you mean?"

"She was a controlling bitch, and she enjoyed hurting people. She would threaten to hurt Ellie if Victoria didn't behave how she wanted. She made life in that house a living hell. I just—I just wanted to help."

"By killing Liza?"

"I had to, don't you see? It was the only way to free them."

"How did you do it?"

"I strangled her outside of the party. Then I dragged her body to the top of the ledge. I took off the trench coat and the shoes—"

My mind flashed back to the red stripe on the back of the coat and the heels of the shoes. "—because they would have shown she was dragged and you wanted to make it look like she'd still been alive and walked up there herself."

He nodded. "And then I pushed her over."

"It makes—" The room started getting blurry around me, and I struggled to stand. Had he put something in my drink? I thought about him pouring out the lemonade for both of us. We both had some, but he—spilled his on me.

So I had to go to the closet.

"My God, you planned this. You wanted me to know. What did you put in my drink?"

"Just something to make you sleep. You were getting too close, asking too many questions, so we decided it was time."

Had he said "we" or "me"? His voice was starting to sound like it was coming from a long way away. He came toward me, and I got ready to fight him. But my hands were like big clumsy paws. Someone else's paws.

I felt myself being lifted up and moved. *Oh good*, a part of my brain said. *He's just taking me to the bed. I'm so tired. Maybe if I just take a nap*, I thought. *Just a little nap and then I'll have more strength.*

The next thing I was aware of was a wall of heat hitting us. Sunshine pricked at my closed eyelids, and I realized we'd somehow moved outside. I struggled to form the words "Where are you taking me?" but I'm not sure if they came out because I didn't get an answer. I tried to open my eyes but had to shut them against the brightness.

After only a few steps he stopped. There was a grunt, and I had the sensation of being lowered, like he was bending over. Then I felt something against my back, and his arms were gone. It was slightly cooler, and the light had dimmed.

I opened my eyes and recognized I was in the trench I'd seen in front of the trailer, the one he'd joked about as the mud baths. He took a step away, and then from over the lip of the trench the blade of a shovel swung into view. I was showered with dirt.

He was going to bury me alive.

I tried to sit up, but my head swam. And at some point when I was sleeping someone had bound my hands behind me. I tried to kick and discovered my legs were bound too. "NO!" I opened my mouth to yell as the next shovelful of dirt fell on me, catching me on the chest and neck. Coughing, I turned my head as the third one was flung over. I took a breath as the fourth one came and got a mouth full of dirt.

I fought against the dirt and the pull of unconsciousness as hard as I could, coughing and retching. I screamed his name, anyone's name, I pulled on the ropes, and I used every ounce of energy I had to keep my eyes open. The light above me began to swim, and then there was dirt in my eyes and a heavy weight on my chest and on my legs. And I was falling backward, spiraling, descending, screaming, plunging.

Into nothing.

CHAPTER 47

*T*here is a phone ringing. I have to get to the phone, but my arms are so heavy. The road beneath me is warm, and I'm crawling toward it on my stomach. The phone I've got to—

I knock the receiver off and try to say hello, but my voice won't come out. I bend down, contorting myself to get my ear near the swinging orange receiver. "Hello," I try to croak again.

"Hello, Ro," the voice, her voice, Liza's voice says. "It's time to wake up. It's safe now. You're safe."

"But how—" I start to say and get a mouth full of dirt.

I woke up coughing.

The sky was a muted blue above me. The earth was cold around me. My head swam. My arms ached in agony.

I was alive.

I listened attentively for footsteps. What had happened? Where was Grant?

The shadows were longer now, and I guessed at least an hour had passed since I blacked out. I forced myself to sit up, sending a chorus of agonizing flares through my head. Shifting slightly, I discovered that someone had unbound my arms. My legs were still tied together, and I tried to reach for them. But my fingers were too numb from being under me. Instead I used my arms to haul myself up to the side of the trough. I sat there, legs dangling into it, catching my breath for a moment, marveling at the feeling of the sun on my face.

I turned and saw him.

Grant was lying on his stomach in the dirt. His face was half-turned, his glasses askew, and the eye I could see was open. A massive pool of blood flowered from his head.

I was sure he was dead, but just in case, I crawled to him. The feeling had begun to come back in my fingers, and I used them to feel for a pulse on his wrist. It was faint. But it was there.

I turned him over. His lips were moving.

"Hold on," I said. "I'll get help."

"No, stay." He held onto me. "It's—"

I was not going to let another person die in my arms.

There was a hammer lying near him covered in blood, which explained his injuries. But not who had inflicted them. Or if the person was still there.

I had to get us away.

I fished my phone out of my pocket but saw that he had been telling the truth about there being no service. With trembling, clumsy fingers, I worried the knot in the rope around my ankles until it loosened enough for me to pull it off. Barefoot, I staggered to his truck.

It was locked. "Where are your keys?" I asked him, but I could have been asking the air, the wind.

I eyed the trailer. They could be in there. And so could whoever did this to him. I was thinking that I had no choice but to brave it when I heard a whinny.

I turned and saw that big wild horse. The horse Roscoe's family had gotten rid of, the horse they called Medusa because she terrified men.

Our eyes met. She stomped her foot and flared her nostrils like saying, *Come on, what are you waiting for?*

I may have been able to fool Bain and Bridgette about my identity, fool them into thinking I was an imposter—but I could never fool a horse.

I knew what I had to do. Grabbing Grant beneath the arms, I dragged him toward the corral. "Here girl," I whispered. She looked at me for a moment, baleful, blaming as though saying, *Oh, sure, you snubbed me before, but now you want me.*

"I'm sorry, sweetheart," I told her. "I had no choice."

As though she understood what I was saying in that uncanny way horses had always understood me, she flicked her mane once and came to me. Just like that. Like no time at all had ever passed.

She bent her head, and I hauled Grant onto her thick neck, then climbed up behind him. Gathering him against my body with one hand and a handful of mane with the other, I clicked my tongue and gave a slight kick, and we were off.

Riding a horse didn't come back to me the way people say riding a bike does. It came the way breathing does, as though I had been missing something vital in my life, and now, at last I was intact, whole, alive again. This wasn't just a ride. I was riding home.

There could be no going back now. No denying I really was Aurora Silverton, had been her all along. When N. Martinez looked for my Aurora Silverton's prints by name, he'd learned my secret—and kept it for me. But it would now be an open one. And somehow all the reasons I'd had for pretending not to be myself didn't matter anymore.

I caught snippets of memory as they rushed by me on the wind. The night it all started, wandering around outside the party whispering, *Colin, where are you? Colin?* Feeling unworthy to be with him because of what Stuart had done to me. Because I was a *filthy slut*.

A flashlight beam slashing across my face. Pain. Darkness. Far-off laughter. Voices whispering.

A truck-stop bathroom in broad daylight.

A newspaper that told me seven days had passed.

I still had no idea what had happened during those seven days. But when I woke up, I learned two things: Liza was dead, apparently of a suicide; and the police wanted me for questioning. I couldn't remember what had gone on at the party or how I'd gotten where I was.

I was certain of only one thing, and that was that I had to run away. That I was not safe. That Liza might be dead, but *I* was the one who had been set up.

As the years went by, parts of my memory came back like the missing pieces to a now lost puzzle, and I became more and more convinced that someone had tried to kill me that night, with no idea who or why. I knew only that I felt confused and frightened when I thought about Colin, Bridgette, and Bain. Colin had no motive to harm me, that I could remember, but Bridgette and Bain did. Or rather, somewhere between twenty and forty million reasons, depending on Althea's will in any given month.

I came back to Tucson after Nina's death to be closer to my family, but with no plan. And then Bain walked into the Starbucks I was working at and gave me the perfect way in. If he and Bridgette thought I was an imposter, I'd be safe. And it would give me a chance to look for the proof I needed. Especially since I knew Colin had enlisted and was away.

What I'd told N. Martinez was true too—I'd wanted to pick my family. And be picked.

Mounted in front of me, Grant groaned. "Torn," he said.

"You'll be fine," I assured him.

He slipped to the side, almost falling, and I had to drag him back up.

"Hold on," I told him. "Just a little more. Hold on."

As Medusa, that glorious, magical horse, and I galloped across the dusty golden earth, I discovered I was sobbing. "You can do it, sweetheart," I repeated, and I don't know if I was talking to him or the horse or myself.

"Just a little longer," I repeated over and over, my tears showering over him. I urged Medusa forward, my thighs clamped around her to keep us steady, my hand knotted through her mane. I would not let another person die in my arms.

A building appeared on the horizon, and I remembered we had passed a fire station. Medusa's hooves pounded the desert, galloping furiously. The firemen must have seen the dust we kicked up because they were standing outside, watching as I came up and yelled, "This man is injured; he needs an ambulance." And they sprung into action.

Someone tied up Medusa, and I rode with Grant to the hospital in the ambulance, holding his hand. Still holding it when, before we got there, he died.

CHAPTER 48

had a broken rib, and the bottoms of my feet were badly lacerated. But I refused to stay still, refused to let them sedate me and put me to sleep. There was one more thing for me to do.

I was grinding my teeth against the pain when I saw her in the doorway. She was wearing a white dress, and she had a paper airplane in one hand. Her braids gave off tiny clicking noises as she spun in a circle, making easy arcs with the airplane, around and around.

"Nina," I said, "What are you doing here?"

She stopped and smiled at me. She looked like she'd grown; her arms were long and so thin. She said, "I came to see you."

"I'm afraid I'm out of stories." I felt horrible as though I were letting her down, but I was so exhausted. I couldn't move.

She looked shy and a little nervous, like the first time I saw her. "That's okay. I didn't come for a story. I came to tell you something. I figured it all out. I know the answer."

"The answer to what?"

She looked exasperated. "How to tell where you're going, of course."

"Oh." *It's too late for that,* I wanted to tell her. "What is it?"

She looked serious. "You can tell you're running toward home when you stop looking behind you."

She was right. It was so simple. I was stunned that I'd never thought of it.

She came and kissed me on the forehead and whispered, "Goodbye, Eve." And then I saw there was another woman standing behind her. Her face was averted but she turned toward me now.

"Mommy?" I said.

She turned toward me and her smile was so radiant it made me feel like there were sparks in me. "How's my girl?"

"Mommy, I'm so sorry," I told her.

"You have nothing to apologize for, baby."

I was crying now, the tears hot on my cheeks. "When you called that day, I was angry at you, so I didn't answer the phone. I just let it ring and ring. I should have answered. And then the next day you— you were gone. I should have answered. If I had answered, if I hadn't been so ungrateful and selfish, you'd still be alive."

"No, sweetheart," she said, smoothing a hand over my hair. "I was calling to say goodbye." Part of me didn't want to believe it, but somewhere deep inside I knew it was true. Had always known. "You couldn't save me. No one could." She kissed my forehead. "You have to forgive yourself."

"I don't know—"

"Shhh," she said, putting a finger to my lips. And disappeared.

I opened my eyes and saw Althea being wheeled in through the door. Her body looked frail, but her eyes were alert and focused. "Help me up," she said to the orderly.

"Ma'am, you should really stay—"

"I'm going to hug my granddaughter, and nothing is going to stop me."

And then she was there with her arms around me, hugging me tighter than I would have expected possible and saying, "My darling girl. My darling Aurora. I love you, girl."

"I love you too, Grandma," I said, and my eyes blurred and I passed out.

I dreamed of N. Martinez in his neat police officer uniform standing above me, smoothing hair off my forehead and giving me a kiss on the cheek.

When I opened my eyes, he was sitting in a chair next to the wall in his uniform, dozing. My heart skipped a beat, and my mind whispered, *Wait, maybe.* He was slightly slouched, his hair was a little bit messed up, and he didn't frown in his sleep.

He opened his eyes, and for a moment he looked approachable and friendly, like in my dream. But then he frowned again, and I knew it hadn't been real.

Tell him how you feel, I thought. *Tell him he makes you feel like confiding, tell him you've never met anyone like him, tell him you feel safe with him, you want to spend afternoons by his side flying kites and eating ice cream and doing nothing and anything and looking at the stars and naming your own constellations. Tell him you dream about him. Tell him you have never seen him smile.*

I said, "I'm sorry I missed your sister's birthday party."

"Yeah. You could have called," he said.

I looked down at my hands. "I know."

He stared at me. And then, as though he'd been reading my mind, he laughed, his wondrous rich laugh, and he finished it with a smile. "You make me nuts," he said.

"I know."

"Why are you crying?" he asked.

I shrugged. How could I tell him it was because hearing him laugh, seeing him smile, were even better than I'd imagined?

The smile vanished, and he went back to frowning and messed up his hair like he wasn't quite sure what to do. He opened his mouth, then closed it without saying anything. Sat tight-lipped.

Finally he cleared his throat and sat up straighter and said in an official tone, "I thought you deserved to know. It's something not being released to the public. I could lose my job for telling you."

"I won't rat you out."

"I didn't think—" He shook his head. "I knew that." He said, "The hammer was the weapon used to bash Grant's head. The murder weapon. You were right."

I sat still, waiting for him to go on.

"It had prints on it," he said.

I knew what was coming, maybe before he did. "Liza's prints," I said.

He nodded.

He cleared his throat again. "I—I guess I owe you an apology."

I shook my head. "I barely believed it myself. It all seemed— I mean you grow up thinking there are no such thing as ghosts. But—"

"But," he agreed. We looked at each other. For a long time. Stretching the silence like taffy until it was thick and taut and far too sticky to be comfortable.

He said, "I seem to have a very bad effect on you. I've seen you with other people, and you're not—like this."

"Yeah." I swallowed. "I suppose it's mutual."

"Yes. I mean, no but—" he began. His frown deepened. "I don't know how else to say this. Being with you is really hard. It—I don't understand it. It makes me nuts. You turn me into a fool."

"I get the picture."

"I don't think you do."

"Fool. Bad. Nuts. I'm clear on that." I turned my face away. "I think I want to be alone." Having him there so close, and hating to be near me, was hard.

I heard him push his chair back. I sensed him hesitate, and then I heard his shoes slip across the floor toward the door. He paused there.

And then he did the worst thing I could imagine. "Napoleon," he said. "That's my first name." His footsteps receded.

I wanted to press the nurse call-button and say I was in pain, but I didn't think they had medication for what was hurting me. He'd told me his name. The name he only told people he wasn't going to see again.

I pushed my face into my pillow and cried.

I fell asleep and had a weird dream in which I realized I'd had the princesses backward and Liza was Cinderella and I was Sleeping Beauty. I was half-awake and half-asleep, trying to figure out what it meant, when I heard footsteps and opened my eyes to see Bridgette and Bain walk in.

Bridgette surprised me by sobbing all over me. "I am so mad at you," she said as she sobbed and hugged me. "You lied to us. Lied. All the time." More sobbing and hugging. "I missed you so much, Aurora. I missed you every day, and you lied. And you thought we tried to kill you. When I saw you on the street, I was coming to tell you that I thought we should end the imposter scheme."

"I thought you were going to kill me."

Bridgette shook her head. "Some family we have. I'm so glad you're back."

Bain was more subdued. After Bridgette finished, he said, "I'd like to talk to Ro alone," and she nodded and left. He sat down on the chair next to my bed and seemed nervous.

"So. They, the police, said, um, your memory was coming back. Not all of it."

"That's what I told them," I said. I stared directly at him. "But it was a lie. It all came back."

He let out a breath and sat back in his chair. "I'm not proud of what I did. And I'm sorry."

"I'm sure." I said, "Why don't you tell me your version?"

"After you disappeared that night, I took off. There wasn't any reason for me to stay at the party once—well, once it was clear my plan wasn't going to work. And then I'm driving by the side of the road, and I see you. Walking there, just strolling along. I couldn't believe it. I'd gone to all that trouble to arrange a kidnapping for you, and you'd somehow disappeared. But then poof you're back. All alone. I pulled over and offered you a ride and—well, it was weird."

"Weird how?"

"I said, 'Aurora, do you want a ride?' And you looked at me and said, 'Who are you?' You had no idea who I was, what your name was, anything. I figured, even better, you won't remember what happened. So I picked you up. You fell asleep, and we drove toward Phoenix. I figured that was as good a place as any to hold you while I sent the ransom note and everything, so I stashed you in a motel. But something must have happened because when I came back you— you weren't breathing. I thought you were dead."

"So you left me there."

"Not like that. I called nine-one-one, and then I took off. I couldn't help; I'm not a doctor. And I figured if you were dead, they would take care of it, identify you, and I'd be home before the Family got the call."

"But the call never came."

His head went from side to side slowly. "No. That was—that was weird. I assumed they just couldn't ID the body. I was so sure you were dead."

"Where was it?"

"On the way to Phoenix. I told you."

"No, I mean, what was the name of the place?"

"Oh. The Highway Motel."

There's a buzzing noise. I'm lying on a bed, my cheek pressed against the spread. There's light coming in from a window, evening light, and I have no idea where I am or how I got there. I look for a clock, but there isn't one. My feet are slightly elevated, on the pillows. I'm backward, my head is at the foot of the bed, and pulling myself up onto my elbows. I see my face in the mirror over the bureau.

I have no idea what my name is. I have no idea where I am or what day it is. I see the window reflected in the mirror. Between the half-open curtains of the room, I can make out a car wash and, closer up, a part of a sign. I lean toward the mirror and stare at the reflection of the sign, spelling the letters out with my finger. T-O-M Y-A-W. Tom Yaw.

In my mind now I flipped the reflection over —WAY MOT. Tom Yaw wasn't a person; Tom Yaw was the middle letters of "Highway Motel," seen in the mirror. Across from the car wash.

So that was it. The story of what had happened.

Or so I thought. There was still one crucial piece missing, although I didn't realize it at that moment.

Bain shifted nervously in the seat. "What are you going to do?"

It was kind of fun watching how uncomfortable he was. "What's in the bag?" I asked, pointing to a pink paper gift bag next to the seat.

"I don't know. It was here when I got here."

My heart stopped for a moment, and my mind screamed, *Liza?* "Hand it to me, please," I said, working to keep my voice level. My fingers shook. I took the bag and spilled it onto the blanket in front of me.

There was a small plastic tiara, an eraser that smelled like bubble-gum, and a butterfly with a suction cup on it. A Post-it note attached to the butterfly said, "My brother says you are sick and like butter-flies. I'm sorry you didn't come to my party. We went swimming. It was gnarly. Love, Josephine."

I must have been allergic to the eraser because as I read it my eyes started to tear a lot.

"Are you okay?" Bain asked. "Do you need a Kleenex or a nurse or something?"

I wiped my eyes on the bedsheet. "I'm fine," I said. "I'm really fine, actually."

"And us?" He gestured between us.

"We're fine too. But if you ever try anything like that again, I'll tell Bridgette."

He looked scared. "No worries."

I put the butterfly and the tiara and the note on my nightstand. I kept the eraser in my hand.

I slept. I slept for days. And when I woke up, I really did know everything.

CHAPTER 49

stood with my toes nestled among the trail of white flowers that stretched from the side of Three Lovers Point and down into the canyon.

Today I will lay your soul to rest, Liza, I thought.

I didn't turn around when I heard the footsteps behind me. I had invited her. I was making a new start, a new beginning.

"Hi, Reggie," I said as she came along side of me.

She gave me a hug. "I was so excited when you called. I didn't really expect to hear from you."

"I couldn't stop thinking about your tattoo," I said. "The butterfly. Or rather, the monarch butterfly. Not because it migrates, or even because it's poisonous, but because of its name. Monarch. I should have gotten it right away. Reggie is short for Regina. It means 'queen', doesn't it?"

"Yes." Her eyes sparkled behind the blue contact lenses.

"Three girls all named after queens. Ellie for Eleanor of Aquitaine. Liza for Elizabeth I. And you. Vicky. For Queen Victoria."

Her smile was radiant. "My secret identity is revealed! I knew you'd get it eventually. How did you figure it out?"

"Three sugars," I said. Her pretty forehead compressed into a frown. "Three sugars and soymilk," I elaborated. "I remembered how Grant knew exactly what you put in your tea that day you ran into us at the hospital café. It's the kind of thing you learn about someone you care about. So I guessed he knew you, and the two of you had some reason for lying about it. I couldn't figure out why, but when he was dying, he kept saying he was torn. Only that wasn't it. He was saying *Tory*."

She picked one of her slightly-too-dark hairs from her sweater and dropped it on the ground. "I hated that nickname. It was so trailer trash. But I guess that was to be expected."

I felt myself starting to get angry. "He loved you. He protected you even when he was dying, you know. He made it seem like he killed your sister himself."

"He did," she said, painting her face with shock. "I don't know what you are talking about."

"When I said I remembered your tattoo, I meant something else. I remembered seeing it the night your sister died. Seeing it after Grant knocked me out instead of Liza and called you in a panic asking what to do."

"What a mess," she said, shaking her head at the memory. "He really screwed everything up."

"Actually it was you who messed it up. When Ellie brought you the note she'd found in the Old Man, setting a meeting with Colin to run away, you thought it was for Liza. You assumed Colin and Liza were a couple. That was why during the party you texted Liza's phone pretending to be Colin. You expected it would be Liza who came running, but it was me, and me that Grant knocked out. He used my phone to text Liza and get her to come out too. But that meant you had two of us to dispose of."

"What an interesting story."

"I saw your tattoo then. When you came to help Grant. You turned me over, slapped me on the cheek to see if I was conscious. I pretended not to be, but I was. And I heard your laugh. You were enjoying it." I stared down at the sea of white flowers. "What I can't figure out is why you did it. Why did you want to hurt Liza?"

Her pretty face grew grave. "You didn't really know her. To you, to her friends, she seemed like a nice girl, but really she was horrible. She only thought about herself and pleasing herself. Having her own way."

"That's not true," I said.

She looked at me guilelessly. "But it is. She only cared about getting what she wanted. She didn't ever think about others. About the Family. She was out of control. I'd tell her to do something, and she'd just ignore me. It had been getting worse and worse since Christmas. Finally, when I saw that note, it came to a head. She thought she was going to leave us!" Her eyes were wide, incredulous. "She thought she could abandon our family. She needed to learn that actions had consequences. Being in a family was like being part of a team—if you do something it affects everyone. And you have to respect the leader. She had no respect."

She is crazy, I thought to myself. *She's absolutely insane.* I said, "So you made her destroy your father's collection?"

"I wanted her to feel what it was like when you ruined something other people loved. That other people had spent time cultivating. That's what she was doing to us. By trying to leave, she was ruining the family. She needed to stop being so selfish."

"But she wasn't trying to leave. The note was for me."

Victoria waved that off. "She would have left at some point." She flicked a piece of dust from her sweater. "I was just trying to teach her discipline. It was for her own good. But even then she was selfish. She *knew* if she didn't destroy those records, I would be forced to hurt Ellie. I made that clear. It was the only way she'd learn. But did she care about that, about my pain or Ellie's? About what a bad example she was setting? No. She still went as slowly as possible, breaking each record into as many tiny pieces as she could because she felt bad about what she was doing. *She* felt bad. She could never stop thinking of herself." She sighed and shook her head. "So I wrote a note of my own pretending it was from Colin and put it where I knew she'd find it."

This was it. The missing piece. The single element that had set everything else in motion. "What did it say?"

"That he realized he didn't love her and had been a fool to think of running away with her." She waved a hand dismissively as though this one thing, the crucial act that had cost more than one life, was trivial and hardly mattered.

But there was a smug satisfaction barely concealed beneath her tone that caught at me. "You hated her," I said with sudden recognition. "You hated her because she wouldn't listen to you, because she was good and kind and people liked her and did what she said because they wanted to, not because they were forced to."

Something flashed behind Victoria's eyes, something like fury, but it vanished almost before I could name it and was replaced by hurt confusion. "You're wrong," she said, sounding near tears. "I loved her. I wanted to help make her better. I was trying to save her. Save our family. She was destroying us. Like a cancer. I had to remove the cancer. Grant understood when I explained it to him. He wanted to help me."

I stared at her. *Did she believe what she was saying?* I wondered. I began to see the contours of her pathology. Whatever had happened was Liza's fault. Liza made her do everything.

This was why Liza dressed like her sister when Victoria was

home and didn't call her friends. It wasn't because she idolized Victoria. It was because if she didn't, Victoria found some way to make her pay. I remembered all her injuries, but only now did I realize they seemed to take place around holidays. School holidays. I'd thought they had been inflicted by Liza's dad, especially after his performance with the police, telling me to stay away, but—

"Your father knew you killed her," I said. "That's why he wanted it to be ruled a suicide and stay a suicide. He was protecting you."

She rolled her eyes. "As though I needed his protection. If he had been able to protect the family, I wouldn't have had to do what I did. He's sweet, but he has really never understood me. When you came back, I was worried you might remember something, so I decided to make sure your memory wouldn't seem trustworthy."

"By making me think I was being haunted."

"And making you think that you'd been the target. That way if they did reopen an investigation they would be looking for who wanted to hurt you and never think about Liza." She said it all in the same calm voice she might use to order lunch. "When I saw you really didn't remember, I realized I could use you. Grant was becoming a liability, and I saw that you could help me take care of him."

"You used him too, though. That first day, when you appeared in front of me at the mall and then vanished, he must have spliced the footage before showing it to me, so I didn't see you go in or come out of the dressing room."

"Grant was a very good editor," she said in the same tone an elementary teacher would have said a slow child plays well with others. "He would never have been a great director or filmmaker, but he had his uses. He just lacked the breadth of vision."

"Not like you." She nodded without irony at my compliment. She was clearly enjoying this and felt no remorse at all. In her mind, she hadn't done anything wrong. It all made perfect sense to her, and she was completely justified. The pretty young woman standing next to me was a psychopath.

I said, "How did you make Stuart's hands blister?"

"That was so easy. I just had to rub poison oak on his steering wheel. Wait a couple of days and *voilà*, blisters."

"And the writing on the sign here? That appeared and disappeared?"

"Hairspray. I barely got away before you came down. I hadn't expected you to try to rub it off. I just thought it would stick and then disappear when the hairspray evaporated. The way it happened—" She hugged herself. "It was pretty amazing, wasn't it?"

It was extraordinary watching her, captivating and horrifying at once. Because it was clear to me now that this wasn't real to her. Liza, her family, me, Grant—we were all just pawns to her in a big game. Life and death didn't mean anything to her because we weren't real individuals. We were just there to serve her ends. Cast member and audience at once. "And the attack on you," I went on. "That was what baffled the police, what convinced me that Liza was really a ghost. But really, it was the simplest one of all."

She chuckled but not modestly. "I couldn't wait to do it. I knew it would play well."

"And Colin?" I asked. "Why did you get involved with him?"

Now she gave me a radiant smile. "That was all because of you." Her eyes twinkled mischievously. "I don't like loose ends, and when you disappeared that night as we were loading Liza into the car, you became one. The danger was minimal—you were probably dead, and even if you did come back, Grant was sure you hadn't seen him. But I still wanted to be careful. So I started writing to Colin while he was deployed to see if he'd heard from you. I considered writing as

myself, but decided to make up the character of Regina instead—
people will tell strangers things they would never tell their friends,
you know." She gazed at me as though she were interested in my
opinion of this random fact, and I felt myself nodding. It was like
being hypnotized.

"After a few months," she went on, "I realized he *needed* me. You'd
broken his heart so badly, he was lost and at sea. He needed someone
who could guide him. He was throwing himself into the most horrible assignments, volunteering for the worst kind of jobs because he
felt guilty about what happened to you. God knows why. Anyway,
when he was injured I went and met him, and we've been together
ever since. And we will continue to be. Happily ever after."

I said, "You sound so sure. But the story isn't over yet."

"My part, no, but yours is." She leaned toward me conspiratori-
ally. "Would you like to know how it ends?"

I thought, *No,* but nodded.

She clapped her hands. "Feeling guilty about having abandoned
your dear friend Liza to a murderer, you came to the place where her
body was found and threw yourself off. It was a last act of penance."

"Like J.J.?"

Her eyes got huge, and she shook her head. "Oh J.J. He saw Grant
up at that house where the party was after he was supposed to have
left. He was a swine, Jimmy Jakes, the kind of creature that has spent
so much time rolling in filth he can spot the tiniest daub on someone else. And of course Grant is easy prey for someone like that." She
sighed sadly. "Poor Jimmy. He was so confused. He wasn't sure what
he'd seen, but he thought it was something. He and I met here, and
he must have misinterpreted my intentions because he tried to take
my clothes off. Can you imagine? He *pawed* me." She paused at the
memory and swallowed. Her face had gone pale, and her eyes were

hurt. "I resisted, and he—he tripped and fell down." Her expression got momentarily bleak. "He touched me. He never should have done that. If only people knew how to behave."

"What about Grant? Why did you kill him?"

"I didn't do anything of the kind. You were there. Did you see me?" She gazed at me as though I were a slightly disappointing pet. "I really had imagined you being more clever. More engaging. I'd hoped we could be friends. But instead you call me out here to accuse me of the vilest things. I can't let you walk around saying things like that about me."

"You don't have a choice. I have proof that you were behind Liza's murder, and you can't have it unless you let me walk away."

She laughed. "That is the oldest bluff in the world."

"The police subpoenaed your phone records. They can prove you were the one behind the ghost phone calls to me. And the ghost knew things only the killer could know."

One of her shoulders came up. "Doubtful. And even if it were true, pointless."

"They know that the shoes Liza was wearing were yours, not hers. They were two sizes too small."

"They said LAWSON in them. Maybe they were hers from before. Won't work."

"They also found the real hammer you used to kill Grant. Not the one you planted next to him that still had Liza's fingerprints on it from before she died. From the time you made her smash your father's records."

There was the slightest flicker of doubt in her eyes. If I hadn't been watching closely, I probably wouldn't even have suspected it, and I would almost have doubted myself when she laughed at the next moment and said, "That's impossible."

"Really?" I looked down at my nails. "When was the last time you checked it?"

It was enough. She didn't relax her grip on my arm, but she pulled out her phone and dialed. "Hi, baby," she said. "Can you hear me? Colin? I know the connection is bad. Listen, have there been any police at your house? There haven't? Good. It's just that they were at my place and were asking questions about you. I know, I'll be glad when it's all over too. Thank you, baby. Love you too."

She hung up and looked at me triumphantly. "Nice try," she said. Then without warning, her leg snaked out and caught mine behind the knee. I staggered to the edge of the ravine, sending a shower of stones plunging to the bottom. "Goodbye, Aurora." I felt a hard, swift kick to my lower back and heard *oof* and began falling headfirst into the canyon.

My arms flailed out wildly, and I stretched for the edge of the canyon. Three of my fingers closed on some kind of root, and I stopped moving.

Looking down, I saw my feet were dangling above empty space with nothing for a hundred feet to break my fall.

The ground swam in front of my eyes. My heart was racing. My shoulder burned, and my fingers got sweaty and started to slide.

"I've got you," a voice shouted, and a hand wrapped around my wrist. I was being hauled up by N. Martinez.

Victoria was sandwiched between two cops, looking at them with wide, scared eyes. "I was trying to help her. Didn't you see? She tripped, and I was trying to—"

I realized I was still clinging to N. Martinez. I let go and stepped hastily away.

His face registered nothing. "There's a car going to Colin's house now to retrieve the hammer," he said. I wasn't sure if it was him or me, but we seemed to be having a hard time looking at one another. "You handled that very well."

"Thank you," I said, keeping it formal. Professional. "For saving me."

"You are welcome," he said in the same tone.

Ask him on a date. Ask him to dinner. Ask him to the movies, my mind raced. *You have nothing to lose now; there are no more secrets.* I said, "I know you don't like me, but would you maybe want to get a coffee with me some time?"

He said, "No. I'm afraid not."

I felt like I'd been punched. After everything, that was where this would end. I felt like my smile was glued onto my face. "Oh. Okay." I turned to go, but his touch on my arm caught me.

He swung me back to him. His fingers laced through mine; his body pressed against mine. I felt like I couldn't stand and like I could fly all at once. "I don't want coffee with you. I want more."

My throat went dry, and my tongue suddenly felt huge. "You said you would never be able to understand me and that I drive you nuts."

"Those are good things."

I let that sink in. I could feel his heart beating against my chest. When my voice came out, it was barely a whisper. "And you told me your name."

He gazed down at me with his bottomless brown eyes and said, "I told you because I wanted to hear you say it."

My heart stopped. "Napoleon," I said.

A slow smile spread across his face like the sun cresting a hill at dawn. "Aurora."

Warmth spilled over me. "When you say more, you mean like—?"

"Like this," he said and bent his mouth over mine. "Aurora," he murmured.

I am Aurora. I am awake. I am home.

ML   6/12